THE
INVISIBLES

The Invisibles

Copyright 2019 by Rachel Dacus

All rights reserved. This book or any portion thereof may not be reproduced or used in any manner whatsoever without the express written permission of the publisher, except for the use of brief quotations in an article or book review.

ISBN: 978-0-578-58758-5

Cover Design by Melissa Williams Design

Interior Formatting by Melissa Williams Design

Editing by Vicki McGough

Published by Time Fold Books

racheldacus.net

For my brother

THE INVISIBLES

RACHEL DACUS

CHAPTER 1
Family Spirits—Saffron

Saffron glared at her black-suited sister across their father's grave in Rome's Protestant Cemetery. It was nearly empty for their father's funeral, only Elinor, this small bunch of stylish Italians also wearing black, and herself in lavender. Was it worth coming all the way from Berkeley, with her domineering sister, for this ritual? Ellie had written a solemn ceremony, as if Dad would have enjoyed the pomp. Okay, maybe he was enjoying it, but Saffron knew he was hating being dead.

She could tell by the purple glimmers that swarmed over his casket that Dad was disturbed by his situation, but he'd soon grow calm.

Her superior sister, with her perfect pageboy and dark suit, looked embarrassed tossing red rose petals onto the casket. Good, she should. The cheesy petal-tossing idea had been Ellie's. She was always planning and calculating. She could never do anything spontaneously. It was as if all the energy in Ellie's body flowed up and gathered in her brain, where it pulsed in constant, bossy motion.

But then Saffron remembered she didn't want to be critical, especially not with her sister, who had invited her to come. She tried to put on a hopeful expression, to please Ellie—and then she remembered Ellie wouldn't like to see her smiling at the funeral.

The judgmental vibes were probably flowing from Ellie, who was always embarrassed by something. Often it was by Saffron and her spontaneity, which was, yes, a little messy. And what Elinor dismissively called *imaginative*. To Ellie, the mix-up with the plane reservations had proved yet again why Saffron wasn't competent. After Saffron booked the wrong dates, Elinor took over with a flourish. Her sister loved to take charge. Ever since childhood, Ellie had honed her management skills by running Saffron's life.

Yes, it was true, Saffron needed help. Of course, she wasn't perfect. Okay, she was about to turn thirty and hadn't yet begun adulting. But at this moment, she was proud of herself for coming along and trying to mend fences with Ellie—as proud as you could feel with drizzle plastering your hair onto your face, your boot heels sinking into the spongey ground, and your sister frowning at your smile.

Suddenly, her confidence dripped away. Saffron saw all her mistakes shatteringly close in the rearview mirror. On this trip to Italy to claim their inheritance from Dad, could she show Elinor she was able to take care of herself? True, Elinor had bailed Saffron out when her recent business failed. And she had picked up the pieces when Saffron was evicted over a silly misunderstanding with the landlord.

But Elinor never gave Saffron the benefit of her many doubts. It was almost as if she relished Saffron screwing up, so she could swoop in as the rescuer.

Ellie glanced over at her, lips pressed and brown eyes squinting. Saffron felt very alone as she listened to the minister's gloomy thoughts on Heaven, in this odd country where no one wore lavender.

Saffron knew if she hadn't come, Ellie would have made this a weekend trip. She'd stay just long enough to pick up the pieces after their father's fatal heart attack, selling his home on the Italian coast as fast as she could, and missing any possible fun she might have in Italy. Without Saffron to inspire her, Ellie wouldn't sample Italian delicacies, or explore Dad's cottage. She'd eat in the hotel dining room in Rome and order nothing more adventurous than Pasta Bolognese and house wine. Life had squashed Ellie. Was there a way to un-squash her?

The trees quivered with a gust of rain. A shower of phosphorescent sparks dazzled up from the open grave as a bird swooped low over their heads. Saffron's stomach lurched as the sparkling atoms swirled up and twinkled through the leaves.

Hella damn. An Invisible.

Not right now, with her sister watching.

The pyrotechnic was probably Dad. He must feel anxious, thinking he was going to stay closed in that box with the polished lid. He must have panicked that his blood was stilled and his body frozen. An active, vibrant man who was always doing, he must be surprised to be dead.

A ripple of fear shot up her spine, probably echoing Dad's uneasiness with his being in *The Room Over There*. He'd settle down. They all did. Invisibles often came to Saffron for help finding their way. Dad would realize where he was. She'd nudge him, they'd talk, and then he'd walk calmly away. And if he didn't walk voluntarily, she'd bully him, the way he had bullied her to improve her grades.

The thought made her smile. She glanced at Ellie, but her sister hadn't caught her finding something funny. Elinor was the kind of woman who didn't see anything she didn't want to.

With a deep sense of irony, Saffron understood Dad's panic. When he'd sent her away, after her mother died, and she had to go live with Ellie and Mom-Betsy, her fear had made her only want to sleep. But she learned to soothe herself, and then she learned to soothe Invisibles. Each time she helped one, a soft ache of gratitude blossomed in her heart.

The minister was going on about Heaven—what did he know about the afterlife? The sparkles billowed higher, unnoticed by the others. Dad would have preferred to write his own eulogy, something poetic and perhaps funny. What this funeral needed was a few streamers and some barefoot dancing.

The mass of fiery dots hung in midair, as if communicating by Morse code. These dancing lights could be saying a spectacular *Sorry* to Saffron. As Dad should for abandoning her.

The phantom twisted itself into eyes, nose, and a mouth. A sad face with large, watery eyes. Not Dad, but his favorite poet, his academic specialty, Percy Bysshe Shelley. Was Dad sending the sad poet?

A small figure darted into her peripheral vision. At her feet was a small gray squirrel. He ran across the toe of her boot to grab crumbs of hotel crackers that must have spilled from her pocket. She fished around, trying to find more. He rushed back, to a safe distance. He munched, sitting upright and keeping an eye on her. Obviously, he was used to pilfering from mourners. Well, why not. Invisibles and tame squirrels at Dad's funeral. Perfect for the eccentric Nathan Greene.

She turned out her pocket, shaking down the last crumbs. She looked up again. Shelley was just vanishing. Had Ellie seen the squirrel? No. Her stoic, prim sister was worriedly looking around. She felt sorry for Elinor, always compelled to assess people and their reactions.

The squirrel edged nearer again. Saffron realized his dilemma. She stepped aside so he could scoop up more crumbs. She loved animals. They followed no rules and made no judgments, except about food.

Past the circle of people in black she saw Invisibles gliding between the headstones and monuments. They all were dressed in contemporary clothes, all in silent motion. Saffron blew a kiss to a young woman dressed in red who had stopped. She looked startled that someone living could see her. Saffron waved, as you do at someone undertaking a long vacation. The woman smiled brightly and waved back, and then she thinned out to nothing. Good. On her way. Saffron wished she knew where they ended up.

If only she could confide in Ellie as she used to. But she couldn't mention the Invisibles to her sister ever again, not after Ellie had undermined Saffron's relationship with her boyfriend Jack by telling him about Saffron's "secret game". When they were kids, it had been different. Saffron had trusted Ellie and told her about the Invisibles. Ellie accepted it. Even though she couldn't see them, she believed her sister.

But on this trip, Saffron would forgo the apology she deserved from Ellie, if only they could get back to some kind of harmony. Saffron missed her sister.

Shelley's face returned, hovering in the air, smiling but even sadder looking.

I'm waiting for you at my cottage. I'm waiting here for both you girls.

A tingle raced up the back of Saffron's neck. Well, triple hella damn. Now they really had to go see Dad's house, to find out why Shelley had just called it his house.

I want my heart back.

Whaaaat? But then Shelley was gone again.

Saffron found a peanut in her pocket, left over from the plane flight. She tossed it on the ground. The squirrel leapt over to grab it. Ellie was watching too. She must think it was super inappropriate, feeding wildlife while burying your parent. The somber Italians, hunched and hatted, clearly agreed. They looked on disapprovingly. Well, why shouldn't she enjoy the event? Dad was just changing from one form of existence to another. Understanding this, funerals in Berkeley were more like weddings. People wore colors. They chanted and danced. Bells were heard.

Death was a myth, and most people only half-lived anyway. Like her sister, moving through life without fully using her senses. If you could make a spreadsheet of your dreams, Ellie would. As a teenager she had thrown away her pointe shoes and wrapped up her box of poems and stowed it on a high, cobwebbed shelf in the garage. She had traded her youth for a calculator.

Would the minister never come to the end? "Nathan Greene, a man of faith, so important to his community."

A man of faith? Faith in his own ego, maybe.

Saffron wished she had brought a sweater. And an umbrella. Ellie began jerking her head with vehement little snaps, signaling Saffron: *Stand up straighter, look sadder.*

She felt sorry for Elinor. What had discipline gotten her?

Infertility, being cheated on, a brutal divorce, and coming down from a luxurious home in the hills to a cramped condo. Slaving away in a hospital. Cementing her pact with bottom lines and dollar signs. After the divorce, Ellie had retreated into her need to outperform others. Elinor's elusive imagination that once roamed nature like a forest sprite was forgotten. But that could change. Elinor needed time away, and Saffron couldn't go back to Justin and the pizzeria right now. She needed time away too.

The minister gave a final prayer. Hands were shaken, solemn nods given, everyone left. Praise the Goddess—it was over.

Chapter 2

A Hidden Manuscript—Elinor

"Well, that went as well as I had hoped." Elinor said, mentally crossing the funeral off her long list of things to do in Italy. What was next?

She grabbed Saffron's hand and tugged. "Come with me. I want to show you something."

Elinor had planned this carefully. It was a little detour to please Saffron, who was looking damp, uncertain, and insecure. A tall girl, her shoulders were always rounded, as if conversing with her heart to agree that she couldn't measure up and therefore shouldn't stand up. They were even more rounded today.

If she'd calculated well, it could be a giant step toward mending everything—their stupid feud, the way Saffron thought Elinor didn't understand her, the years of petty disagreements. And if she had planned this trip right, and she could make peace with Saffron, she might have a chance to help her sister make the most of this inheritance. She could help her wisely invest and make a more secure future.

Elinor led Saffron down a narrow path, over stones slippery in the mist.

Saffron suddenly stopped, and then she threw herself into Elinor's arms. "I didn't get to say goodbye."

"To the minister?"

"To Dad!" Saffron wailed.

Elinor patted her sister's back until the sobs quieted. "He left us so many times, I thought it was a practical joke. When I got your call, I laughed."

"You were always so mad at him, I thought you were happy he was dead."

"Ellie, I thought you were kidding! Dad just couldn't have died."

Elinor let go. "When did he ever fail to surprise us?"

"And never in a good way! But now I can't tell him . . . anything."

Saffron sniffled hard, fruitlessly fishing in her pockets for a tissue. Elinor pulled the loose ends of her wool scarf around and dabbed Saffron's nose. Amazing. The woman who had refused to speak to their father was now distraught that she couldn't speak to him ever again.

"Come and see. You'll like this," Elinor said gently, and started walking.

Saffron followed. From behind, she chanted one of their favorite lines of Shelley's poetry.

"O wild West Wind, thou breath of Autumn's being!"

How perfect was that, Elinor thought. She answered. "Thou, from whose unseen presence the leaves dead are driven, like ghosts from an enchanter fleeing."

"Hail to thee, blithe Spirit! Higher still and higher. From the earth thou springest like a cloud of fire."

Because of their father, they knew buckets of this stuff.

"Here we are." Ellie stopped at a section of headstones set in mossy grass. "The Poets' Graves."

Her sister was surprised. "Whose grave is this?"

Elinor pointed down at a small granite stone sunk deeply into the grass and read the inscription aloud. "Percy Bysshe Shelley, 1792-1822. 'Nothing of him that doth fade, but doth suffer a sea-change, into something rich and strange.'"

Leaning over and then looking up, Saffron smiled her approval. "This is a perfect gift from the universe. Someone whispered the idea to you—Dad?"

"Dad would want us to pay our respects to his favorite poet." What she didn't say was that she hoped attending this funeral and visiting Shelley's grave might also lay Saffron's Invisibles to rest.

"It's so tiny. Look how small the plaque is. You'd think he was curled up or sitting cross-legged to meditate."

"His body isn't in there," Elinor reminded her.

"I read that." Saffron touched her own heart. Her deep breath was rough and her face pale as she looked at her sister.

Elinor said, "After his body washed up on shore, his friends burned Shelley's remains on the beach." Elinor took her sister's hand.

"Dad told me the story."

"Dad was obsessed with Shelley. After all, he named his literary hero Lorenzo Shelley."

Saffron nodded. "Dad's *Metaphorical Detective* series always has a Shelley. And so do all of Dad's essays and books."

"He's the family poet."

Saffron looked up at her with a strange smile. "The family Invisible, too."

Elinor dropped her sister's hand. Had this been a bad idea, coming to Shelley's grave? Or even bringing Saffron to Rome at all. Elinor was never sure about people, their feelings and reactions, often so irrational, especially those of her intense and mercurial sister.

"I felt him," Saffron said, staring at Elinor. Suddenly she smiled, her green eyes wide. "He's with us."

Elinor said, "You mean, right now, here at his grave?"

"No, before. At Dad's grave. I think Dad sent him."

She stared at her younger sister. Saffron's Invisibles again. Unpredictable was the mildest word for Saffron, and yet Elinor's heart had lurched into a protective throb watching her little sister hug herself during the funeral, letting herself get soaked, strands of curly brown hair blowing around her face.

She touched Saffron's shoulder. "Let's go."

The funeral had understandably upset her sister. This hadn't been the worst funeral in Saffron's life. That was her mother's, when she was only nine. Elinor had miscalculated.

She should think carefully before she spoke to Saffron. Inviting her sister along was supposed to repair this stupid feud, not worsen it. And Elinor didn't ever want to be called a meddler again. A furious Saffron had called her that after that disastrous Thanksgiving. If Elinor could roll back time, she'd erase her dinner table snark about Saffron's then-boyfriend (predicting the then-ness of him). She'd uninvent her phone call after the holiday to let the boyfriend know he had been missed and that his absence wasn't appreciated. Hearing about Ellie calling him, her sister's sizeable temper had flared and stayed on high burn.

Was that why they hadn't spoken in two years? Elinor could have picked up the phone or sent a text. But she hadn't. She was unsure of how to make amends when her sister was so angry. Plus, the peace of no Saffron in her life. Not having to extricate her sister from all her predicaments.

Now Saffron was shivering. No wonder, with no sweater, no shawl, no umbrella. Elinor pulled off her scarf and draped it over her sister's shoulders.

"Keep it until we get back to the hotel."

"I'm fine," Saffron protested, trying to hand it back. She wouldn't let herself be protected, even from the cold.

"Wrap it around your neck!" Elinor said, hearing her harshness.

Saffron giggled. "You mean strangle myself with it!" She tugged the scarf closer. "It's nice, Ellie. Thanks. I should have brought something warm."

Elinor tried to be gentle. "If wishes were fishes..."

"Remember the wishing game we made? *The Romantics?*"

"The one we made with cardboard, paper, and jelly beans for markers. Cards of hopes and wishes."

Saffron nodded with a fond smile. "My favorite was one you wrote and always made sure I pulled out. *Make something of feathers and hope,* it said."

Elinor was surprised. "You remember that!"

"You must have written more than ten of them to make sure I always got it. Every game."

"I wanted you to be able to hope. You got shortchanged." Elinor watched her sister's smile vanish. She was just trying to help, but everyone resented her help, even her ex-husband. He had taken to saying, "Thank you, Mr. Fix-it!" whenever she tried to make things better.

"But I grew up, Ellie. I learned that hope doesn't

change anything. It's what you do going after your hope that changes things."

She was right, of course. "When did you become such a wise little owl?"

Her sister looked up at the sky, and Elinor wondered what she was seeing. But Saffron looked back at her and grinned. "Arabesques through pen and pain . . ."

It was a line of Elinor's from a long-ago poem. She gave Saffron a mock punch on the arm. "How did you remember that?"

"You put your poems away, but I remember them."

Saffron took Elinor's hand and squeezed. That squeeze was worth flying across the Atlantic for.

Suddenly, Saffron was dancing with impatience. "Ellie, let's go! I don't like graves."

With good reason. Her first funeral had been her mother's.

"Okay. We have to get to the lawyer's office for the reading of the will."

She grabbed Saffron's hand and pulled her away.

What other kinds of distress was Saffron in? Had she gotten in another financial mess? Were her Invisible visits taking over again, tipping her mental balance?

The inheritance could help stabilize Saffron, who was thirty-going-on-seventeen. For years, her proto-hippie sister had bounced from one dead-end job to another, one ratty apartment to another, never finding her direction. Saffron also had a talent for attracting irresponsible men. There was no reasonable prospect of Saffron stabilizing on her own, but money could do it. Enough money, the money selling Dad's cottage would bring.

Elinor blamed their father. If Dad hadn't left Saffron

with them, if he had raised her after Saffron's mother died, her sister wouldn't be so desperate and damaged.

As they walked to the lawyer's office, the tense muscles in Elinor's neck began to relax. The air was warming, the clouds parting, the golden sunlight brightening Rome's Baroque facades and many sparkling fountains.

The lawyer, *Signor* Capelli, was an elderly man in an ancient black suit. His office was, like him, cramped and airless. He greeted them in a tenor voice that surprised Elinor. She guessed he had read lots of wills to Americans, because his English was good, if elaborate. He sat behind an immense, ornate desk—a mahogany fortress. The windows were velvet-draped, the books were deep in dust, and small copies of classical sculpture graced the side tables.

He gestured to them to sit in the big, uncomfortable chairs. Elinor smoothed her hair after adjusting herself forward and nodded to him.

Signor Capelli took out a folder and laid it on the desk. Looking up, he put on red-rimmed reading glasses, and with this Italian sense of style, began to read. After several long passages, he stopped and translated the wishes of their father.

"To make it simple, you have jointly inherited the house in Lerici, your father's sole property in Italy, with all its contents."

"I knew that there was a house, but I don't know anything about it," Elinor said.

"Your house has a view from the top of a cliff," he told them. "From hills above the sea, hills full of herbs and flowers and majestic trees." Very poetic, for a lawyer. He went on. "They have made movies about this place. I believe your film *Enchanted April* was one."

"That sounds beautiful!" Saffron said, smiling at Elinor. She turned back to the lawyer. "Have you seen it?"

His pale, wrinkled face wasn't capable of blushing, but Elinor thought she detected a small tinge of warmth. "*Si*, your father generously invited me for a weekend. Lovely area. Many Italians vacation there."

Capelli adjusted his tie and continued. "The rest—the most substantial of his other assets being his copyrights—are willed to several parties. The University of California becomes the heir to his academic works. For the novels, both of you and his ex-wife Betsy Greene share the rights and royalties. A small collection of Italian jewelry, once belonging to his late wife, who died without another heir, is given to Betsy Greene as well."

Saffron got up and went to the window. She stood in the deep casement looking out on the Roman streets. Elinor doubted she was hearing a thing.

"He says Mom shares the copyrights to Dad's novels with us," Elinor said to her sister.

Saffron turned. "I know," she said, looking startled.

Elinor rose and reached across the wide desk to extend her hand, assuming they were finished. "Thank you, *Signor* Capelli."

He shook his head. "Oh, but that isn't all. There are two special provisions of Nathan Greene's will. He wished me to explain them to you."

Signor Capelli looked down the length of his Roman nose at Elinor, who promptly sat back down. He waited until Saffron came back to her seat.

"First, Nathan Greene has left you the rights to a manuscript. It is to be found at his property in Lerici. Its value will be divided equally between the two sisters, but he stipulates that you must discover its whereabouts together and present the evidence to me that you have done so."

"Discover it?" Saffron leaned forward, her eyes bright with intrigue. "Why? Doesn't he say where it is?"

Capelli leaned back, holding the will to his chest. He looked first at Saffron over his red reading glasses, and then at Elinor. Then he answered with slow, measured words.

"*Signor* Greene has hidden the document at his home in Lerici. You are to locate it together and present to me evidence that you have fulfilled these terms. *Signor* Greene was clear that its discovery by both of you, together, was a condition."

"What if we don't fulfill that condition?" Elinor's throat filled with a surge of anger. Dad and his games, and now from beyond the grave. It was far from funny. This time, instead of helping her, he was damaging her future, because a treasure hunt didn't fit into her schedule for keeping her job at the hospital. Let alone a hunt with the help of her train wreck of a sister.

Capelli motioned calm with a horizontal swish of his hand. "Please, do not distress yourselves. The provision further states that if you do not locate the document together and provide proof, the manuscript is to be donated to the University of California, Berkeley. So, it will not be lost."

Cool relief spread through Elinor. It was just one of Dad's academic papers, with little monetary value, and nothing she needed to care about, its value one for the scholars, not to enhance their inheritance. He just wanted them to have one last game together, of the kind he'd always devised.

"What's the second provision?" Saffron asked.

The lawyer looked at her, and then at Elinor. So serious. His pause sent a chill through Elinor.

"*Signor* Greene's second provision establishes a trust for the benefit of Saffron Greene, into which is to be placed the proceeds of her inheritance, and supervised by the sole trustee, which is Elinor Greene. This trust will expire in five years, and its remaining proceeds go to the sole beneficiary, Saffron Greene."

Elinor looked at Saffron, slumped in her chair, pale and open-mouthed. She looked like Capelli had punched her in the stomach. Her own stomach felt hollow, and her pulse tripped a nervous rhythm. She was being placed in charge of her adult sister's financial welfare. It wasn't exactly going to mend their rift.

But having always looked out for Saffron, she was also relieved. This was exactly what Saffron had meant when she objected to Elinor's "meddling." Dad had made a provision in his will that might keep them forever feuding. What had he been thinking? She guessed he'd been thinking that Saffron would take a large bequest and, as Dad liked to put it, "just piss it away." And that was, Elinor had to admit, a likely scenario, given Saffron's past.

"There is one more thing." Capelli opened his drawer. He pulled out a cream-colored envelope with Saffron's name on it and handed it to her. "*Signorina* Saffron, your father has left you this letter, to be opened in private."

Saffron's eyes widened as she took the envelope and looked at Elinor.

"I don't know anything about it," Elinor said. "Clearly Dad didn't want me to."

Signor Capelli rose and extended his hand. They shook hands with him. He assured them he would be happy to assist them further.

Elinor walked out of the building taking deep breaths and headed over to a large fountain to sit on the wide ledge. Adorned with leaping dolphins, its spray wet her back, but she wanted to think before deciding what to say to her sister.

"How could he do that?" Saffron shouted at her, swarming over to sit too close beside Elinor. "For five years I'll be your slave!"

"Don't exaggerate. I'll just make sure your inheritance is safe. Well invested."

Saffron looked at her with fire in her green eyes. Her loose hair seemed to have picked up electricity and crackled out around her, despite the mist from the fountain. "No one in this family takes me seriously! Now you'll lord it over me. Why did I even come with you?"

Saffron scooched away, turning her back.

Elinor tried reason. "I didn't know he'd do this!"

Looking away, Saffron gave her nothing. "You must have put him up to it."

Again, being logical, Elinor said, "How could I? I didn't know he was making out his will. I didn't know he was going to die so early."

Saffron's stiff body relaxed. Good. How could she think Elinor had planned—or wanted—to be Saffron's trustee?

Her sister turned back to face her, and Elinor saw her defiance. "You're my guardian now. You've always thought you should be!"

"I'm not your guardian. I'm just your trustee, and only for five years. Listen, I can help you think over your financial decisions. That's all. We both need to agree about the house. Dad wanted us to agree. Maybe that's why he did this."

"Ha!" Saffron stood up, facing her, intimidating her

with her wild expression. "What about this manuscript? What if it's worth a lot of money?"

Elinor tried to imagine why her father would set this game up. He hadn't liked their feuding. Saffron had always been his favorite. He had implied to Elinor that it was her fault, when of course it was Saffron's temper that kept them apart.

Saffron tugged on Elinor's sleeve. "What if it's a lost collection of Shelley's poems?"

Elinor considered. "But how would Dad have found a thing like that?"

"Maybe he didn't find it. He could have bought it on the black market."

Again, Saffron had picked out a zebra instead of a brown pony. "A black market for old-fashioned Romantic poetry?" Clearly she had never heard of Occam's Razor or Sherlock Holmes.

This ridiculous treasure hunt was probably Dad's trick to lengthen their time together. He'd probably written the manuscript as another of his games. But what if it was worth real money? It might be the last of his novels. His popularity had grown ever since the first *Metaphorical Detective* appeared and gained a wide audience. There had even been a movie option, though it came to nothing. A thirteenth book could be worth a lot. His American publisher could make a splash out of its being found after his death, in his home in Italy.

"Whatever it is, we have to go and find it! Dad said so."

Saffron had that magic-glazed look in her large eyes. "Let's go tomorrow."

Elinor countered with facts. "I have to meet with Dad's Italian literary agent, talk to a real estate agent, and consult *Signor* Capelli about inheritance tax in Italy. It will take at least two days, and I have to get home soon, or lose my job."

Saffron jumped up. "But it's ridiculous to come all this way and not spend time at the cottage! I'm getting too wet. Let's go eat."

"Okay. Find us a trattoria around here. I'd like a real lunch."

Saffron consulted her phone. "Okay, there's one around the corner."

When they settled into the small, cafeteria-style bistro, Saffron asked, "Couldn't that manuscript actually be Shelley's? Why else would Dad keep it mysterious?"

"How on earth would Dad get hold of a lost Shelley?" Elinor stumped her sister long enough for them to finish their sandwiches and then start walking back to the hotel.

Saffron wouldn't let go of the idea. "What if someone stole it and contacted Dad? Everyone knew he was the expert. Wouldn't he try to buy something like that?"

"You don't just trip over lost masterpieces. Even thieves would have a hard time. And why wouldn't Shelley have published everything in his lifetime? He wasn't shy!"

Saffron said, "Can you walk a little slower, please?"

Elinor stopped and waited, and then continued, Saffron behind her, huffing with questions. "Okay, maybe not a lost Shelley. But why do you think Dad wanted us to look for it? Why would he make it so mysterious?"

"Because he was a manipulative, game-playing—" Elinor stopped herself from calling their father a son of a bitch on this, the day he was buried. "You and Dad are both goofy romantics. He probably enjoyed the idea of having us play one last game."

"Maybe Dad will be watching us."

Nathan's games, intrigues, and mysteries had driven them crazy. His author slogan had been *What fun is life without mystery?*

"Why do you suppose he hid it instead of telling us where to find it?" Saffron wasn't going to give up. She used to like Dad's games better than Elinor did.

"Dad never thought enough about the practical consequences of his games."

She thought of Saffron's letter and wondered if her sister would tell her what was in it. That, too, was like Dad. Another mystery.

Passing by a trash can, Elinor tossed her wad of used tissues into it with force. She saw Saffron flinch.

"What?" she said.

"I feel like you're tossing Dad's spirit in there," Saffron said.

Oh, good heavens. Elinor's shoulders hunched. She was about to embark on two weeks in close quarters with a sister who said such things. As if anyone could toss a spirit anywhere. As if spirits were crumpled, cried-into tissues. As if Saffron were a touchy teenager. It was time she grew up.

The clouds had lifted. Sunlight bathed the buildings in a mellow glow. *Signor* Capelli's description had been intriguing. Although she needed to get back to work, it made Elinor want to see what they had inherited before she sold it. And maybe Saffron was right. Seeing Dad's house could be fun.

But it had to be short-term fun. A crisis was brewing at work. Elinor had made hiking dates with girlfriends. She had joined an expensive cooking course and already missed several of those meetings. She couldn't afford to indulge Saffron for long. Unlike her sister, she had a real life to get back to.

CHAPTER 3

On the Road—Elinor

Elinor hung up the call with her boss. "Understandable request," Bill had said. "It takes time to dispose of property. Get it done as expeditiously as you do everything."

Bill extended her leave to three weeks instead of two, but with a hint of warning. "Just remember you're needed here."

"Saffron!" Elinor called into the bathroom, where her sister was getting ready to go out for the day. "I got the okay on extra leave from work. So we can drive up to Lerici and spend time in the cottage."

Her sister rushed out, one hand still holding onto the end of a half-made loose braid. "That's so great! Can we go tomorrow?"

Elinor's phone buzzed. A text from her boss. *Our best to you. From the office.*

The office. Couldn't he have at least said "from us all", or even from himself? How many people in the office even remembered that her father had died?

"Not tomorrow, but the day after."

"Yes! We have to have time there. We won't get to keep the manuscript unless we find it together, remember."

"That manuscript isn't important, I'm sure."

Why had she said that? Saffron frowned.

"I'll need a couple more days with the lawyer, so keep enjoying Rome."

For once, her sister was quick to take Elinor's advice.

She came back in the afternoon, having met a guy named Gino. She described him as "leather jacket, Vespa, one of those Italians who zip around on motorbikes, saying, *Bella, scusi*!"

Elinor tried not to say anything negative when Saffron went with him that night to a club. Gino was a good dancer, apparently, full of compliments, and had a great if lopsided smile. He sounded just right for a few days with her sister—the whole *braciole*, a delicious spicy meat roll Elinor had once made in a cooking class on Italian cuisine.

The best part was that Gino would soon be left behind. Saffron had said something about his possibly coming to visit them in Lerici, but of course that was nonsense. The guy had probably been looking for a hook-up. He'd soon forget Saffron, not that her sister was forgettable, but traveling up the Italian coast would have been a long drive to chase a casual connection.

Elinor was eager to meet with their father's Italian literary agent. Nathan Greene had bequeathed the most lucrative rights, those of his popular murder mysteries, to all three Greene women. The poet-sleuth, Lorenzo Shelley, had become popular, with his knack for applying the rules of metaphor to murder clues. Every killer in his books was compelled to leave literary scraps as a trail. Readers ate these books up, and they were still selling. If the missing manuscript was another of Dad's mystery novels, they might get an advance plus more royalty income. The Italian translations had done well, and were still bringing in good royalties, maybe because Nathan was available to speak at bookstores and at the university in Rome.

When Elinor reported on the meeting, Saffron said, "It's like owning a little piece of Dad, getting his royalties."

Elinor nodded and added, "The agent said an odd thing, when I told him we were going to see the house. He called it 'The haunted house'."

"Really?" Saffron sat up, excited. "He said that?"

"Yes."

"Did he say who was haunting it?"

"Saffron, stop."

Saffron smiled. "We can go to Lerici tomorrow. See our cottage. And find the manuscript."

"He probably just stuffed it in a drawer. We can present it to *Signor* Capelli on our way to the airport."

As she watched Saffron's smile wilt, Elinor wished she hadn't jabbed the bubble of her sister's imagined vacation.

The next day, they put Rome in the rearview mirror of a tiny, yellow, rented Fiat. Elinor could finally take off her suit and relax into jeans and a loose top. It was going to be a long drive, and she was pretty sure Saffron wouldn't do much of the driving. If any.

As she drove, Elinor talked about what she had learned and what she planned about their inheritance. "If we get as much for the house as I think we will, I can hire a financial advisor and have him invest the funds for us. We'll be set and can stop worrying."

"Who worries?" Saffron reclined her seat until she could tip her head back and then look at her sister. Her long hair fell away from her face as she shook it loose.

Elinor noticed again how her sister seemed to shrug off worry as easily as she shook her hair out.

"You should worry. Everyone should." Elinor kept her gaze on the horizon, imagining Saffron's way of driving would be to look all around constantly, and never at where she was going. Because that's what she did in life.

She had to make her sister quit fooling around. "We'll go see the house but then we have to sell, if we want to have any hope of realizing our dreams. It's what Dad wanted to give us."

"A house."

"A future."

Saffron was looking out the window, elbow propped on the window frame, her fingers lazily sieving the wind. The plains and cypress-dotted hills of Tuscany streamed by. "You're the finance person, Ellie. You do the worrying for us. You always do."

Elinor's grip tightened on the wheel. "Imagine what this can do for you. You could build that animal shelter. It's a good idea, and you've got people interested. Find a veterinarian partner, and with money you can do this."

Elinor smiled. Saffron's heart was always center stage, but her sense of practicality had left the building. She could help bring it back inside.

"I'm going to build the shelter, but I'm not in a rush," Saffron protested. "Why not stay for a whole month? We'll go back soon enough."

"Yes, but the sooner we sell, the sooner we can move forward. There are things you want to. Things I want to do."

"Name one," Saffron replied.

Elinor considered. She wasn't going to say what she thought, that she wanted to move forward with setting up an unwreckable trust fund for her sister, with a reasonable allowance.

Instead, she said, "If you roll up the window, we can put on the air conditioning."

"I'm not hot." Saffron was looking at her. "And you're dodging."

Elinor countered. "Why don't you want to go home?"

"I don't need to." Saffron's face was now averted.

"Did you and Justin break up?"

"Not exactly."

Elinor snorted. "Breaking up is a yes or no." She tapped her forefinger on the wheel, waiting to hear the definition of "not exactly."

Saffron turned back to her and stared. "I didn't tell him I was leaving," she admitted. She turned back to the window.

"Didn't you tell Justin that Dad had died?"

"Oh that, sure. I just didn't say when I was going. I just went. He got pissed off."

"Why?"

"I borrowed some cash from the register. For spending money. My paycheck will come while I'm here."

"Borrowed? Oh, Saffron!"

"Don't take that *Saffron* tone! I'm not twelve."

"But, you're on the lam."

"On the lam! What are you, Sam Spade?"

Elinor gave her a quick glare. "All of Dad's mysteries used the phrase, so don't blame me. Were you planning to avoid Justin, after stealing from him?"

"I didn't steal! I'm paying him back with my car. I'm just—don't you ever feel like escaping?"

Elinor was distressed to hear herself lying. "No. I like my life."

"If your life is so happy, quit throwing shade on mine."

Elinor wanted to let her have the last word. She truly did. But she couldn't. "What makes you do these things, Saffron?"

"What makes you hate your life so much?"

"I don't." But too many meetings clogged her calendar. Collapsing at the end of the day into a battered leather armchair, Elinor spent most evenings half-aware of the Chopin or Mozart she streamed to calm herself, while thinking, *Is this all there is?*

A cushy inheritance would let her stop wondering. Despite her thrift and caution, divorce had left her without a nest egg and only a few working decades to build one. This trip would give her a future and also help her be close again with her sister. Why did these important things have to be in conflict?

Elinor tapped the steering wheel with impatience. "I could have written a better eulogy."

"No! It was perf."

She turned and caught Saffron's insincere smile. "Seriously? 'Nathan Greene, a man of heart and community, of art and humanity'?"

They stared at one another and first Saffron, then Elinor laughed.

"Dad would have found that hilarious," Elinor admitted.

"I'm sure he was laughing," Saffron said.

They laughed some more.

Good brown wren, Nathan Greene would have told Elinor, if he had been standing beside her at his own grave. *Leave the peacock stuff to me.* She might be a brown wren, but wrens were good executors of the missed details that peacocks trailed behind their showy tails.

Saffron now surprised her. "Ellie, you've had a hard time for so long. Taking care of everyone. You need a for-reals vacation."

How ironic, Saffron comforting her. Elinor took a quick look at herself in the rearview mirror, assuring herself that beneath her perfect hairdo and careful makeup, you couldn't see life's scars. After almost forty years of life, Elinor had enough of them to make her psyche look like a roadmap.

Like the roadmap Saffron was now trying to puzzle out, holding it upside down.

"You can't read it that way! Tell me if we're going to come to a turn soon, will you?"

The road became narrow and curvy, winding around hills, dipping up and down.

"It's coming up. I just can't tell by this how soon."

"You have to tell me where we turn before the actual turn."

Saffron crumpled rather than folded up the map and let it fall. "It says we keep going. I'm excited!"

Elinor looked over to catch Saffron's grin. "The house is probably rundown, you know. Judging by how Dad took care of his things. But the lawyer said it's probably worth something because of the location, near the Italian Riviera. You know, like Portofino, where they anchor yachts. We'll make a lot of money."

Saffron stared, her green eyes wide. "Don't you already have enough money?"

What fantasy world did she live in? "No one has enough money! I don't want to work this hard. If I have some money, I could find time to write."

Saffron heaped this wish with lavish sarcasm. "You're such a romantic!"

"And you're an incurable one."

"But this is our first vacation together since we were kids. Don't let's spend it squabbling. And I don't want to go home without having adventures!"

Elinor was firm. "Okay, but you have to help get the house ready. I mean really help. We have only three weeks."

"I'm sure your boss will let you have another week if we need it," Saffron said airily, as if it were nothing to ask. "Just remind him how indispensable you are."

"How do you know I am?"

Her sister's smile curved wryly and she sweetly said, "It's your way, Ellie. Being necessary."

As Saffron turned back to the open window, a question formed in Elinor's mind, and she considered before voicing it. "So, did you ever open Dad's letter?"

Her sister waited a moment and then turned to face her. "Yes."

"I'm not asking you to reveal what's in it. Just—are you happy about it?"

Saffron got a dreamy look and nodded. "Yes."

A memory bloomed in Elinor's mind, of a small, weepy nine-year-old girl coming to share her bedroom. That first night together, Saffron had wept so quietly into her pillow Elinor wasn't sure if she was crying or if it was the wind coming in through a slightly cracked-open window.

Finally, she had gotten up and picked out her best rag doll, the one she kept tucked away for safekeeping in her closet, now that she was too old for dolls. Elinor took the doll to her new little sister and tucked it under Saffron's cheek. The girl looked up and smiled. Then she went right to sleep.

Elinor smiled at her now, silently tossing Saffron the

memory, wishing her sweet dreams in this new phase of their life together.

Elinor was to be the guardian of Saffron's good fortune, if only she could get her sister to see it that way. As the miles rolled past the windshield, she began to rehearse what she'd say to Saffron to get her to accept Elinor's new role.

Chapter 4
O Wild West Wind—Saffron

As the car crested a hill, Saffron saw the town of La Spezia spread out before them, a golden rose sky above the small town. Her breath caught in wonder. Even from far away, the Mediterranean glittered.

"Wow!" The sisters said simultaneously.

At the next turnout, Elinor pulled over and they got out.

Signor Capelli had said their house had a view of the sea. "A lovely place. Hills of herbs and wildflowers, and the bay is very beautiful. They made movies of the Ligurian coast. I believe your film *Enchanted April* was one."

Seeing the setting, Saffron was thrilled. His description was just right. Enchanting.

A grateful warmth spread through her chest, as if someone had overturned a pot of warm honey inside her.

Elinor found words. "Lerici, *il Golfo dei Poeti*"—the Bay of Poets." Elinor spread her arms wide and told Saffron, "All the Romantic Era poets lived here." Her perfect hairdo was ruffled by the crosscutting breezes, whirling strands straight up into the air. She looked like a smiling Medusa and taller somehow than her usual petite height.

"Shelley," Saffron added quickly. "He was here."

"Yes."

Her sister agreeing? Saffron continued. "Maybe he even lived in Dad's house."

"Oh my god! Quit with Shelley." But Ellie was smiling. She turned to Saffron and took her hand briefly, then let go. "We're not too far, but this is a perfect place for a stop."

Ellie went around to the back and opened the door to get out the thermos. She poured and offered the cup to Saffron, who took it.

She took several sips. "Why you never put sugar in your coffee, I'll never understand. It's as if you like bitterness."

"I do. If I put gobs of sugar in like you do, I couldn't taste the coffee."

Saffron handed the cup back, stretched her arms out and traced circles with her outstretched hands, relaxing her shoulders.

Ellie drank and looking up and down the coast, said, "If Dad's house has even a smidgeon of this view, it will be worth a lot." She handed the cup back.

She liked that her sister was enthused, but Saffron felt the glow of something else. She remembered that Mary Shelley, wife of the poet and the author of *Frankenstein* had described this region as having "rich tints of Italian heaven."

"This is bliss!" she said.

As they stood looking at the coastline, she knew Elinor badly needed a break. She'd grown so thin in the two years they'd been apart. She even looked old, a few tiny silvery threads in the dark hair at her temples. The corners of her mouth sagged more often than lifted. This was all wrong. Saffron had to save her sister from this premature descent into withering.

Another sudden gust sent Saffron's hair flying. It carried a tang of brine and scents of grass, soil, and flowers.

The wind threw the hair back from Ellie's face this time, and she stared into it with a wild impulse, chanting, "*O wild west wind!*"

Saffron giggled and raised her arms, too. She added the next line of Shelley's poetry, in deep, prayerful tones. "*Thou breath of Autumn's being.*"

"*Thou, from whose unseen presence the leaves dead are driven.*" Ellie matched the depth of Saffron's voice, making her laugh. It was like the old days, when they swapped verses from memory in their room, sometimes making fun of their father's sententious readings in the lecture hall.

"*Like ghosts from an enchanter fleeing.* Only there are no dead leaves. It looks like spring today." Saffron loved the feeling of sharing things as they used to. She wanted to stay right here, so as not to disturb this fragile harmony.

"Yes." But Elinor lowered her arms and her voice became businesslike. "Let's get going. It would be nice to settle in while it's still daylight, and we have to pick up keys first."

As they pulled onto the road, Saffron chanted out the open window, "Lerici in the province of La Spezia! What do you suppose those words mean?"

"I looked it up," Elinor said, keeping her eyes focused on the twisting road.

"Of course you did."

"La Spezia means 'Spice'."

"Perfect! We're going to own a spicy home. Let's call it The Spice."

"It already has a name. *Signor* Capelli told me it's called *Casa Magni*."

"Our house has a name! That's so Italian. What does it mean?"

"It means *big house*. It's not a special name."

As they drove toward the water, the lowering sun on its surface, twinkled like a skirmish of knives.

Saffron sang out the window into the wind. "We're going to The Big House in Spice!"

She hoped that the House in Spice would give her sister the warmth that had seeped out and left her clutching through life's storms to the pitiful raft of money.

And she wondered why Shelley was waiting for them.

Along with that thought, she remembered her letter from Dad. Opening it again in his cottage would be the perfect place. She'd read it there. And then she'd decide if she was going to share its contents with her sister. The way the day had gone, Saffron felt like sharing everything. But she knew Ellie too well to imagine that every day of the next three weeks was going to be this tranquil and fun. No, she could see the To-Do lists forming in her sister's brain, even as Ellie looked out toward the sea.

Chapter 5

The Big House in Spice—Elinor

By the time they found "The Big House in Spice", Elinor was exhausted. She wished she could turn down Saffron's enthusiastic chatter to a whisper. Or silence would be good.

She turned into the narrow, hill-hugging street on which their cottage was located. She found the number on a mailbox at the street. It was a tiny vacation place down a slope, at the bottom of the driveway. Elinor was afraid she wouldn't be able to get even their small car back up that driveway again, so she parked on the street.

Elinor and Saffron wheeled their bags down the gravel path. It led through a small garden of roses, thyme, and rosemary to the front door. The garden hadn't been recently tended and the roses needed deadheading. Weeds shot up through the rosemary, but the disarray was still charming.

Casa Magni had obviously been named "Big House" with a sense of irony.

The door was made of thick, blue-painted wood planks.

A small window with an iron grille at eye level gave Elinor a peek into a large, sunny living room, with big windows and glass doors looking west. Obviously, the view was the reason for situating a cottage here.

She put the key in the lock and twisted both ways, but it wouldn't turn. Had they given her the wrong one? She jiggled it once more, and yanked. With a hard squeak, it opened and they stepped into a stone-floored great room with French doors that opened onto a patio overlooking the sea.

Elinor and Saffron both gasped.

The large open white-walled room shone with afternoon sun. The light slanted through the trees that partially screened the view of the sea and made the golden stone glow.

The living room's angled sofa and love seat backed up to the wall and the view, creating a conversation area with an armchair and stool. Elinor thought it was quaint for Dad to create such a conventionally social arrangement. The dining table nearly backed up into the living room space. Their father had clearly wanted a table long enough to have company for dinner. The dining table and chairs left just enough room to allow passage between it and the pass-through bar that opened the kitchen to the dining and living areas. The kitchen was apartment-tiny, a glide-through space into which was crammed a large refrigerator with steel doors and a matching oven and microwave, inadequate counters, and as part of the bar, a sink and a counter containing an elaborate espresso maker.

Off the living room they found a small bedroom painted dark green. It had a single bed and a desk and chair. The bed was half-made, as if their father had just gotten out of it and wandered away to make breakfast. Never to come back. Elinor stepped into the room and tossed the comforter over the pillow, as if to complete his thought.

It wasn't a big house. Maybe the name Magni was because of the spacious views of cliffs and the sea from so many windows. They walked out onto the patio. From its hillside position, the patio had a wall-to-wall view of the water. The low angle of light made the waves glitter, a net of gold.

Elinor's breath sped up as she realized that they owned this shamble of a cottage and the land, a small, breathtaking piece of Italy. For the moment it was theirs, a home in a land that had weirdly become part of their family. She made a mental note to come out here for breakfast, even if it was just a piece of toast. What they had to eat were the leftovers from two quick stops on the road, but Italian sandwich leftovers were so delicious you could call them a feast.

The downstairs bedroom was more of a study, but there was an adjoining guest bath. Elinor decided they could call it a child's room for purposes of the sale.

Upstairs three more bedrooms shared a bathroom. Hardly a casa, but certainly big enough. Elinor imagined the feeling of not having to check her bank balance and budget before buying a new car, after they sold this definitely charming cottage.

"I guess this is my room, then," Saffron said, dropping her bags in the smaller of the three upstairs rooms.

"If you like it. It has a view," Elinor said, happy to have the roomier one.

"Sure, the view is great," Saffron said, taking her bags to the chair next to the window.

Elinor nodded, wondering what offense she had committed now, judging by Saffron's tone. But it made sense for her to take the bigger bedroom and have a table for paperwork. There would be lots. She didn't have enough outlets to work on her laptop but she could set up in the small bedroom downstairs, where there were several outlets, a giant mess, and which obviously had been Nathan's study.

Elinor went into her room to unpack, but Saffron followed.

"Let's go out before we're too tired. We need food. We need to find a shop and get some stuff."

Elinor noticed Saffron didn't offer to go and spare Elinor the chore, after she had done all the driving. Her sister was relentlessly cheery to be here, because she hadn't done all the work to get here.

Sinking into the chair, Elinor tilted her head onto the back of the chair and closed her eyes. She could fall asleep right here, sitting up.

"We can go out in the morning," was all she could murmur.

But Saffron's voice rose into a soprano that made Elinor's skin twitch. "Come on, Ellie. Walking will make you feel better."

They found a small supermarket four blocks away. At first glance, it looked like neighborhood groceries at home, but Elinor was surprised that they charged a fee to use a cart. She found a stack of handbaskets and took one of those, not wanting to deal with foreign coins just yet.

She hadn't thought about having to shop in an Italian grocery. As she looked down the aisles marked with strange words, the shock of inheriting a home in Italy sank into her heart with a leaden thud. She wasn't home. She had a lot to do, and no language in which to do it. She couldn't even find the words to buy some food.

Tears forced themselves up her throat and behind her eyes, spilling so fast that she turned away from Saffron, picking up a tomato and pretending to be fascinated. She must be simply too tired to manage her feelings.

"Look, they have plastic gloves in a dispenser," Saffron said, distracting Elinor. "I guess you're not supposed to touch the fruit. But how can you tell if it will be good?"

"We better not touch it without the gloves, then." Elinor grabbed plastic gloves, put them on, and picked up the tomato. The Italian sign told her nothing, but she pulled out a bag and put four tomatoes in it. She thought that if they had good flavor, she'd simply slice and salt them, maybe with a few sprigs of arugula. A piece of focaccia bread would accompany that nicely as an appetizer before whatever they could find for a quickly thrown-together dinner. Possibly the store offered cooked chickens the way her neighborhood store at home did.

Surprising herself with this impromptu menu—Elinor was a cook-by-the-book girl—she led Saffron through the market, deciphering words on containers, picking up milk, cheese, and eggs with plastic-gloved hands. The store didn't offer whole cooked chickens, but it had sliced chicken for sandwiches. And of course, focaccia.

"Look at these tomatoes!" Elinor said, opening her bag to show Saffron as they stood at the checkout. "They're half again as big as anything at home. I just hope they aren't overgrown and tasteless."

The clerk was fluent in English, thank goodness. She suggested they buy fabric bags to carry their groceries home, as paper bags weren't sold here.

In the kitchen, Saffron tinkered with the espresso maker. "Hey, this machine is like the one at Justin's. I'll make us some cappuccinos. You put together our plates and go sit."

Elinor arranged the slices of tomato and arugula with the focaccia and chicken, an arrangement that seemed to order itself. She took the plates to the dining table near the open kitchen and went back for jars of mayo and mustard.

"Decaf for me, please!" she told Saffron. "If I don't sleep tonight, I'm coming into your room to haunt you."

They sat down. Elinor again had a funny feeling of home, the comfort that glows in your stomach as you eat in a familiar place. But Italy was hardly that.

She hurried her food down because she needed to unpack before falling off the cliff of exhaustion, but Saffron insisted on finishing their coffees together.

Upstairs in her room, Elinor found sheets and blankets in the closet. She put them on the bed and lay down, so tired her limbs melted into the rough cotton. Forcing herself up, she staggered to make the bed and unpack, and then she shrugged off her clothes and dove into bed.

She heard Saffron shut her door, but instead of falling into the sleep that was at her fingertips, she got up and went back downstairs. What was all this cheap furniture doing in Dad's house? It wasn't like Nathan. Maybe it was the Italian's taste. But so un-Italian. Weren't they all into great design?

Inside the fridge was another tomato bursting with promise. Before she sliced into it, she smelled its earthy warmth. Flavor, she'd learned in class, was a thing anticipated in the nose and flowered on the tongue, in various places on the tongue, depending on what type of flavor. Slicing it up, she salted and ate the slices off the cutting board. Tomatoes grew so differently here. Maybe these were from kitchen gardens. None of the tomatoes at home had so much flavor. You could make this a main course!

That midnight meal did it. Upstairs, Elinor threw herself into bed and then sniffed. Were these sheets fresh? Tomorrow, the laundry. Tonight, she was done, drifting off with the scent and savor of a shiny red tomato.

CHAPTER 6
Loving Lerici—Saffron

He found Saffron in the night, buried under the comforter. His coolness as he approached stirred her and she woke. Without moving, she breathed. Could he tell if she was awake?

The soft male voice spoke inside her ear.

I am happy you have come.

The air was coffee-dark. She heard the slightest sound of breathing, a sensation that lifted the hair on the back of her neck. She shivered.

He was keeping himself invisible. She could only hear him breathing, which was odd. Invisibles rarely made breathing noises. After all, they didn't need to breathe.

"Do you come with the house?" she asked into the darkness.

A rustle and deep sigh.

A secret is beating in your heart. We are tied by a silver thread, as are you and Elinor.

She remembered Dad's wordplay and how much he liked games.

"Thread? Is this Dad?"

A figure wavered into shape, features dim, as if in twilight. Small and thin, not Nathan's tall, athletic shape, and wearing a long black coat, holding a top hat.

"What do you need?'

The reply was quick. *To help you both find what you need.*

"What we need? The manuscript?"

His words were faint as he faded away.

I have been waiting a long time.

She shivered and shook herself truly awake. Maybe he was Shelley. He didn't sound like Dad.

She turned on the light. Getting up, she threw on her robe, and though still sleepy she pulled open the bureau's drawers. She looked under the clothes she had hastily thrown in one drawer last night in a frenzied emptying of her suitcase. She found some clothing—maybe Dad's wife, the Italian? They were pretty stylish.

She looked around the mostly empty closet and then under the bed. Two sneezes from all the dust balls. One drawer in the night table was empty, except for a pencil and a wadded chewing gum wrapper.

That manuscript had to be somewhere. It wasn't that big a house. If she found it tonight, would it be a sign that their new home embraced her? Wanted her to stay? She considered going downstairs and searching, but sleepiness caught her and she went back to bed.

Sunlight from the west-facing window touched her awake. Saffron sat up. She remembered the midnight encounter. Shelley in their house. Exhilarated, she grabbed her robe, pulled on socks and padded downstairs. She started up the espresso machine. Having worked in Justin's pizzeria, Saffron knew how to use all such devices.

As a thank you to her sister for the driving, and a great start to their first full day here, she was going to make Ellie a great breakfast. The first espresso wasn't bad. She dumped it in the sink and made another, adding the milk they'd bought yesterday. She foamed it with a loud, short hiss. No sugar for Ellie. Dark perfection.

Still no sign of her sister. Saffron went into the living room. She saw a bureau and began opening drawers. Seemed too obvious to hide a secret manuscript under the placemats, silverware, and napkins, but you never knew. And Ellie had said Dad might have just stuck it in a drawer to make sure they'd arrive at the house. She tried each drawer again, to make sure she hadn't carelessly overlooked anything, but there was no manuscript box or pile of papers. One drawer was stuffed with decorative napkin rings of many colors and materials. She wondered how many people Dad and the Italian had entertained here. Looked from the number of placemats, napkins, and napkins rings like lots.

Saffron wandered out onto the patio, the small mug warming her hand. The air in the shade was cool. She stared at the sea, the pale, watery blues and sky pinks meeting in a luminous lavender at the horizon. The view sent thrills through her. Setting the cup down on a table, she spread her arms wide, as if to hug the whole gorgeous coastline. Their coastline, now. The azure sea glistened far below the steep hills where Casa Magni perched. Small trees and flowering shrubs, wafted up to her their herbal and floral scents. All this was theirs!

It could be Saffron's, if Elinor went home and left her here. She could immerse herself in this beauty without being under the thumb of her sister. Maybe there was a way to keep the cottage while sending Elinor home with her money. In Rome, Gino had given her an idea, and Saffron was going to follow up on it.

Pulling her cotton robe tighter, she turned to look behind her at the sky above the house, where the sun had already risen enough to warm up the day. Soon, as it had yesterday, it would feel like summer.

She had the sense of someone behind her. Expecting Ellie, she turned, but there was no one. The feeling was of her nighttime visitor, and it felt like a soft blessing. Yes, she needed to stay here.

"This place is just perf," she said mostly to herself, but maybe to him. "I'm going to find the manuscript. With your help."

A cool thrill ran up her back, an answer perhaps. It must be Shelley—who else would belong to the house? This was the coast where he had lived and drowned. He had told her that in the cemetery, saying he'd wait for them. Saffron felt the hum of a widened awareness in every cell, and she knew there was a rightness about all this. She just had to get her sister to see it.

After a timeless moment, her atoms shimmered back into place. The ocean murmured beyond the hush of the trees. She felt at home here, in a way she didn't in Berkeley. A pair of finches swooped down with giddy trills. They, too, were welcoming the sisters.

Shoving her hands into her pockets for warmth, she found the letter.

What a perfect morning to open it. The flap on the thick cream paper was easy to slide back, as if her father had only licked the tip of it, wanting Saffron to open it quickly. She took out a single-folded sheet of heavy cream note paper that bore the name Nathan Greene in gold letters at the top. The message was written in his signature green ink:

Listen to Shelley. ~ Dad.

So, he had sent Percy Bysshe Shelley to her. There was more, but that was the most important part. The rest made her know that Dad believed in her and her gifts.

In the kitchen, Saffron found a crusty cast iron skillet, a mixing bowl, and a cheese grater. Eggs, cheese, and toast. She'd been right to insist they shop. Another miracle! The toaster worked. She made toast and munched a piece as she scrambled the cheesy eggs. If only she'd thought of getting oranges to make fresh juice, but they had bought the bottled kind. She poured herself a glass and one for Ellie.

"My gift. Breakfast." Saffron said, when Ellie came down.

Her sister's smile filled Saffron with hope. The cottage, the spirit, and the ocean. A little heaven they had stumbled into that would make them feel winged. Here they'd both find what they needed.

They ate at the dining table, and then they took their plates to the sink and their coffee onto the patio.

"You won't believe the view this morning." Saffron picked up both cups and carried them out through the glass doors.

When she saw the panorama, Ellie gasped. "The ocean! It's periwinkle blue. And look at these gorgeous terra cotta pots. Wouldn't they be beautiful filled with pink petunias and marigolds?"

She went over to inspect the pots. They were as tall as her knees. She scratched in their dry soil. "Planting them would make the patio an even sweeter place."

Ellie wasn't thinking about selling, but about sitting

here herself. As if it were home. Saffron could see Ellie bonding with this patio, this air, this ocean.

"Look up! Grapevines." Saffron pointed to the lattice overhead. Her fingers reaching the low, dangling twigs. "Must be wonderful when the grapes are growing."

Ellie reached for the hanging, hand-sized grape leaves.

"I'm just . . . dead!" Saffron exclaimed.

"What?"

"Sorry. Millennial-speak. I'm very happy." Saffron got up and walked over to the pots, then past to look around the side of the house.

Ellie lay back on the chaise. Looking up through the leaves, her eyes relaxed and her smile curved with wonder and peace. Saffron noticed how Ellie's toes pointed with joy, and then she stretched her arms up.

This place was what they both needed. Beauty made you peaceful. Or creative. Or both.

She got up and took a few steps. She pointed up the coast as she said, "Up there is Cinque Terre. We should go. I read about it. It's hella beautiful."

"If we have time."

Ellie sat up and swung her feet around onto the flagstones. Saffron was sad to see her go back into business mode.

She pushed it a little. "They say it's a wonder of the world. Ancient villages on cliffs."

Her sister had always been adventure-averse. While Saffron was having fun in Rome, Ellie was finding her bliss in the business of death and inheritance. Saffron had read in the hotel's brochures about the tiny farms of Cinque Terre, how they grew organic fruits and vegetables and made traditional Ligurian dishes. Ellie would love that, if only she could get her sister to travel up there.

Saffron walked back and sat at the table.

"This place does have charm," Ellie said, closing her eyes to better soak up the sunlight that peeked between grape leaves and sense the hillside aromas.

It was a good sign that Ellie was using her senses. Lerici could reach into her sister and loosen those anxious coils.

"I could live here," Saffron said.

Ellie's reply made her wish she hadn't said it. "We're going to sell this place in a few weeks and go home. I'm taking my whole year's leave time. That's three weeks, all the time I've got. Your job isn't hanging by a thread."

"The struggle is real," Saffron said, dripping irony.

"We have to sell this place in a few weeks. That's it."

A shout welled up out of Saffron like a spitting cobra. "You're always taking away what I love!"

"And you're always pilfering things that aren't yours!" Ellie retorted, with an icy calm.

Saffron ran back into the house. They were back in their old patterns, Ellie manipulating her into rage. Saffron did some deep breathing, but a bitter taste rose into the back of her throat as she remembered the time her vindictive sister had called the police on her. Saffron was fourteen. She had just borrowed some cash from Mom-Betsy's Blue Fish Jar. Nothing. A couple of fives. The police, of course, had just given Saffron a warning, and the younger cop even winked at her.

Would Ellie ever forget? Then she remembered the night she came to stay with Elinor and Betsy. She didn't want to be hugged, because nothing could ever make things right after her father had left her with these strangers. Saffron spent her first night trying not to let her new sister hear her sobs into the stiff pillow. But Elinor had gotten up and brought Saffron a soft fabric doll. After a while, Saffron had fallen asleep with the doll. Maybe she could forgive her sister. Someday. But her heart still shrank, expecting criticism whenever Ellie walked into the room.

Saffron went back onto the patio and sat down.

Ellie said quietly, "I'm not trying to take anything away. I want to make things good for both of us." Ellie pushed away her cup and reached for Saffron's hand.

"Okay, we'll work it out," Saffron said. "Just keep your mind a little open, okay?"

"Okay. Three weeks is a nice vacation. We have until mid-October. We can explore the area. But we have to inventory everything, and you have to help. Agreed?"

"Agreed! I just want you to absorb the beauty and healing in this place, Ellie and to relax. You work too much."

Saffron looked over, worried she'd made a statement that sounded like an accusation, but Elinor got up with a smile and slid her feet into her sandals.

"Let's start going through Dad's stuff. We'll make a list." Ellie started into the house.

Saffron smiled. Lists were Ellie's happy place. "And while we're making lists, we can look for that manuscript box," Saffron said.

Elinor turned around quickly. "Who said it was in a box?"

Saffron shrugged and shook her head. "I assumed."

"Maybe it's nonexistent," Ellie said.

"I don't think so. Dad said something about a book when he called me last April."

"For your birthday? What did he say?"

"Yes, my birthday. He asked if I'd read his last mystery novel. I fibbed and said yes. And then he said I'd be surprised by his next."

"But why would he want his novel donated to Berkeley? It's not academic. They wouldn't even want it."

Saffron shrugged. "Maybe that was just a threat. You know how Dad liked to put spooky consequences into his games."

Her sister shook her head. "I'll never in a million years understand our father. I'm going to change into my grubs and get my notebook. We can start with that small bedroom. It's complete chaos. We can sort as we inventory."

Ellie was truly in her happy place, organizing a mess. The chaos room.

CHAPTER 7

Harmony in Autumn—Elinor

Elinor began the inventory in the "chaos room", as Saffron was now calling it. She didn't intend to search for the manuscript. The room had been used as a catch-all. Knowing her father, the best place to look for something important was in a jumble.

She said to Saffron, "This room could take all afternoon."

"Clearly where Dad threw all the stuff he was working on. Ellie, this might be where we find it!"

Her enthusiasm was like fingernails raking down a blackboard, making Elinor flinch. Three weeks of this was going to be a challenge, but she'd put all that restless energy of Saffron's to better use than playing Dad's ridiculous game. Elinor handed her a pad and pen.

"We'll write down every stick of furniture and piece of décor—and I use the term décor loosely."

Saffron took the paper. "You used to be a poet. You describe and I'll write it down."

In the closet, they found Nathan's rickety metal bookcase.

"Look!" Ellie exclaimed, picking up a paperback. "A signed copy of *The Metaphorical Detective*!"

She read aloud, "Lorenzo Shelley knew that the pen in question had been used to stab the poet. 'Of course, he deserved to be put out of his misery for that famous sonnet, but to die like this—by his instrument of fame!'"

Saffron cracked up. Ellie could be so funny.

"Never one to disguise his sources," Ellie commented. "Write down the title, published by Morning Glory Press, 1979, 294 pages."

"Do we have to write down every single detail of each book?" Saffron asked.

"Every single one, otherwise it's not accurate. Vagueness hinders truth."

She continued to pick up books and describe them in detail as they went down the row, a complete set of Nathan's twelve mystery books, all signed with his large, flamboyant signature in green ink.

"We could have a big garage sale," Saffron suggested, "if they do that here."

"They do them everywhere. People love to buy old crap."

Saffron picked up a book and brushed off the dust. She reeled off the details. "*Shelley: The Final Year*. Academic, hardcover, published in 2002. But I've never done one. I hear they can make a lot of money."

"I want to keep that book. Please go slower. Saffron, why don't you want to go home?" Elinor asked, turning around to stare at her sister.

Saffron looked up from the notepad. "Not that it's your business, but Justin and I did break up."

Elinor shook her head and raising her eyebrows said, "I'm sorry. That must have been sad for you."

Saffron looked down, avoiding Elinor's sympathy, but obviously sad. "Yes. I guess. Stupid me, thinking he really cared."

"I liked him better than the other one, but if he didn't care, he's a schmuck." Elinor turned back to the bookcase and picked up another book. "Look, a piece of paper inside with Dad's writing."

"A letter? A note?"

Ellie read a little, hesitated, and read it out loud. "Shelley came to me again last night. He has ideas for my new book, not the one about him, but the new mystery. He wants to be my muse. This could be a good game."

Saffron hopped up and down. "Shelley and Dad!"

Seeing Invisibles must be genetic. Or having a huge imagination, more likely. Whatever it was, Saffron had inherited it, and that wasn't a good thing for her future.

"Can I have it?" Saffron stretched out her hand.

"Sure." Elinor handed over the note and turned back to the bookshelf.

Saffron was too excited to continue in the closet. She had gone to the desk next to the door and was opening drawers.

"This one is locked," she said, turning back to Elinor.

"Look for the key in the other drawers." Elinor stayed in the closet, making sure they'd catalogued all the books.

"Oh look, the clock is all wrong."

Elinor emerged to see Saffron staring up at the old-fashioned mahogany clock that hung above the desk.

"It probably just needs winding."

Elinor went over to it and started to open its glass face

to see if there was a winding mechanism, when her sister interrupted her.

"Let's take a break, Ellie. It's too pretty to be stuck in here all day. I want to go out."

"Break? We just started."

But there was no point trying to tame a wild pony inside a small room. "Okay. Let's stop now and go to town for lunch." Elinor promised herself she would hold the line tomorrow.

Sunlight mellowed the facades of Lerici's buildings. As they walked downhill, Elinor forgot about the inventory when they came face-to-face with the aqua sea. The view from the top of their street was even more breathtaking than the view from their patio. They stopped, taking it in.

Saffron was right. Italy could change you, but Elinor hadn't come here to be changed. She had come to wind up Dad's estate and have this last opportunity to spend time with her sister before life spun them off in opposite directions.

The breeze had picked up and tall clouds formed over the water. Striding through the sea air, inhaling deeply, Elinor thrilled to the salt tang and a feeling of autumn.

Behind her, Saffron bounded downhill as if on springs. "We have a guardian, you know," Saffron said, raising her voice over the breeze.

"A guardian? You mean an angel?"

When Saffron had first told Elinor about her Invisibles, Elinor had told her best friend in secret. Of course, the friend didn't keep it secret. She spread a rumor. Saffron became "the weird Greene girl." She said she could never forgive Elinor, but she got her accidental revenge. The term "the weird Greene girl" acquired plurality, and they both became "the weird Greene girls." After a while, Elinor had come to like it. Her little sister had originality and the spirit to stand up to bullies. Even to her.

Two neighbors were out in their yards gardening as they passed. Talking to each other, they held up ripe tomatoes, comparing them. Though they were speaking Italian and Elinor couldn't follow, it was clearly a genial competition. They didn't of course recognize them as neighbors. Elinor wanted to say something, but they'd be going home soon, so why make friends.

Entering the outskirts of town, the leisurely pace of Lerici swirled around them.

"I love this place!" Elinor burst out.

"It's gorgeous, isn't it?" Saffron's smile was beatific.

Elinor liked seeing her so happy.

They stopped at a sandwich place with a patio overlooking the beach and settled in. Elinor tried not to think about the inventorying ahead.

Saffron looked over at her. "'There is a harmony in autumn, and a luster in its sky,'" she quoted.

"Shelley," Elinor said.

Saffron hesitated and then said, "I saw him last night. He's here in our house."

A shiver crept up Elinor's arms. "What do you mean, you saw him?"

"He came into my room while I was sleeping. I didn't see-him, see-him, but I felt him. He wants to tell us . . ." She hesitated. Elinor saw her grow cagey. "Tell us something."

Elinor reminded her of her agreement. "You've talked to Dr. Conrad about this for a long time, and you both agreed that the Invisibles are part of you, part of your subconscious."

Saffron crossed her arms, looking away. "Yes, I know.

Jung said the universal subconscious contains everything. Like poetry does. Or maybe you've forgotten poetry."

"I haven't forgotten. I often read poetry. It does contain everything. It opens you to new possibilities."

"You may read it, but you keep your heart closed."

So judgmental. Elinor was tired of parrying with her sister, and she let her temper fly. "Oh no, I think you're the one whose heart is closed. For all your freedom, you're afraid to open it to anyone. You run away!"

Saffron glared and then turned to her menu.

Elinor leaned back, halfway sorry. She softened her voice. "Are you ready to order?"

"You pick for us."

"The basil chicken sandwich looks good."

"Okay."

The waiter came and Elinor ordered Italian sandwiches, *paninis*.

As they were eating, Saffron said, "Ellie, he's part of our house."

"Shelley—your ghost?"

"I don't like that word. It's a mean way to describe them, the Invisibles. They're just people, spirits in a different phase of life."

Elinor dug down to find sympathy and acceptance. She found some as she chewed the last of her sandwich. "Of course he's part of our family. Dad told me he loved this coast. Shelley did too. So, it makes sense you'd feel his presence."

Again, a shiver danced up Elinor's back. Saffron seemed happy with this. It was nice to be sharing again, even if it was a ghost.

"Tell me more about why you don't want to go home yet," she asked Saffron as they walked back to their house.

"Berkeley doesn't feel like home right now."

Elinor shook her head. "It's home. You have always had me and Mom."

When they got back to the house, Saffron rushed onto the patio. She kicked off her sandals and took her turn on the chaise as Elinor poured them each glasses of orange juice and brought them out to the table.

After just a few minutes, Saffron got up. She tiptoed downhill over the small lawn and around the house. What was she looking for?

Then she was back, her face blazing with wonder. "Ellie, I saw a baby deer! With the beginning of horns. A he-deer."

"Antlers. A buck."

"Yes! He was just standing there and I startled him. I followed him and he stopped, and we looked at each other. It was magical!"

She smiled. Sightings of wildlife—much better than spirits.

"Come and see! He scampered away but he can't be far."

Elinor got up and put on her sandals. They cautiously walked around to the spot where Saffron had seen the deer.

"He's gone, but look!" Saffron whispered. "A rabbit!"

A wild hare bounded away, past the bank of rosemary. "Nice," she said.

As they went back, Saffron said, "I'll make dinner."

Saffron went inside, but Elinor lingered, looking out to Shelley's sea, in which he'd drowned when his sailboat capsized in a sudden storm. A poor sailor, not very good at knowing where he was going and how to get there. Much like her younger sister. If only Shelley had had someone wise to look out for him.

She sat down at the table, her leather-bound notebook in hand, intending to make notes on the inventory pages. Looking out over the ocean, Elinor caught the reality of her father's permanent absence as hard as a blow to the stomach. Death, so complete and immutable—and yet the house was full of him. His CDs, the replicas of his favorite Gauguin and Van Gogh paintings, and books by his favorite poets all seemed like things he'd walk in and again start to use.

The only things that weren't Nathan Greene were the furnishings. Not so much Dad's taste. Probably the Italian had chosen them.

And there was that bookcase of his mysteries in the closet. A weird thrill ran up to the top of her head. The wind, or the thought of death. What if Shelley came to her, too? She could book two counseling appointments with Dr. Conrad—one for Saffron, and one for herself.

There is a harmony in autumn.

The line of Shelley's gave her an idea. She turned to her notebook and wrote a note on a blank page.

There is a blue of cloud whose shadow called up the greater sea blue whose luster whistles the whitecaps.

She had always thought she should honor inspiration, but she hadn't had any for a long time. That door had been shut so tight it might have been nailed closed, but now the words sprang out in her mind like leaping deer, followed by what she used to call a panther thought. *When you find a place that loves you, love it back.*

Before she could think better of it and erase the surprising line, she shut the notebook. This place was doing things to her.

What was important was restoring her relationship with Saffron. She had to make their three weeks a game-changer. No, that was wrong. This wasn't a game. She shouldn't be thinking of scoring points. Saffron would hate that term. Elinor wanted to meet her sister more on her own terms. The problem was, she had no idea how. They had grown into such different women, with Saffron stuck in a proto-hippie haze. No, that wasn't right. She couldn't mend their tattered sisterhood by criticizing her sister. But what *could* she do? Right now, all she felt like doing was melting into this beautiful day and perhaps inviting a few more words onto her page.

But her serenity was jarred by another impulse. Elinor got up and went inside. In the chaos room she was using as an office, she went to the narrow bureau next to the closet and opened the drawers, starting with the bottom, inspecting the contents thoroughly. So typical of her father: pens and pencils without a container, socks, half-filled notebooks, novels, and matchbooks. No manuscript.

Elinor shook off the impulse to keep searching in the rest of the house. Of course this was Dad's game, launched through his will. He was the game player par excellence. Dad would have gone to the trouble to write a manuscript just to leave them with this treasure hunt that was supposed to be conducted together. Nathan Greene was a man of many dimensions. Perhaps this was one last book, to be published, but only as a joint effort by his daughters. Or perhaps it was nothing, and at the end of hunting for it, they'd find a note with yet another riddle, or a joke, and they'd laugh at the way Dad loved to keep them in suspense until he delivered a punchline.

She felt as though Dad were watching them, with his amused smile.

Chapter 8

The Invisibles—Saffron

Saffron startled awake in a dark room. Where was she? She remembered this was the cottage in Lerici. Her chosen bedroom.

A strip of light glowed under the door. The window, which she had left cracked open before she went to sleep, let in gusts of chilly, damp air.

She was about to fall back asleep when, despite the coolness, electric prickles sizzled up her arms and the dark came unmistakably alive.

"I know you," she said aloud, sitting up and turning on the light. "You can't hide."

But of course, he could. Any Invisible could hide, though most wanted her help, so what was the point of hiding?

She fumbled around on the bedside table. Trying to remember the lamp and where the switch was, she touched the leather cover of the book of Shelley's poems. The last verse she had read before falling asleep now came to mind.

In the golden lightning of the sunken sun, o'er which

clouds are bright'ning, thou dost float and run; like an unbodied joy whose race is just begun.
I am an unbodied joy.
He was talking to her. She whispered back, finishing the line. ". . . whose race is just begun?"
Shelley had been dead for more than a century. Why hadn't he moved on to *The Room Over There*? Invisibles had to move on, didn't they? Yet she felt him here, breathing, as if his breath blew gently on her forehead. She couldn't see him in the dark, but maybe if she could turn on the light.
Her skin crawled. She reached farther over and found the light switch. In the suddenly bright room, she saw a misty form in midair. Sitting up now, she waited to see what he'd do.
The poet's pale, round face became clear.
She spoke again. "A Poet hidden in the light of thought, singing hymns unbidden."
But you are bidding me to come.
"Am I?" How was she calling Shelley to come to her?
Shake your chains to earth like dew.
"But they're not mine. Ellie's the one with chains!"
She felt a subtle weight join her on the bed. She gasped. "What do you want?"
Peace between my girls.
Peace. My girls. The word grated on her wounds. She winced, feeling the many criticisms from her sister over the years, the scars that never quite healed.
Tears rolled down her cheeks. "Ellie doesn't want peace. She wishes I'd never come to this family. That you'd never sent me to them."
The voice, melodious, deep, and familiar rang out.

"Saffron dear, I had to send you somewhere. I couldn't care for you, and you never forgave me for that."

"Dad?" she called. "You're breaking my heart all over again!"

No reply. Then, "Your heart must become unbreakable like mine."

Unbreakable? She'd never be that. Was it her father or his favorite poet? Or could there somehow be a merging of the two spirits? Nothing like this had happened before, a blending of Invisibles. But honestly, what did she know about them? She was just a greeter for *The Room Over There*, someone who smiled and waved them through. No one ever came back and told her anything.

Saffron fell back on her pillow and cried harder. No one ever wanted to stay with her. Not spirits, not sisters, not mothers, not fathers. She must have a gene for spoiling everything and repelling everyone.

Lying in bed sniffling, she reached out for the tissue box. Pathetic, slobbering thing that she was, she located it, pulled out a wad, and dabbed at her nose. A metaphor for her life—a soppy wad.

But she had to take the risk of this next week with Ellie. She had to change the fact that truly her older sister had never liked her. Why would she? Saffron had taken up most of the attention as soon as she arrived, the space Ellie rightfully should have had to herself in Mom-Betsy's heart. Saffron had to try, in just the few days they had left together, to do something that would change her sister's opinion of her.

Or—and maybe this was a better idea—she had to do something that would give them more time.

Sleep wasn't going to return. Saffron dried her nose and pushed off the covers. She sat up and swung her feet onto the icy floor, toeing around for her slippers. Failing to find them, she hopped over to gather socks and robe from the chair.

Downstairs it was even colder. The window was open, and the French doors let in the nighttime chill. Saffron sat on the couch and hugged a big pillow. She thought about the Invisible. Or two Invisibles, or the two in one. Dad didn't seem to have settled. Was it because "his girls" weren't settled with each other? And why was Shelley restless, after more than a century of being dead?

She opened her laptop and wrote to Gino, the guy from Rome.

Half out of spite for her sister, and half out of hope that it might provide a compromise, she typed the email.

Looking good about going ahead on the rental plan. I'll send photos to you later. How many do you need?

Gino could do an online trial listing of their house to rent to vacationers. It would test response and see what income they could earn. Five thousand euros a month, that's what Gino had said. That was a lot of money. It could change Ellie's plan about rushing home, and everything might change.

What if the Invisible she'd felt was actually Shelley's shadow? What if Shelley's boat sinking had actually been murder? Someone might have tampered with the *Don Juan* that day, puncturing the hull. Someone could have been hired to do it. It could even have been the poet's unhappy wife, tired of his outrageous philandering, his having an affair with her sister, fed up with the husband who often ignored her. Perhaps Mary Shelley made sure to put her husband into history, a history she could revere from the distance of death.

What if their hidden manuscript made it clear that Shelley knew what Mary planned to do?

Saffron's head prickled with a cold thrill. She hugged the pillow. Would Dad have made a mystery story out of Shelley's murder? A murder could be the reason Shelley's spirit stayed here. Perhaps he wanted justice. She had to look into the history of Shelley's life. If he had been murdered, surely there would be something in the stories of his life to suggest that.

She started upstairs, then thought better of it and instead went into the chaos room. She looked in all drawers, except the locked one, for Dad's manuscript. After finding nothing there, she went into the kitchen. Hiding it in the kitchen, on a top shelf or in the back of a cupboard would be a clever spot. Very like Dad to pick an unlikely place.

Finding nothing, she turned up the pillows of the couch. Surely she'd have felt something if it was under there, unless it was a slim manuscript. Would Dad hide something so valuable in a couch? She looked over the back of it to be sure, and then got on her knees to look under. Nothing but dust balls and floor.

She went into the chaos room and opened all the drawers again. Then she came to the locked one, but she was too drowsy to think about it just then.

She went back up to her room and got into bed. She had one thought about her email to Gino, maybe she had worded it wrong, but she pulled the covers up to her chin and fell asleep.

* * *

The next day, they walked back to town, to the same place for another delicious lunch. Saffron followed her sister, enjoying the fact that Elinor wanted to explore beyond the house.

Ellie suddenly patted the top of her head, as if bothered by flies.

"Ellie, what's the matter?"

"Something buzzed me." She again swatted.

Saffron watched an Invisible cohere from a swarm of dots, teasing her sister's hair, and amazingly, Ellie could feel it.

Elinor had once seen one of Saffron's Invisibles, the Swedish lady. Ellie had described the woman who walked into their bedroom one night. Then Ellie had forgotten.

What do you want from us? she thought. Apparently, she said it aloud.

"You're talking to flies now?" Ellie swatted the last imaginary fly off her hair. "Or are you talking to one of your imaginary beings?"

Imaginary. In those lonely childhood days, when the Invisibles had first started coming, Ellie could catch glimpses, or so she had said. But then she developed psychic armor and lost the ability to believe in anything.

Saffron's phone vibrated. A text from Justin, demanding she return the petty cash and justify leaving without notice. Demanding, ever demanding. *And I expect to see you immediately when you get home. —J*

She texted back: *Don't count on seeing me soon. Staying for now. Sell Elvis. Keep the money.*

"Elvis" was her ancient, dinged-up car. It was unfair of Justin to make a big deal. She needed spending money. What did Justin know? He knew pizza, and all he dreamed of was the next pineapple-mushroom-sriracha pizza topping.

She needed to dream bigger. *Because. Freedom.* She had seen it scrawled with a marker on a street sign in Berkeley.

If they were staying another week or two, and Saffron was sure it would happen, she should email her dog-walking clients. She didn't miss Justin, but she missed her Keegan, Nissa, and Silver, the terrier, bichon, and collie mix she walked regularly. She had left in such a hurry that her furry friends and their families would wonder where she was.

The Invisible was again circling Ellie's head.

Elinor swatted, stopped, and glared. "You're playing with my hair."

Saffron cracked up. "Dr. Conrad would say you're projecting."

CHAPTER 9

Cosma Takes Charge—Elinor

Three weeks obviously wasn't long enough to inventory, clean, prepare, and sell a house of this level of dilapidation.

So a week after their arrival, Elinor emailed her boss, Bill, again. She wrote first thing in the morning, knowing it was the end of the day there, when he'd be tired and liable to make snap decisions. Bill was not only going to be day's-end tired, but end-of-Friday fatigued. The best time to twist his arm. People got special leave after a *bereavement*, didn't they? She used the word twice in her email and asked for an additional month.

Her boss' reply gave only mild pushback.

I just granted you three weeks, and now you want even more. As you know, we frown on utilizing all of your annual vacation leave at one time. But in this special circumstance, you may have the month. And you can throw in two weeks' sick leave. Just remember you're needed. And don't get sick for the rest of the year.

Such a huffy, stuffy note. Utilizing. Couldn't he just say

"using"? And why did he have to remind her of the policy she knew well, since she had helped write it? But she couldn't afford to anger her supervisor or lose this job, so she'd suck up the tone. It was nice that he'd reminded her that she was central to the department. A department for which people lined up seeking positions, especially for jobs like hers. She wouldn't ask for a minute more, and she'd be sure to be on a plane home by the end of November.

But she needed time to prepare the house properly for sale, or they wouldn't get everything they could. If she got some help to spiff the place up, soon they should be getting offers. Once that happened, Elinor could leave, providing she could leave the details to a wonderful local realtor. She had yet to find one, but that would happen any day, since she had contacted a few.

So now she also had more time to mend things with Saffron. That would be good, too. Not to mention time to soak up a little Italian charm.

Since they had arrived, Lerici had blanketed them with its magic and Saffron seemed like a changed person. Less odd, less quarrelsome. She had relaxed into the town and its style, its beaches and shops. Saffron was taking advantage of the vacation from worry Elinor provided by taking charge of the sale, and she was sleeping in every morning. That gave Elinor time to savor a little of the local charm herself, from the comfort of this cottage and its beautiful patio.

Having received Bill's email, she closed her laptop, got up, and walked around the living room. Saffron must have had one of her nighttime vigils. In the room they had shared as children, Elinor had often awakened to find Saffron's tee shirt, sandals, and robe strewn on the floor, an open book on her bed, and the carpet covered in crumbs.

Elinor now picked up socks from the couch, took a half-filled glass of water and a plate with half a banana to the sink. Her sister must be sleeping late to make up for it.

Since it was a bright morning, with light coming into the now tidy room, Elinor used her phone to capture pictures for listing the house. She took a shot of the beautiful turquoise and gold Murano glass candlesticks. Those were truly lovely pieces, rescued from the chaos room and placed on the dining table to catch the light and sparkle. Soft, reflected light glowed on the white walls and pastel-colored couch and chairs. Elinor tried to imagine her father riding down Venice's Grand Canal in a gondola, with his Italian wife, but she couldn't picture the woman. But Dad must have been happy with her. The candlesticks glowed with a light suggesting harmony.

She should buy a few more pieces of local art and pottery. With some sprucing up, the pluses of this place would overshadow its deficits of cheap window frames and a dingy ceiling.

Wandering out to the patio, she looked for good shots. If she planted the terracotta pots with purple petunias and cascading white alyssum, it would be the highlight before the spectacular view. She'd get new throw pillows for the couch. She could do this all in a week or two.

A burst of nostalgia interrupted her—a sense of having been here before. Was it sadness about losing Dad, with the certainty of his being dead so new?

She went over to the edge of the patio, sat at the table, and looked out. She pictured her father sitting out here enjoying this view. But now he was gone. Dad would never walk through the double doors and sit down with her. He wouldn't ever again call to make excuses for not having called sooner. She'd never again hear his disparaging witticisms that made her laugh despite herself, nor would she wince at the sarcasm she had picked up from him, but could never execute with the same flair. Her peacock of a father would never dazzle and disappoint, dazzle and disappoint, never again.

An epiphany of loss. She tried to slam shut the door in her heart. Tears slid down. She knuckled them off her cheeks with two swift dabs. This wasn't like her. She didn't allow herself nostalgic moments. She had to again root herself in what she could see and touch and count. That's what grounded her in the kind of reality she could plow through without falling apart.

That's how she had gotten through marriage, infertility, and infidelity, and how she'd get through death. She had learned to perfect this after a brutal divorce, coming down from a beautiful home in the hills to a cramped condo on student-ridden Northside. She had then determined to take no chances with her security, no risks with her feelings ever again. And she wouldn't do it now. She'd focus on selling this place, not on imagining a visit with her father here that had never transpired.

Because hope always brought disappointment. Elinor knew that. Even the poetry she had tried to write in her twenties had brought a string of rejections. Wanting to be a poet was paired with the indelible knowledge that it was hopeless, with a poetry professor for a father, one given to the quick, slashing critique that left you nowhere to go.

She had rebelled by writing *haikus* on scraps of paper and leaving them in bookstores, cafés, and libraries. That had felt satisfying, until she got a phone call after she mistakenly left one written on her business card. The ensuing date was the worst blind date ever, when he reached over and pulled her almost off her barstool to kiss her with way too much tongue.

Saffron came outside as she was sitting here, eyes still moist. Elinor pretended to cough and surreptitiously pulled out a tissue to blow her nose. It didn't matter. Her sister wasn't up to noticing things.

"I need caffeine." Saffron's eyes were at half-mast.

"Let me make you a cup. It's after ten."

Saffron shook her head, saying as she went back inside, "I make it better."

Elinor went inside. Saffron handed her a cup and Elinor sat in the armchair while her sister settled onto the couch.

"Did you have trouble sleeping?"

Saffron nodded. "I was up a long time. What have you been doing?"

"Taking pictures for the lawyer's inventory."

"Can I have copies?" Saffron asked.

Elinor was puzzled. "Sure. I'll finish taking them this morning."

She hesitated, her conscience wrestling with a desire for harmony. "I've called some realtors to drop by and take a look." The pinch of anger on Saffron's face made her quickly add, "We need to get a professional to give us ideas."

Saffron snapped, "I need more sleep. We can talk about this later."

She stomped back upstairs with her cup, robe flapping and sash dragging.

Just as well. Elinor didn't need a grouchy, half-dressed sister when a realtor might drop by.

Briefly, she wondered again why Saffron wanted the photos.

She took pictures in the chaos room, doing her best

with the lamp, chair, and not-so-bad bureau. The cheesy replicas of famous paintings would have to go before anyone viewed the house. Maybe she could find some prints of local views, maybe even a watercolor from a local shop. It was funny that Nathan Greene had such bad taste in decorating, while his taste in poetry was admirable and praised. He loved his Romantic Era poets and Impressionist artists. He didn't care that the frames were cheap or the selection of art clichéd.

She went back into the living room to photograph the patio doors, first with curtains closed and then open. She looked at the images and was satisfied. Next she'd try to capture the patio and view, the house's biggest selling point. But when she went outside, instead of shooting the panorama, she sat down and made notes. Notes for another poem, of all things. This house was having an effect on her.

The breeze gusted. A sudden whistle, a bird call sharp as a summons. The next line that came pierced her.

He lived here a lonely bird, to end life as a strange neighbor.

She felt her father's loneliness for home here. That silly mahogany clock, emblem of an America he was cut off from, among people with other traditions and languages. His impossible yearning for home. He must have often wished to go back.

A sudden, electric buzz jarred her. The doorbell. She wasn't used to its tinny sound, as if from a dented bell. It rang again and she rushed inside to the front door. It could be the first agent. Good that Saffron had gone back to sleep.

On the narrow front step stood a small, dark haired woman dressed in a shade of green that defied a name.

"*Prego*, are you *Signorina* Greene?" she said, holding out her hand.

Elinor shook it briefly.

"I'm *Signora* Cosma Gavazza, your new real estate agent."

Her suit, a color between teal and olive, was topped with a bright red scarf wrapped loosely around her neck, ends tossed back over her shoulders. Colors that might have been nice in a salad, but on a woman made her resemble a tropical lizard.

Cosma barged in, hardly giving Elinor time to get out of her way. Surveying the living room, she turned back as Elinor shut the door. "*Signorina* Greene, this will be easy to list."

"*Signora* Gavazza, please call me Elinor. We're starting to get the place ready to sell, so it won't look like this . . . It's too soon, but I'll work fast."

"Call me Cosma," the woman responded. "It's never too soon to list a house in Lerici. The market is always good."

Cosma made a gesture, wiggling her raised hand with its dark red, pointed fingernails. Elinor thought it must be an Italian gesture that meant she should believe what Cosma said.

The realtor walked in a semi-circle around the great room, her teetering heels clicking on the stone floor with smart little taps. Everything about Cosma was smart, and that made Elinor nervous.

Over Cosma's shoulder, she saw Saffron approaching, still in her robe, hair wild. Her sister was frowning alarmingly.

Elinor tried to smooth things. "Saffron, come and meet

Signora . . . meet Cosma. She's going to help us determine the value . . ."

"Saffron Greene," Saffron said with as much ice as a half-dressed woman could pack into an introduction. She didn't extend her hand for a shake, and Cosma wisely didn't offer hers.

Elinor could see now that it would have been better to prepare Saffron for this first visit. She hadn't realized that *Signora* Gavazza would show up so quickly. But of course, real estate agents were always quick, probably to edge each other out with exclusive listings. Elinor wasn't sure she wanted to work with this woman, but maybe her aggressive qualities would help sell the house.

"Can you give me a rough idea of the value?" Elinor said, as much for her sister as for the realtor.

"We're not in a rush to sell," Saffron added, glaring at Cosma.

Then she went into the kitchen and noisily made an espresso. She took it upstairs. Elinor was relieved to have only one pushy person to deal with.

"*Signorina* Greene . . ." Cosma began.

"Please, it's Elinor."

"*Signorina* Elinor . . ."

"Just Elinor."

"Elinor, let me tell you one big thing. It's complicated to sell real estate in this region. You must consider the zoning regulations, taxes, and whether or not you have earned income from renting it—and if so, how much—to consider before you decide about selling, or can qualify to sell it. May I look around now?"

"Well, of course." Elinor took her all the way into the living room. Cosma glanced quickly into the kitchen with a look of disdain and brushed her manicured fingers over the dining table.

Cosma kept up a monologue as they walked. "You know, I'm familiar with this property. It's rumored that the great English poet Shelley once stayed here. But nobody knows for certain."

"It's truly a local rumor?"

"From long ago, but it persists. Everyone loves a ghost story."

"Ghost story?"

The realtor walked quickly around the living room. Facing away from Elinor, looking out at the view, she said, "Everyone in Lerici knows of it, the death of Shelley. The English poets all loved this area. As who wouldn't love it. Especially the English. You Americans too."

"So, the Romantic poets did come here."

"Oh yes. And the area is known for their presence."

"Huh." The connection between poetry, Lerici, and this house made Elinor's face tingle.

"Yes, definitely. The rumors are promoted to increase property value."

"Oh, they're just urban legend?"

"No, the poets definitely came here. May we step out onto the patio?"

Elinor nodded, and Cosma opened the doors and went out.

"Do you know where the poets lived?" Elinor asked as she followed.

"We simply aren't certain which houses they rented. They were all poor at the time, except for Byron. That's why they came to Italy. It was cheap."

"What else do you know about this property and the poets? Anything that might increase its value?"

Cosma gave her a quick, suspicious look. "Are you thinking to sell it furnished or unfurnished?"

Elinor was hopeful. "Can we sell it furnished?"

Cosma shook her head, embarrassing Elinor. As she led Cosma back inside, she saw through Cosma's eyes the rickety dining table painted deep blue, the mismatched sofa and armchair, the whole jumble of a room. Saffron had said she liked the homey feeling. Saffron was not representative of most buyers, Elinor was sure.

"The furnishings are certainly poor," Cosma said. "So I don't recommend selling it furnished. Perhaps you could hold a yard sale."

"So they have them in Italy too?"

Cosma gave her a glare. "Of course. You must get better furnishings to stage the house. I can help you. You may need repairs, too. This table is nice," Cosma said, passing the blue dining table on into the kitchen.

"Is there anything about the house's history that will help it sell?" Elinor asked.

"The house is on our local registry. I will check, since you're interested, but so many buildings here are old. You know, you could divide this into apartments to rent. It's big enough and that would produce good income."

But renting the house wasn't part of Elinor's plan to sell and invest the proceeds in bonds to yield each of them a meaningful and secure income. After she had enough money to fund her retirement, maybe she'd go back to writing, or even take up her photography again. She could take more culinary courses, hike every trail in the Bay Area.

If she had enough money, she could make art and food to her heart's content. Her life would change and become a lot freer, like Saffron's—only with security. Long morning coffees here on the patio. But not necessarily here, just somewhere like here. Unlike her sister, she wasn't going to indulge in an easy life at the risk of eventual poverty.

She came back from these thoughts to hear Cosma enthuse over her idea. "If you wanted to split this into rental units, I can act as your local rental agent. My fee is very reasonable. We could rent it out so you can wait for the best time to sell. And in the meantime, make repairs."

Hadn't Cosma just said this and every season was a good time to sell? Why was she quick to provide alternatives?

Elinor would have to find another realtor.

"Shall we go upstairs?" Cosma inquired.

To be polite, though she wanted to throw Cosma out, Elinor nodded and led the way up to the first bedroom, hers. She knew it was in good shape, and perhaps she could get rid of Cosma before Saffron woke up again.

Cosma took a few steps inside, looked around, advanced into the room a little more, and pronounced, "Adequate."

Adequate? Elinor led her into the bathroom, which Cosma inspected with more interest, opening drawers and cabinets, sliding back the shower door and even turning on the tap. She put her hand into the water.

"The hot water comes quickly. Very good," she said, and left.

Cosma walked down the hall and stopped at Saffron's door. She waited. Elinor hesitated, and then she opened the door a crack and peeked. Saffron was up and in the bathroom, with the shower going. Perhaps it was safe to give Cosma a glimpse, but no more. If Saffron came out and saw them in her room, she'd flip.

Elinor opened the door on the colorful disorder of

Saffron's bedroom—only two days' worth of strewn clothes created a patchwork of vivid pink, green, apricot, and blue. The tossed-back comforter revealed wrinkled sheets, one corner pulled off revealing the naked mattress. The pillows were crooked and one pillow had fallen onto the carpet. A bureau drawer was slightly open, while the drawer below it was open wider, showing a pale cream nightgown creeping over its edge as if trying to escape and join the party of clothes below. Saffron's suitcase was open on the only chair in the room, its contents rummaged in as a robber would.

Elinor tried not to gasp. "My sister is spontaneous," was all she could say.

Cosma shook her head. "A mess. But a good room. Nice window." The realtor walked over to the window and pronounced, "A good view. Very good feature."

The shower stopped. Elinor hastened Cosma out and closed the door, relieved to have missed annoying Saffron with their intrusion.

Cosma said, "Before we can show this house, the mess must be cleaned up. You understand, people don't want to see a house that's lived in. They want to see a model house, so they may imagine themselves living here, with their things. Or better ones. This—" She swept her arm around—"needs a great amount of work. You cannot show it this way."

Cosma was apparently used to bossing her clients. Disappointed, Elinor followed her on down the hall to the third bedroom. Cosma walked in and looked briefly around at the single bed pushed against the wall and the half-painted feature wall and bookshelf. She was clearly not pleased.

"Not adequate for a bedroom, but we could call it a study."

They went downstairs. Elinor ushered Cosma outside to see the patio, the garden, and of course the exquisite view. Cosma's brief nodding told Elinor that the house had scored with her in this area.

Lastly, she had to show the realtor the chaos room.

Cosma walked in first, turned, and said, "You know this floorboard feels soft. I have a cousin who works on houses and can go underneath and look for you to see what might need repairing."

Eleanor nodded before she had time to think. "But we're not interested in extensive repairs."

"Have Matteo go under and see what's what. No need to make up your mind at this point." Cosma forced out a grin. "If you wish, I can contact him."

Elinor reluctantly agreed. It sounded like a scam, but finding local contractors she could trust would be time-consuming. For some reason she couldn't explain to herself, the more aggressive Cosma was, the more Elinor was inclined to put herself and her house in this realtor's hands.

"This is a nice desk, and the clock is good too," said Cosma as they left the room.

As they stood at the front door, Saffron came down and went into the kitchen without saying a word.

Cosma asked, "Will she be gone when I'm showing the house?"

Embarrassed, Elinor assured her they'd both stay away. She took Cosma's card.

"I will email you," Cosma said, and she left, her heels making determined thumps on the flagstone path.

Maybe the next agent would have a more promising view of the house.

Elinor sank into the couch. Disposing of the house in a foreign country, with this junk furniture, overseeing contractors, and with Saffron resisting, weighed her down. Elinor leaned her head back and stared at the ceiling.

Saffron came out of the kitchen. Tersely, she said, "You can't hire that woman without my agreeing!"

Elinor decided at that moment that she would hire Cosma. Agreement or not.

"Please sit down and listen before you get worked up."

Saffron frowned but sat. Elinor told her about Cosma's suggested repairs.

"At least someone else is telling you to take more time!" Saffron fumed, arms crossed.

"Saffron, you've never stopped thinking life works by hopes and wishes. But here are some facts. This house seems to need repairs. And this realtor can help with them. So that gives us more time here. I wish you'd stop pouting. We can't afford not to sell."

Saffron turned to her. She unfolded her arms to twirl a strand of hair around her finger, a habit she always had when thinking. "All I want is more time. I'll help."

Saffron took a sip of her coffee and asked, "Want some?"

Elinor nodded and let her head fall back on the cushion.

She was suddenly tired, and it was nice to have help, even if only with a cup of coffee. The prospect of managing repairs and the sale, and Saffron, made Elinor want to go back to bed and pull up the covers.

"Short pull or long?" Saffron asked.

Elinor managed a smile. "Long, please."

Saffron brought the cups over and sat down. "Tell me everything the realtor said."

Sipping her coffee, Elinor summarized the visit. "Cosma thinks we need a lot of repairs, some big, like the floor in the room down here, and also to get some new furniture. She says the property could be more valuable if we do all that."

Elinor hesitated, considering whether or not to be honest and tell Saffron that Cosma had suggested a way to turn it into rental units. Honesty won.

"She said we could turn it into two separate apartments, for—"

"For rental!" Saffron finished with a flourish of her hand.

"That's an idea, but no way can we afford to do that. It would cost more than I have to invest, and you don't have any cash, so I'd have to pay for it. But I need all my money to live on. It's just not an option."

She noticed that Saffron didn't suggest the one thing that might make it possible, a mortgage.

Instead, her sister finished her coffee, swung her feet off onto the floor, and said, "Let's go explore Lerici. We need some adventure."

Startled, Elinor nodded and finished her cup. Getting out of the house of contention might sustain Saffron's good mood. For today, anyway. She'd take tomorrow as it came.

Chapter 10

Local Dinosaurs—Elinor

Elinor walked downhill behind Saffron as they headed toward town and the sparking harbor. Cobblestone streets were lined with red-roofed buildings painted bright colors. She took deep, measured breaths as they walked. Around the curve of the coastline, in the distance, another castle towered over a small village, a piece of Italian medieval history.

For a moment, Elinor pictured the medieval towers and villages, the fortresses of nobility and the people who served them. As they descended, she thought with satisfaction that for the moment she owned a piece of this history, like a lady with her own small tower. But soon she'd go home and leave this nostalgic fantasy of a town.

They stopped when they reached the foot of the hill. Looking up and down the beach promenade, which hugged the coastline, they could go in either direction.

In front of them, at the intersection of the street they had walked along and the promenade, was their town's medieval castle. Huge, stark stones piled it high on a promontory in the harbor. In its time, it would have been nearly unbreachable. Now it was a tourist stop, housing a natural history museum.

"Want to take a look in the castle?" Elinor asked.

"Let's first walk up along the beach," Saffron said, pointing north.

The tree-lined promenade was lined with shops, cafés, boutiques, and patio restaurants. They turned and strolled. Adults and children splashed in the water and soaked up sun in beach chairs. It was surprising that anyone would wade into the ocean on this cool day, with the waves crashing and foaming. Signor Capelli had told them that Lerici was a vacation place for Italians, a modest version of the exclusive Italian Riviera resorts that lay north, beyond San Terenzo.

Children kicked soccer balls on the grass that lined the promenade and white-haired men sat on benches chatting as they faced the sea with their wrinkled, tanned faces. Everywhere ebullient Italian bounced its consonants around like the thwok of balls the kids kicked high.

Hungry now, Elinor pointed to a restaurant. "How about lunch?"

They settled at a rickety table on the patio facing the harbor. Clay pots overflowed with red, blue, and yellow flowers.

Elinor caught a waiter's eye. He came and handed them menus.

Saffron said, "You order for us."

Elinor glanced through the menu and when ready she signaled him. "We'll both have *caprese* salad, pasta bolognese, and artichoke *torta*."

When the food came, Saffron dug in and chewed vigorously. She was a believer in chewing, Elinor remembered, having learned from her onetime macrobiotic diet that food was best digested in the mouth.

Ellie couldn't finish.

Saffron stopped eating. "I'm sad," she said. "I know you're sad too, Ellie. I can't imagine life without him. I'm used to being angry because Dad isn't calling me."

"Yes. It's sad because it's so final."

"I feel like I never knew him. Why did he leave your mother?"

Elinor didn't know what to say. She pushed her plate away and looked Saffron in the eye. "He left because he met your mother."

"Oh," Saffron said. "Then why should we miss him? Dying was one of the best things he ever did. We wouldn't be here in Italy if he hadn't."

Elinor had a moment of imagining if Dad had stayed with her and her mother. Imagining a life without Saffron twisted up such a knot inside her that she gasped, tears welling up.

"You may not believe it, but Dad loved us," Elinor said. "Or he wouldn't have given us his house." She blinked the tears away.

Her sister's gaze was drifting. "I guess we should be grateful. I sometimes feel thankful . . ."

Saffron looked lost. Elinor knew this was the moment for action. For an adventure. She caught the waiter's eye and signaled. He quickly brought the bill. Calculating a tip and counting out cash restored Elinor's composure.

"Let's go see the castle," she said.

Saffron grinned and nodded.

They went up the hill and entered the fortress through a doorway in the thick circular wall. They were greeted by life-size reconstructions of dinosaur skeletons—huge, ferocious beasts in skeletal form reared up in the semi-darkness of the museum.

"This is a museum of the Prehistoric savannah of Lerici," Elinor read from a sign.

"It's amazing!"

Elinor raced over to another sign, grateful to have shelter in the world of facts. "Dinosaurs lived in the Ligurian area two hundred million years ago."

"*Pareiasaurus Dilophosaurus*," Saffron read.

Ellie walked past to a smaller dinosaur. "This one's called '*Giant Ceratosaurus Vulcanodon*'."

Their voices sounded faint in the high-ceilinged space. Around the walls were dioramas and two small robot dinosaurs that at the touch of a button gnashed their toothy, clamping jaws.

"This is so cool," Saffron said. She reached out to touch a small one. "This one's so cute. I'll take him home."

"He can be my pet dino."

Saffron's laugh echoed wild in the tall, dark space. "Normal people have cats, Ellie, but you would have a dino."

"Are you saying I'm fossilized?"

They smirked at each other. They next came to a replica of *Tethyshadros*, one of the smallest duck-billed dinosaurs, native to Italy.

"Ellie, do you know the theory that the dinosaurs evolved into birds?"

"It's not even a theory now. They say it's a fact."

"Can you imagine what dinosaur songs would have been like?"

"Like Beethoven played on a pipe organ!"

"I want to include birds in my shelter."

"You're still thinking about it then?"

"Of course I am. At Thanksgiving, you told me it was a silly idea. But I've never given up. And you said the money from our house could fund it."

"I'm sorry I called it silly. That was dumb of me. Tell me more about your idea."

"It's a humane shelter that could also bring trained animals into nursing homes, so old people can pet them."

Elinor smiled and said, "I envy the way you can dream. I lost track of mine."

Saffron smiled at Elinor, who said gently, "*Hope, the thing with feathers*. Remember the card in our game? I always planted extras for you to draw."

"Ellie, we should make our hopes a reality," Saffron said. "That's what life is for. Don't you think?"

"I think we should see the gift shop now."

They stopped at a display and Saffron held up a pair of potholders with dinosaur drawings. "Don't we need these?"

Elinor shook her head and moved on. Saffron persisted, finding a frilly pink apron decorated with a Tyrannosaurus Rex wearing a frilly apron.

"You should start cooking again," Saffron said. "You took classes at home. Take a class here in Italian cooking. And wear this," Saffron said, holding it up.

Elinor laughed. "That may be why the dinosaurs are extinct. Funny aprons."

"I'm buying it. I dare you to wear it on Thanksgiving."

Elinor was surprised Saffron mentioned a holiday that had driven them apart. "You know, if we're staying to fix up the house, we might be here for it."

Saffron's eyes welled up, and that told Elinor everything. She decided to ask for more time off work so she could make a great holiday meal, one that would erase the other from memory. She'd begin researching recipes and ideas when they got home.

As they came down the walk to their cottage, Elinor saw a man kneeling beside their front door. He was chipping away at the stucco with a chisel and hammer. His dingy overalls and tanned arms made it clear he was a handyman, and used to working outside. But why on their house?

Elinor shouted. "Who are you? I'm going to call the police right now."

He turned around and got to his feet, letting the tools drop. Startled, he had an innocent expression. His tanned features and dark eyes seemed shy as he ducked his head briefly.

"*Signora, scusi, la signora Gavazza mi ha mandato a riparare questa porta. Mi dispiace! Dispiace.*"

He took off his cloth cap and held it to his chest, waiting while Elinor shook her head. His obvious innocence calmed her.

"Do you know . . . ?" Elinor asked her sister.

Saffron shook her head and snapped at the man. "We don't speak Italian! Did you say *Signora* Gavazza sent you?"

"*Si, si,*" he said, still intimidated.

Elinor asked, "What's your name?"

He shrugged, looked like he still expected to be attacked.

Pointing to herself, Elinor said, "*Signorina* Greene. Your name? *Nome?*"

He pointed to himself and replied, "Matteo Poggi."

Whatever the reason for his destroying their doorway, Matteo Poggi looked helplessly pinned to the spot. Elinor

89

used her best broken Italian while waving him away. "*Non e . . . necessario . . . Arrivederci!*"

Matteo Poggi picked up his tools and speedily left.

"I'm going to call Cosma," Elinor said once inside. "This has to be her guy."

Saffron went out onto the patio, and Elinor decided to go upstairs to make her call privately. She didn't want Saffron to overhear her hiring the realtor.

On the way to her room, she glanced into her sister's. An unfolded piece of paper lay open on the top of the bureau. Mildly curious, Elinor went in and picked it up.

> *My dear Saffron, By the time you read this, I will be gone. I want you to understand why I arranged things as I did between you and your sister. I put her in charge of your share of everything because Elinor is a bit obsessive-compulsive. She loves the fuss and detail of handling practical matters. She loves it the way you love your Invisibles and animals. She'd be miserable if she wasn't managing you!*

Elinor's hand shook a little as she held the letter. She was shocked to discover that Dad had this private understanding with her sister. Somehow Elinor had always thought she was his confidante, the one he trusted to understand things Saffron couldn't. She read on, afraid to find out more.

> *I'm giving you something Elinor doesn't value, but I know you will. It's a treasure, everything you could imagine and more, even with your great imagination. I hid it because I want you*

to take time to find it together. It will change your lives. I want my girls to come back together. Remember how well she cared for you when you first went to live with them. A treasure hunt should help. You both always loved games.

~ Love, Dad.

Elinor stood still, the letter in her hand. Her father thought her obsessive-compulsive—in other words, as flawed as Saffron.

When tears came they were tears of anger. After all she'd done, all she tried to do to make things go well for everyone, including her father. Making excuses for his absences, smoothing things over when he insulted her sister or her mother with his clever sarcasms. All her life, Elinor had tried to please and impress her father. And now—obsessive-compulsive. A private letter to Saffron, the one who needed support. Not Elinor.

What could Dad have meant by everything Saffron could imagine? Her sister's power of fantasizing was prodigious, and yet Dad always encouraged it. You'd think he would want her to grow up, if only a little. You'd think he'd write her a letter encouraging her to listen to and trust her older sister.

A hidden treasure, Dad had written. Elinor marveled at the idea that something might be missing in herself. The dinosaur apron Saffron bought. Did her sister think of her as a dinosaur? Elinor considered the idea that Dad and Saffron knew something that she didn't. It was the first time she'd ever had such a thought.

She came to, put the letter down, and silently fumed

out of the room. Glancing at herself in the hall mirror on her way to the stairs, she saw her stern-looking face surrounded by perfectly combed hair. She grimaced at her compulsive self. Obsessive. No, she was not those things.

Shaking her head, Elinor decided to re-assert her sense of control. She'd make Saffron a fantastic pasta dinner, wearing her dinosaur emblem proudly.

Chapter 11
Midnight Tidying—Saffron

It was cold. Saffron looked at her phone. Two-thirty a.m. What was that strange noise? It seemed to be coming from downstairs. *Swish, swish, swish*, like someone dragging a cloth across the floor, or the curtains blowing from an open window. But they hadn't left the windows open.

Grabbing her robe, she went downstairs. One light was on in the living room. Her sister was sweeping, making the shushing sound, bristles across the stone tiles.

Swish, swish, swish the broom echoed. Middle-of-the-night neatening—what thoughts filled Ellie's mind when she did this? *Swish, swish, swish*, as if tidying could straighten the messy world. Or her sister's fears. She had always done this, gotten up at night because she needed to sweep a mess into little piles and scoop it up to throw in the trash. The way Ellie had made her poems and her creativity disappear, a mess in her mind she seemed to want to eradicate.

Saffron stood on the lowest step for a few moments, watching her sister sweep away her troubled thoughts. This cleaning quirk was a secret between them. Ellie had started this in their childhood. Saffron would get up because of a noise and find her sister in the kitchen or living room. When she asked Ellie what she was doing, the defensiveness more than the reply told her Ellie was unable to control this impulse.

Ellie would say. "Mom doesn't like to do dishes at night, but I don't mind."

Once, Saffron had said, "Why did you wake up and think about it?"

Elinor had stared at her, looking guilty. "Just did."

Saffron tiptoed back to her room. The pillow was her boundary.

Later, Saffron woke up again, this time to a different noise. A soft male voice in her head.

Find my book.

"If you keep waking me up, I won't be able to do anything!"

The Invisible didn't so much appear as become a clearer voice.

Don't raise your voice. I'm a sensitive poet.

Saffron stifled a laugh and readjusted the pillow to block him out. She needed sleep.

You need me more than sleep, and I need you.

"Why do you need me?" she asked, rubbing her eyes and sitting up.

Make me thy lyre, even as the forest is: What if my leaves are falling like its own! The tumult of thy mighty harmonies will take from both a deep, autumnal tone, sweet though in sadness. Be thou, Spirit fierce, my spirit! Be thou me, impetuous one! Drive my dead thoughts over the universe like wither'd leaves to quicken a new birth!

"Um, are you saying you need me to be you? Or what, exactly?"

When she was twelve, on one of her rare visits to her father in his home in Vermont, Dad had read a Shelley poem aloud to her. "We should get started with the classics," he had said. "Shelley wrote some of the most beautiful poetry in the English language."

She liked the music of the poem, but she couldn't understand what Shelley was trying to say. "He's telling a lot of secrets, but we don't know what they're about," she told her father. "So how can we understand?"

"That's what poets do, they tell secrets, but those secrets are wrapped inside other secrets. You have to unwrap them carefully, like a present, and slowly open them up. You need to look for what's at the bottom of all the secrets."

Her father smiled. Saffron understood that he meant poetry was a game. He liked to play games, saying games were good for your brain and your heart. So she had always thought of Shelley's poetry as a game of secrets. Maybe one day it would become clear to her, but so far it hadn't.

But maybe this was the day. The Invisible echoed her thought.

You're right, this is the day. And the secret I'm going to tell you is that all secrets lead back to love, one way or another. I want you to follow the thread between me and your sister.

This wasn't the way things worked. She was supposed to help the Invisibles move on. They weren't supposed to be her spirit-gurus, nor her pals.

Your sister keeps you out. She has a secret to guard.

"If it's about her midnight cleaning, I already know."

It's a secret she doesn't even know she has.

This was intriguing. "Then tell me!"

When it's time.

"Is this one of your games? Dad?"

As I said, he asked me to take care of you.

She had never walked out on an Invisible before, but most of them had better manners. Saffron lay down and pulled the pillow over her head.

Pay attention to what I say, or one of you won't be here in the New Year.

Even with the covers over her head, she felt his voice reverberating within her. What did he mean, one of them might not survive?

She felt alone, cold, and without an answer. With a dry sob, she wondered why everyone wanted her to change. How many times had she tried? She sucked in another little cry, remembering how on this trip she wanted to show Ellie she was now a better person, but she was failing.

She had once been good at changing. In ninth grade, Saffron had changed her name and her whole personality, becoming *Marnie*. For a while Ellie liked Marnie better. But when Saffron entered high school, she introduced herself to new friends as *Lila*. She read *Gone with the Wind* and became *Georgia*. Her friends made fun of her name changes, so she rebelled and required everyone to call her *Scheherazade*. Making friends with a Goth girl, she put a crimson streak in her hair and sported the name *Jet*. *Jet* went off to college and came home Saffron.

All that time, Elinor had remained Elinor. Maybe that was their problem. Elinor never changed, and Saffron was too good at it.

* * *

When she woke up the next morning, Saffron came downstairs to find her sister had gone out. This was the perfect moment. She called home.

"How are you girls getting along?" Mom-Betsy asked first thing.

Saffron's sigh answered her.

"Are you giving your sister the benefit of the doubt?" her mother asked, and Saffron felt the same old suspicion that her adopted mother gave her sister preference because Elinor was her natural daughter.

"But Mom, she treats me like I'm still nine! She's been named trustee for my share of the inheritance, and she's acting like she's been appointed god."

A pause on the other end. Then Betsy said, "You know I'm not always going to be here to referee between you two. I hope one day you can learn to get along with each other. Try tolerating her peculiarities."

Saffron was briefly enraged. Then she felt the wisdom in her mother's words. "I'll try, Mom. She makes it hard. But I'll try."

"When are you both coming back?"

"It's up to Ellie. She thinks she's going to sell the house in a couple of weeks, but I can't see how even she could do it that fast. She's charging around here with a dust mop in one hand and a list in the other. She's a blur, most days. And this is the most beautiful place on earth. She can't even see it."

Mom-Betsy sighed. "Dear, you have to help her see it. I'm counting on you."

Saffron hung up, wishing she were at home and could get a hug from Mom-Betsy. She sure wasn't going to get one from Ellie any time soon.

CHAPTER 12
Baby Boy—Elinor

A week after their visit to the dinosaurs, Elinor emailed her boss and requested more leave—unpaid this time. She needed more time to ready the house, and they had no idea where the hidden manuscript was. Saffron kept insisting they hunt for it, and now Elinor knew why she made it such a priority. Even if she was putting her job at risk, she knew she had to ask.

Bill wrote back with a one-line zinger.

Just make sure you're planning to be back on the date we agree on, and don't ask again or this is it.

What he meant by "this is it," Elinor didn't want to find out. Did he think she didn't value her good position?

After reminding him that she had valued her job for ten years, she finished the inventory. With a flush of satisfaction, she emailed it to *Signor* Capelli and Cosma. Now that Cosma was involved, however, a number of To-Do items had been added to her spreadsheet, not the least of which was to deal with the furnishings. On separate lines, Elinor had entered "Research estate sale services,"

"Appraisal of best furniture," and "Yard sale." Then she deleted the yard sale line. By showing the house furnished, crummy as these pieces were, she could save days of work.

Cosma insisted on repairs. Finding workmen and supervising them would take up most of Elinor's remaining time.

She had relented about hiring Matteo Poggi. According to Cosma, he was the best handyman in Lerici, and sought after. Elinor secured his services for small things that would make a difference, like chipped stucco. He came and went quietly, a gentle and unobtrusive presence. Though the tapping of his hammer made his whereabouts known, he was as stealthy as a cat. He didn't talk much— no English—and that was fine. But he couldn't do the bigger repairs. She still had to find a contractor for those.

Another big To-Do item was Thanksgiving. Although she didn't enter it on the spreadsheet, Elinor thought sharing the holiday with Saffron was a great idea. Her sister was enthusiastic, but now with so many To-Do items and deadlines, making an elaborate dinner added to her sense of pressure.

The next big item was cleaning. This place had corners and edges that hadn't seen a wet rag in years. Dad must have had a housekeeper, and she must have been half-asleep while she worked. The flimsy construction meant that edges didn't always come together squarely, and crevices let in dust blown by the constant marine wind. Once you let a place like this start to go, recovering it took a huge effort.

Elinor located the supplies, bought more, and thought of asking Saffron, who had helped with inventorying, but she wasn't to be counted on. And the last thing to help their relationship was for Elinor to turn into a nag about cleaning—bringing back echoes of their childhood fights.

Besides, Saffron would be poor at scrubbing baseboards and dusting ceilings. Her sister had developed a routine of spending her time on the patio, her laptop open. When Saffron did pitch in, her standards made more work for Elinor. She could only imagine the current condition of Saffron's apartment at home.

"How do you use this?" Saffron had asked, when handed the string mop.

How could someone reach thirty without learning to use a mop? Her thin hands with their long fingers didn't seem to firmly grasp the mop handle.

Not that Elinor minded working alone. There was a meditative quality to scrubbing, sweeping, and dusting this house that she enjoyed. She melted into the rhythmic movements, and then when she took a break, she'd go out and ponder the view. The blue of the ocean beyond the trees smoothed out the kinks in her, renewing her energy for the next tasks. And it was satisfying to see the house shine. The place was beginning to have savor, like a soup when its flavors combined to release an herb-laden aroma.

Saffron came out of the chaos room holding the mop. "Hey, can I mop something else? Now that I know how to use this."

"Seriously, you want to clean?"

"Yup. You work so hard. It's my house, too."

Elinor was skeptical of this sudden, generous offer, but it might contribute to their harmony to put her sister to work. "Why don't you dust baseboards in the hallways, upstairs and down?"

Saffron smiled, setting the mop against the corner. "What do I use?"

"A wet rag is the only way to get the grime off. There are some under the sink." As Saffron went to get rags, Elinor had an insight. "Have you been looking for the manuscript?"

Saffron, holding a rag in each hand, turned and tilted her head. "Not much. We should, though!"

Elinor gazed at her. The light dawned. "You take that room, and I'll take this one."

"No, let's do each room together! Like Dad said."

They hurried to the chaos room. Saffron was first in. She turned and immediately savaged through the desk, opening all the drawers and tossing their contents around.

Getting to the bottom, she shook her head. "This drawer's locked."

Abandoning the desk, Saffron went to the bed against the wall and crouched down to look under it.

"Come on! Dad wouldn't hide something under a bed." Elinor looked at her and then opened the closet.

Wedged next to the bookshelf in the closet were a few pairs of slacks and two jackets, a straw hat on the shelf above. So few things, but most of his clothes were in the closet of Saffron's room.

What if there as something behind the bookshelf?

Elinor began to pull out all the books. Saffron was watching with interest as Elinor stacked the books behind her and carefully pulled out the wire shelf. Nothing was behind it but dust balls so thick you could knit with them.

Elinor stood there looking at the dusty wall and carpet, deciding whether to tackle the cleaning job this minute or save it for later, when Saffron's exclamation made her turn.

"Look what I found!"

Her sister had opened the clock face. She turned to Elinor and held up a small, scrolled silver key.

For a moment they stared at it and each other, and then in unison said, "The drawer!"

Saffron tried it in the desk lock. The key turned. She pulled out the drawer and held up a stack of papers held together with a rusty clip. She thrust it forward and Elinor took the papers. She nearly dropped them when she read the name of the organization at the top. *Bethany House Anonymous and Private Adoption.*

She scanned quickly down the top page and saw "Nathan Greene" listed as the father. A woman named Yasinia Alvarado was listed as the mother, and both had signed on the third page. "Baby boy" was the child's name. The birthplace was Oakland, California.

Elinor looked up at her sister and handed the papers back.

"We have a brother," Saffron said. She looked at her sister, mouth open, until she grabbed Elinor by the shoulders and shook her. "Say something!"

"What. The. Fuck."

Elinor hadn't realized she'd said it until Saffron echoed the words. But Saffron kept shaking her shoulders.

"What?" Elinor asked.

"But Dad never told us. Why didn't he?"

"Maybe he hadn't decided what to do. He didn't know when he was going to die."

Saffron finally let go. "When was the baby born?"

Elinor looked at the top page. "From the date, it looks like it happened before Mom and Dad got married. Before I came along."

"Let me see." Saffron reached with both hands, wiggling them. Elinor handed the papers over.

Saffron scanned through all the pages and looked up. Her eyes filled with tears. "Why wouldn't Dad tell us we have a brother?"

Disgust rippled through Elinor. "Dad loved keeping secrets. Especially when they kept him from inconvenient truths."

"Ellie, that's horrible! Don't say that."

Elinor's voice was as flat as an untuned key. "Why not say it. That's how Dad was. Give me the papers."

As Saffron handed them over, she said, "We have to find him!"

Elinor stared at the adoption papers. "Or we can shove these back into the drawer and lock it up. Let the new owners find it."

"What? How can you just pretend we don't know?"

"Oh, Saffron. You think everything is sweet and hopeful. What if our brother doesn't want to know us? What if he wants to sue? We probably can't even find him. Look at the stationery. It's a closed adoption."

Saffron's voice was low. "But we have to try."

"No, we don't. And how? They don't let out information on closed adoptions unless you go to court."

"But you can find anyone online."

"And how are we going to search, under 'Baby boy'? Born in Oakland in 1981? Good luck with that."

She saw Saffron wilt under her sarcasm. But she persisted. "Don't you want to try? Don't we owe it to Dad?"

Elinor's sarcastic laugh erupted. "Yeah, we owe it to Dad. Who never even mentioned him to us or to Mom. Did 'Baby Boy' ever try to find us?"

Elinor reached a hand out for the papers. Saffron handed them over. "But if he's our brother—don't we owe him something? Aren't you interested in knowing a part of our family?"

Elinor glared. "He's not part of our family! We don't owe him anything. Certainly not a share in our inheritance."

"I can't believe you'd put money above family!"

Saffron ran out of the room. When Elinor came out, she was lying on the couch, an arm over her eyes. Of course weeping. Saffron wept at the wrong spin on a word. She was still such a child.

Elinor summoned her patience and said gently, "I didn't mean it like that."

Saffron shouted. "Yes, you did!"

"How is he part of our family? He was an accident of Dad's."

Saffron sat up and said, "We. Have. A. Brother."

She leapt up and stood in front of Elinor, hands clenched at her sides. Then Saffron stalked to the door, picked up her bag, slung it over her shoulder. The door slammed behind her with a reverberating shudder.

Elinor went to the couch, thinking to smooth out the indentation her sister had left, as if to erase the argument. But instead she sat down and swung her feet up. Everything in her body hurt suddenly, her eyes, her head, and most of all her heart.

Dad had done it again. Turned their family into a seething pool of chaos.

"Where's that broom?" she asked herself out loud.

She remembered leaving it in the corner of the kitchen, which needed sweeping after Saffron had made breakfast and spilled coffee grounds.

Elinor got up and went to the broom. She energetically swished the mess into the dining area in a pile, then swept under the table, pulling out each chair, making more piles. She swept the piles up, took them to the kitchen trash and dumped the detritus onto a welter of old food, wrappers, paper towels, and plastic wrap. Brushing off the dustpan, she felt as if she were removing the last hour, making her life again orderly. This wasn't compulsion. It was the way mature people dealt with crises.

With the dining room and kitchen floors clean, Elinor decided the living room deserved the same treatment. She swept that floor and then moved out onto the patio, where she set the broom down on the flagstones and sank onto the chaise. Staring at the sea beyond the trees, she let the word enter her brain. Brother. They did have a brother.

What other important things had Dad hidden from them, things that could potentially change their lives?

Chapter 13

A Getaway Place—Saffron

Saffron walked downhill as fast as she could. She had no idea of where she wanted to go, only away from Elinor. Away from her heartless, domineering sister. And now, not her only sibling, for there was Baby Boy to think about.

Lerici seemed to have changed color because of the massive new knowledge. There were now three of them, not just two. Was Baby Boy still alive? If he wasn't, would she be able to sense him?

What she wanted in the immediate future was a good café. She needed a place to settle, to absorb all this.

At the bottom of the street, she turned north through the harbor part of town, and walked along the promenade. She was looking for a café where she could unpack her laptop, order a coffee and a roll, and stay for a while. A place like those at home, a place where the patrons weren't the come-and-go, fast-latte kind. Where they didn't mind if you lingered. A café where everyone stared into their laptops when you were looking at them and stared at you when you weren't. In other words, a room of caffeinated introverts.

These ocean-facing cafés were full of noisy families. Adults rushed in and out with their children, shouting and shrieking. These places wouldn't work.

She turned up a side street. After a few steps, she spotted a window painted with gold letters: Caffe La Scala. She walked the half-block to it. The doors were open and the large, sunny café was filled with empty tables. The barista had his back turned to the door. He was warming up the espresso machines. She couldn't order over the noise of the steamers, so she sat at a table by the window. A choice spot.

People walking by on both sides of the narrow street seemed more like residents than vacationers, mostly elderly men in sweaters and caps. Two young women were talking as they pushed their strollers up the street. No one hurried on this street. No one was wearing bathing or business suits.

After getting her latte, dumping in three heaping spoons of sugar, and settling at her table, she opened her computer. She was going to figure out how to search for someone who had been anonymously adopted. Elinor had been right. She couldn't simply search on "Baby Boy" born in Oakland in a certain year. She needed some idea of how to unseal a closed adoption, whether it was even possible. After a few searches, Saffron felt hopeless. She'd need Elinor to help figure this out, and right now all her sister wanted to do was lock away the secret again.

She decided instead to tackle a simpler project and email Gino. The guy from Rome was her big Italian adventure, and probably her last one, given how much Elinor wanted to rush home.

Saffron wanted to hear more of Gino's ideas about renting their house to make money. Maybe it would enable them to keep it.

Beginning the email, she paused to think up a jaunty salutation—something better than the generic *Hey*—something that evoked their connection in Rome. After all, Gino might even follow up on his promise to come and see her in Lerici.

Ciao, Gino! She typed. Yes, that was good, better than *Hey*. She wondered if there was an Italian word for *dude*.

Saffron remembered their evening together in Rome. Gino had taken her to a music club, told her he had visited America. His English was good. He was nice, Italian-charming, and polite.

"Did you like America?" she had asked.

"Yes. I'd like to live there. I have a plan."

"And I'd like to live in your country one day," Saffron had said.

"Do you have a plan also? It's good to have plans. Even if they go—what's your word for it? Wryly."

When she laughed, he leaned forward—she had thought to kiss her, but he stopped and said, "You have such beautiful eyes, *Bella*. Green with flecks of gold."

He had stopped in the middle of the narrow sidewalk, half a block past the nightclub, pressed her against the fence around a house, and kissed her. Their smoldering kiss went on a long time, and she had to catch her breath. But then Gino took her hand, turned, and walked her back to the hotel.

Her Italian adventure turned out to be more of a gentleman than she would have liked. So disappointing. But Saffron gave him her number. They met the next day for breakfast, and Gino had talked about his uncle's vacation rental business, and said he'd come to Lerici. Of course, that was a brush-off. Had she given him the cottage's address? Or had she done it the other night, after the Invisible had unsettled her? She remembered sending Ellie's pictures to Gino, but that was just an excuse to say hello.

That cute barista was no longer so busy. Saffron went up to the counter, ordering a pastry with her second latte. She smiled her biggest smile, the one she knew created a dimple on her left cheek. His smile turned one side of his mouth up, while the other stayed put.

"*Prego, signorina,*" he said.

Her stomach fluttered. Tattoos cascaded down his arms from under a tight black tee shirt. You wouldn't get those muscles by hefting cups of espresso. He probably lifted weights. Maybe women too.

"I'll have a caffelatte," she said, signaling that she had no intention of trying to speak his language.

He raised an eyebrow. "*Certo, signorina.*"

"Aren't you going to tell me that no one orders a latte after breakfast?"

"Certainly not. You're American. You drink Starbuck's." He winked a very Italian wink. "I'll bring it to you."

She went to her table and watched him work the machines quickly, like someone playing pinball. Quick hands. What would they feel like on her? A hopeful thrill expanded in her heart, along with a stir of something hotter.

Saffron stayed for a generous hour, and then she window-shopped along the promenade, stretching out the time away from home. She bought a pair of espadrilles from a sale table outside a boutique. She found a gelato place that served right onto the promenade from a window.

Ambling back uphill, she considered the possibilities. Baby Boy took a kaleidoscope of forms. She remembered the date, and realized he would be their older brother. Would he look like them? Why hadn't the mother decided to keep him, and why had Dad never stayed in touch? What had happened that her father felt he had to hide it from everyone for his entire life?

But she couldn't talk to Ellie about it. Ellie had dropped the steely barrier of her will to remain ignorant of their older brother. She was selfish, ungenerous, and worst of all, not in the least bit curious about something that had to do with her own life. She made the decision to learn more about how to look for him, but without telling her sister. If she found him, it would be time enough.

At the front door, Saffron remembered that this whole thing had been uncovered because they were looking for Dad's manuscript. He'd sent them on this treasure hunt. Did he expect them to find the adoption papers—and if he did, was he trying to get them to continue the hunt at home, where they might be able to locate him through the hospital?

She pushed the door open quietly, hoping Ellie was somewhere else. But she was in the kitchen, making something that smelled like tomato sauce.

Ellie looked up as she came into the living room. "Did you have fun in town?"

Saffron nodded, relieved to find at least a sham of peace. If Ellie was uninterested in family secrets, she wasn't going to reveal any. They'd be polite strangers under the cottage roof. Not really sisters at all. Just half-sisters. With an almost-brother out there somewhere.

Chapter 14

The Americans—Elinor

Early the next morning, Elinor sat alone on the patio. Her blue robe was wrapped tight around her legs because of the brisk breeze. She ruffled her hair into obedience with her fingers, having forgotten to brush it before coming downstairs. She reminded herself it didn't matter; Saffron wouldn't care, and there was no one else to notice.

She was trying not to make mental additions to her spreadsheet of things that needed doing, but simply to appreciate the beauty.

Warm September had given way to October's chill, but the place was still a charming cottage, with the purple petunias and white alyssum she had bought still blooming, spilling from the clay pots. The house still would show like a summer cottage, if they didn't wait too much longer.

She thought about Baby Boy. Leaving the patio, she carried her mug into the chaos room and stood in front of the clock. They had put the key to the drawer back inside after locking the drawer and the documents away. The shock of the discovery had made Elinor forget to look for a way to wind the clock or locate its batteries.

Opening the glass face, she saw that there were two keys. One was the drawer key. The other must be the key to wind the clock. She tried it, and after a few dozen turns, the clock sprang to life. She adjusted it to the time on her phone and stood back, satisfied. Putting time right gave her a small thrill, the way getting spreadsheet formulas to work together did.

But this was her moment not to think about these things. Soon the sun would reach the west-facing patio and warm it up. She went back outside and sat at the table, sinking into the hush of morning with a tiny sigh.

I'd stay on this patio until my life slipped aside, and the hands of the clock intertwined like the blooming petunias.

But petunias wasn't a poetic word. She wanted another flower-name—

Before Elinor could finish the thought, she heard a loud knock on the front door. Eight o'clock—too early even for Cosma, which was too bad. She hadn't been able to reach her, except to leave a few voicemails about Matteo's latest project, the squeaky front door hinge, and the fact that she had received no invoice from him. What was all this costing?

The knock repeated five times, sharp and insistent. Elinor went inside. She pulled the sash of her robe tight and opened the door to a blond man in a turquoise polo shirt. A short blonde woman stood beside him, wearing a gold pleated skirt topped with a burnt orange paisley blouse. They had to be American, maybe asking for directions

"May I help you?" She tried to seem friendly, though it

was annoying to be disturbed at this hour, even for directions.

"We're here to move in."

The man smiled and started forward, as if expecting to come in.

Elinor stepped forward to block him. "Move in?"

"To take possession of the house for our vacation, starting today. That's what the company said. Are you the caretaker?"

He picked up the suitcases she hadn't noticed before and gestured that he expected to be let in, but she still blocked his way.

The woman was amazed and then angry. Her cheeks grew pink. Gripping his arm she said, "We rented this from Gino's Properties, and you're supposed to have been gone by now!"

Elinor said, as calmly as she could, "What are you talking about? We own this home. You have the wrong address."

"But we rented it."

"You can't have. We're not renting our house. You're mistaken."

Now everyone looked confused.

Elinor pursued her advantage. "Go back and call your rental agency. They've obviously mixed up the addresses. Our house is not for rent—though it is for sale, if you're interested."

The offer further confused them. The woman tilted her head and said to her husband, "Let's go back."

He wasn't persuaded, but at last he shrugged. They turned and left.

As she closed the door, Elinor wondered if her sister had somehow manipulated things to summon people to rent their house. It was a wild idea, but all Saffron's talk of rental meant she had to be behind this.

"Saffron!" Elinor unleashed the full power of her voice, in a soprano register.

A sleepy Saffron appeared at the top of the stairs. "What is it?"

Elinor knew she must have heard the knock on the door. Saffron must have known something was up, but didn't want to come out and face the music. How had she arranged to rent the house—and why?

Two could play the innocence game. "Let's talk, now. Come downstairs."

Saffron came down and said, "Let me make you some coffee."

"No, I'll make you a cup while you sit down and tell me what's going on."

Saffron sat, looking surprised. Elinor brought the coffee over and sat across from Saffron.

Crossing her legs, she sipped and asked, "How did you get those people to rent our house?" Her voice was sweet but the question direct. It landed just as Saffron lifted the cup and was about to drink.

Saffron set down her cup. "What do you mean?"

Elinor's voice purred. "You didn't think you could keep it from me once they were to move in, did you?" Hands on her knees, Elinor gazed steadily at her sister, who avoided her eyes.

"Move in? Who?"

"The people who came to the door. I convinced them their rental agency, some shifty company called Gino's Vacation Rentals, had mixed up the addresses."

"Gino's?" Saffron squirmed on the couch, crossing and

then re-crossing her legs. Finally she tucked them up under her.

"Stop playing dumb and tell me how you're mixed up with this."

"What makes you think—"

Elinor leaned forward. "I know you did this. Now tell me."

"I met that guy in Rome, remember? Gino. Maybe you were too busy to remember, but I told you. I met Gino at the Pantheon. He invited me for coffee. We talked. And we've emailed a little."

"Talked? What did you tell him about our house?"

Elinor smelled the familiar whiff of her sister's offbeat ideas. Ideas perhaps meeting a predatory stranger's ambitions, and creating a whirl of shady dealings. Was this Gino a scam artist? Was Saffron so gullible as to have been taken in? Italy seemed full of avaricious people with talent for conning visitors.

Elinor took some deep breaths, reminding herself to keep her voice level. "You let Gino set this up and go forward with it, didn't you?"

Instead of answering, Saffron got up and took her coffee back to the kitchen. "You always accuse me of messing up. And you still don't know how to make coffee right."

Elinor jumped up and paced a tight circle, her body tense with anger. "What did you say to Gino that made him think it was okay to list our house?"

Saffron slowly came back into the room. She looked dazed, eyes wide. "I didn't tell him to! When I met him in Rome, he asked why I was here. All I said was that I had inherited property."

"Did you tell him it was in Lerici?"

Saffron hesitated, and then she sat down, tucking her

legs under her. "Not at first. But then, yes, when we got to talking."

Elinor realized Saffron might well have made a mistake in sharing too much information without understanding how it could be used. Perhaps she had let slip some information to this stranger, Gino, and he had devised a way to collect deposits on "renting" their house, without actually renting it. A scam. But what kind of a scam would succeed if the "renters" were turned away? Wouldn't they demand their money back as soon as they could dial Gino's number? Or perhaps "Gino" was already long gone, a con man fleeing from the phony setup after pocketing their deposit. Saffron had no idea about people. She was wrapped in her dream world of helping Invisibles, having casual affairs, and walking other people's dogs.

Elinor sat down, feeling the burden of responsibility that was her lot in this family—a weight of awareness that pressed on her head and shoulders until they ached with martyrdom. She had to work so hard to keep her mother and her sister in their dreamlands. And now that she was Saffron's trustee, she had to think of the future not just for herself but for her sister.

She lowered her voice to disguise her frustration. She had to lure out some information to deal with this. "Tell me everything you know about Gino and what you told him about our house."

It worked. Saffron relaxed and stretched her arm out along the sofa back. "I'm trying to recall everything. You remember, I met him in Rome. Gino had told me he helps with his uncle's rental business, and I'd told him about this house. After we got here, I described it to him in an email, and he wrote back that Lerici is a prime vacation area for

Italians, but not so much for foreign tourists. People pay a lot to take vacations here." Saffron emphasized. "A LOT."

"But these people who came to the door were Americans. What else did he say?"

"He told me about his uncle's business. Ellie, I liked him and I thought he liked me. We were just having fun emailing. I swear I didn't tell him to rent the house."

"Oh, Saffron! Don't you ever imagine that people can be dishonest in order to manipulate you?"

Saffron's voice rose. "He said his uncle's business represents lots of properties on the coast. They get huge fees . . ."

"Was that why you asked me for my photos?" Elinor snapped. "To give this stranger pictures of our property?"

Saffron looked panicked. Elinor wasn't going to get more if she was criticizing instead of engaging her sister. She willed herself to be patient. She had to contact Gino herself and do damage control. She couldn't leave it to Saffron.

"Gino's business is legitimate!" Saffron said. "He showed me the website. When he emailed me, I might have told him we're considering it. But I never told him to go ahead. It was just a little fender-bender of miscommunication."

Vagueness was the enemy of truth, Elinor believed, and her sister was a pile of vagueness, loose ends wrapped in a tattered mist. Rage suddenly pumped fire through her and she couldn't stop herself. "You're going to give their money back and apologize to those people! Honestly, do you ever think about growing up?"

Saffron squirmed to the far end of the couch, as if she expected her sister to come at her with fists. Elinor took a deep breath. She folded her arms, as if to prove she had no physical intentions, but it was too late. Saffron had completely wilted.

She had to leave the room, or things would go from worse to impossible. Elinor was about to stomp into her office, when Saffron jumped up, grabbed her laptop from the table, jammed it into her backpack and her feet into sandals. The door, thick as it was, quivered with her slamming.

The house was peaceful in Saffron's wake. Elinor knew why her sister had become fixated on staying here. Evading her ex-boyfriend, no doubt some debts, and undoubtedly another failure to launch. Her sister was in love with her own escapism, and Elinor despaired of ever changing that. The Shelley visitations were a manifestation of her little sister's deep denial of reality. But even for Saffron, it was unusual to be so obsessed. Why Shelley—was it all about their father's death?

She supposed this idea of renting the cottage had to be based on something.

Elinor went into the chaos room and opened her computer. Saffron had to be exaggerating about the rental prospects. She looked up a local agency. Her eyes widened. People did pay thousands for a month's house rental here. Their house was dilapidated and small, but even the small ones fetched good summer prices. But the idea was absurd. Compared to selling, reinvesting to enlarge her balanced portfolio of investments, the rental income wouldn't be advantageous. She had crunched the numbers many times, and these didn't come close to what she needed for monthly income.

Suddenly, Elinor's hair ruffled up. With the windows shut, she thought it must be a descending spider or large fly and she brushed frantically at the top of her head. She felt nothing crawling.

She went out into the living room and sat on the couch, gazing at the ocean. Taking deep breaths, she focused on the leaves in the trees dancing alternately dark green and gold in the sunlight. A sense of peace reigned over her, and she fingered the nubby fabric on the sofa's arm. Another line of verse might be coming through. It had been so long.

Maybe Saffron was right. They could stay through Thanksgiving, and it would give them a holiday together. An erasure of the past. Saffron would never change, so she just had to accept her wayward sister and stop trying to expect Saffron to become responsible. Elinor would try to love her as she was.

At the same time, she'd have to manage Saffron better. Step One: fix things with Gino and the Americans. Make sure he took the house off his website and refunded their deposit money.

Elinor got up and paced the living room, trying to come up with Step Two. Her bare toes became chilled by the stone floor. When the answer coalesced in her mind, her feet stopped. She leaned against the back of the armchair and savored her own brilliance. Then she took out her phone.

"Cosma? This is Elinor Greene. I'm calling to say I want to put the house up for long-term lease, until we can get it on the market in a better season. And you'll have to work with me long distance . . . Yes, I'm going home soon. I can handle the sale from Berkeley."

Clicking off the call, Elinor was glad. She missed being home, where everything was predictable and orderly. Saffron had been right about leasing the cottage. It could take off the pressure to sell, if Cosma could find someone to lease it for a few months. Thanks to Saffron and Gino, Step Two had become clear.

Step Three suddenly popped up. No, it was crazy, impulsive, and Elinor never acted on impulse.

Before she knew it, she had pulled out the phone and hit redial.

"Hello, Cosma? Elinor again. I had another thought. I want you to look around for a small condo here in Lerici. No, not for rent. To purchase . . . Not for me, no. For my sister. She wants to stay."

Chapter 15
Michael Shelley—Saffron

After their second fight in as many days, Saffron went to Caffe La Scala. Her sister was more toxic than ever, ready to blame Saffron for anything and everything.

As she walked to town, each lungful of fresh air pumped up the balloon of injustice inside her heart.

She should just book a flight home. Just go and leave everything to Elinor. That would serve her right. Let the obsessive, judgmental elder sister do her thing and stagger under the burden of it all while missing Italy's beauty, and the lovely patio where they could feel like real sisters. Let her miss real life and love.

She walked faster, trailed by her sister's angry judgments, ribbons of fire swirling around her, invading her lungs.

Suddenly she stopped. Well, damn. What an effed-up mess she had made.

Of course, Ellie was right. Saffron walked slowly, the realization dragging at her ankles. Why did she always let Ellie be the fixer? That made her always the screw-up.

She should fix her own problems, and not always lean on her sister. Ellie had managed Saffron's airline reservation flying to Rome because Saffron had gotten the wrong dates. Intending to fly separately, because she and Ellie weren't speaking, she had booked the wrong month. When she confessed, they fell into their old pattern. And then Ellie fixed it so they were flying together. And now her sister was in charge of her fortune. And her whole life, really.

It was so clear what she had to do. She had to be the one to get in touch with Gino. Not Ellie. She had to fix this thing with the Americans.

And then she had to find that manuscript. And persuade Ellie that a lost brother needed to be found. Needed to be offered a part in their family. Then she had to keep her sister from making snap judgments about their future. Ellie might be her trustee, but Saffron knew, as her Dad had said, that her sister had a piece missing, a piece she could gently put back into place in the puzzle that was Elinor Greene.

She started walking faster, with the mantra *I got this*. She could change Ellie's attitude. She could stop giving in to the magnetic pull of her sister's competence. She could assert that, since it was half her house, even if Ellie was her trustee, they belonged there. Shelley knew it. She knew it.

Thing was, she couldn't explain to Ellie why they belonged here. But the evidence was clear, her sister was melting into Lerici life and their cottage. Ellie was cooking in a meaningful way. She was spending dreaming time on the patio, and she wasn't always making those damn lists. Ellie had even started writing again. Though she tried to hide it, Saffron had caught her dictating on her phone, things that sounded suspiciously poetic.

When she pointed that out, Ellie had said, "I'm writing to my boss."

Yeah, yeah, yeah. Writing to your boss about the periwinkle blue sky. About autumn crickets and their mournful songs.

At Caffe La Scala, she went up to the counter and ordered. The barista gave her mildly flirty face, but not enough to satisfy her. She got her coffee and then took it back to her table, keeping an eye on him to wait for a more auspicious moment. Flirting across a room was always fun.

Saffron started an email to Gino, then trashed it. A jaunty tone wasn't going to cut it. Sorry-so-sorry girl had to do better. Maybe she should call him, as Ellie had said she was going to do. Would he be the one to answer the phone number on the rental agency website? Or would it be Gino's uncle, and if it was the uncle, how would she explain who she was and why she needed to talk to Gino? What if it turned out that the uncle was furious at her?

The more she thought about it, the more she knew the best thing was to let Ellie handle it. The mess with Gino, the sale of the house, dividing up the proceeds. Whatever. It was Ellie's thing, and after all, Shelley had said to trust her sister.

Saffron looked over to see if she could catch barista guy's eye, but a tall guy in a ratty, rust-colored sweater came in and stood at the counter, blocking her view.

"*Ciao*," he said to the barista.

If only he'd get out of the way. Ordering in fluent Italian, he leaned on the counter. Clearly, he was a regular.

He turned around and spotted Saffron and they sized each other up. Wavy hair, large eyes, features that astonished her. It was almost as if Percy Bysshe Shelley had walked into the café. His blue eyes surveyed her, and then he turned around to talk to the barista.

When he got his cup, he turned and came straight over to her, settled at the table next to hers, slung his pack onto the floor, and sat in the rickety chair too small for his tall, lean body.

He set his cup down and leaned over. "I'm Michael, and you're too gorgeous to be sitting alone."

A pushy Englishman, judging by the accent. He must have thought she was looking at him.

She must discourage this. "I'm Saffron. Busy, though."

She looked down at her screen.

He smiled. "I can see."

In her peripheral vision, she noticed the way his brown hair curled up from his forehead. As he raised the cup to his lips, his biceps bulged under the terrible sweater. A tempting package, despite the brashness.

She realized how rude she'd been. "Sorry. I was concentrating."

He grinned and held out his hand. "Michael Shelley."

She shook it firmly. "Did you say Shelley?"

"I did."

"You're not! You can't be."

"Well, in fact, I am. Why do you say that?"

"Your name being Shelley."

He raised his thick, sandy-colored eyebrows. His eyes were just too blue. The blue of the deep end of a swimming pool or the shallows of the sea.

He said, "I am. In fact, the poet Shelley is a distant forbear. Is that what you meant?"

She abandoned the attempt to look busy. "Seriously, you're related?"

"'Related' makes the connection too close. Half of

England appears to be related to Shakespeare. But I do have lineage in common with him. And the name."

Michael Shelley turned his chair all the way around and faced her. Tall and strong in the lean way of a runner or a rower.

"If you're going to do that," she said, "you might as well scoot that chair over."

Smoothly, he scooted. She looked over his shoulder to see if the barista was watching, but he was busy at his machines. When barista guy turned, he gave her an all-too-professional wink.

She turned back to Michael. He said, "Tell me why you're a fan."

"Of Shelley? I like the skylark poem best. Freedom is my wavelength. And my father taught and wrote about his work."

"What are you doing here?" he asked.

"Having coffee, of course." Listening to that English accent was mesmerizing.

"I mean, in Italy. Lerici isn't exactly a tourist hotspot." His smile was wide, a mobile mouth with excellent teeth. "You're very beautiful, you know. Dramatic. Like fireworks."

Points for originality and audacity, but minus points for acting like such a puppy. Even if a cute puppy.

"Thank you," she said coolly. "A very poetic compliment. What I'm doing in Italy is inheriting a house. And writing. It might turn into a novel. Or a memoir."

"Aren't they very different kinds of books?"

"I can't pigeon-hole my creative process. If you label everything, you miss the excitement."

She turned to her laptop screen pointedly, signaling that it was time for him to move back. He did.

She opened an email and began vigorously typing.

A young woman came in and went up to the counter, where barista guy leaned over and kissed her quickly on the lips. Saffron tried not to show her disappointment. After the Italian girl sat down, Saffron went up to the counter and got another latte, along with another quick, professional wink. She got the message.

Going back to her table, Saffron gave Michael a brief smile. She could cultivate this guy if the barista wasn't showing interest. Maybe barista would notice she had the attention of someone else. Avid attention.

"Tell me about how you write," Michael said. "I do a little writing, but I have a hard time getting started."

"I have no trouble starting because first thing in the morning I journal. Free write. I let the whim take me over, maybe turn it into an essay, or add some line breaks and let it be poetry. It might be something, or only warming up."

"Thanks for the tip."

"What are you working on?" She looked over to his table at his open laptop.

He shrugged his angular shoulders and smiled. "Oh, not much. Maybe a poem."

"Lord, not another poet!"

"Don't you like poets? But you like Shelley."

"I love poetry, but I don't always like poets," she said darkly.

His sudden laughter was an abrupt bark, almost a cough, a very un-English sound that she liked.

"My father was a writer, so I guess I inherited the habit. My sister has an even worse case, but she squashed it with large doses of accounting."

He chortled again. Saffron liked being able to make this man laugh.

"Okay, show me some of your writing," she said.

"Now?" His pleasure showed in his broadening smile. What straight, white, very-un-English teeth. In fact, the whole picture was giving her stomach throbs.

Michael tilted his head. "Sure. Why not?"

He went back to his computer and typed, then brought the computer, setting it on the tiny table. She moved hers to give his room and looked at his screen.

"Nice." After a few lines, then, "Very nice!"

He flashed the full smile on her now, and the throb was definitely exciting.

"Thanks. I'm not exactly a poet, but I like writing when something moves me." He closed the laptop. "Show me yours?"

"Oh, no. It's not ready for prime time."

He jerked his head back slightly. "Okay, then just tell me the most surprising thing that's happened to you this week."

Staring steadily at him, she gave him the truth. "A spirit came and told me how to be a better sister."

His lips parted. They were nice lips. He shook his head in surprise. "Really? Who was it?"

She smiled, ready to spring the full secret. "Pretty sure it was Shelley himself."

"You're messing with me!" That laugh again. It was hot, the way he laughed. And weird. And cute.

She shrugged. "No I'm not. He came with the house."

His large eyes widened. "Tell me more. What did he say you should do?"

She inhaled and caught his scent, a woodsy aftershave

and well-lived-in cotton and wool. "He implied that my father had been able to see him."

Michael nodded. "Makes sense Shelley would haunt this area. He and the other Romantic poets all lived here," he said.

He had the most *amazing* blue eyes. Lashes not long but curving like his light brown hair.

She told him about her last-night's reading, how she learned that Shelley brought his wife Mary Shelley for a summer in Liguria, along with Mary's sister Claire, and Shelley's son. In that time, 1822, the area had been a fishing village. Shelley bought a small sailboat and anchored it in the harbor, christening it the *Don Juan*.

"An apt boat name for someone who believed in free love," Michael said. "The boat sank just off this coast and Shelley drowned. Do you think that's why he haunts your house?"

"Maybe."

"In England, we have so much history the spirits have to queue up and take turns haunting."

She laughed. "The realtor didn't mention it, but he might have even been living in our house."

"Are you selling up?" Concern lifted his adorable, thick eyebrows.

She nodded and said, "Yes, if my sister has her way."

Saffron saw over his shoulder that the barista had brought coffee to his girl. When he went back behind the counter, he looked in her direction. She found she cared a lot less than she had.

Michael saw her looking away and said, "You know not just Shelley, but Petrarch and Dante came here too. Down the street is a Hotel Byron. George Sand had a house. Would you like another espresso? Or a sandwich? My treat."

She agreed. It was fun to have an admirer. Especially one with such beautiful eyes.

He brought her a doppio with succulent brown bubbles in the crema, sprinkled with chocolate. She smiled and sipped, deliberately giving herself a milky moustache, then licking it off. Michael watched, entranced.

"What were you reading?" he asked, looking at her laptop.

"A book about the life of Shelley."

"You're that interested in him?" asked his more attractive descendant with that smile that landed with a thump inside her.

"Well, he is haunting my house."

"Maybe you should get haunted by a more popular poet. Shelley's rather out of favor, unless you plan to teach the Romantics."

"Teach! I wouldn't be caught dead teaching," she said, holding up her hands, palm out to hold off the idea. "My father was a professor. Facing bunches of bored adolescents every day. No, thanks. Not my thing."

Michael smiled. "I didn't think it would be. Besides, you're too beautiful to teach. Your students would just stare at you."

The espresso machines whirred as they stared at each other, conversation cut off by the noise. The jazzy whine held them, and Saffron's pulse began to throb. Heat spread up into her face.

"What brings you here, to Italy?" she asked when the noise stopped.

His fine English complexion grew into a blush. "I was kicked out."

"Of your country?" She leaned in and again his short bark of laughter made a tingle spread from her core out to her fingertips.

"I was kicked out of my ancestral home," Michael said. "But I'm kidding. The ancestral home is just a family row house in London. My father kicked me out. He said I should live on the Continent for a time before deciding on my future. Either I'll go into trade with him, or go back to university and into teaching."

Saffron was confused. "Trade?"

"What you call business. I'd rather die. But like you I don't want to teach, so death may lie before me."

"Why don't you want to go into 'trade'?" She couldn't help putting air quotes around the word.

He smirked. "I need adventure and independence."

The words rang gongs in her heart. She smiled. He was a kindred soul, and a Shelley.

"Have you had adventures here?" she asked.

"Not enough," Michael said. "Teaching might suit me after all, but I lack the credentials to teach at the Oxford level, or something like that. If I do go that way, Oxford is my goal. So, I'll have to go back to get a higher degree, and then get lucky with my father's connections."

So he was ambitious. "Why only Oxford?"

"Because I wouldn't want to do the kind of teaching that deadens my mind. I'd like to be exploring, learning, and improving my own understanding along with that of my brilliant students."

He had a vision of his future. She leaned slightly toward him, crossing her arms, and then uncrossing them. She touched her cheek quickly, wondering if it was as warm as his.

"What repels you about teaching, and business?" she asked.

He ducked his head, embarrassed—or was it just the English way of answering probing questions. "I was somewhat kidding. My mum works in the groves of academe. She says it's a fine life. She loves her students. Dad has never said he loves his clients."

"And here you are in Italy, thinking about all this from a distance."

He grinned. "That's about it."

If he shifted an inch closer, his knee would touch hers. She crossed her legs to create more space, but in doing so bumped his leg. His flicker of a smile said he liked it.

"What are your goals?" he asked.

"I'm planning to open a humane animal shelter. In Berkeley, where I live."

"Are you a veterinarian?"

"No. I'd hire a vet. My plan is to get rescued animals adopted through a pet lending program. And to comfort people in nursing homes. I had this in motion when my father died."

"Are you going home soon?"

"The thing is, I don't know if I want to go home."

Michael's smile was broad. "So for now, you're staying."

She wondered if he thought she was of a higher class because she owned a house. He sounded and looked like he might be one of those English aristocrats, like the Shelleys.

"The house my sister and I inherited is called *Casa Magni*. It's up on the hill overlooking the sea."

"Grand views, I imagine."

"We look down at the beach and up to San Terenzo."

"The beach is great, though it's past time for swimming."

"Why? It's still so warm. I haven't been down to the beach yet."

"You must walk with me on the beach! I can show you a lovely horse-shoe cove called La Baia Blu."

She resisted only a little. "I usually take my walks alone."

Michael found the way to persuade her. "I could show you the harbor where Shelley anchored his boat."

Clever man.

"Finish your coffee and we can go."

"Now?"

"Why not?"

She liked Michael's laughter, a deep and musical sound that rippled up the scale. It sent a light thrill up her spine and a thump down deep in her core.

She was going to say yes to more than the beach. But she was going to make him wait. "Meet me tomorrow, and you can show me Shelley's harbor."

He swept a pretend bow. "As you wish, my lady."

Saffron recognized a great exit moment when she saw one. Rising, she packed up and gave him her most alluring smile on her way out.

CHAPTER 16
Tonio and the Aubergines—Elinor

They needed something for dinner. Elinor got her purse and jacket and headed for the store. She had concentrated on peacemaking for the last week, after their argument about the Americans. She was glad Saffron had left for a café to chill out. She didn't know if she could spend too much time with her sister and keep the peace. When Saffron's presence irritated her, she went to buy groceries.

Today she had a mission. Thanksgiving was coming in a month, and all the cleaning and repairs to stage the house for sale would take at least that long. Her boss had, amazingly, agreed to lengthening her stay yet again, though now she was not only on unpaid leave, but judging by the curtness of his emails, on very thin ice. Now she emphasized the phrase *settling the estate*. Maybe he was impressed that she owned a house in Italy. Maybe he thought she was going to be rich and leave her job. If only.

As she walked, glimpsing the sea to her left, between houses and apartment buildings, Elinor let herself enjoy the beauty and feel expansive again. And that made her sorry about the fight with Saffron over the Americans. She'd been too harsh, letting her sister get under her skin. If Saffron had just been thoughtless, and not calculated, harsh would have been justified, but of course she was just doing her usual messy, careless thing. She'd said something to this Italian guy that created the misunderstanding. Elinor should be the one to clear up Saffron's mess, and without resenting it. After all, Dad had named her the trustee, and she had always looked out for her sister. It was the big sister's role, wasn't it? Especially with such a fey soul.

Now that Elinor knew there would be closure, the house would sell, and they'd share the proceeds, she was inclined to be more generous. She wished she could unsay some of the meaner—but true—things she'd said. She wished she could erase them from Saffron's memory. You couldn't fix people by yelling at them. Marriage had taught her that. If only she'd learned it sooner, maybe she wouldn't have had to suffer things like being called 'Mr. Fix-It' by her husband.

A holiday with her sister would be the perfect way to mend fences. An antidote to that last, toxic holiday meal two years ago. Elinor planned to use all her knowledge from cooking classes to create something special, a delicious piece of home, and a reminder that might tempt Saffron to miss their home.

She realized it was too soon to shop for the meal, but not too soon to get ideas. The menu should feel traditional but incorporate Italian elements. A pasta course instead of the sweet potatoes. A chianti instead of sauvignon blanc. Perhaps something with local fish sold fresh at the harbor. She had high, but vague hopes. A grand menu design hovered in the back of her mind.

She smiled as she thought about buying Saffron a condo here. Maybe Cosma could find a small apartment, and Elinor could dip into her savings for the down payment, then let Saffron use the trust income for the payments, until they could sell the cottage. Elinor could even help her sister find a way to earn income and have a fresh start in life. Because clearly Saffron was once again escaping a bad relationship. Maybe setting her up to stay in Italy would help stabilize her. She felt hopeful.

At the market, she got a cart and began browsing. Being among vegetables and fruits always cheered her up, their colors and textures like a painting of abundance. Surplus. Plenty. Having enough and not having to worry.

Who knew if you could get whole turkeys and sweet potatoes. Italy didn't have Thanksgiving. She hadn't thought about the fact that they didn't stock up on these crazy big fowls. How could she make anything traditional? Pushing up the produce aisle, she tried out some new ideas. A couple of whole chickens to roast. She could still make a feast, just a different kind. After all, they could call any good feast Thanksgiving.

A tall man was annoyingly moving ahead of her, slowly, with a basket over his arm. He looked too Italian to be any help. She moved to the zucchini bin but he came around the corner the other way and again blocked her, zipping along the row. He must be Italian, because he took so much time over the vegetables that he seemed to have an intimate relationship with artichokes. He was crowding her, and yet he didn't seem approachable, holding his basket carefully away from bumping her cart. All she could do was wait and try to be patient.

They inspected the squashes and aubergines in tandem, apart just enough. Elinor surreptitiously watched him, trying not to be frustrated. He was middle-aged, tanned, and slim except for a slight paunch. He picked up eggplants thoughtfully, seeming to inquire of their special characteristics. His slightly large nose gave him a thoughtful expression. Suddenly, he looked over at her and smiled broadly.

"*Prego, ti piace carciofi?*" he said, in a deep and quiet voice.

"American. Sorry, I don't speak Italian," she said.

When he smiled, he was handsome. His wavy, dark hair softened the severity of his features.

"American! I speak English, *signorina*. I was wondering if you like artichokes. You were standing by them. May I assist you?"

She knew enough Italian to understand his calling her *signorina* meant he assumed she was single. Was he coming on to her? She did like them, and hadn't actually noticed she was standing in front of a huge bin of tiny artichokes.

"Maybe these artichokes are unfamiliar to you, because they don't grow in the United States," he explained. She could see he was trying to be helpful, and she appreciated the help in this aisle of half-unfamiliar vegetables.

"These are smaller than the ones I usually see." She noticed his nose was very long.

He smiled and again became handsome. "These are the best Venetian lagoon artichokes. It's rare to get them here. They're completely delicious when sautéed in olive oil and sprinkled with lemon juice. You eat them whole."

"What about the thorns?"

"This variety has no thorns."

"Wonderful! I wouldn't have known. So many vegetables are different here."

"May I help you with anything else? What are you looking for?" He looked at her empty cart.

She realized she hadn't picked out a single vegetable. Was he thinking she was trying to pick him up? She'd heard of grocery store pickups at home, but was it a thing here too? Embarrassment warmed her cheeks.

"Actually, I'm trying to find arborio rice. I'm making an American Thanksgiving dinner. Rice would be standard, and arborio is the best."

He nodded thoughtfully. He wasn't coming on to her, or he would have been pushier. Had she made some terrible Italian social mistake? Of course, he was middle-aged. He must have some experience with women and knew enough not to behave like a teenager when interested in one. So maybe it was just what it seemed, two strangers chatting in the vegetable aisle of an empty store. Was this the wrong time to be grocery shopping, according to Italians?

"That would be a good addition," he said. "But what about a more Italian style dish? Orzotto with prosciutto and mushrooms is delicious. It's a rice-shaped pasta."

"Oh no, I don't eat wheat."

"Eating here must pose some challenges for you." His deep, melodic voice was free of sarcasm, so she accepted the statement. It was a challenge.

They moved further down the aisle in silence.

Then he said, "You might enjoy aubergines. We prepare them here in a dish called *Melanzane alla Parmigiana*, simple and delicious. Layered and baked, with some tomato and parmesan cheese. You can make it even in America, when you go back."

Subtle. He was fishing to find out when she was going back.

"Our Thanksgiving holiday is coming soon, so I don't know if I can make too many complicated dishes. I was thinking more of our traditional feast."

"Of course! Thanksgiving. When your founding pilgrims discovered America."

"Yes, sort of. Not discovered, but survived their first winter."

They stopped at the aubergines. "Have you been to the U.S.?" she asked, breaking the ice.

"Yes, once, to New York. I visited with my cousins who live there. On a vacation after my wife died."

So he was a widower. "I'm sorry you had to undergo such a thing," she said.

He put his basket down. Elinor ceased pretending she was browsing and they faced each other. His had such a nice smile, wide and easy, showing an eyetooth lapped slightly over the one next to it, an imperfection that made his whole face handsome.

"I'm Elinor," she said.

"Antonio Vassallo," he said, "but please call me Tonio. It was my grandfather's name. Our tradition, to keep names in the family."

He was older, maybe even by ten or twelve years. She wasn't sure if he was flirting, but she liked the way he kept the conversation going. This was, after all, merely a supermarket encounter. She was likely to run into him again, if he was shopping in her neighborhood. It made sense to be a good neighbor.

"I think I'd be up for trying the orzotto—what did you call the dish?"

"Orzotto with prosciutto and mushrooms. It's not too difficult. I could email you a recipe."

He wanted her email.

"That would be nice, thanks. Something more festive than plain rice would be great." Of course, she had taken a gluten-free baking course, but in Italy she had eaten lots of pasta. She probably wouldn't have a problem with orzo.

"Is this the best store around here? My sister and I moved in recently. We don't speak Italian, and we're just getting to know how to buy groceries."

She hadn't intended to reveal so much, but she liked the way Tonio nodded, receiving the information with seriousness. She liked not feeling stalked, but befriended. It would be nice and potentially helpful to have a local Italian friend, especially when she had to negotiate something as complicated as selling a house.

Another shopper turned the corner with her cart. Elinor and Tonio became aware they were blocking the aisle. They moved farther down.

"So, you and your sister are here with your families?" he asked, clearly fishing.

"My sister and I inherited a house down the street. We came here to sell the house, but first we're making some repairs. I'm divorced."

Why had she revealed to Tonio why she was here, owning property, and divorced?

"You're not planning to stay?" He looked disappointed. "Of course you must have good reasons. But Lerici is a wonderful place to live."

He was well dressed. He had no ring on his hand. She didn't mind his curiosity. "I have a job, and my mother to take care of. But I have no one else. Oh, well, my sister, but we don't talk much."

Elinor moved her cart. He followed and they stopped again at the tomatoes.

"You have a lot of different tomatoes!" she said.

"This is Italia, after all!"

So he could be funny. Elinor replied, "Of course. You make your tomato sauce from scratch while in America even Italians use the canned stuff."

"Please! Don't bring me down with the misdeeds of my countrymen."

She grinned. His English was good. "Where did you learn English?"

"In my job. I used to work in a hospital in Genoa. I studied English and became a translator for foreign patients."

"You worked in a hospital? I work in a hospital!"

He nodded and gave her a dose of that surprising smile. "*Simpatico*. Fellow sufferers of the medical system."

He put on a plastic glove and picked up a large tomato. Holding it up next to his cheek, he said, "Oversized. Big as a baby's head. Grown too long and will be tasteless. Better to make friends with it than eat it."

He put the giant tomato back down.

"I would be happy to show you how to make true Ligurian tomato sauce," he said, picking up smaller tomatoes.

"What else would you suggest? I don't see any turkey. Perhaps chicken?"

"I have some good recipes that might come close to your Thanksgiving turkey. Also, in Lerici, the fish is spectacular. You pan fry them and drizzle olive oil, top them with chopped basil. Instead of one big bird, two fresh meats."

He was a cook! "Tonio, why don't you join us? After all, you've made the menu interesting!"

"Oh, I couldn't intrude on your family festivities," he said, looking hopeful.

"It's just me and my sister. You'd make it festive!"

She felt shy, inviting a stranger met in the vegetable aisle to a family holiday. It was the sort of thing Saffron would do.

He nodded. "*Signorina*, I would be delighted."

She rushed to qualify that she wasn't hitting on him. "Our tradition is to have lots of people at the holiday. You'll be our Italian guest. Actually, our only guest."

"I can recommend other neighbors if you wish to have a big table. If you haven't met the pharmacist next door, I can introduce you. It's important to know the pharmacist."

He was joking. "I think one guest may be the right number. Let me give you my address." She fumbled in her purse for a scrap of paper and a pen.

"What street? Does your house have a name?" he asked. "Maybe I know the house."

"In fact, it's named Casa Magni. On Via Nino Garini."

"Ah! I know it. Not far from here, which is why you shop in this market."

She stopped searching for paper and pen and made a mental note to pick up a notebook. "Is your house nearby?" she asked.

"Yes. Nothing so grand as Casa Magni. An apartment on Salita A. Canata."

So, Tonio was a neighbor. They browsed together down the aisle, now turning a corner into the section containing a stunning variety of bottled water, sodas, and juices. Tonio pulled out a large bottled water, an American brand.

"Are you always funny around food?" she asked.

"Hopefully."

Tonio walked with her as she picked up their overnight needs. It was too soon to buy for Thanksgiving. She

141

bought the tomatoes, the aubergines, and at Tonio's urging, also persimmons. They would keep.

"Try one of these," Tonio suggested, picking up two large honeydew melons.

She picked the right hand one and put it into her basket. He picked up two bunches of purple grapes so large they must be hybrids. She took both. Great. Now she had a basket of fruit and vegetables.

"Where's the meat market?"

"The Italian *supermarcato* is a little different than the American supermarket," he said. "This is the section with cheeses and cured meat."

Elinor browsed the large cooler alongside Tonio. It displayed an amazing variety of things: prosciutto, pancetta, mortadella. Mozzarella, parmigiano, pecorino, ricotta and other cheeses.

"In Lerici, you do well to go to an independent butcher for fresh meat. A *pescheria* for our mouth-watering seafood. I can show you where to find the best."

Elinor nodded. "It's a wonder Italians have any time left for other things, after the shopping, cooking, and eating of this wonderful food."

Tonio's smile again startled her. Her pulse sped up briefly, and then she calmed herself.

He said, "We find time for the important things of life!" He seemed to be saying something more.

They walked out of the store together. Tonio offered to take her to the *pescheria* and butcher. They walked up the street. The lowering sun had painted everything a glowing gold.

"What a marvelous place!" Elinor exclaimed.

"Enchanted Lerici. That's on the banners." He grinned with pride for his town.

They came to the door of the *pescheria*. Tonio pointed out the butcher shop two doors down, and then gave her his number and left. As Elinor watched him walk away, her stomach lurched and her pulse pounded for a few moments. He was older, but handsome and funny. Kind. Charming, and not aggressive. She had made a friend, maybe something more. An odd rush of her pulse acknowledged the wish for more.

When she got home, Saffron was upstairs. She sat down at the table and opened her laptop to begin her research on Ligurian cuisine. Tonio had promised to email recipes, but she couldn't count on it. He might not even come. Who was he, truly, anyway? Was anything he told her true?

Her invitation had been rash, and unlike her. She was becoming as impulsive as her sister. But it was too late now to take it back. Maybe Saffron would enjoy having a third at the holiday table. Or perhaps her sister had invited a homeless family of gypsies! Although her whole idea for Thanksgiving had been about their twosome. Damn. Elinor wondered if she had just spoiled everything.

She smelled smoke. It had an herbal scent and was coming from upstairs.

Saffron came down.

"What are you doing?" Elinor sked.

Saffron smiled shyly. "Just a little smudging."

"Why?"

"Exorcizing some memories."

"Where did you find sage sticks?"

The shake of Saffron's head made Elinor feel she'd asked something silly. "Italy has civilization, you know," her sister said.

"Are you trying to get rid of Shelley?" Elinor asked.

"Never!"

"What then."

"If you must know, I'm sageing away your bad vibes."

Elinor shook her head, but with a smile. When Saffron's smile in response got a sly tinge, Elinor had a suspicion. "Were you at the café today?"

Airily, her sister admitted it. "I've had some adventures."

Adventures! Saffron's magic word.

Elinor's suspicion confirmed, she asked, "Met someone?"

"Sort of. Maybe."

Elinor's grin made Saffron turn and go into the kitchen. Taking leftovers out of the fridge, she looked over at Elinor and smiled. "Want me to make you a latte?"

"Sure, I'd love it."

Generosity seemed to be flowing. Elinor broached the subject. "Let's figure out about Gino. I'd be happy to talk to him about the misunderstanding with the Americans, and how to make things right."

She saw from Saffron's quick smile that this offer was acceptable.

Saffron brought their cups over and sat at the table. She took out her phone and typed with her thumbs. "I forwarded you Gino's email. You can take care of it."

While Saffron nibbled at last night's pasta with chicken and broccoli, she offered more information. "Honestly, I didn't tell Gino to go ahead. I'm sure. So it was a mix-up of some kind."

"Can you give me a little more information?"

"Gino works only part-time for his uncle. He also sells Vespas. I have his email. Don't know if I have a phone number, though. This is even better cold than it was hot!"

Elinor nodded. She had the ace card—the condo idea

for Saffron—and she corralled her temper. She could afford to take time.

"Tell me more about Gino and how you met. Did you sleep with him?" Elinor thought it was wonderful she could toss it out so offhandedly.

Her sister was ready to confess. "No, we just went out dancing. I did ask him to give us a proposal when I went to breakfast with him. I wanted to be able to tell you how much income we could make. Of course, later, after we got here, he emailed me and said to send pictures, that he couldn't estimate the income without them. So I sent yours."

Elinor didn't look at Saffron. She worked to slow her voice. "If that couple paid Gino, and he hasn't paid us, then he is stealing from them. What are we going to do about it?"

Saffron's voice rose into soprano. "You think I'm a crook too? I guess you still do, just because I once borrowed money from Mom-Betsy's jar."

Elinor was still calm. "Once a thief . . ."

"I guess you'd still want to have me arrested for taking a few dollars from Mom's jar. Calling the police on your fourteen-year-old sister?"

"You knew that jar was off limits. And I said I was sorry."

"You aren't my mother, but you seem to think you are!"

Saffron's abrupt rise made Elinor think she was leaving. The room or even the house. She said, "Please don't yell. The past is the past."

"What else do we have between us?" Saffron said, quietly miserable. "You always took a dollar or two. Nobody told me I wasn't enough of family to do it too. I wanted an ice cream cone."

Elinor tried to sound sympathetic. "How could you be so gullible with Gino?"

Saffron folded her arms. "Gino said houses here get thousands of euros a month. His uncle takes a commission, and that doesn't make him a crook."

Elinor got up and went into the kitchen. She wanted to think about dinner and to stay calm. She picked up a mixing spoon, looking at it as she thought about what Saffron had said.

"So you didn't actually put our house up for rent?"

"No! Besides, you talked to a realtor about selling it, and you didn't tell me!"

Elinor leaned against the counter. "It's not the same. I'd tell you before signing anything. Why don't you let me call Gino, and I'll sort the whole thing out. What else did Gino say?"

Saffron's voice was softer. "He said we might need repairs, and that he knows people here."

Elinor sighed and gave a small laugh. "Does every single Italian have relatives in the renovation business!"

Saffron went to the couch and plopped down on it. She picked up a pillow and hugged it as if it were a teddy bear. Elinor could see she'd made her sister retreat, so she softened her voice.

"What else did you write to Gino?"

"I was sleepy when I wrote. It was the middle of the night."

"Can you please show me all your emails?"

Saffron's beaming smile showed her giving in. "I'll forward them to you. By the way, did you just pick Cosma out of an ad?"

Saffron's sarcasm was a fair pushback, but Elinor knew she had won. "As a matter of fact, yes. I'm going to find a few more agents and compare them. Do you want an alert every time I email a realtor?"

Saffron leapt up. "Yes! You can't sell without my signature."

"How do you know that? Maybe I can."

"Because *Signor* Capelli told me. Maybe it's not in the terms of the trust."

Elinor's laugh was short and sarcastic. "Who are you? And what have you done with my sister?"

"I called him," Saffron said, as if it were a victory. "I have his phone number. He said we could ask any questions we want. He said that's the one exception to your making decisions as the trustee. You can't sell without my agreeing to it."

Elinor laughed. "But you can't hold up the sale indefinitely."

Saffron paused. "I might decide to live here."

Again Elinor laughed, and even more sarcastically said, "You might just do that."

Surprised, her sister sat back down. "Why do you say that?"

"I'll tell you tomorrow."

With a wry expression, Saffron changed the subject, "So why were you at the store so long?"

Elinor felt the cheesy smile swarm over her face.

With her annoying intuition, Saffron said, "No, you didn't! Who is he, and when can I meet him?"

"His name is Tonio, and you're going to meet him at..." She hesitated to admit her rash invitation, as she knew any impulsiveness delighted her sister. "At Thanksgiving."

"Get. Out!"

"You're so unattractive when you're gloating." Elinor couldn't help saying it with a smile.

"Romance in lovely Lerici!" Saffron crowed.

Elinor knew she was going to have to endure weeks of teasing and questions. Somehow, she didn't exactly mind the way it made her smile.

Chapter 17

Shelley's Castle—Saffron

The next morning, as Saffron was finishing her coffee at La Scala, Michael came in. Without even ordering, he came over and held out his hand.

"Pack up your stuff. We're going to see the real Bay of Poets."

She liked this boldness. He was more confident than yesterday, and his tone sent a zing up her spine. She held out her hand and he gripped it, helping her up. The next zing raced from his hand through hers to the top of her head. Adventure sparkling on the horizon, she gathered her stuff and followed him toward the door, hand in hand, as the feeling tingled in her stomach.

He pulled her down the street. They turned right at the bottom of the hill and onto the beach promenade. Walking alongside the water, today full of white curlicues, Saffron looked up at the green hills. In the clear light, they looked fresh-minted.

The pressure of his hand intensified. "The hidden beach is wild and perfect, he said. "Like you."

Dazzled by this compliment, she walked along, more aware of Michael's hand than of the wide swath of beach, dotted with beach chairs. The benches were nearly empty, the wind driving everyone indoors.

"Just a bit farther," he said, tugging her along.

Their speed throbbed in Saffron's pulse. The hidden cove, they both knew, was a pretext and a preamble—a pre-amble. Excitement tightened her throat, making her breath catch as she trotted beside him. He was so tall and his hand never loosened its grip.

She was going to have an adventure in Italy. His hand kept her locked into it, any doubt falling away.

They came to a sign: "Beach Behind Castle." A few more signs directed them to a marble arch over a tunnel beneath the building. They darted into the darkness holding hands, the path level, though impossible to see underfoot. They came out at a small, brilliantly white beach. The surf seemed higher now, pounding the shore steadily with dark, frilled swells. "Do people swim here? I mean, when it's not so windy?"

"They do. No one's here yet, but by afternoon I bet the beach will be full. People who know the secret of this place love it."

They took off their shoes and walked closer to the surf. Saffron scooped up a shell and put it in her pocket. "A souvenir." Of more than the beach.

On the way back, Michael stopped at a corner and pointed up a steep cobblestone street. "My little castle's up there. I bring home all the goddesses I meet. Would you care to visit?"

The rash compliment went to her head like a quickly quaffed glass of champagne. "Sure." This was it. The real adventure, not the hidden beach.

"Come, my Artemis," he said.

They climbed a short distance and turned down an even narrower alley. He stopped at a turquoise wooden door with a lintel low enough that he had to duck his head entering.

"The gate to my modest tower."

Saffron paused long enough to wonder if she was stepping into another mess with someone she hardly knew. But if she stopped now, she'd never find out what it was like to be a goddess.

When they were inside the doorway, he hesitated, but didn't kiss her. What would his lips feel like? Instead, he led her up narrow stairs that turned on a landing with a small window. She glimpsed the hills, and then they went up the last few steps.

Michael opened the next door, which had no lock. He held it for her, and Saffron entered a small studio apartment. Bedroom, kitchen, and sitting area were all in one room, with a separate bathroom.

"Welcome," he said with a sweep of his arm that came close to knocking over a lamp.

She giggled. "Cozy for a castle."

She walked around, looking out the one window onto the alley, trailing her fingers across the top of an armchair that was nearly at the foot of the small bed. Two reproductions of Renaissance paintings graced the wall above the bed, both Da Vinci's.

"You're a very beautiful goddess," Michael said, coming close to her. "I'd say you're the goddess of adventure."

His compliments were ridiculous and made her skin burn. Ridiculously hot, the way he didn't touch her, even now. So she made the first move, as befitted a goddess of adventure, and she kissed him.

151

That's all it took. Michael pulled her over to the bed and they sat to kiss again. His lips were delicious and the kiss just kept going as they toppled over.

"Soul meets soul on lovers lips," he whispered.

"What, Shelley too?"

"Because of you," he whispered and went back to wordless kissing.

She was surprised by the sudden passion from this deferential, soft-spoken guy. His kisses became wild as they roamed her face and neck. He pushed her down and pulled up her sweater, his fingertips rough, but his touch tender.

What had given him callouses—did he play guitar? She saw an instrument in the corner, a mandolin. Even more romantic. She gave in to sensation, as his mouth replaced his hands.

By the time she woke up, morning had turned into afternoon. Michael was asleep—no wonder, after all that expenditure of energy. She looked down at his handsome face. Those good looks were a trap. She had made a mistake, though it was out of a sense of adventure. And yes, because he was exciting once he took charge of the situation. She looked at him, asleep next to her, his mouth slightly open, his rhythmic exhales echoing the rough breaths in her ear that had thrilled her. A jolt in her core reminded her how thrilling.

She considered inviting him to Ellie's Thanksgiving dinner. She liked Michael, but soon they'd be gone, and in any case, he was trouble for sure. The sort who pinned you down. Soon would come requirements and conditions, and she wouldn't be free anymore.

Pulling on her sweater and pants she went to the window. The sun was blocked by buildings on either side of the street, but she could tell from the shadows that it had moved a lot. They had slept half a day.

As she watched Michael sleeping, a surge of warmth spread through her. His chest rose and fell, hairless, half under and half outside the sheets. Saffron thought of the morning she left Justin to come here. She had slid out of bed early, silently, knowing she had to get to the airport. Debating whether to wake him and tell him she had the flight to Rome today, intending to be a good person after all and not leave without saying goodbye. She watched him breathing and when he suddenly took a big breath and held it, she panicked. She couldn't face his questions. *Why didn't you ask me to come? Why are you so secretive? What do you think I'd do at the funeral?* She had managed to get herself and her suitcase out without waking him.

She was holding her breath now. She'd be a terrible person forever. Justin already knew that, which was why she had left him. Saffron couldn't bear for Michael to find out. He was so nice, so full of compliments. His body and charm could devour her caution, and those muscular arms and legs—what did he do besides drinking coffee to keep in such fantastic shape? He was going to trap her. She had to escape, because he had made it clear he was going to hold on with everything he had, and what he had was a lot.

Saffron took one more look at Michael and slipped out of the room, hoping to untangle the knot of emotions that threatened to choke her.

How good she had become at escaping her own feelings and the complications of someone having feelings for her. Too good to be a truly nice person, the kind of person that Michael deserved.

Tripping lightly down the stairs, she emerged into a mellow late afternoon. Her body was warm and tingling from physical excitement. She was slightly, pleasantly sore, a talisman of her adventure.

But she couldn't leave him entirely behind. This was a small town. She'd see him in the café or somewhere, and she'd have to make her *I-am-so-sorry* excuses, but he'd have gotten the message: she had to be free.

She turned down the street. An old woman passed her carrying two shopping bags, wearing a green scarf on her head to keep her white hair tucked against the wind. A ginger cat and a black cat played a leaping game down the alley, pouncing on each other and racing away, pouncing again. A deep breath of salt air tingled through her.

On the promenade, two elderly men side by side on a bench leaned together, hands on their canes, talking, probably gossiping. The ocean's engine was racing but everyone walked with a sense of permanent leisure. Her heart was racing along with the choppy sea. She sensed the many possibilities in her future, making her breathing deep and quick. Yet everyone around her seemed to move slowly, as if now and forever were entwined in time. The earthy colors of the buildings, the deep and twinkling blue of the sea—it sank into her that this was a moment she'd never forget. She had to show Elinor the enchantments of Lerici. Her sister needed to feel some Italian magic steeping in her blood. Ellie needed to hear the whisper of adventures in her ear.

A small bookshop with a cart of books in front enticed her. Most books were in Italian, but one title in English leaped out: *I Am Shelley*. She picked up the slim, well-thumbed paperback and skimmed. It was a fictionalized recreation of journals written by the poet. As she read here and there, she realized that this was too much of a coincidence—she was leaving behind a Shelley descendant, who quoted Shelley, and now finding a book on Shelley. Some invisible hand was drawing her into Shelley's net. To find this book in English, here, ready for her—it wasn't an accident.

Could their hidden manuscript really be one of Shelley's? It would explain why Shelley's spirit was hanging around their cottage. He wanted to help them find his book.

She went inside and bought the book, asking if they had any more books in English about Shelley. An older saleswoman dressed in black understood her question.

"We have books of his poetry, books about his life, and books about all the Romantic poets who have stayed in the region of La Spezia. Do you know this is called the Gulf of the Poets?"

Saffron was excited. "I did know, thank you. I'm the new owner of *Casa Magni*, a house on Via Nino Garini. Do you know it?"

The woman shook her head. "I know the street, of course. But not your house. Why do you ask?"

Saffron took a breath and asked her big question. "Is there any possibility that Shelley lived here?"

"Ah, no, *signorina*. He rented a house in San Terenzo, around the other end of the bay. The house is well marked. But he moored his boat here."

Saffron was annoyed that this woman was deciding whether or not Shelley had lived in her house. *Casa Magni* might well be where he had lived. She had asked a mere bookseller an important question, when she should instead find a local historian.

"Thank you," she said. "I'll take this one." She browsed around the counter display while the saleswoman rang up

155

her purchase. "I'll take this too," she said, pushing forward a volume of poetry.

It would be her Thanksgiving present for Ellie.

That night, Saffron read her new book, most interested in Shelley's death. The book said he'd drowned because a sudden storm overturned his boat, but it also mentioned a local rumor that pirates had rammed the boat. That was dismissed as lore cooked up to draw tourists. She wondered.

She read about his funeral on the beach. Lord Byron and Shelley's other friends had searched for his body for several days before his remains washed up, so decayed and putrid that even Byron couldn't stand it. They decided to have a cremation on the beach, and they built a pyre, set Shelley's body on fire, and watched it burn. They watched the flesh melting and the seething brains of this gentle soul boiling out of his skull. Most left before the end, but Trelawney stayed. He saw that one part of Shelley's body remained: his heart wouldn't burn.

Trelawney had snatched it out of the embers. When Mary Shelley learned of the funeral and the unburned heart, she begged Trelawney to send it. He did, and Mary Shelley kept her husband's heart in a box in her desk for years. All that time later, Shelley's heart was still unbreakable.

My heart is unbreakable, Shelley had told Saffron. *We must give our best.* Now she understood that Shelley's heart was his best—his compassion. But what did she have to give her sister—what was her best?

Soon it would be Thanksgiving. She could maybe give Ellie a token of her gratitude for bringing her here, where she felt her real life was going to start.

Shelley came, this time in her dreams. Comforting

her, he whispered that he understood her work with the Invisibles. He whispered into her ear, as the dream vanished:

While yet a boy I sought for ghosts, and sped
Through many a listening chamber, cave and ruin,
And starlight wood, with fearful steps pursuing
Hopes of high talk with the departed dead.

But that was the trouble. Her high talk with this dead poet never amounted to an explanation. He never told her why he was lingering—taking care of the sisters seemed to amount to interrupting her sleep—or where the dead were supposed to go when she waved them away. Shelley should have shared a few secrets with her, if he was going to bother her so often.

* * *

The next morning she went back to La Scala for a latte. Of course, Michael came in. He grinned, but when she didn't immediately smile, he looked hurt.

He came over, shrugged, and pointed to a chair beside her. "So . . . ?"

Saffron nodded and he sat. She didn't look him in the eye, but his being so close made heat flare in her, along with the memory of his body on top of hers, the delicious touch of his hands, the sound of his breathing as he fell asleep afterward.

"So," he said cheerfully, "you left while I was sleeping." Not a question. Not exactly an accusation.

This was going to be awkward. She quickly made her apology. "I'm sorry I dipped. Not much on repeats." She couldn't help staring at his very blue eyes, questioning her.

A flame of desire shot through her. She tamped it down, into ash, looking down.

"I'm sorry." It sounded like a *sorry-not-sorry*. Hella lame.

"Oh, I get it," he said.

He got up and backed away. She realized too late that she should have touched his arm or his shoulder in a friendly way.

He went to another table, disappointment trailing him like a sweet scent going rotten. She was sorry to leave it like this. Maybe she was sorry she had let the whole thing happen. Lerici was a small town and they both liked this café. She couldn't easily avoid him. She was forever too late realizing her mistakes. And here was another, hopefully to be undone by cheery smiles across the café and brief conversations about the coffee and the weather.

Michael opened his computer without looking over again.

She hoped she hadn't made an enemy. A surge of longing rushed through her, with a flare of physical desire for his touch. Why did she have this absurd urge to go over and tell Michael she'd just been joking? They could laugh about it. But then she'd have to be with him, and she wasn't ready to make a commitment to a stranger. Why had she let herself be drawn to him and stupidly sleep with him? They hardly knew each other.

An urge to get away rose wild into her throat. Then she remembered Shelley urging her to be kind. She'd been mean to her sister and mean to an Invisible. Now she'd hurt this sweet man. She'd fix it with Michael another day, she promised herself as she packed up and left without even glancing at him.

When she arrived at the cottage, she found Cosma Gavazza waiting on the doorstep.

"Isn't Elinor here?" Saffron asked, opening the door.

"Oh no, I didn't come to see *Signorina* Elinor. I came to see you."

Saffron smiled, wondering if Ellie had somehow conveyed to the realtor that in Ellie's absence, Cosma could talk to her about the house.

"Come in. What can I do for you?"

Saffron indicated a chair, but Cosma didn't sit. "You can come with me to see the condo for sale. Your sister asked me to look for you, but of course you must be the one to decide."

She could only stare at the woman and wonder if somehow Ellie could have mixed things up. Could perfect manager Elinor have miscommunicated a crucial fact? Unlikely, but then could this pushy Italian woman have invented such an elaborate maneuver for selling their house? Equally unlikely.

"Who said I was in the market for a condo?" Saffron asked.

"Your sister told me. Now we have an appointment to see it, do you want to come or not?"

Saffron looked at Cosma, trying to decide if she was being poor with English or simply rude. She decided it was a combination.

She shrugged. "Okay. Let's go."

Cosma's car was tiny, dented on the rear bumper, and had cracked leather seats. When Saffron opened the passenger door, it emitted a rusty croak, like a bullfrog, one opening and one again closing.

They drove downhill, turned left, and then went uphill again. The view from this street was promising. Cosma parked in front of a brick colored apartment building set right at the street, with almost no entry garden, just a concrete walkway that surrounded a pool. There was no elevator, so they had to climb a set of stairs.

The doors were all tan, almost as uninspired a color combination as in American apartment buildings. But Saffron didn't care about the colors. She was curious what her sister had in mind, and why Ellie hadn't mentioned setting up this appointment for her.

Cosma stopped halfway down the hall and opened the door on an apartment. She held it for Saffron, who saw it was a small place. The windows didn't face the sea, but rather looked out on the hill across the street, so there wasn't much light.

Saffron walked quickly through to the bedroom. Inside its pale lavender walls, she felt uneasy. As if someone had been unhappy, a teenager who cried a lot, but then left home and got free. Cosma took her into the living room, which did have a picture window, but even in this midafternoon hour it was dim.

"I'm going to step out on the deck by myself for a few moments," she told the realtor.

Outside, Saffron leaned on the balcony railing and drew some healing breaths. This place was all wrong for her, or she was all wrong for it. A confusion of resentment and gratitude to her sister whirled through her, until she could calm her emotions.

A group of boys bounded up the street, chasing and kicking a ball back and forth. Shouting in Italian, their high spirits sent an electric thrill through her. Their boisterous energy evaporated thoughts of Ellie and Ellie's constant manipulation of her. Among the children playing in the alley was a boy even younger than the rest. He had a baseball cap on backward. It loosened as he jumped back-and-forth, trying to catch their ball with hands that couldn't grasp it. The other boys were only using their feet. He seemed not to understand the game.

Suddenly, he looked up at her. Saffron smiled and nodded her head. Then she waved and said under her breath, "Go on home, baby." He gave her an uncertain look and then smiled back. His image softened and went out like a small candle flame. Good. Another one on his way.

She was startled by the sense of someone touching her shoulder. Cosma? She turned and felt rather than saw Shelley's faint outline.

This isn't your home. You don't belong here, and I don't either.

She laughed.

You won't find my manuscript here.

"Why is it important to find it?"

But he was fading away. All she heard now was the soft sighing of the breeze and the shout of a child running down the street.

"I don't think this is quite right for me," she said when she came back inside.

Cosma waved her extravagantly manicured hand. "I have several more to show you. This is just the first."

"Okay," Saffron said.

They went back to the car and back to what now felt much more like home.

Cosma let her out without turning off the engine. "I'll be in touch!" she said. "*Ciao, bella!*"

Saffron had settled prostrate on the couch, head on the armrest and feet propped up on pillow, when Ellie came in with bags of groceries.

"Why did you set me up?"

"What do you mean?"

"The condo. Cosma took me to see it."

Saffron could hardly have shocked Elinor more if her face had suddenly sprouted green spots.

Elinor cleared her throat and said, "I know you want to stay. I'm going to make that possible."

Saffron tried to think of a way to convey to her sister that this wasn't going to make either of them happy. She thought of her relatives, in order of their happiness, and Elinor was at the bottom. Saffron had never seen Ellie truly happy.

"We have to find another way," was all Saffron could think of.

She should have known her sister wouldn't accept it.

"You don't have to pick the first condo you see!" Elinor protested. "Look at others. It's a perfect way for you—for us both—to get what we want."

"But you don't understand. It's what's here in this house, the feeling and the *feathered hope*."

She wondered if Eleanor would even remember the reference.

"What are you going to do for a living, if I let you stay in this house?"

Saffron tried to make it light, but she was getting sadder by the second. "Maybe they'll hire me at the café. I make a pretty good latte."

"And how are you going to pay me back for my share? Surely you think I deserve my inheritance too!"

Saffron looked down, walked away, and tossed a reply over her shoulder. "I'll figure it out."

Elinor called after her as Saffron climbed the stairs. "Have you no ambition whatsoever?"

Saffron stopped before she disappeared. "You have enough for both of us. How happy has it made you?"

They stared at each other. There was no winning this. She'd have to give in. Or something. Maybe the spirit of Shelley, as full of advice as he was, would have an idea.

Home. On a sudden impulse, she took out her phone and typed a text.

Hey, Michael! Have you ever been to an American-style Thanksgiving dinner? Come over to our place if you want. Sis is cooking up a feast. Five pm. Spiff up.

Chapter 18

Thanksgiving, Italian Style—Elinor

Tonio had come through with recipes—lots! Elinor read her email from him and realized if she followed his suggestions, it would be by far the most daring meal she had ever created. And one of the biggest.

He had confirmed he was coming. Re-reading it, a prickle ran down her arms and she swung between delight and stage fright. She was going to make the first big feast since her divorce and make it for someone who knew about cooking and was a virtual stranger.

She looked up from her laptop on the dining table and saw the room with the eyes of a first-time visitor. The dingy corners of the ceiling, the dust on the floor and surfaces.

When she was part of a couple, it had been easy to throw dinner parties. They had thrown quite a few, mostly to promote his business. They could afford a house cleaner and takeout dishes from the gourmet shop.

Now she was going to do a big dinner solo, because of course Saffron didn't maintain a friendly relationship with any menu that didn't center on eggs or pizza. And she didn't help much with house cleaning. She reminded herself to ask her sister to at least dust these surfaces before Thanksgiving.

First on Tonio's list of Ligurian dishes, Elinor was pleased to find an item she knew well: focaccia. She had often made this flattened bread brushed with olive oil in her cooking class. At home, it was often paired with cheese and sausage. She could buy it readymade, if she ran out of time.

Artichokes, definitely. Here they were small, thornless, and delicious. One recipe had them dipped in batter and browned in olive oil with parsley and onion, to eat whole, tender and crunchy. Tonio's recipe said minestrone originated from soldiers making soup in their helmets during the First Crusade. He had suggested both chicken and fish, as seafood was so plentiful here. She didn't think making tiramisu would be too hard.

The menu, finally set, was spectacular, in Elinor's view.

Battered and Fried Carciofi, small thornless artichokes
Minestrone Lerici Style, a soup originating in Liguria
Roast chicken with peppers and olives
Ligurian Swordfish and Potatoes
Orzotto with prosciutto and mushrooms
Colline di Levanto, a white wine from Cinque Terre
Focaccia
Tiramisu
Cinque Terre Sciacchetrà, dessert wine
Espresso

It was to be Thanksgiving, Italian style. Elinor hoped Saffron was going to love it, and it would be the peace offering needed to win her sister's agreement to do the only reasonable, practical thing. To sell the cottage. And yet here she was, gaily planning a homey holiday.

When Saffron came in that afternoon from her daily rambles, Elinor laid out her plan. "We're going to have a nice Thanksgiving here, and I want the house to be perfect. You need to help out more."

Surprised, Saffron cocked her head and looked around. "You're right, Ellie. I can help out. What do you want me to do?"

Elinor considered Saffron's probable cleaning skills and changed her mind. "I don't know. Take your pick. Walls, surfaces, floors, bathrooms, windows . . ."

"I'll take hidden manuscripts."

Elinor was now the one surprised, but on second thought, "Good. Find that thing and I'll count it as full participation. Find it before Thanksgiving, if you can."

Saffron laughed. "You drive a hard bargain, but I'll do it. Watch me."

"I'll send you a spreadsheet to use. You can cross off every place in every room you've searched, and even if you don't find it, looking will count.

That cracked her sister up even more. "Ellie, keep your spreadsheet. I have my own system."

"As long as it's systematic."

"You'll see."

On the Tuesday before Thanksgiving, Elinor shopped. She wanted to take home all these recipes to show her cooking class and ask the instructor for a referral to a class on Italian cuisine. She'd bring Lerici home, and come home sharing a new closeness with her sister—if this meal succeeded.

A beautiful Italian holiday to erase the miserable event two years ago. Surely Saffron was ready to forgive and forget. Elinor had been rotten to her about Jack, but now she had this chance to cap off their time in Italy with a gift from her heart. She was going to make it a thoroughly delicious gift.

On the way back from the store, Elinor noticed a nursery. She remembered the terra cotta pots and her vision of them overflowing with petunias, marigolds, and alyssum, ivy too. She went into the nursery yard, but she couldn't remember how many pots there were. She could go home, count, and come back. Few of these plants were flowering and most looked bedraggled.

She went inside and asked the nurseryman if they had any more flowering plants.

"Not at this season. Not planting time, *signorina*," he said.

She nodded and went outside again on the nursery patio, where she spotted the perfect addition. The one flower in a sea of greenery was a large potted pink camellia. Salmon-pink petals radiated from a large gold center. The terra cotta pot was shapely and large, enough for the plant to grow. The nurseryman recommended not buying it until spring. He said that in this climate, in November, flowering camellias are reduced to their essence of sap and seed. He couldn't promise the blooms would last, and it was unlikely to open any more in time for a dinner in a week.

Elinor bought it anyway. What was wrong with her? She was planning to sell and leave Lerici, and yet here she was, going all Saffron about a flowering plant.

It was too big to bring home. Elinor had it delivered. The next morning, two men wheeled the pot on a dolly around the side of the house and set it in place on the patio. Elinor had it placed to be visible from the dining table. The bush had opened one more pink bud overnight, a sister to the first flower, like twin corsages. Its golden center was full of tall stamens. It would look lovely for Italian Thanksgiving. Going all Saffron had its satisfactions. Saffron came out onto the patio, and Elinor showed her. "Don't you think Tonio will enjoy it? Flowers in November."

Her sister's eyes opened wide. Elinor realized she hadn't told her sister about him. What was there to say? But there was something. The feeling clogged her throat.

"You invited someone you just met to Thanksgiving?" Saffron grinned. "He must be handsome."

"Don't be such a romantic! This has nothing to do with attraction."

Saffron pointed to the flowering plant and grinned again. "Okay, I won't be romantic. What's he like? Is this the man you met in the market?"

That sly smile of Saffron's made Elinor's shoulders hunch, as if she'd been caught half-undressed. "He's a nice man, but just a neighbor. Older guy. He helped me shop and gave me some recipes."

Saffron tilted her head. "Ellie, come on. You can tell me."

Why was she covering up the fact that yes, Tonio was handsome, and yes, she was intrigued?

She forced her voice low. "I thought it would be fun to have an Italian person at Thanksgiving. You should invite someone. You must have made friends in the café."

Saffron looked away. That meant she had.

"I don't have anyone special. But I don't mind your friend."

Saffron was such a bad liar. So there was someone, and someone Italian, someone her sister had slept with. Did he, too, have a rental business, or relatives who were carpenters needing work?

"I can cancel with Tonio. Just tell me."

Saffron smiled that I-know-your-secret smile. "Can't wait to meet him."

"And I can't wait to meet your friend. Ask him to come"

She got a huge laugh out of her sister. "Okay, you're good. Yes, I have a friend. I invited him already. His name is Michael."

"Does this Michael have a last name?"

Saffron's smile was sly. "Shelley."

To her credit, Saffron did some looking for the manuscript. She also brought home two packages of mixed flowers from the store and arranged them in the tall ceramic vases she found in the closet of the chaos room.

The house was clean, thanks to Elinor's midnight prepping, and fresh-looking, thanks to Saffron's flowers.

Promptly at five on Thanksgiving, Tonio knocked on the door. Tonio's double-cheek kiss caught Elinor by surprise. A lovely European custom, it shot warmth through her, though his lips' touch had been feather light.

"Welcome!" Elinor said. "To Casa Magni. It's a little small to be called Big House, and it's slightly haunted, according to my sister."

He smiled and looked around appreciatively. "Haunted? Excellent!"

"Come in!"

Tonio stepped further into the great room. He handed Elinor a wine bottle and set the tiramisu he'd brought on the bar between the kitchen and dining area.

Saffron stood up from the couch at the far end of the

room and held out her hands. Tonio crossed the room and shook both her hands, smiling that handsome smile.

Crazily, Elinor felt proud of Tonio as she introduced them. "This is my sister Saffron."

How nice that he had dressed up. His tweed jacket and teal colored silk turtleneck with gray slacks was elegant but not stuffy. Comfortable shoes—very un-Italian, but it made her feel better about her American loafers. After all, she couldn't cook a feast in heels, though an Italian would have.

She had learned about the Italian thing with shoes in the hotel lobby in Rome, when a young Italian woman had asked if she was American. She asked how she could tell, and the woman looked down. "Your shoes." Elinor looked at her pointy-toed, peach suede heels and realized she would never be shoe-Italian.

Elinor had then made a study of shoes, and learned of the two kinds of Italians: young Italians of taste in torture shoes and elderly Italians who had given up their taste. Americans, she realized, never had any taste to start with.

Tonio had clearly not given up his taste except that he was wearing comfortable shoes. Probably fallen arches. He was middle-aged. Elinor liked him better for not wearing pointy shoes, but she appreciated his elegance.

"I'll check on dinner and pour us some wine," she said, retreating into the kitchen, feeling giddy.

Tonio sat in the armchair next to Saffron on the sofa, while Elinor lifted lids on the simmering pots. She turned to work at the sink and counter, facing out of the kitchen. Tonio and Saffron were at the far end of the room, but she could listen if not participate.

"How long have you lived in Lerici?" Saffron asked him.

"Nearly fifteen years." Tonio leaned forward, crossing his legs to avoid their being crowded by the coffee table. "My wife and I retired here after living in Genoa."

Elinor tried to catch his expression, but he was half-facing away from her.

"Where is she now?" Saffron asked.

"She died five years ago." Tonio said it easily, as if he was used to saying it.

"I'm so sorry." Saffron reached over and touched his arm.

He nodded and turned around to look at Elinor. "May I help you with anything?"

"No, thank you." She smiled at him, finding his offer sweet.

A timer dinged and Elinor turned back to the oven. She took out the chicken and tested it. Herb-scented perfection. But she wanted to hear more. Another timer buzzed, and she stirred the soup and reduced the flame to a flicker.

Elinor turned back to face into the living room as Tonio asked Saffron, "And you? How long have you been in Lerici?"

He turned his head and look over at Elinor. She made her smile sympathetic as Saffron said, "Three months now."

His gaze made her flush. She looked down and began to slice the focaccia.

A knock on the door, distinct and rhythmic.

"Must be Michael!" Saffron exclaimed and went to the door.

Elinor reflected that he was only twenty minutes late. Perfect for a friend of Saffron's, who wouldn't then expect her to be punctual to anything.

Elinor stepped out of the kitchen as Michael Shelley

came in, holding out a bottle of wine and a bouquet. Saffron took them. He slipped his arm around her waist and gave her a quick kiss on the lips.

Then he nodded hello's to Elinor and Tonio and came into the living room. Saffron said, "Ellie and Tonio, this is Michael Shelley."

"Delighted to meet you both," he said.

Elinor noticed that his English accent was cultured, but flavored with a northern region. She liked the sound of his deep but musical voice. And he was outrageously handsome with a wholesome flair. Saffron's taste was improving. And except for the tardiness, Michael was courteous.

"So you're a Shelley? Any relation?" Elinor asked.

He flustered slightly in the charming English way. "Barely. A distant descendant."

"Then you should feel at home here," she said, gesturing around the living room. "Some believe that the poet lived here, even possibly in this house." She looked at her sister, who winked.

They settled in the living room and Elinor went back into the kitchen to take things off the stove. She put the chicken back into a warm oven and poured wine from the bottle Tonio had brought. It seemed a safer bet that it would be the best wine, between the two bottles. Although Michael was polite, his sweater was frayed at the collar, and Tonio could afford silk turtlenecks. Michael's bottle would make a nice follow-up to Tonio's.

She took the tray of fried artichokes out of the fridge and brought it to the coffee table, gestured that they should help themselves, and then went back and brought the tray with wine glasses.

Sitting down on the love seat, she turned to Tonio. It

seemed an appropriate moment to say it. "I want to say again that I'm sorry about your wife."

Tonio nodded. "After you've loved someone a long time, you never completely lose them, even after they die."

His warm honesty touched Elinor.

Michael murmured, "I'm very sorry to hear it."

Tonio nodded to Michael and smiled, lifting his glass. "A toast to our hostesses. It's a special wine from our region. I thought you would enjoy it. The Albarola grapes are grown north of here, in Cinque Terre. The wineries are delightful to visit."

Elinor sipped and said the wine was delicious.

Tonio was pleased. "Wonderful!" He plucked an artichoke from the plate and cradled it in a napkin. "Our local artichokes are too. We eat them whole, with our fingers."

Elinor watched him eat with pleasure that kindled her own, knowing she'd made the dish correctly.

Saffron asked Tonio, "So what job are you retired from?"

Though Elinor winced at her sister's intrusiveness, she was interested to hear Tonio's answer. She was embarrassed to realize that she knew so little about him, and yet she had invited him to an important family occasion.

Tonio's voice in answering sent thrills through her. He had beautiful, mellow tones. "I worked for the hospital in La Spezia. Management work. I enjoyed it. The atmosphere of saving lives every day—it's exhilarating and rewarding."

Saffron gave Elinor a look. "That's such a coincidence, both of you in hospital work. You're colleagues. Or would be, if Ellie got a job here."

"And if I hadn't retired," he reminded her.

Elinor got up and lit the candles on the dining table.

The kitchen timer buzzed. She brought out plates and bowls of food and invited them to bring their wine and sit.

She put herself at the head of the table, closest to the kitchen for convenience in serving. They all sat, and Elinor looked around. A glow that matched the array of candles on the table lit up inside her, calling up memories from a family holidays, times when even Dad showed up. She had forgotten what it felt like to be part of a warm family. Funny that two strangers at her table could make her feel this.

Tonio caught her eye and then looked at Saffron. "Do you have special traditions to start your holiday meal?"

Michael said, "I've heard Americans express gratitude on this day. Something to do with pilgrims surviving the wilderness, isn't it?"

Saffron got a laugh from everyone when she said, "We give thanks, eat, and watch football."

"Mainly we drink and overeat," Elinor said.

Tonio said, "We simply call that being Italian."

Elinor liked his humor and his manners. She hadn't remembered him being this handsome when they met in the grocery store.

Saffron then improvised. "We usually say a blessing before the meal. We do it holding hands."

She glanced at Elinor, who remembered that it was definitely not a family tradition to hold hands. Her wicked sister held out hers and they all clasped hands. Tonio's hand took Elinor's with a quick and strong grasp, and her face grew hot.

Saffron continued with her fabrication of family tradition. "Our family doesn't say blessings, but we each say something we're grateful for. Ellie? Do you have something you're grateful for?"

Elinor said, "Oh, no, Saffron. It's your privilege to go first. Since you remembered our family tradition." She emphasized the words and aimed a sharp glance at her wicked sister.

But she didn't mind that Tonio kept holding her hand as Saffron gleefully extemporized. Elinor couldn't concentrate on her sister's improv. She was fully and exquisitely aware of the pressure.

"Dear . . . Lord of the harvest . . . we thank Thee for the bounty before us, and for the fruits of this beautiful new land. Thank You for bringing us to Italy—well, You brought us here because of Nathan's dying—but however, thank you. Amen."

They each added 'amens'. Tonio's grasp lingered one more moment after the rest dropped hands. Elinor flushed with warmth, and she had to take a big sip of wine.

She rose to ladle out soup from the tureen. "May I serve you all a *primo* of minestrone?"

"Genuine Lerici minestrone! Wonderful," Tonio said, lifting his glass to salute her.

Elinor's hand shook slightly as she handed him the first bowl. "I wouldn't dream of heaping everything on one plate, although that is the Thanksgiving tradition."

Michael laughed. "And the English traditional feast, though of course we don't have your holiday."

"But we're here, so we're feasting the Italian way," Elinor said.

She took a spoonful of soup, and they all started eating. This felt like a real Thanksgiving. Her cooking class teacher had said that holiday meals were social art more than culinary events. Through the flickering candle flames, she saw that it had been a wonderful idea to have this one.

175

Tonio scooped up his first spoonful of soup and shook his head, alarming Elinor. "Is there something wrong?"

Tonio paused, savored, and swallowed. "No, it's—simply *perfetto*!"

She relaxed into a smile. "It's your recipe. I'm glad I did it well. Do Italians have any traditions at this season?"

His brown eyes warmed up over the smile that made him even more handsome.

"We don't have pilgrims, but the ancient Romans celebrated a harvest festival. It's called Cerelia, and it's in October, in honor of Ceres, goddess of agriculture. They ate and drank, like your Thanksgiving, with music, parades, and games."

"I guess everyone has harvest feasts," Michael said. "Though the Italians make these things so much more fun than the English. Ours was transported to America and became your Thanksgiving."

Saffron smiled politely at him and turned to ask Tonio, "What made you decide to live in Lerici? Why not somewhere more dramatic on this coast?"

"You want more drama than Lerici's beautiful views and marvelous food?" he replied.

Saffron laughed. "I'm always looking for drama. What do you suggest?"

"I could take you to the big castle up the coast. Both of you! You're welcome too, Michael."

Saffron clapped her hands. Michael nodded, smiling.

Elinor cleared the soup bowls and served the main course, the roast chicken with its side of peppers and olives, and orzotto with prosciutto and mushrooms. She had decided not to attempt the swordfish, and so she held her breath as they started on the chicken. It was the main event.

For a few minutes, they all ate appreciatively. A glow of pride swept through Elinor as each of them caught her eye and smiled or nodded, chewing.

Then Tonio turned to Elinor. "What kind of hospital work do you do?"

"Human relations in our local hospital." She laughed. "Our departments would be next door if we worked in the same place."

"When do you plan to return to your job?"

Tonio's question made her a little breathless. "I'm almost out of leave. And I have to decide whether to ask for more. But I could lose my job."

"Do you ever plan to come back?"

She tried to be casual under Tonio's dark gaze. "Hopefully. As you say, what more could I want than Lerici?"

Trying to keep the conversation balanced, she turned to Michael. "Where around here do you live?"

"Not far away. I have a room in the Guadani home. Started in the summer, and here I still am," said Saffron's interesting friend.

"Are you a student?"

Michael took a generous swig of wine. "Not anymore. I'm taking a gap year. I'm supposed to be deciding whether to pursue a doctorate. My parents thought a bit of Italian living would suit me, before I succumb to academia."

Elinor now understood that she was talking to a young man of means. "Where in England do they live?"

"London. I mean, the family castle is there—that is, the old Shelley abode. Not a castle. More of a large flat, really."

"The family abode? You live with your parents?"

Michael was getting more embarrassed. "They're good roommates, actually. But of course, I'm up at Oxford."

He was willing to be grilled by a relation. That said something.

As they savored the dessert, they each sampled two versions of tiramisu, Tonio's and Elinor's. He offered to show Elinor how to make the one he'd brought and hastened to assure her that every version of tiramisu was *"perfetto"*, especially hers. Such a gentleman.

Michael, she noticed, had taken Saffron's hand under the tablecloth. When he did, she looked at him in a way that seemed like a promise.

One thing Elinor would surely take back home. Every time she entered a kitchen, she'd think of Tonio and his contributions to their Thanksgiving. She'd make them a new tradition. But Italian cuisine was the least of Tonio's talents. That was something else she'd have to think about.

* * *

The day after Thanksgiving, Elinor made her decision. She called her boss and explained that the realtor couldn't put the house on the market yet because the repairs had become complicated.

He listened, giving terse *Uh-huh* replies, and said, "This is unpaid leave, as we agreed, but we need you back. Or we need a substitute. Anyone you'd suggest?"

Elinor hadn't thought about this, and it made her go blank for a moment. Then she had an idea. "What about Harvey? He's taken some of my workload when we got into a crunch. He knows the organization of my filing system and can handle the phone calls to employees."

"Harvey would be good," Bill said thoughtfully.

Why did Elinor suddenly feel she'd made a terrible mistake? "I'll be back at the end of December," she offered, wondering if by then Bill might say she didn't need to come back at all.

What if Harvey proved to be too good?

The pause on the other end was somehow threatening. Then Bill said, "When you get back, be prepared for some changes. Things don't stand still because you're *bereaved.*"

The sarcasm chilled her.

He ended the call and she stared at her phone. Her hand was shaking. When she went home, was she going to be demoted—or worse? What would life be like without this job? Her life revolved around it. Did she have much life outside it? She woke up in the morning thinking about tasks and meetings. She went home after work with that glow of knowing she was necessary and competent. The faces of her boss and colleagues followed her into the evening's relaxation, confirming her important place in the life-saving machinery that was a community hospital.

In a daze, Elinor went out and sat at the patio table, looking out over the hillside, wondering what her place in the world was supposed to be, if she was no longer part of that institution.

Her phone rang. Cosma Gavazza, with excuses. "You see, *Signorina* Elinor, people in Lerici are always wary. There have been rumors, you know. Your father wasn't often here. He didn't keep the place up, they say. Outsiders aren't looking for property so late in the season. It isn't a good time to list the house."

"When will it be a better time?"

"In the spring is better. We get our best prices then."

Spring! Long after she would be gone. Elinor wished

she had never signed with this woman. Cosma should have told her this critical information in the beginning.

"Why are they wary?" Elinor replied. "It's a beautiful property, and most people don't believe in ghosts."

"*Si*, it is beautiful. You have a fantastic view. But the history is a slight problem."

"I thought history was a bonus around here."

Cosma replied, "Of course."

"Did someone die in this house?"

"We think so, yes. They talk of an unhappy spirit. You see, these subtleties influence people in this region. Of course, outsiders don't hear of this."

Elinor was silent for a moment, contemplating the silvered stretch of morning sea below their hillside. She decided to be direct. "You're saying people think our house is haunted?"

"The neighbors used to spread silly tales. We could come down on the price, and see if that brings more interest."

Coming down on the asking price was exactly what Elinor didn't want. Why should Cosma care if they lost money? Here she was, with a reluctant realtor who wasn't on their side, weakly negotiating for a good price. No other realtor in this small area was likely to take on the property now. And in any case, Elinor had signed an agreement, and it might be hard to get out of it. Cosma had her over a barrel.

Elinor sighed. "I'll think about it."

"It would be best to lower the price this week. With the weather changing, there are fewer buyers," Cosma said, her sharp voice bearing down on Elinor. "Let me know. *Ciao.*"

Saffron came out and joined her at the table.

Elinor said, "Want some Thanksgiving leftovers? I can make us some plates."

She needed to savor this time with her sister. Everything was going to change. She would have to lower the price, sell, and go home soon.

Saffron nodded cheerfully. "I'd love some."

Elinor went back inside. Opening the fridge, she saw chicken, pasta, and artichokes. She made plates and brought them out to Saffron.

Chewing, mouth full, Saffron said, "Everything tastes even better today."

Elinor smiled and nodded, her own mouth stuffed with pasta. This was the way the days after Thanksgiving should be, stress-free and fun. With delicious leftovers.

She told Saffron the news, good and bad. "I called my boss. He said I can have more leave. But they need me back by the end of December. So we have to lower the price and sell this place soon."

Saffron's shoulders hunched. "What did you say to him?"

Elinor picked up a drumstick. "I told him I'd be back at work by the end of December."

Saffron jumped out of her chair and came over to sit next to her. "We can't sell that fast, Ellie. Let me stay here and handle the sale."

Elinor's breath sped up, but she tried to slow it down before answering. This wasn't the moment for an argument. "Let's figure it out later."

"Can't we talk about it now?"

Saffron sat up and leaned forward to look at Elinor, who relented. "Okay. Cosma says we have to get an offer soon or we might not get one this season. We might have to wait for spring."

Saffron's eyes widened. "Sell before Christmas? But what if you don't go back then? Would they really fire you?"

"Yes, they would. And there would go my pension. And . . ." She started to say "my life" but couldn't. Sadness clogged her throat. Things were changing, and the meaningful parts of her life were balancing on a perilous edge. "Can't we talk about this another day? Let's just enjoy our leftovers."

"Time for more tiramisu!" Saffron jumped up and went into the kitchen. "Want some?"

"Sure." She loved seeing Saffron bounce again. Elinor wanted to stay too. She needed her sister now.

Saffron delivered their dessert with a big smile. Elinor tried not to show her tears welling up.

"Ellie, you're worried."

"Yes. I'm—going to make sure we have Christmas together." She reached out to Saffron and they held hands, gazing at each other.

So much had happened between them in these three months. How could she go back without Saffron, and how could she prevent her little sister from reverting to her problematic style of living?

Elinor was suddenly determined to get another week off, to stay after Christmas, until New Year's. She was so far out on a limb with her job now that another week wouldn't make a big difference. She needed time to see about that condo for Saffron.

Chapter 19

O Wind, If Winter Comes—Saffron

Saffron had promised to search for the manuscript because Ellie was busy doing things to get the house ready to sell. Saffron looked, mostly in her own room and in the living room, but after pulling out drawers and looking under and behind them, and moving furniture, she realized it wasn't going to be easy. When that surprise clause in her father's will had set them on this treasure hunt, she had been sure it wouldn't be hard. Dad never made his mysteries too hard. But this one was proving the exception.

With time ticking away, she felt the pressure to find it. This afternoon, while her sister was at the market, she tackled a new room. Had they looked for the manuscript through the kitchen? It might have been Dad's nod to Ellie's cleverness with food. Or possibly they were supposed to find a clue in Shelley's poetry. Saffron remembered the lines.

Though we eat little flesh and drink no wine,
Yet let's be merry; we'll have tea and toast.

She had pulled all the dishes out of the upper cabinets, when her sister came home with groceries.

"What are you doing?" Elinor asked, her arms full of bags.

Saffron quickly cleared a space on the counter and Ellie set them down.

"Keeping my promise. Looking for the manuscript."

"Good. Now can you suspend the operation until I put this stuff away and make some lunch?"

"Sure."

"Are you hungry?"

"No. I might go out."

"Are you keeping a list of places you searched?"

"In my own way."

"I'll leave this for you to put back when you're done."

Saffron had a great urge to give Ellie the house to herself for a while. She could see her sister was in a spreadsheet state of mind. "Can I do it when I get back?"

"Sure," Ellie said.

Thinking of Shelley, Saffron remembered another promise, this one to herself. She needed to feel this Bay of Poets embrace and let the water buoy her. Shelley's spirit had encouraged her to douse herself in the water here. Late November weather was getting unpredictable, as it often was in the Bay Area. But at home, lots of people went swimming at this time of year. She could just dip in a toe, not full immersion, but it would make her feel herself as one of Lerici's own. She decided this was the day. She went upstairs and changed, putting her bathing suit under her dress. Then she went to the café.

Michael came in. Wow. He was showing up often. Every time she came to the café he was here, and despite her brushoffs, he was always smiling.

He came over. "What are you up to?" As if he didn't even realize she was pushing him away.

"Going to put my feet in the ocean," she said. She heard herself sounding cold and wished she had first said hello.

His voice deepened and he looked away. "Sorry. Didn't mean to intrude."

She relented. "Sorry. Hi. Good to see you, Michael."

"Putting your feet in the water? Seems awfully chilly for it."

He pulled over a chair and sat. Why couldn't he take a hint? Why did she want him to back off? He wanted her and she wanted him, but if she went back to "Shelley's Castle" she'd be lost, and she was tired of being lost while trying to find herself in the arms of some guy. Hadn't she come here to leave that pattern behind?

"What are you doing today?" she asked, as if she didn't know. Stalking her.

Michael put his hand over hers on the table and said warmly, "Getting my fill of seeing you. Seriously, why would you dip even a toe in that freezing water?"

"I just have to. Okay, gotta bounce." She took back her hand and stood up.

Michael frowned. "Have fun."

Hoisting her backpack, she walked out and headed down to the promenade, both resentful and regretful.

But Michael was beginning to hover. Real men didn't hover. They slept with you and then ran. Or they suffered you to hover around them, but never too close. She didn't know what to do with Michael. Why did he like her so much? Why did any of them ever like her, enough for them but never enough for her, and when this one did, why was it bothering her?

Her head vibrating with impossible questions, Saffron

cruised past the main beach, full of tourists. She wanted to sample the water of that hidden beach Michael had shown her. That deep, dark water. She needed some darkness today.

Spotting the sign, she turned and went into the tunnel, keeping her eyes on the lighted end. The place smelled of brine and something less nice. She became aware she was alone, and if someone came in and meant her harm, no one would know.

The sound of footsteps made her hurry forward and out into the beach behind the Castle. Saffron took off her sandals and squished through the silky sand. The water was the deep blue she craved. Forested cliffs rose up steeply behind the castle, casting shadow on the beach. Clouds mounded high overhead, crossing the sun.

She'd put one foot into the surf. It looked wild, crisscrossing itself in endless froth.

Doubt knocked her knees soft, but she was only going to wade in a little. She dropped her bag and stepped into the surf. It wasn't as cold as she expected. She took off her dress and threw it back to the sand, and then she went further, until she was ankle deep. Surprisingly, not at all cold, so she went in up to her knees. The sand was soft and silty. She was now mid-thigh into Lerici's ocean.

Suddenly, her legs were knocked out from under her. She was swept out on a muscular wave. Reaching down, she couldn't touch bottom, so she began to tread water. Okay, this was the full baptism. Time to go back.

Swimming toward the beach, Saffron found herself unable to make progress. She swam and swam, but couldn't get closer.

Panic. No, this sea wouldn't beat her. She swam sideways, to find a better current, keeping the castle in sight, and then she made progress, but she was moving parallel to the shore. She needed to get back in.

A second moment of panic. She couldn't go toward the beach and she was getting tired. She kept swimming parallel to shore, trying to find a current that would let her in.

A man come out of the tunnel. He was too far away to see. At this point, anyone was welcome. Could he see her out here? She stopped swimming to tread water, gathering her strength. Her eyes level with the surface, she relaxed. The silver tips of the water and the billowing clouds. Beautiful. Was this where she would just go down and stay?

She felt him there, amid the gray, chopping waves. Was he beckoning her? She swam toward him, but she couldn't reach him, her arms and legs tiring. As she struggled, she heard the poet's line.

Death is the veil which those who live call life.

Gulping water, she pushed harder, but she was gasping and sinking and couldn't keep her mouth above the surface. Were those Shelley's long arms reaching under her, around her? The pull was strong. She was sinking. If she died in the sea, Ellie could have her body cremated on the beach, like Shelley. But if she died today, who would search for Baby Boy? And the lost manuscript might never be found.

The light disappeared. She was below the surface. Looking up through the water, she saw the air as a country she might never again reach. Should she just let it happen? But her lungs wouldn't stop desperately trying to breathe.

A sharp pull. Everything went dark.

When she came to, she was heaving quantities of water onto the sand. A man was pounding on her back. She retched up more and then nothing, though the spasms kept on.

He rolled her over and she lay on the sand, sputtering and coughing. Michael had followed her after all. For one moment, a surge of gratitude made her intensely love him. Then she rolled back onto her side and retched some more. Shaking, she rolled onto her back again and lay there breathing until the nausea subsided. Grateful, angry, happy—he made her feel a bunch of impossible things all at once.

"Thank God!" Michael said, and kissed her forehead. He grinned down at her, proud of his achievement.

She helplessly gasped. At last her breathing slowed. She turned on her side and threw up a little more sea water. At last she was still, though the light hurt her eyes. She shielded them with her arm.

"Can you stand up, do you think?"

She shook her head.

"You're shaking. But I don't have a jacket."

Saffron shook her head again. He took her hand and helped her sit up. "Thanks, I can stand now." Talking was an effort.

Her knees buckled, so she let him hoist her up and hold her.

"You shouldn't try to walk."

It was so unnecessarily romantic. She turned and threw up a last bit of water on his shoulder. He looked down at her with his too-blue eyes and ready smile, letting her head collapse onto his wet shoulder. He didn't care about her making a mess. He had her gripped in his arms. She almost wished he'd never let go.

He tried to carry her and succeeded for almost a block

before he set her down and said, "I'm sorry. Shall I call a cab?"

"I can walk. Just slowly, please."

He offered his bent arm and she put hers through it, leaning heavily and directing him to take her home.

"No, I need to get you to my car."

He did and drove a coughing Saffron uphill to the cottage.

Helping her out, he gave her his arm and they slowly made their way to the front door. Saffron felt in her pocket for a key, and he simultaneously knocked. Then he laughed, embarrassed.

Before the door opened, Michael scooped her up in his arms. When Elinor swung the door back, Michael held her out, like an offering.

To Saffron's great satisfaction, Elinor gasped.

Chapter 20

A Drowned Mermaid—Elinor

Michael Shelley stood at the door, cradling a wilted, coughing Saffron in his arms.

"What on earth!" Elinor stepped aside to let them come in. Saffron seemed unconscious until her eyelids fluttered open.

He let her down gently onto her feet. Saffron hobbled over to the sofa, leaning on her savior. She sank dramatically into the cushions, her long, wet hair spiraled over her shoulders.

Thank goodness she was alive and dripping all over. Elinor asked, "What happened?"

"I saw her floundering in the waves, so of course—anyone would—I jumped in. Luckily, having been on rowing club, I was able to bring her to shore. Dangerous to go swimming in that cove, particularly in the autumn. Waves get turbulent. She was lucky I was there."

She looked at Saffron. Her sister was shaking, wet, and weak—a drowned mermaid. Elinor sat next to her, trying not to get wet, and draped the couch shawl around her.

Even if Saffron was overly dramatic, she had clearly survived a close call.

"Silly girl," she said, her relief spiced with anger. "What were you thinking? It's going to storm out there. You could have drowned!"

She looked at Michael.

"I'm sorry I didn't get there sooner," he said, bowing his head.

Elinor shot back, "Why? Did you tell her to do it?"

"No, no! I told her not to. I should leave you in peace now."

"Don't go," Elinor said quickly relenting, getting over the shock. "You're as wet as she is. Stay for coffee—or would you prefer whisky?"

"Whisky would be nice."

He was even nicer than she had noticed at Thanksgiving. And brave to scoop her foolish sister out of the waves.

Elinor said, "Please sit down and let me get it for you."

"Whisky or even tea would be lovely, thanks."

A man who could say the word 'lovely' without blushing. Elinor remembered from dinner that he was well educated, not actually poor, though he liked to wear old, scuffed shoes and unraveling sweaters. Hard to tell about his clothing today, plastered to him as it was.

Elinor poured Michael a whisky and put on the kettle. Tea for them all would be good. She got out three mismatched mugs and tea bags. An Englishman wouldn't love tea bags, but that was too bad. No honey or sugar, only sugar substitute. She remembered the English often put milk in tea, so she poured milk into a glass, lacking a pitcher. When the kettle whistled, she poured hot water into the mugs, put the whisky and tea things on a tray, and took it all out.

He was hovering over Saffron as she reclined, a shawl pulled around her.

"Do you want tea with your whisky?" He nodded enthusiastically. She asked, "With milk?" He asked for "one lump" and she offered the sugar substitute.

Elinor handed her sister a cup of tea. "Here's something to perk you up."

Saffron smiled weakly. "I guess I'm not meant to drown," she said, and closed her eyes. "If I'm up to it, I'll drink it."

Elinor was suddenly furious. "You weren't meant to be so stupid, either! Not everything is determined by fate!" She turned to Michael. "So how did you happen to spot her?"

He was startled. "We were both in the café. I didn't exactly follow her, you know—well, just going in the same direction, in case. I saw her heading for the hidden beach, and I thought I'd go along to make sure . . ." He faltered into silence. Then he got up. "I'm in the way here. I should let Saffron recover."

He didn't go, though. Clearly, he wanted to stay.

Michael was visibly shivering. Elinor went to the closet, got out her own heavy wool shawl, and gave it to him. He accepted the purple shawl without question, draped it around his wet sweater, and smiled. "I must look ridiculous."

He did, a little. Elinor laughed. "Drink your tea! And your whisky."

Saffron sat up, sipped her tea, but seemed genuinely exhausted. She lay her head back on the sofa, eyes closed.

"So, Michael, how did you meet Saffron?"

He said with a proud smile, "I ingratiated myself by buying her a cappuccino. Caffeine brought us together."

Saffron's eyes were still closed as she said, "And then he showed me his beach and his castle."

Elinor turned back to Michael. "Let me get you something to eat. It's tea time in England, isn't it? And that means food, if I'm not mistaken."

He nodded enthusiastically, still shivering. She went into the kitchen and found some cheese and crackers, and an apple to cut up.

"You're selling this house?" Michael said as she foraged.

Without turning around, she knew Saffron was frowning. "Yes, we're trying to. Seems to be the wrong season, though."

Elinor added, "We have a local realtor but she's finding more problems than buyers."

"That's what they do around here. You get it in the shops too," he said.

"Really?"

"If you express interest in something, you have to hear the story of why you shouldn't buy it, or they can't sell it. That raises the price. In London, they practically grab the credit card out of your hand, saying 'May I run this through for you?' before you've even said you want it."

"Same in the States. Here, they want repairs first. You'd think a realtor would jump at the chance for a big fee." Elinor brought out the snacks and offered some to Michael.

He said, "Here, storytelling is a form of bargaining. And Italians are fabulous storytellers."

Still half-dozing, Saffron added, "Because they value feelings."

Elinor was pleased that Saffron felt enough better to try

to manipulate her. "Italians value displays of emotion. I'm not sure it's the same thing."

Michael was quick to sense the tension and said, "But they love emotional displays because their feelings overflow. It's a warm culture. You'll see when you've been here longer."

Saffron had successfully recruited him to her case for lingering. Elinor wondered how her sister attracted men so quickly. Michael was definitely in the throes. She hoped Saffron didn't use him up. He was too good for that.

On impulse, she said, "Michael, why don't you come back tonight for a meal? At the Italian hour, eight o'clock. That is, if you don't have any other drowning mermaids to rescue."

He was pleased, and offered to bring wine. Saffron agreed, though with less enthusiasm than Elinor would wish for.

After he left, she asked, "Are you interested in this guy?"

Saffron shrugged. "Maybe, maybe not."

Michael was undeniably handsome, a combination of rugged and sensitive. Her sister had terrible taste if she wasn't thrilled at his interest. She'd help Saffron see it. It wasn't meddling, it was facilitating.

When Michael returned that night he was completely dried off, better dressed, and yet it seemed he owned more than one ragged sweater. Michael offered a bottle of Sangiovese, a generous choice.

"Please sit down," Elinor urged as he stood in the living room looking around to see where Saffron was.

She took the wine into the kitchen and Michael offered to open it for her. He worked the corkscrew easily, popping out the cork. The lasagna was in the later stages of baking, wafting out an aroma of pasta and tomato sauce. Elinor poured wine into two glasses.

"Smells fantastic," he said, as Elinor gave him a glass and steered him to the living room. They sat together on the sofa.

"You know, my sister's always late," she said. "Right now, she's somewhat scattered. She'll be down in a minute."

"I can imagine," Michael said, "what with losing your father."

That proved to Elinor that Michael and Saffron weren't well acquainted.

"We weren't close to Dad."

"Even if you weren't close, still, he's your father. I'd miss mine very much."

So Michael loved his father. That was even more endearing. In a rush of hope, Elinor imagined Saffron and Michael as a couple—two sweet, good-looking oddballs.

Elinor went into the kitchen to get the plate of antipasti, saying, "I'm glad to know your father is alive. Your mother too, I hope."

"Yes, dear old Mum, very much alive and lively, as everyone says."

She returned with the plate, set it down, and asked, "Did you grow up in London?"

"I did. In the family estate, as we laughingly call our townhouse in Chelsea."

She wanted to ask if he planned to move out on his own after he took his degree, but she remembered how sensitive young people were about living at home.

"Saffron is sensitive," he said, as if picking up on the unspoken word. "She may not consciously miss your father, but I'm sure she does."

"My sister has been grieving our father for a long time."

Michael was startled. He set down his wine glass. "Sorry? I thought he had died recently."

"He did, but he sent Saffron to live with us after her mother died. His traveling and teaching schedule was too rigorous for raising a child."

"How terrible. To lose her mother so young, and then be separated from her father."

There was compassion in his gaze and the sympathetic shake of his head. He was a keeper.

He picked up his wine and sipped. Saffron hadn't yet come down. She wasn't exactly being enthusiastic.

"Grieving for a love you never had enough of is terrible," he said.

"For her, yes."

He nodded. "No wonder she was wading out into the sea."

"I'm so grateful you followed her, Michael. I can't think about what might have happened if you hadn't."

He gave an embarrassed laugh. "I had to make sure she was all right. Even if she didn't want me to."

Saffron came down, barefoot and wearing a big, loose green tunic over blue palazzo pants. Elinor knew from her dangling green earrings that Saffron had made an effort. When he saw her, Michael jumped up, a dazzle on his face. He wasn't merely an admirer, Elinor realized. He was in love.

Chapter 21

Two Shelleys—Saffron

Michael dropped by first thing the next morning. It had to be love, Saffron realized, and it had to be stopped. Reclining on the sofa, a bowl of cappuccino in her hands, she watched Ellie answer the door. She accepted the bunch of coral roses he'd brought and invited him in. Ellie was smiling like a teenager being asked to dance for the first time. Good, let Ellie have him.

"These are for you both, my thanks for hosting me last night."

Of course, Michael had brought the flowers for Elinor too. Clever man, to try to get to her through her sister.

Saffron swung her feet off the sofa as Michael came toward her. She gestured to indicate a space on the sofa. He sat too close, turning sideways to face her.

"Would you like some coffee?" Ellie asked him.

He turned to Ellie and nodded. "Yes, thanks."

He turned back to face Saffron. He might not be able to get to her through her sister, but he might through those blue eyes. "Oh, maybe you'd rather have tea?" Ellie asked.

Michael shook his head, smiling at her. "No, thanks. Coffee is my morning drink. Tea is for afternoon."

"We have wonderful blood orange juice, too. It's local, a guy down the road has orange trees and puts out a basket. You pick up a few and leave some cash."

Michael grinned. "Sure, I'll have both. Don't you love the locals and their gardens? A guy around the corner from me has a grove of lemon trees and makes homemade limoncello. Ruins you for the shop stuff."

Saffron replied, "Elinor is getting into local cuisine. Well, you know from Thanksgiving. But then of course, she'll go home and go back to cooking with plain old ingredients."

With a squint at her, Ellie went into the kitchen.

What to do with him? While Saffron regretted the unexpected consequences of having slept with Michael, she now remembered the soft strength of his hands gently sculpting her skin. Maybe Ellie sensed their chemistry, and had decided to match-make. Ellie had a long habit of deciding what, and who, was best for Saffron.

From the kitchen, Ellie asked, "Would you like to come back for dinner tonight?"

"You're too kind. Yes!" Michael said, grinning at Saffron, as if the invitation came from her.

Yes, he was pleasing to look at. And the flowers, and the compliments. That charming English accent. The manners to go with. He was just fire, and fire wasn't what Saffron wanted right now. Besides, he was going home too, to England, so what was the point of his hanging around with her? Saffron was clear on the lack of their future together. And if they flung the fling she felt like continuing, then what? What if he didn't go, or what if Ellie succeeded in selling this place, and she had to leave? Any way she could see it, the future didn't bring them together.

If she could have hooked up that one time and then ghosted him, it would have been different.

That night, Michael brought a homemade risotto with roasted shrimp.

Saffron didn't see the need of his cooking, and said so. "Why put together your own ingredients when there's such fabulous takeout from the market?"

"Saffron!" Ellie protested. "Don't be rude."

But Michael was definitely trying too hard.

Ellie was so pleased that Saffron wondered if she was interested in Michael—and maybe she was, despite their age difference. Her sister, once interested in something, was unstoppable.

"Oh, I didn't mean anything. That was cool of you to make it," Saffron said as she started to bring a tray of water glasses to the table.

He deposited the risotto on the kitchen counter. "Let me help you," he said to Saffron as she came through with the tray. He bumped her shoulder gently, not hard enough to ripple the water in glass. His gaze was longing. So annoying.

"Excuse me!" she said and went past him.

During dinner, Ellie invited him to come to dinner again tomorrow. Time to have it out with her sister. This was outrageous. Unless Ellie was interested in Michael herself, she was being more manipulative than Saffron ever remembered.

"What's your favorite Italian dessert, Michael?" Ellie asked as they sat down to dinner, passing around Michael's risotto and a big salad.

Missing Saffron's laser glare at Ellie, he replied,

"Tiramisu. It's like having a hundred favorite desserts because no one makes it the same way as anyone else. I make one with extra chocolate. Should I whip that up for tomorrow?"

"That would be fantastic!" Ellie was so leading him on. Saffron was disgusted.

Michael stayed late, so Saffron would have it out with Ellie in the morning. She did, as they sat for breakfast at the patio table.

"What are you doing with Michael? You're going to get his feelings hurt!" Saffron said.

Ellie angrily launched her reply. "You're the one being unkind to this terrific guy. You haven't even expressed your gratitude for his saving you. You owed him at the very least a dinner, but you act like he's a pain. Why?"

Elinor put down her mug firmly, with emphasis.

Saffron's voice rose. "Oh jeez! How much gratitude do I need for one little rescue? You invited him to dinner—twice!"

Ellie was disgusted with her, and Saffron felt a little ashamed, but her sister just didn't understand. She was acting this way to spare Michael's feelings, not hurt them further.

But her sister wasn't done. "You could have drowned, Saffron. What were you thinking, swimming alone, and with so much wind?"

"I was following my instincts. You wouldn't understand."

She couldn't say she was following Shelley. Ellie would think she had some suicidal urge, when in fact it was an affirmation of the life—a vivid, memorable life like Shelley's. A life of being who you are.

"Did you sleep with him?"

Without waiting for an answer, Elinor got up and went into the kitchen for more toast. So she was making a statement, another judgy proclamation from her mom-sister.

Saffron raised her voice. "Michael took me to see what he calls his 'castle'. We did what we felt like. End of story."

When Elinor came back, she kept the toast next to her. She picked up a piece and bit into it, then shoved the plate toward Saffron.

They chewed in silence.

"So he's coming tonight," Saffron said. "But after this, stop."

Ellie's voice softened and she looked at Saffron. "Why don't you like him?" She really was curious.

"I do like him."

"So why are you avoiding him?"

"Because. It's complicated. It's for his own good."

Saffron could see her sister was even more puzzled now. "What does that even mean?" Ellie asked. "Are you trying to spare him the heartbreak of your dumping him? So in order to accomplish that, you're dumping him?"

"You don't get it at all. We hardly know each other, and I do like him. But . . . I don't know. He makes me feel . . . crowded."

Saffron realized it wasn't a real answer, and Ellie wanted one. She wanted an answer too, but it truly was complicated.

Ellie turned away abruptly and went into the kitchen. Saffron gave a deep sigh. She was always disappointing her sister. That wasn't what she wanted, but Ellie was always telling her how to run her love life. How little her sister understood relationships.

Michael showed up for dinner five minutes early,

bearing the tiramisu, which did look fantastic, dark chocolate pieces and melted streaks on top.

"Elinor, tell me about yourself," he said cheerfully as they sat down.

Ellie's reply was, "There's not much to tell."

Saffron thought that was silly. She wasn't going to let her sister get away with it, so she elaborated. "Ellie wrote a whole book of poetry that she won't show to anyone. Maybe she even threw it away."

Saffron was delighted to see Ellie's irritated frown.

"Wow," he said, head turning from one sister to the other. "Is it true you're a poet?"

"That's a gross exaggeration," Ellie said, spooning penne pasta onto their plates and passing them. "My sister loves to overstate. I once wrote some poems. I put them together. They're in a box somewhere."

Michael persisted. "Did you publish some?"

He thought he'd flattered Ellie. What a miscalculation.

"Maybe a few in some long-dead literary journal. Would you like more pasta?" She passed the bowl, and having already finished the dainty portion, he took it and spooned out a much better portion for someone over six feet tall.

Ellie smiled, pleased that he liked the food. "Tell us about your family."

"My father collects rare plants. We have an immense garden at home. Immense for a London row house, that is."

Ellie gushed. "What an interesting hobby. I assume it's a hobby. Is that his work?"

"No, he's in trade. Sorry, in American that means he's in business. Dad has a company called Shell Game. It creates Internet platforms for virtual conferences. Harold—that's my father—wants me to join him, but he's not pressuring. Hence the sabbatical. So I can decide my fate."

"Not a bad fate, either way," Ellie said. She turned to Saffron with pointed smile.

Was her sister thinking that Saffron should be part of that and marry Michael? Or maybe Ellie was imagining herself as part of the Shelley family.

"And what does your mother do?" Ellie asked.

"Vivian is a barrister. Sorry, lawyer. I'll get the hang of translating into American, I promise! She handles divorces, family law, things like that. And she also teaches law."

He stopped talking and consumed his second helping. After it was gone, he asked, "Elinor, what do you like to do here?"

Ellie smiled at being asked. A minute ago Saffron had wished him gone, but now jealousy bells rang in her head.

"Mostly just getting this house ready to sell," Ellie said. "At home, I hike in the hills."

Saffron helped herself to more pasta and said, "Obviously nature is my love, too. Or I wouldn't have gone swimming."

Michael cracked up and gave her a look of gratitude. Was he glad she'd nearly drowned? Maybe he was, because otherwise he wouldn't be sitting here with them, ingratiating himself to Ellie and making it clear he intended to stick around Saffron.

If he thought he had won, he could think again. Because.

He reached for a piece of bread, but then thought better of it and offered the breadbasket to Ellie and to Saffron. When both declined, he tore off a large hunk and poured more olive oil onto his plate, dipping the bread and biting off a chunk.

While chewing, he winked at Saffron.

"Ellie's divorced," Saffron said. "Messy divorce, though. I'm sure your mother could have helped her."

Ellie gave her a furious stare. "Saffron likes to share intimate details of everyone's life, including her own. My divorce wasn't dramatic or messy. Just sad."

Michael shook his head. "I'm sorry," he said with feeling. He turned back to Saffron. "I'm sure you were a great help to your sister during all that."

"I did what I could," Saffron said, knowing she had hardly been any help. "Now you know all our secrets."

He smiled. "I don't know much about yours, Saffron. Do you plan on staying in Italy for long, after you sell this place?"

Saffron shook her head and then changed her mind and nodded. "Maybe."

Michael took his time with another helping, as they politely picked at theirs and waited for him to finish.

Finally he did. "This is another delicious dinner you've given me. I wish I had more family secrets to offer up. Something more to bring than tiramisu. Next time I'll bring some of that delicious local fish stew. You can get it at the fish market by the harbor."

Next time. Saffron restrained an urge to eye-roll. She got up and took the plates into the kitchen.

"I'll make coffee." She turned back to the table and Michael. "Or is it tea for you?"

"Whatever you're making."

Ellie asked him more about his father's interest in botany. As she rinsed the plates, Saffron listened to them talk about plants. She could imagine that he was getting interested in Ellie. Elinor needed someone to shake her up. A younger man would be perfect.

For a reason she didn't want to investigate, a surge of

fury heated her. A good thing she was still in the kitchen, her back turned to them. Her sister was once again invading her territory, ready to take away something that belonged to Saffron. Did Michael belong to her? Of course he did!

The tiramisu was delicious, and Saffron calmed down, but then Ellie welcomed Michael to drop by anytime—what was she thinking, after what Saffron had told her? Ellie looked over at her with a 'gotcha' smile. Saffron was going to have to do a lot of gentle snubbing, if Michael was going to be around all the time. She'd have to spend more time in town and at La Scala. Now she was determined to push Michael away, if only to annoy Ellie. Or would Ellie pick up the pieces of his broken heart? Michael seemed too ready to fall in love. Maybe it didn't matter with whom.

The next morning, Saffron went out early. The whole town was hardly open. She walked up the promenade, enjoying the emptiness of the beach and the way the shops were just opening their doors, shopkeepers setting out displays and signs. A young boy on a bicycle zipped past her, the breeze ruffling her long skirt.

"*Ciao!*" he shouted back.

"*Ciao!*" she called after him, delighted.

She turned back toward the center of the port, intending to go to the café. A shopkeeper came out of his door with a sign board and waved her a salute. The day felt so promising. She wondered briefly if Shelley and his poet friends had often walked up and down the beach promenade in the morning, as she was doing.

At La Scala, the barista was still warming up the machines. Except for an older man seated at a corner table, the place was empty. She got her coffee and sat by the window, opening her laptop. As she did, an email popped up.

Ciao, bella Saffron! Are you and your sister ready now to list your beautiful home for rent?

Gino the unreliable, Gino the charmer, Gino the crook. After Ellie had called him, he'd said he would refund the money to the Americans. Did he ever do it? And how would she and Elinor ever know for sure?

The email put her in an awkward position. She decided to play along.

Ciao, Gino. We might still like to list our house, but not yet. Did you refund the Americans' money?

Nothing came immediately back. After fifteen minutes, another email arrived.

Lovely Saffron, I only put up a partial description and the Americans said they wanted to go and see, as they would be in the area. I took a small deposit from them and told them to knock on your door and inquire. They misunderstood and thought they were moving in. Didn't you get my email? But your sister and I have worked it out.

Saffron wasn't buying any of this, but she wanted to see what he'd say, so she emailed back.

I need to take some better photos and talk to my sister.

He was quick to answer.

Does the house need repairs? We have people in the area. I can send them to give you estimates.

Yes, send me their names and contact info.

After only a few minutes, Gino replied, giving her names of three contractors. She looked them up, but everything was in Italian. She browsed through Gino's website.

How would you like the heading of your listing to read?

Clever man, to get her thinking about their listing, when she hadn't agreed. But it was irresistible to imagine the listing.

She shot back: *How about Vacation in Lovely Lerici?*

Saffron knew enough about advertising from the pizza shop to know that was a good tag line.

She got a quick reply. *Romantic Vacation in Lovely Lerici!! Brava, cara Saffron.*

Cara. Didn't that mean "Dear" or something? She smiled at her screen, and then checked on a translation for *Cara.* "Dear, darling, beloved, charming." Wow. But she had to find out what Ellie had talked to the lawyer about, and if he confirmed that everything had been worked out. In the meantime, she was keeping Gino on the hook.

She emailed Gino again.

How much do you think we can get for a month's rental?

The reply came back fast. *Maybe five thousand euros a month, in the summer.*

When Saffron went home, she told Ellie about the email. "He said it was his mistake, and it was due to his poor English. He thought I told him to go ahead. And then he asked me what I wanted for a tag line to list the house."

Elinor was quiet for a few moments. "He promised he'll refund their money. He understood, I'm sure, that this was the end of it. But now he's trying to get us to advertise?"

"Maybe I shouldn't have emailed with him. I thought I should find out what was going on. You never told me. I'm so sorry!"

Saffron couldn't stop a few tears falling. She had messed everything up, again.

Ellie touched her hand. "Some Italians don't speak as much English as they think they do. Just don't let him put the house on his website!"

Saffron felt both grateful and sad. Her sister forgave

her, but then Ellie's impression only deepened that Saffron was hopeless at being a responsible adult.

That night she again read about Shelley's life, taking comfort in his sense of natural freedom and social injustice. He'd been so opposed to his patriarchal society that he'd given up his fortune and lived his definition of freedom on the Continent. *Because, freedom.* Pushing the book aside, she switched off the lamp and fell asleep.

Her eyes fluttered open. He was hovering, misty and morose, his loosely tied silk cravat tumbling over a billowing white shirt. His large eyes gazed steadily at her.

"Hello," she murmured, trying not to flinch.

He was so close. And visible.

Sorry to wake you.

His voice was for the first time strong, higher in register than before, with the same upper-class accent Michael had. Of course, they were both Shelleys.

She smiled sleepily. Maybe he was just a dream.

But a dream was sitting in the chair across from the foot of her bed.

We need to talk.

He pulled his cravat loose and leaned forward, hands on his knees.

"Did I do something wrong?" she asked, trying to remember.

You have an intuitive way. Your heart is wise.

"No one ever called me wise!"

You need to understand yourself. You belong here in my house, with me.

That made her shiver, but she had to ask. "Is this really your house? Did you live here?"

Yes. But you must stop arguing about the house with your sister. Stop being a child.

"Why are you here?"

He asked me to stay and watch over his girls. One of you may cross over soon.

A freezing chill swept through her. She was going to die?

"What's it like there?" she asked.

You're not ready to be here. Nor is she.

"You mean Ellie?"

Shelley tilted his head, looking sad. Then his head kept tilting and rolled up in a swirl and disappeared.

She couldn't go back to sleep now. Was one of them going to die? Could Dad have appointed him the family spirit? Why would their absent, neglectful father care?

Until she had nearly drowned, she'd never pictured herself actually dying. She couldn't die yet. She wasn't even thirty.

Chapter 22

Olio d'Oliva—Saffron

Walking to town with her sister the next morning, Ellie told Saffron that her boss had approved her to stay here through the end of the year.

A surge of happy surprise excited Saffron, and then Ellie followed it with, "I love our being here together."

Saffron stopped. She turned and hugged her sister long and hard. Lerici and their magical home here was changing her sister's heart. "Let's go buy something fun," she said. "Something very Italian."

Elinor laughed. "Sounds great."

They browsed shops along the promenade, looking for the right place to buy fun things.

"Let's go in there," Elinor said, pointing to a sign '*Olio d'Oliva Superbo*'. Superb Olive Oil.

"Do we need superb oil?" Saffron asked.

"I do, for cooking. I want to make an authentic *Inslata Caprese*, and the best oil is essential, Tonio says."

The shop was tiny, hardly three steps deep and ten steps wide. The proprietor was behind the counter making notes in a ledger. He was thin, balding, and elderly with straight posture obviously meant to correct the impression that he was tiny in stature.

"Welcome," he said in English. "Americans?"

Elinor looked down at her feet and nodded, mystifying Saffron, who replied, "How did you know?"

"Shoes," he said, shrugged, and went back to his ledger.

"Do you have any special olive oil?" Elinor asked.

"Why?" he said, looking up sharply.

"Why? Why not? Isn't this a shop that sells superb oil?" He shrugged.

This strange attitude challenged her. "Please show me your best olive oil."

"It's all the best," he said, waving an arm around vaguely. "Choose one that suits your price."

Saffron could see that Ellie was annoyed. And that would make her determined. This shopkeeper had no idea who he was messing with. Elinor had to be in control, especially where her purchases and money were concerned.

Ellie came to the end of the left side of the counter and looked at a tiny bottle with no price tag. The oil inside was a dark yellowish-green. To Saffron it looked like the leftover from the good pressing, though why the man would display his leftovers she had no idea.

"There's no price marked on this one," Ellie said with a smile.

"Not for sale."

Ellie's smile deepened and hardened. Saffron knew that smile. It didn't bode well. "If it's not for sale, why are you displaying it?"

He shook his head. "It's for locals, *signorina*. You would not enjoy this oil."

Saffron could see the insult land. Her sister's posture straightened.

"You save the good stuff to sell to tourists, is that it?" Ellie inquired gently.

He looked canny. "Or something like that."

Ellie and Saffron stared at each other, and then Ellie said, "Or you don't want to sell your premium oil to tourists. But you know, we aren't tourists. We own Casa Magni and we've been staying here."

"Oh?" he said.

"Or maybe you don't care for Americans." Ellie's voice was syrupy sweet, and Saffron knew what that meant.

"No, *signorina*, I love Americans. I lived in your Philadelphia for a year. But this oil is not for you."

She was almost purring. "What would I have to do to get you to sell it to me?"

He gestured with both arms now, indicating the whole shop. "We have many beautiful olive oils, oils superbly crafted, ones whose taste will make all your pasta and focaccia sing in the mouth. Why do you want that one? It's not a good one for you."

Elinor was digging in her heels, Saffron could see. Too bad the shopkeeper didn't know her sister. He would have given up right now.

"I'll pay whatever you want," Elinor insisted. "But I want this bottle."

He shook his head. "I cannot sell it. It's promised to someone."

"What do you mean, promised? I'm here and I have cash. What good is a promise compared to cash? I'll pay more than they promised."

"*Signorina*, this is not how we do things in Lerici. This oil is for residents only."

Elinor's cheeks had grown pink. Saffron was a little afraid for the proprietor.

"I own a house here. That makes me a resident. Tell me how much."

Saffron thought it was time to intervene. "Ellie, maybe we should go have some breakfast," she said, putting a hand on Ellie's elbow.

Ellie shook it off, picked up the little bottle, and went to stand in front of the proprietor.

"How much do you want?"

He folded his arms and refused to speak.

"You know, I could put this in my purse and walk out. But I'm offering to pay."

He considered his options. "You may be a resident in legal terms, but you are no resident until you have been here for a year."

Ellie went back over to where she had picked up the bottle and replaced it.

"I will take that one," she said, pointing to a larger bottle with a price tag that stood on the counter near the register. "How much?"

"Ten euros," he said.

Saffron was relieved. No glass was broken, no faces were slapped. Ellie was backing down.

She pulled out her wallet, counted, and handed over the bills. He took them and she picked up the bottle.

"Let's go," she said, taking Saffron by the elbow and hurrying her out.

When they were outside and again in the sunshine, Elinor stopped being angry and laughed. "That's one for the books. Italians!"

Saffron was relieved it had ended without something

being broken. Not even genuine Lerici olive oil would be worth that.

Ellie vented. "What an insufferable Italian ass! Wouldn't sell me his damn oil. Who cares? How good can olive oil be?"

Saffron wisely didn't answer that one.

Chapter 23

San Terenzo's Shelley House—Elinor

Elinor tucked her bottle of olive oil into her bag. She had felt challenged, and she didn't react well to being challenged or insulted. The silly man probably thought all Americans were crass tourists.

"Michael!" Elinor nearly ran into him as they swung around the corner onto the promenade.

"How lovely to see you!" He made a slight bow.

He was so adorable. Why couldn't Saffron see it? "We're out for a walk and coffee. Please come along, if you'd like."

Saffron flashed her a dark look as Michael fell in step next to her. He took her hand and Saffron let him. She was smiling. A wise fellow, to push his accidental advantage.

"It's a glorious morning, isn't it?" he asked as they walked. "This is the start of fall weather, I'm told."

Elinor nodded. "Like Berkeley, the subtle change. Cooler but not many falling leaves."

"Are you looking for coffee? Most places don't open

early with the summer visitors gone. I know a good place in San Terenzo. Have you been over there?"

"No, we haven't."

"It's a hike, but I have a car. I'd be happy to take you. San Terenzo is fantastic."

Why had her sister pulled away from this young man? Aside from his failure to conceal his feelings, and the fact that he often wore the same sweater, he seemed perfect.

"Michael, that's kind of you," she said and looked to Saffron, who was smiling at Michael.

Elinor said, "We'd love to."

"Great!"

They sat on a bench as he sprinted away to get his car. The beach was nearly empty and the waves thundered onto the sand with white lace.

"You're okay with this?" she asked.

Saffron, looking out at the ocean, smiled. "I'm absolutely okay."

A glow of happiness kindled in Elinor. It grew when Michael pulled up in his small, dented Fiat and parked in front of the sign that read, "No parking any time."

Getting out, he opened both passenger doors. Elinor dove for the rear and Saffron sat in front. He beamed as he unlocked the parking brake and turned onto the road.

"We can drive through here. In summer, you have to have a special pass. Autumn is the best time on this coast."

"Like in Northern California," Saffron said.

The road to San Terenzo climbed. Elinor could see why he hadn't advised walking. It wasn't far, but it was steep. Michael parked at the top of a hill and they got out.

They walked around the small central square, Michael giving them local history. "San Terenzo has ancient origins. There's also a castle, like Lerici's." He pointed to a neighboring hill.

"Let's see it," Saffron said, "to see if it's better than ours."

"Yes," Michael promised. "And the Shelley House isn't far. Shall we go?"

The minute he said it, Saffron's face changed, but Michael didn't notice. He had no idea he'd stepped in an emotional sinkhole.

"It's only a rumor," Saffron said airily. "Lots of houses are probably called the Shelley House. It could actually be in Lerici. I've talked to people."

Elinor was glad she didn't say she had talked to invisible people. She didn't want Michael to think her sister too odd.

"True, there's doubt about which one," he agreed.

Michael led them downhill to the beach promenade. It was a short walk to a white house with a sign that said "Villa Magni." Its arched entrance to the park-like grounds.

"Villa Magni—that's funny!" Saffron said. "Our house is Casa Magni."

Elinor's breath caught when she saw another sign: "Percy Bysshe Shelley's Villa," along with a white plaque bearing a Shelley quote:

I still inhabit this divine bay, reading dramas and sailing and listening to the most enchanting music. – Shelley, 1822

"Touristy advertising," Saffron scoffed. "The whole area must be dotted with 'Shelley slept here' signs. Rumors and advertising."

Michael smiled and seemed not to understand. They

went up to the entrance, and he read aloud from the poster. "Shelley left San Terenzo aboard his boat, the *Don Juan*."

With his back to Saffron, he couldn't see her wide-eyed shock. He continued. "A sudden storm arose and the boat capsized. All aboard were lost. People say that the spirit of this romantic English poet still lives on between the inlets and the rocky points of Marinella, which had bewitched the English poet."

Saffron's voice rose into a sharp soprano. "It's not true! He sailed from Lerici, not San Terenzo! Just because you put something on a wall doesn't make it true."

Elinor heard panic in her voice and she began to feel some herself.

Michael was baffled. He plucked a leaflet from a box next to the plaque, opened it, and said, "It says here that San Terenzo was at once a small village and an independent township during the Napoleonic times. It began to be noticed because of the Romantic poets Shelley and Byron. Shelley lived in Villa Magni, the white house facing the sea; his wife Mary Shelley, author of the famous novel *Frankenstein* also lived here."

Saffron was nearly shouting. "That's completely wrong! I know, because Shelley came to visit me and said he'd lived in our house."

Elinor rushed to explain. "Saffron has these deep experiences . . ."

Turning on Elinor, Saffron lowered her voice, but still angrily said, "Don't explain away my Invisibles!"

Michael tilted his head and looked at them. "We don't have to go in."

"Let's don't. We can walk around the park," Elinor suggested.

Saffron walked away and they followed into the small, grassy park screened from the street by tall hedges.

As they walked together, Michael told Elinor, "I've blown it."

She hoped he was wrong. "No, you haven't. Just let her blow off steam."

"I forgot she believes your house is the real Shelley house. How could I do that? And it might be. Italians have all sorts of rumors about history."

She blurted out, "Saffron needs someone like you."

He looked pleased, but then he shook his head. "No, I've messed it up. I've dissed her ghost."

"She likes you. I know it. And I'm getting her a condo in Lerici, so she can stay." She hesitated, then fudged. "She told me she likes you."

He was eager to believe. Cheerful again—the man had a talent for happiness—he pointed out the camellias and shrubs. "Oh look! A rare species of hydrangea."

He went ahead to admire it. While he was examining the plant, Saffron circled back.

"Why do you do this, Ellie?"

Elinor lowered her voice. "He said he forgot our house was the real Shelley one."

Michael came back to them, all enthusiasm. "There's a Yulan magnolia over there. It's one of the oldest flowering trees on earth."

Saffron turned and walked away.

He said, "Has she always seen people on the other side?"

"Since she first moved in with us."

"You know, in England, we're used to hauntings."

"I don't suppose, *being* a Shelley, you've ever seen . . ."

He smiled. What could be more perfect than for Saffron

to actually marry a Shelley descendant, one who didn't disbelieve her Invisibles?

Finally he said, "I don't see them, but the whole family believes our house boasts a few spirits."

So he wasn't disturbed by Saffron's Invisibles.

"Michael, you know so much about plants. Did you study horticulture?"

He smiled. "No. I took my degree in English Literature. I would love to study it, but soon I'll have to turn to serious pursuits. My father gave me a year to decide."

They started walking, following Saffron, who was leaving the park and heading back to the house.

"When you say whole family, does that mean you have brothers or sisters?"

"No, I'm an only child. But the three of us seem like a big family."

He smiled down at her as they strolled. She was beginning to imagine a wedding. He might be a loafer now, but he had a future and a family. Probably an inheritance.

"And how long have you been here?"

"Six months. It's probably getting time to go back to university and then into teaching. I'm no businessman."

"Saffron's also trying to decide her future. She's always been original, and that makes it harder to choose a path."

Michael saw Saffron at the entrance. "Maybe she wants to go in after all."

He sprinted ahead. As they caught up, Saffron said, "It's not the real Shelley house, but I want to see it."

They went through the house quickly. Elinor was glad to see Saffron walking next to Michael, having overcome her upset and paying attention to the only Shelley that mattered. When they reached the car, Michael invited them both to drop in for tea at his 'castle'.

"I'm too tired," Elinor said, hoping her sister would go alone.

"I'll take a rain check," Saffron replied, her voice soft. "Maybe tomorrow?"

She looked at Michael, and he eagerly nodded.

In Saffron's smile, Elinor saw pleasure, and it ignited her own. Perhaps her sister would find her way with Michael.

CHAPTER 24

Shelley's Castle Again—Saffron

The next day, Saffron texted Michael and asked to take him up on that rain check. He picked her up in the afternoon and drove her to his place. She liked zipping down Lerici's narrow streets in his small, rattling car, back windows rolled down, the wind streaming through her hair.

A sure driver, he made quick time. He parked in the alley, came around to open her door and led the way up the staircase. As they climbed, he said, "You know, history is mostly nonsense. You're so right about that."

She appreciated his respect for her ideas. He understood her feelings about Shelley. After all, he was a Shelley.

The stairway's blue walls were filled with tattered film posters. At the turn of the landing, Michael looked back. He reached for her hand. She had missed his touch. A flush of warmth speeded her pulse, and desire streaked through her as she remembered the way their bodies had fit together.

Inside, Michael offered her a chair at the tiny table. His studio was so small that to fill his teakettle, he had to take only one large stride to the sink. He turned on the flame under the kettle and pulled out two teacups with saucers. So English he didn't even ask if she wanted coffee instead. Maybe it was the late afternoon hour.

If only she could have both Michael and freedom. Because. He was too good for her, somehow. She never had good boyfriends.

Michael went to a drawer and pulled out a small blue box. The kettle started whistling. He pulled it off the fire and put the box on the table, looking at her with a question in his eyes. Was he giving her something? But he didn't offer it.

She looked into his eyes. He was so easy to read, and now she read hope, doubt, and affection. Ignoring the tea water, he sat at the table and offered her the box.

It had no wrapping or ribbon. She opened its lid .

"Just something," he mumbled.

Inside the box was another box, this one brown. She opened that one. On a wad of tissue lay a silver charm in the form of a tiny mermaid.

"For me?" She felt a rush of excitement.

"To put on a necklace or a bracelet." He was embarrassed and happy, which made his eyes sparkle.

"I've never seen you wear a charm bracelet, but maybe you could just keep it. As a memento of when I fished you out of the sea."

Of course. "Thank you, Michael."

Saffron leaned over to him. Putting her hand on the back of his neck, she kissed him. It was as intoxicating as she remembered, sending thrills through her. His lips were soft and pressed back urgently.

"Come on," he said, rising and taking her by the waist, the idea of tea forgotten.

Expecting him to pull her toward the bed, she rose, keeping his fingers tight on hers. He pulled her toward the door.

"Let's go out. I want to show you something."

Surprised, she grabbed her purse and followed him down to his car.

Pulling away down the alley toward the setting sun, he said, "I'm going to show you an unforgettable Ligurian sunset."

He drove north, the road winding into the hills. The dark sea appeared far below. He pulled over and they got out. Arm around her, they walked to the edge, of their lookout point. Cove after cove dipped in and out up the coastline. The sea was dark blue, embellished with restless black scallops while the clouds blazed red gold against the deep teal sky.

"Are you warm enough?" Michael asked.

She nodded.

He whispered, "I don't want to ask for a commitment now, but I can't let you go."

She looked up at him. Sunset warmed his face and made him glow like a young god. He smiled. Their gazes held. Her freedom slipped a little away. Saffron didn't mind.

His arms went around her so gently, hers going around him. Their kiss was almost ethereal, lips gently touching. For an instant, they might be one person, warm and light as that last apricot-colored cloud, flesh glowing softly. Saffron felt something change inside her, like the flash of a first evening star, a key turned in a forgotten lock.

Chapter 25

Castello Brown—Elinor

When Elinor came downstairs the next morning, Saffron was up and dressed.

"Are you going out?" Ellie asked.

"No. I thought Michael might come early, but he hasn't."

"It's only eight-thirty," Elinor pointed out.

She saw Saffron's disappointment and wondered what had happened last evening. Whatever was going on, this was a new Saffron, impatiently waiting for Michael instead of trying to escape him. She was glad to see it, and then she thought of Tonio, and wondered if he'd ever drop in without calling. But that wasn't his style.

Saffron was restlessly changing positions on the couch while Elinor made coffee.

It was another balmy day, maybe even warmer than yesterday. An autumn heat wave would help the house show well. And she could have more breakfasts on the patio. With the cleaning and accessorizing done, the house was now charming and comfortable. She understood why her father had made this a home. She almost didn't hear the knock on the door until Saffron leaped up and opened it. Tonio stood there, wearing a summer suit and a Panama hat, and carrying a picnic basket.

"*Ciao*, Saffron. *Ciao*, Elinor!"

Enthusiasm carried him into the room.

"Hi," Saffron said, stepping back and then closing the door as he came in.

Elinor stood up and wrapped her robe tighter. "It's good to see you!"

"I'm taking you both to Portofino today. For a picnic! And a special tour. It's all organized—if you want to go."

Elinor said, "I'd love to! I need to change."

Saffron offered. "I'll make Tonio some coffee while you get dressed."

Tonio said, "I give you twenty minutes. Because you're American, and Americans do everything quickly." He laughed, took off his hat, and sat on the couch.

"What a nice idea! You're very generous," Elinor said.

Tonio looked pleased, that handsome smile briefly flashing. "Would you like some coffee while you wait?" Saffron asked.

He declined, and Elinor ran upstairs to change, hearing Saffron tell him that she was going to change, too.

As she came back down, she saw her sister sitting next to Tonio, wearing a gathered skirt, a tee shirt, and sandals, holding her large-brimmed hat. Saffron's outfit made her feel prim in her black slacks and black-and-white striped top, but she wasn't the type for peasant skirts.

"We'll have a special tour of Castello Brown in Portofino!" Tonio said, standing up. "With my friend Enzo, the museum director. And then we can picnic in this fine weather."

"Castello Brown, is that the villa high on the hill?" Saffron asked. "Where they filmed the movie *Enchanted April*? I love that film!"

He nodded. "The very place."

"Is it haunted?" Saffron asked.

Elinor gave her a look.

"Haunted?" Tonio said. "Ghost stories are only legends. Part of the history of a place."

He was at ease now, more relaxed with them—with her. Her heart sped up a little. What could come from getting interested in someone she'd be leaving? She couldn't lead him on. But it would be wonderful to spend a day with him.

They drove to Santa Margherita in Tonio's classic Alfa Romeo, arriving at a town even smaller than Lerici, full of colorful buildings tumbling down a hillside to a harbor. Then they took a boat ride, curving along dramatic cliffs, past dots of civilization clinging to tiny beaches and harbors. They arrived at the tiny cove of Portofino, the most elegant place on the Ligurian coast.

They docked at the horseshoe harbor and got off on the promenade. Tonio led them to look around the "fishing village," as Portofino described itself. It had once been a fishing village, but now its permanent denizens were shops like Gucci and Prada, and yachts were moored in the small harbor. Even the trees and shrubs wore expensive-looking manicures.

As they climbed the steep hill to the castle, Tonio took Elinor's elbow. She looked up into his tanned face, worn with lines of smiling and kindness. To think that he had arranged all this as thanks for their simply giving him Thanksgiving dinner.

Saffron sprang ahead enthusiastically in her flimsy

sandals. She stopped and turned back, long hair fluttering in the breeze. "This is perfect!"

Elinor was proud of her sister's beauty and warm nature, even as she was always on edge about Saffron's impulsiveness.

The path curved and rose more steeply. Tonio helped her, holding her hand as she navigated a tight turn. Though she had shaken his hand in the supermarket, this felt different. Gentlemanly, and maybe more. His hand lingered on hers as she smiled up at him and went on. He helped Saffron, too, over the steep part.

The sea spread out far below as they climbed and reached the hilltop grounds of Castello Brown.

"It began as a Roman outpost," Tonio explained as they walked toward the castle with its round tower and ancient battlements.

At the entrance stood a thin, dark-haired man in a charcoal gray suit. He opened the massive front door. "Hello!" he called out.

"*Ciao*, Enzo, my friend! May I present Elinor and Saffron, my American friends who have inherited a home in Lerici."

Enzo greeted them, extending his hand, and then shaking Tonio's. "Welcome to Castello Brown! I'm Enzo Deste. You've picked a fine day for touring, and I'm glad to be your guide. We have few visitors at this time of year so it's an exceptional pleasure to host a private tour."

The man was understated but elegantly dressed and impressively fluent in English, with hardly a trace of Italian accent.

"This castle must be enchanted," Saffron said, surprising them. "I smell spirits in the air."

Elinor hoped Saffron wouldn't keep talking like that

around Tonio and his friend, but Enzo just nodded and smiled.

He narrated in a cultured voice, easy with English. "This headland has always been a strategic location on the coast. The castle in which you stand was built probably around the tenth century, and remained under the rule of the Visconti of Milan until 1425, when Tommaso di Fregoso occupied Portofino."

Enzo toured them through the museum and then led them into a salon with a large wooden table and tall, leather-upholstered chairs. His assistant came and set down plates of antipasti and glasses of sparkling water.

"How did the castle become a museum?" Saffron asked.

Enzo gestured down the length of the table. "As you can see, it was a residence before becoming a museum. In the late eighteen-hundreds, a British Consul, Montague Yeats Brown, had admired it from the sea. After the Vienna Congress in 1867, when Portofino became part of the new Kingdom of Italy, the castle lost its strategic importance and was disarmed. Brown was able to buy it for his residence for only seven thousand lire. In 1961, the castle became part of the Municipality of Portofino."

"So this was where they filmed *Enchanted April*?" Saffron asked.

"Yes. The filmmakers wanted an Italian location, one overlooking the sea and a picturesque town. We charged reasonable fees, considering that they tied up the property for three months."

"They couldn't have chosen a more beautiful spot," Elinor said.

"It's enchanting! Love and happiness are swirling around here," Saffron added.

After visiting with Enzo, they went outside to picnic on

the lawn. Tonio had brought a lavish lunch. It was hard to say what went to her head faster, the wine, the sunshine, or Tonio's smiles.

Going down, the path seemed steeper. Ahead, Saffron was wobbling in her shoes. She felt a flare of anger at her sister, who always put herself at risk, as though accidents were just badges of adventuring honor. Just as Elinor had the thought, Saffron's ankle buckled and her sister went down, almost falling off the path.

Almost in slow motion, she saw Tonio grab Saffron's arm in a strong grip, keeping her from tumbling downhill. He held onto her, despite the momentum carrying them both off-balance. Even in his fancy Italian shoes, Tonio held firm until Saffron sat down on the path.

"Ow!" she wailed, hands on her ankle.

Elinor rushed forward, with half an urge to slap Saffron. She was ruining a great day with her stupid shoes. Instead, she let Tonio support Saffron the rest of the way down to the car. A pang of envy rooted in her heart when her sister leaned on him, smiling and talking, his arm encircling her.

Tonio drove them home and helped Saffron onto the couch.

Elinor showered him with effusive thanks and an invitation. "Will you come tomorrow for dinner?"

He lit up, a warmth in his brown eyes. Her knees might be melting. He said he'd love to and hoped they hadn't seen too much of him.

Elinor was certain of one thing: she hadn't seen too much of Tonio.

She went into the kitchen and foraged for leftovers, while planning tomorrow night's dinner of broiled chicken, penne pasta, and broccoli with pine nuts and mushrooms.

It wasn't exactly a feast, but he already knew she could cook.

Leaving Saffron settled on the sofa, Elinor went out on the patio. She watched the sun setting, savoring the golden light and memories of the day. Every look Tonio had sent her way came back and was caught with that sunset radiance.

She saw her life in the hospital administration office in cinematic detail. It was a movie that wouldn't draw a crowd. In fact, she was the only one in the audience. Standing on the patio, looking out to a sea of revolving colors like a bowl of liquid jewels, Elinor turned off the projector.

She went inside and sat at the dining table, opening her laptop to check her email. Her boss. Bill's tone wasn't pleasant.

"Elinor, we've given you ample time to deal with your bereavement and inheritance. We now require your presence. Otherwise, we will be forced to find a replacement, possibly a permanent one. If you aren't back at work by January 3, don't bother to come in."

Elinor sighed.

Saffron asked, "What's up?"

"My boss. He insists I be back in the office right after New Year's. We'll have to pack up and deal with the sale from home. It's a mess."

Saffron was quick. "I can stay. I don't have a job."

Or a boyfriend, except a promising candidate here, if only you'd get a clue. Elinor managed not to say it. She looked at her sister. After these months of changing, Saffron looked like someone who could actually manage things. She had finally agreed that they had to sell, it was just a question of timing. Sadness plummeted through Elinor at having to leave this place, leave Saffron and . . . everyone. *Leave Tonio.*

She shook it off, remembering her plan and the estimate for the last repairs from Cosma Gavazza. The wily realtor must have realized that a compromise was the only way this was going to remain her listing, contract or no. They agreed to a list of repairs, and no more could be undertaken without Elinor personally approving it.

Now they had just a couple of weeks to find that damn manuscript. She could take it with her on her way home and check in with *Signor* Capelli—or maybe not. Possession was nine-tenths of the law, they said. She could simply take the book home and do whatever she and Saffron agreed should be done. A little of her sister's lightness of touch with morals must be rubbing off.

"You're sad," Saffron said. "Me too."

Elinor smiled. "I'm coming back. I just have to. You're going to take care of everything, and I'll be just a text or call away."

Just two more weeks, through Christmas and New Year's. And *Tonio.* Nothing about that was set at all. Maybe she could ask him to help Saffron, to be available in case she needed more than Elinor could give over a call. And of course, she'd have to periodically check in with him about how things were going. The thought of remaining in touch with Tonio . . .

"Why are you smiling?" Saffron asked.

Her sister was too quick. She could always catch a feeling floating in the room.

Winter

Chapter 26

Christmas in Liguria—Saffron

On this dismal, overcast December day, with the fog's gray curtain erasing Lerici and the sea, Saffron worried about Ellie leaving at the end of the month. Saffron would have to go eventually, too, once the house sold and she bought an apartment. It would never be the same.

Curled up on the couch, she escaped these depressing thoughts by reading about closed adoption. She learned that you had to go to court to unseal it. You had to have a reason that was more than personal. A medical necessity, something else legally compelling. Would the possibility of an inheritance qualify? Baby Boy could share in the windfall from their father.

That thought made her fingers pause over the keys of her laptop. Could Saffron persuade her sister to share? It seemed like the right thing.

And where was Michael? He had been scarce this week, after their sunset kiss. Why was he putting distance between them? More discouraging thoughts wove into her gray mood, so Saffron focused on the hidden manuscript.

Ellie said she had no more time to search. No matter what she thought about today, Saffron couldn't settle into happiness. She needed a walk, or a small adventure. Maybe she could stop thinking about herself and make dinner for her sister, with a readymade lasagna, a bagged salad, and takeout tiramisu. Maybe Michael might show up. He ought to, really. It was time, unless he meant to cut things off. It would be ironic, since she'd done that to him, so . . . instant karma? When Saffron came in with the groceries, she said, "Dinner will be ready at seven. I bought a lasagna and a salad. Dessert too."

Ellie's amazement was a thing of beauty.

Saffron added, "I'll call Tonio and invite him. I'm sure Michael will come by. Or maybe you should call him."

Elinor looked at her with curiosity, but agreed. "I'll call Michael."

Saffron gave Tonio a call. When he was around, something like perfume wafted from her sister, an essential sweetness Saffron knew well. The real Ellie. So why was she going home—just for a job?

Michael showed up early and walked in without knocking. He was wearing his old fraying sweater, the one she had helped pull over his head the day they had made love. As she looked at him, her pulse did two backflips. She knew he was thinking of that day too.

Tonio was precisely on time, at six-thirty, and dressed in a refined caramel colored sweater and brown suede jacket. Of course, he brought a bottle, but instead of wine, it was a deep green olive oil. He also had a bag wafting the aroma of fresh-baked focaccia.

"*Ciao, bambini*!" he said. "I come bearing gifts for dinner."

He came into the kitchen to put down his offerings and

then went back into the living room to take off his jacket and hang it on a peg near the front door.

Tonio and Michael shook hands and Saffron poured wine for them.

While she was heating the lasagna and putting the salad into a big bowl, she listened to them talking. Tonio's voice blended well with Ellie's, a well-tuned duet.

Michael's voice was in a different choir. "What is there to do around here at Christmas?" he asked. "Never been here at this season."

"It's a resort town," Ellie said. "I imagine there's not much at Christmas."

Tonio gently contradicted her. "Liguria has some of the most spectacular celebrations in Italy. In this season in La Spezia we bring the Christ Child out of the sea with fireworks!"

"Fireworks!" Michael said, and Saffron felt something like a small burst of fire in her chest.

Ellie added, "Christmas fireworks—I'd like to see that."

"Then you will," Tonio replied. "I'll take you all."

Saffron turned around to see the affectionate way he looked at her sister. Ellie was simply blind. She turned back to her chopping board, dicing tomatoes for the salad.

What if Ellie lived the rest of her life without having Tonio in it?

She chopped the strange thought away. Tonio was telling them more about the local celebrations. "In Liguria, we celebrate the birth of the Christ Child. For us, birth is one with the sea, and so the statue of the Christ Child comes from the sea on Christmas Eve. We must all go to Tellaro and see this sacred spectacle."

Saffron brought the salad bowl and plates to the table.

"Tell us more about it," Ellie said.

"There are so many candles you could never count them all! And great songs, everyone singing. The Holy Child is brought up from the waves and carried to the church in a candlelight procession."

It made Saffron think of a long-ago Christmas, her first at the Greene's. They had a pungently scented tree, dazzlingly full of tiny lights and glass ornaments that caught the glints. It was the best gift she'd ever had, her heart exploding with the warmth of belonging.

"We all have to go!"

Saffron didn't look at Michael, but was happy he agreed. "We must!"

CHAPTER 27

More Christmas Gifts—Saffron

Saffron and Ellie made an agreement about holiday gifts. They'd each buy one for the other, two for Mom-Betsy for Elinor to take home. If they found things while they were out shopping, they might buy a gift each for Tonio and Michael.

"I don't feel comfortable about buying Tonio a Christmas present," Ellie said. "I haven't known him long."

Saffron shook her head. "What if he buys you one? You'll feel terrible if you have nothing to exchange."

"Did you and Michael agree to exchange?"

Saffron plopped herself down on the sofa. "Oh, Ellie. You make everything about lists and rules. We didn't talk about it. He's spontaneous, like I am."

Ellie came and sat beside her. "What if he buys you one and you have nothing to exchange?"

Saffron laughed. "Of course, I'm going to get something for him. I just have to decide how much to scale it up or down."

Ellie poked her. "What does that mean? Is your relationship scaling up or down?"

Another shake of the head was Saffron's answer. Then she thought better. "I know! We can go in together on a gift for Michael. I have the perfect idea."

"What?"

"A sweater!"

They laughed for a long time about that.

"What would you get for Tonio if you decide to splurge?" Saffron asked.

Her sister got up and walked away, finding yet another cobweb to swipe at. Saffron felt her conflict in even thinking about it, let alone answering.

Finally Ellie turned back to her. "If I were on those kinds of terms with him, what I'd like to give him is an elegant silk scarf. You know, the kind that comes from the best Italian shops around here. But he probably has plenty of them."

Saffron's voice was warm. "That would be wonderful. Do it."

"But he probably isn't giving me anything, and I don't want to embarrass him."

"He will give you something."

"I don't know where to find anything like that."

"I do."

Ellie insisted they only take one day for gift shopping. "We'll waste too much time, otherwise. And time's getting short. We have to get the house on the market."

Being reminded, Saffron said, "Then let's go now. Today. Christmas shopping is best the earlier you go."

"But where?"

Saffron knew that the shops in Lerici weren't exactly of the Christmas gift variety. They were more the vacation memento kind. But she had spent more time in town than her sister, and she told Ellie about a beautiful store tucked away just off the town square. It had men's and women's clothing of the kind she hadn't considered being able to afford. It would be perfect. And there were two other shops, one for stationery and one for gourmet food. Maybe they'd find things in those.

Saffron led Ellie across the hill from their house, and after a few minutes they arrived at the historic Lerici town center. Her sister was impressed by the quaint, elegant shop tucked into a tall Baroque building facing the square. Its window displayed an array of colorful silk mufflers—just the kind of thing Ellie had said she wanted to buy.

There were two narrow aisles through the shop, which was crammed with display cases and shelves. Saffron told Ellie to be careful about picking things up. Italian vendors didn't like their wares being touched.

In the end, it was impossible to shop for each other without spoiling surprises, so they agreed to meet at the *gelateria* in an hour. By the time Saffron got there, Ellie was already seated with her cup of gelato. Well, of course she was. She probably had made a list before they even left the house, while Saffron had nothing in her mind about the gifts she would choose. She liked shopping as a free association exercise.

She set her two full bags down and got her gelato.

"All set?" Ellie asked.

Digging into a pistachio gelato, Saffron said, "Oh, more than set. You?"

"I'm happy."

On Christmas Eve, Tonio arrived at the same time as Michael for wine and snacks before the excursion to see Christmas fireworks.

As soon as he came in, Tonio handed Elinor and Saffron gifts wrapped in brocade cloth and tied with velvet ribbons. "Here we give presents on Christmas Eve. I know Americans do it on Christmas Day, but that's a day most Italians are in church, so the night before is our time."

Ellie looked flustered and happy, Saffron thought, as she took the beautifully wrapped gift. She accepted hers and waved Michael further into the room. He wasn't holding anything, and Saffron wondered if she should give him the large package she'd wrapped for him. It was too big. She had been too spontaneous and generous, but then being generous couldn't be wrong, could it?

The sisters had piled their gifts on the coffee table, and they now placed their gifts from Tonio among them. It meant they had to be opened before anything could be served.

Tonio sat on the loveseat, but Ellie sat on the armchair instead of crowding next to him. Michael hesitated to see if Saffron would sit on the couch, and then he sat close to her. He met her glance with a secretive smile. So Michael was okay with the gift-giving, even though he hadn't brought anything. Good. It shouldn't be a rule. Saffron smiled back, confident again about her gift.

"Elinor, would you like to open yours?" Tonio said, handing her the gift.

Saffron enjoyed the blush on her sister's face as she accepted the present and untied the beautiful ribbon. The pink on Ellie's cheeks deepened as she pulled open the fabric and held up another piece of fabric, a shining paisley brocade shawl of interwoven teal blue and forest green, threaded with gold silk highlights. She gasped as she held it up between her hands.

"Tonio, it's gorgeous! Thank you so much. Shall I try it on?"

"Yes, try it."

Saffron tried not to roll her eyes at the reserve between these two. But at least her sister gave Tonio an enchanted smile. And then she actually blew him a kiss. Saffron looked at Michael, who seemed to understand her every thought. They grinned at each other.

When Tonio opened his gift from Elinor, the awe on his face was a thing of beauty to Saffron. There was no way her sister was going home. Not to leave this wonderful man who clearly adored her, in his quiet, polite way. If only Ellie could understand Tonio's way of expressing his feelings, everything would go the right way. But Ellie was often blind to emotional signals, or flustered by them.

She grabbed her gift for her sister and handed it over.

Ellie smiled, and her smile grew when she lifted out of the box a leather-bound notebook with Venetian paper covers, and a large, scrolled pen. It looked antique but held rollerball cartridges, her favorite kind of pen.

Opening the thick pages, Ellie saw that they were blank. "Oh, Saffron, thank you! I will treasure this. It's so beautiful."

"Just fill it! This one's for Michael," she said, reaching for a package on the table. "Open this."

Elinor smiled at her as he took the package.

Michael's face lit up as he unwrapped the box and lifted out a gray-blue linen pullover sweater. "I guess I won't have to wear frayed sweaters for a while!"

Saffron had picked well, she could tell. The shopkeeper had suggested it, and when she saw the color, she knew how it would look with Michael's blue eyes.

Michael laid it down on his lap and turned to kiss her on the cheek. "Thanks."

He pulled something out of one pocket. "For you," he said, handing a silver bracelet with seashells to Elinor, who was surprised and thrilled. She put it on and thanked him.

"And this is for you, Saffron." Michael handed her a silver chain, just the right length and weight for the charm he'd given her.

"Thank you, Michael! I can put the mermaid on it." She leaned over to kiss his cheek, but he didn't turn, so she kissed him on the lips, lingering longer than she had planned. Nothing with Michael worked out as planned, and she liked that.

Ellie handed him his gift from her with a smirk Saffron didn't understand, until he unwrapped it and held up another sweater. Saffron and Ellie laughed.

"Great minds..." he said. "Thank you! I'll toss the others, I promise, now that I have a complete wardrobe."

Tonio handed Saffron a beautifully wrapped box. In it was a large picture book on Castello Brown, accompanied by a small novel about Shelley. She was touched by his thoughtfulness, remembering how much she'd liked their outing to Portofino and her fascination with the poet.

Last, but definitely not least, Saffron opened her gift from her sister. Opening the big box, she pushed aside the magenta tissue paper and pulled out a white straw panama hat decorated with a band of seashells and flowers. "Lerici" it said on one side. Saffron put it on her head and raced to the mirror, delighted to see how perfect it looked, and racing back to hug Ellie.

After having coffee, Tonio drove them all to Tellaro. The small, colorful town cascaded down the steep hillside toward the sea. Like all these coastal towns, it had almost no parking near the beach. They parked at the top of the hill and walked down, wading into a large crowd of people talking, singing, some with already lit candles.

Following Tonio, Saffron looked back to see if she could manage to exchange places and put Ellie next to him. Michael reached for her hand, and pulled her back to make the exchange. She was pressed back against him as they stood in the crowd.

Then they all surged down toward the beach, candle flames flickering all around. People began to sing in unison.

Astro del ciel, Pargol divin, mite Agnello Redentor! Tu che i Vati da lungi sognar, they sang.

"What does it mean?" Saffron raised her voice to ask. Then she recognized the melody: "Silent Night."

She hummed along. Ellie was next to Tonio, but looking up at the sky, waiting for the promised fireworks.

Michael sang the English version into her ear.

Close to the beach, the singing stopped and everyone hushed.

Tonio said, "Now the divers bring up the statue of the infant Jesus from the sea."

Suddenly, fireworks sprouted. Pop-pop-pop, the soft explosions penetrated the song. Many voices rose up to the pinwheel-lit heavens. Saffron turned her face up to the lights. Her mouth dropped open, ready to catch on her tongue each sparkling drop of colored light.

A rustle through the crowd. Tonio gestured and led them forward until they could see the beach, where divers in black wetsuits emerged from the tide. Caught in a spotlight, they held aloft the statue of infant Jesus. The crowd applauded and cheered. Saffron could see the colors of the painted statue, the baby draped in a blue robe, its round face rosy with melon colored cheeks and a cherubic smile. The chubby little arms reached up.

The crowd parted right in front of them and the divers carrying the statue started the procession up to the church. As everyone thronged ahead in a dense line, Tonio held them back until he pulled them into the end of parade, up the winding street. The church doors were wide open, revealing a wall of candelabras, gilt scrolls, and marble sculptures. Most of the crowd wouldn't be able to get inside and stayed outside, singing, holding up their candles.

Tonio asked if they wanted to go in for Mass, or alternately there was a local trattoria, where they could have a traditional Ligurian Christmas meal. Gleefully, Saffron, Ellie, and Michael voted for the meal.

Sitting at a small square table, they read the paper menus as Tonio gave suggestions. "Usually here, according to the fasting rules, one eats no meat today. The dinner tables often have *ravioli in brodo*, that's cheese ravioli in broth. Maybe *cappon magro*, a fish and vegetable salad. And *pasta con le sarde*, or pasta with sardines. Also *spiedini di pesce*. These are fish kebabs."

"How about we have it all and share?" Saffron asked.

Elinor nodded. "Yes, please."

"Everything times four!" Michael added.

Tonio was pleased and gestured the waiter over to order. "We're lucky they're open. The family keeps it staffed as a service to the community. After Mass, many people will come in."

"What did you order?" Elinor asked.

He smiled. "As Michael said, everything times four! I also ordered *vin brulè,* another tradition here. Mulled wine."

"I could use some spirits, after standing outside with that ocean breeze!" Michael said.

"I like all your Ligurian traditions," Elinor said.

Saffron watched Tonio's eyes brighten at that, even before he smiled. She sensed the *ping* of something between him and Ellie, something like the gentle popping of tiny pink fireworks. She saw that something would come from the dazzle in Ellie's eyes. They ended with dried fruits and *pandolce*, a Ligurian fruit cake.

"What's in it?" Ellie asked.

"Sultanas, currants, glacé cherries, almonds, and candied orange peel," Tonio said.

Saffron loved her sister's radiant smile at Tonio. Outside, fireworks were still spangling the sky. It was nearly one in the morning. Magenta pinwheels sparkled against the dark. They got in the car, Saffron and Michael in the back. She saw that Tonio and Elinor were still making their own silent, pink sparkles in the air.

CHAPTER 28

Christmas Fireworks—Elinor

Elinor looked back at her sister from the front seat. A childlike rapture on Saffron's face reminded her of their first Christmases. On Saffron's first with them, Betsy had made angel tree decorations. To the raffia and crepe paper forms she had added tiny cutout photos of Saffron's face, so their tree was covered in with Saffron-angels. On Christmas morning, Saffron was speechless at the tree and her piles of gifts, each tagged with her name scrolled in gold ink.

Tonio looked over at Elinor and smiled. She smiled back, the moment's perfection lighting her up inside. Seeing Saffron and Michael holding hands also delighted her.

When Michael had brought her fainting, dripping sister home after nearly drowning, he showed his devotion. Elinor thought her sister had finally found someone worthy, not those jerks she always picked up. But each day since, Michael had hung around their house, keeping up good cheer, despite being held off by her sister. He was determined. He would be so good for Saffron, if only she could see it. But her sister liked her men bad, men sure to dump her—or in Gino's case, scam her and then dump her. She seemed to expect to be abandoned, and to look for guys who would act out that role.

As they drove away, she saw a fresh volley of red and green fireworks splash over Tellaro.

Tonio looked at her and again they exchanged smiles. A burst of fireworks went off inside Elinor, spangling her face and heart.

When she woke up on Christmas morning, she remembered that sparkling warmth first thing, and again it spread through her. Elinor stretched her body under the covers, from toes to fingertips, feeling the sheets against her skin. She sat up, eager—to do what? She couldn't call him. Could she?

Practical considerations ticked off in her mind and made her swing her feet over onto the floor, taking root and settling this flighty feeling.

Elinor stood up and marched to the closet. Shrugging efficiently into her robe, she decided on the usual breakfast, even though it was Christmas. Eggs, toast, juice. Predictability and routine, her anchors.

Saffron was already up and sitting on the couch with her cup, reading. The opened gifts they had exchanged were on the coffee table, making the room festive.

Elinor checked the clock. She had slept late.

"Good morning. Merry Christmas! Is that your new book on Shelley?"

Saffron looked up, surprised. "Merry Christmas! Yes, The one Tonio gave me."

"You have a stack of books on your night table. Every one of them is about him."

Her sister smiled in recognition of the truth. "I found an article about a series of Shelley poems. Shelley wrote about them to a friend, but no one knows what happened to them. Ellie, what if he was writing the manuscript and Dad somehow found it?"

Elinor went into the kitchen and made herself toast and coffee. Saffron had washed the four champagne glasses and set them to dry on the counter. Munching on the toast, she looked back at her sister.

"It would be amazing if you spent more time looking for the manuscript than trying to figure out what's in it."

Saffron glared and picked up her book. "Sorry not sorry," she said.

Elinor stared. "It would be even more amazing if you'd round up some plates and napkins for our guests tonight."

"Wow, you haven't been this snarky for weeks and weeks. Is it because Tonio said he's not coming tonight?"

Elinor swerved around and brought her food into the living room, the comment blistering her ear.

"Why do you always make assumptions? Tonio might change his mind. And what difference does it make? I'm going home soon."

Of course her sister had everything mixed up. In a salad of wishes, romantic feelings, and improbability, Saffron was pairing her with a man fifteen years older and soon to be six thousand miles away. Her sister was the dreamy one, never Elinor. Why would she say that?

Elinor looked down and saw that she was holding two cups, her tea and Saffron's half-filled cup left in the kitchen. Standing there, she realized she was definitely not herself.

Saffron was trying not to laugh.

"Fair enough," she said. "I like him. There, I said it."

Saffron's slow shaking of her head told Elinor she

wouldn't get off that easy. "Say it—you love him. You might even want—"

"Don't get carried away. Yes, I really-really like Tonio."

His name warmed her mouth and slid down to expand her heart. That floaty feeling again. What was wrong with her? It had been so long since she'd fallen in love that she couldn't believe it was still possible. A pulse beat *Yes* into her heart, and she realized the truth.

She stepped into the hug Saffron was all too ready to give. She had forgotten how physically strong her sister could be. The hug anchored Elinor's dizziness and let her feel her feet on the ground again, along with relief at having admitted her feelings.

They separated. "I'm sad to have to leave. What if I never see him again?"

Saffron shook her head with a snap that reminded Elinor of her own gesture. "You can't let this be the end, Ellie. You have to come back. Lerici is our home."

She took Elinor's hand and led her over to the patio doors.

"What are you showing me?" Elinor asked.

"Look out there. Look at this patio and the view. Look at the garden. You love it here!"

Elinor looked out at the bare limbs of the trees and shrubs and the darkened ocean. Yearning unwound from her, curling around everything she saw. But Berkeley was where she belonged.

She faced Saffron. The same tug in her heart. "I hate leaving you," she said.

Saffron grabbed her into a fierce hug. She whispered, "It's Tonio you hate to leave."

"Him too. But you! Mostly you."

The ache burned in her eyes and threatened to spill out.

Saffron brushed her shoulder with a soft hand. Elinor was both comforted and sad.

"Okay, so New Year's is coming up in a week. What do you want to do?" The New Year would take her away from this. What she wanted was to call her boss and tell him to go jump off a bridge. What she said was, "We could have champagne here for New Year's, and invite Michael and Tonio."

"But I want some time with you, time by ourselves," Saffron said fiercely. "It might be our last night together for—a while."

Saffron's pleading eyes decided it.

"Okay. We'll stay home and invite them to come. We'll tell them we're finishing the year early, and send them away so we have the rest of the evening to ourselves."

"Yes!" Saffron's hug sealed the deal.

CHAPTER 29

New Year's—Saffron

On New Year's Eve afternoon, Saffron sat on the couch trying to read. After turning a few pages, she put the book face down. Staring out at the waving trees and restless sea beyond, she thought about Elinor leaving in two days. She was staying, but nothing would be the same. It was the worst way to start a year. She needed to talk to Ellie about things. What things? It didn't matter. They needed time together, and the time was fast diminishing.

Ellie came into the living room and sat next to her, looking tired. "I'm half packed," she announced. "I'll do the rest tomorrow. While I'm gone, will you help Cosma get the house on the market as soon as possible?"

Saffron was startled. "We didn't agree to sell this season. Cosma said spring was best, remember?"

"We agree to do it as fast as possible. Remember, you can get Cosma to find you a condo. You can stay in Lerici."

Saffron reached forward and touched her sister's arm. "Let's don't hurry. You know, a house that contains our own family spirit, that's different than anything I can buy."

Her sister surprised her by giving in. "Okay, let's wait till spring. Let Cosma figure out the timing."

Ellie really didn't want to leave, Saffron could tell. Maybe her sense of belonging here had grown stronger and her sense of belonging to Tonio growing.

Saffron couldn't resist asking, "What are you going back to that's so wonderful?"

"My job. Mom."

"You hate your job. And Mom makes you nuts. She could come here and live with us."

"She couldn't leave her cats."

"Mom could bring the cats."

"You're bored with your life."

"I am not!"

Anger surged inside Saffron. "You even dress for boredom, in your gray suits! No one in Berkeley dresses like fog."

"You're *too* Berkeley! You couldn't exist outside that anti-establishment bubble. You wear your big floppy lavender dresses, but you'll never grow into them."

Saffron wasn't sure what the insult meant, but her own voice rose to a soprano pitch. "I live authentically. And you're a coward. Leaving just when you're falling in love!"

Elinor's reply was calmly snide. "You wouldn't know 'falling in love' if you tripped over it. Why don't you marry Michael? That would be authentic. But you're too swept up in your 'freedom'."

Saffron shouted. "You impose your judgments on everyone!"

Ellie leaned forward. "I told Michael you like him. So sue me. Oh, and sue me over the house, too, because that's what it will take."

"You think I'm still your little slave, like when we were kids!"

Saffron jumped off the couch and ran upstairs. The hell with celebrating a new year with her sister. She sat on her bed, by turns fuming and feeling like a giant failure. Why had she let herself be goaded by Ellie, once again? So what if her sister wasn't ready to admit they had to keep this house? Saffron knew Ellie would come to it. She would go home and regret having left. She'd come back. Tonio would persuade her to stay.

She closed the door to her room firmly and sat in the chair by the window. The anger ebbed. Her breathing slowed. She should calm down.

As she calmed, a shimmer in her peripheral vision made her catch her breath.

"Are you here?" she asked without turning. She felt his presence.

Oh, Saffron.

Great. She had disappointed a spirit, the way she disappointed everyone. Why were they all against her, even people in The Room Over There?

I'm not disappointed. You are. Think about what you'd like to do next, not what you just did. Think about the future, though I know you don't like to. Fear not for the future, weep not for the past. Because, dear Saffron, you're stuck in the present and the other two are mythical.

How did Shelley know so much about her? And why was he sounding more and more parental?

I know you because you're sensitive like me. Imaginative, and astride that wild horse for your whole life. I know how that is both blessing and curse. I will help you make it more a blessing, if you let me.

Saffron wasn't sure she wanted to be tutored by an

incorporeal person, even one who was a great poet. Look at Shelley's life, that wreckage of fine intentions, adequate means, and genius talent. He seemed well able to live on that galloping steed of imagination, but not very well in the practical world. She wasn't sure she wanted his guidance.

The silence gathered. She had hurt his feelings, but what she felt was the truth. She stayed still until the shimmering subsided, and then she went over and lay down on her bed. She'd take a little nap before getting dressed for the evening, whatever it brought.

The knock on the front door roused her. She went back down.

Michael was all dressed up, if you could call wearing his new, good sweater over a faded lavender shirt dressed up. They had agreed not to make a big deal, and yet here he was, fancy as anything.

And she was in a sweater and sweatpants.

He was early, no doubt hoping to have dinner. He thrust a large bottle into her hands. "To start celebrating," he said. "Vintage Veuve Clicquot. The good stuff. After all, it's New Year's!"

Ellie came into the room. The slacks and sweater she had been wearing all day weren't festive, though Ellie had added a necklace.

She offered him a chair and said, "How expensive. I suppose you take New Year's seriously."

Ellie said, "Tonio won't be coming after all. He's going to drink champagne with his elderly neighbor. She'd otherwise be alone."

Michael smiled. "Typical kindness from Tonio."

But Elinor wasn't smiling.

"Too bad he'll toast the new year with a charity case instead of us," Saffron said.

Ellie went into the kitchen. Over her shoulder she said, "Michael, I hope you like minestrone. It's our dinner, and you're welcome to join us, of course."

"I love minestrone! I hope you like this champagne. It's the best I could find."

Ellie's enthusiasm surprised Saffron, and not in a good way. "We can have soup with champagne! And I wouldn't mind going out later, to see how they celebrate New Year's in Liguria."

The traitor. The plan was to toast the coming year here at home and send away their guests about nine o'clock. If they didn't have this evening together, Saffron wouldn't be able to have a real conversation before Ellie left. Her sister would start rushing around tomorrow, packing, giving instructions about caretaking the house.

Ellie put the soup and bowls on the table, along with a ladle and spoons and bread. The three of them sat to eat.

"This is great," Michael said, spooning down some soup.

Saffron got up, went into the kitchen, and brought back the bottle of champagne. "Let's open it now!"

"You could change clothes," Ellie said. "We could go out instead. You might like exploring New Year's in Lerici."

Saffron looked to Michael. What did he want?

Looking at Saffron, he said, "There are nightclubs in La Spezia. I know one you might like, techno-pop meets Italian *discoteca*."

"Sounds loud," Saffron said.

Ellie said, "Sounds fun."

The double traitor. Saffron had almost never heard

Ellie use the word *fun* except with a pejorative tilt, as in 'all you want to do, Saffron, is have *fun*.'

Michael seemed to realize he was caught between them, which made Saffron smile.

"Come out," Michael said. "Please, Saffron."

He reached for her hand, and she felt the strength of his grasp with a fire that shot through her anger and melted it into something else. Her lips remembered their sunset kiss. Why had he been avoiding her this week?

"Your choice, of course," he said softly. "Elinor, what do you say? A little New Year's Eve adventure?"

Ellie smiled at him. "Sure."

Saffron said, "New Year's is just a quirk of the calendar. But I'm willing."

Michael gave her his big, warm smile. "All right! I'll get us a taxi. I don't want to have to drive."

The doorbell rang. Being nearest to it, Saffron jumped and then hopped up to answer it. She found Tonio on the step, holding two bottles. He was dressed up, in a dark suit and muffler. She invited him in with a nod.

"My New Year's date fell asleep on me," he said. "So I've brought you a gift from the Ligurian sea, just like the statue of the Christ Child." He held up the two bottles. "This is a very special sparkling wine made here in Liguria from local vineyards."

"How is it from the sea?" Michael asked.

"It's aged in steel cases underwater. It's a technique invented by a local vintner."

"How marvelous," Elinor replied. "Why do they do that?"

"The temperature is right, there's no light, and the sea rocks the cradle of bottles. The wine emerges from its marine aging pale gold with bubbles like sea foam. Peach and mineral on the palate."

Elinor's appreciation of both giver and gift softened her voice. "What a special treat!"

"Now we have three bottles!" Saffron exclaimed. "We can have a nice party here. No point going out when we have the best wine and company."

Michael held up his bottle, "We can have some of this before we go and the special wine when we get back."

Tonio untied his Christmas muffler and draped it carefully over a chair back, with a look at Elinor. "Do you like this idea of going out?"

Saffron was infuriated to see her sister betray their plan. "It sounds like fun, if you're up for it!"

He looked at Ellie and that lit up her sister's smile. She obviously could have a future with this wonderful man. Her sister always said Saffron had no common sense, but she was the one who was going to ruin everything for herself.

Saffron went into the kitchen to get glasses for the champagne. Perhaps if they had a few glasses, they'd give up the idea of going out.

"There's a great little club in La Spezia," Michael said, pushing his idea. How had Saffron not noticed that he could be stubborn? "We could rock in the new year."

Staying here would be so much more intimate than going to a noisy club. Now that Tonio was here, they could all have a happy night. Why was Michael being such a jackass?

But he persisted. "We can go and be back before midnight, and then we'll toast in the year as we planned."

Maybe if she resisted, he'd come to his senses. "We'd have more fun—and be able to hear each other—if we stay in. We can put on some music, and better music! You said it was techno-pop. Does anyone here like techno-pop?"

Saffron look at the three of them. Tonio and Elinor shook their heads. Michael nodded.

"You would!" she hissed.

Disgusted, she retreated to the far end of the living room, turning to look out the window. She made the decision and tossed over her shoulder, "You all go ahead. I don't want to go out."

She still hoped to change Michael's mind by resisting.

"We'll miss you," he said sarcastically.

So that's how it was. No more adoration.

"You kids have fun," she retorted, her back still turned. Even as she willed herself to stop, she added, "I'm going to curl up with my book—"

"Couldn't Shelley do without you for one night?" Michael said, with both pleading and annoyance.

She turned her around and came back. "I guess you can do without me for one night. Oh, and break a leg while you're all dancing!—Oh, wait, that's for performing, isn't it? Well, break something."

Michael shrugged. He was angry.

After they had gone, Saffron stood at the patio doors looking out at the fog swirling up. It blanked out even the closest bushes. If only it could blank out the mess she'd made. But she was alone now. It felt comfortable. And sad.

She went upstairs and got on the bed, but couldn't decide to get undressed. Maybe they'd come back for champagne.

She was tired now of Shelley's whining, tired of his inscrutable poems. She aimed her anger at him like a ball of darts. He was an easy target.

Going downstairs, she helped herself to a big bowl of vanilla ice cream, grating pieces of dark chocolate on top. Taking it over to the French doors, she opened them and stepped out into the chill. Her bare feet freezing, she stood there looking into the fog, and then stepped back inside when it began to feel like frostbite.

The uneasy feeling caught her as she remembered saying "break something."

She ate her ice cream standing in the middle of the living room. Although she was staying, she was losing this place where she and Ellie had lived together.

Turning back to the patio doors to make sure she'd secured them, she felt Shelley step through the glass, a white face above a white silk cravat, spilling over his long, dark coat.

You made a mistake.

"Obviously," she said. She took another bite of ice cream.

Feeling sorry for yourself.

"You're a judgy spirit."

She finished the ice cream and set the bowl down on a side table. "I'd offer you some, but . . ." she giggled.

I watch over both sisters. But I worry about you.

"I thought that was a guardian angel's job. Your job seems to be accusing me. You should haunt my sister. She'd agree with you."

Nathan asked me to. You have something to give your sister.

"Dad could see you?"

Of course.

"Why would he want you to take care of us? He was a crappy father."

As I was. Perhaps we are both making up for that failure in life.

Saffron retreated to the couch and put up her feet on the coffee table.

This is a bad night to have alienated your sister. And also a poor thing, to have pushed aside the young swain you bedded.

Saffron stared. "What, were you spying on me? If I'm so terrible, why do you visit me?"

I'm the only one who can help you.

"Aren't you supposed to be the poet of equality and kindness?"

He wavered and dimmed until she saw only the side table with the potted orchid and outside, the thickening sea of fog.

Saffron went back to the kitchen, wondering if she wanted another glass of wine. Deciding she didn't, she went out and into the chaos room, intending to open up the drawer and again look at the adoption papers. Baby Boy was out there somewhere in the world. Grief plummeted like a stone through her heart. They'd never find him—like they'd never find the manuscript—if they weren't united. And because she'd lost her temper, she and Ellie had never been so alienated.

She looked up. The clock had stopped at exactly midnight.

Chapter 30

Nightclub, New Year's Eve—Elinor

The taxi crept cautiously through the fog. Wishing she could see something, Elinor put her fingers on the window. The searing chill seeped through the glass.

"Typical Lerici winter," Tonio said. Sitting next to her, he asked. "Are you chilled?"

"Freezing," she said, pulling her coat tighter and wishing he'd put his arm around her. "But I'll be fine once we get to the club. I'm sure it will be warm."

"It will be sweltering," Michael said cheerfully from the front.

Was Lerici decked out for New Year's? Elinor wished she could see.

As they rode into town, she promised herself to drink only one glass of champagne. Remembering her limits kept her life in balance and helped her make good choices. It was her way, even on New Year's. What a mess life would be without limits. Just look at Saffron, who was always making impulsive choices she was sorry for later.

"Too bad we couldn't get Saffron to come," Michael said.

"She always does things her own way, and she's not always happy with what she chooses."

Elinor hoped she could rely on Michael to look out for Saffron while she was gone. He understood and tolerated her better than Elinor ever would. Saffron liked him, but kept him at a distance. Was that why Michael hadn't been around for a while?

She'd urge Michael and Tonio to get her back before midnight, so she and Saffron could see in the New Year together by themselves, as planned. Why had her sister made such a fuss because Elinor wanted to go out for a couple hours? But she realized she had gone back on her promise to Saffron.

The driver spoke no English, so Tonio gave him directions. He took them to La Spezia and parked at the intersection near the club.

They walked to a brightly lit doorway where a sign read "Club Cavina."

Tonio insisted on paying for them all at the door. They descended the narrow, curving metal stairs into a loud subterranean space packed with people. Most were young, all were moving and drinking as they danced to a frenetic beat so loud and dominant that it vibrated the metal railing under Elinor's hand. She held tight, as if afraid of being carried away on a riptide.

The music was a series of electronic pops and fizzes, threaded through with a rock guitar melody line and relentless drums. The singer screamed in Italian into a mic. Most of the women wore tight, revealing tops and the men were in ripped jeans. Elinor felt overdressed and old in her black dress.

Michael grabbed her arm and eased her onto the floor while Tonio went to get them a table. For a few seconds she steadied herself by holding onto him. His reassuring smile eased her into dancing a little. He was so nice. If only Saffron had agreed to come. What made him think she'd like a deafening *discoteca* on New Year's Eve?

The maroon walls were lit by swirling blue and gold lights. People packed into every crevice of the large room, some crammed onto this dance floor, more at the banquettes lining the walls, some at tiny round tables edged closely by this dancing mob. She could smell the sweat of people around her, feel their heat.

"It's so loud!" she shouted.

Michael nodded as if he could hear and smiled. She gave up trying to be herself and began to hop like the dancers around her. Hopping seemed to be the Italian disco dance. Everyone was jumping up and down.

She let Michael dance her further into the melee. When she looked back, she saw that Tonio had claimed a small table and three chairs tucked under the stairway. He sat waiting for her, watching with a smile as they danced.

Finally, the music stopped. Over the din of the crowd, Michael said he was going to get them some drinks. He led her over to Tonio and the comforting, dark corner, seated her in a gentlemanly way, patted her arm, and left. She felt like a child who had received a good grade on a test.

"Strenuous!" she shouted to Tonio, and was about to continue when the music started up again.

Michael returned with three glasses of wine. He sat and they picked up their glasses.

"What do you think?" Michael shouted.

Neither of their replies could be heard, but Tonio raised

his glass, and she could see he was toasting. "*Salut*!" he probably said.

"*Salut*!" she replied, as did Michael and they all drank.

"It's new for me, this kind of place," she shouted fruitlessly, to no one.

Tonio and Michael smiled and nodded. The mere presence of her two gentlemen escorts was a blessed buffer against the wildness all around her. Elinor was having fun. Enjoying something new wasn't a bad way to start a new year.

They drank more, and then Michael rose and again held out his hand. With a smiling shrug, she got up and followed him onto the floor, right up to the stage. He was so gentle and so happy. She would have done just about anything to keep him that way and hope he and Saffron could get over being angry.

Too tired for the jumping anymore, she slowed down, and Michael followed suit, flirting a little as they danced. She was sure he'd rather be jumping. He grabbed her hand and they danced something new that he was showing her. As she mimicked him, he grinned and nodded, and danced close.

"You're a great dancer!" he shouted in her ear.

She shouted back her thanks and said she had to sit down. He escorted her, shouting that he'd get more drinks.

Tonio shouted and gestured. She understood that he was excusing himself to go to the men's room. As he slipped gracefully between the dancers, she wished she had danced with him first. Disappearing behind a large post, he melted into the darkness.

Deciding to be adventurous, Elinor stood up and danced on her own, facing the bar. Lots of people were.

She moved farther into the crowd and raised her arms as they did, feeling a rush of exhilaration and alcohol.

The shock wave roared out—a wave of noise so high and hard it gained heat as it blew straight into her ears and knocked her over onto her face as the lights went out. The music stopped. Something sharp hit her in the back. Elinor drifted into darkness.

Mist over the water, so peaceful. No, smoke from a chimney. Cottony silence. Deaf. Oh. So still. Where. Am. I? Shock. Is that what you're in?

The ceiling had a hole in it and a foggy sky above that. She was underground somewhere and something had her pinned to the floor, feeling wet.

Mist again. Silence. Fall into it.

The silence grew into sounds. She blinked and found herself swaying back and forth. Was she in a hammock? Voices, garbled words. Italian? She was put into a vehicle. They closed the doors and it moved forward. Strange faces looked down at her.

Someone said, "*Una grave!*"

The mist closed in again.

Chapter 31

An Explosion—Saffron

Saffron's phone chimed, waking her. She reached for it on the bedside table.

Michael's voice swam through her sleepiness. "There's been an explosion at the club. Ellie's in the emergency room in Sant' Andrea Hospital in La Spezia. Tonio and I are with her."

Saffron sat up. "What? Say that again! Where is she?"

"Explosion. She's at a hospital in La Spezia. She's stable. That's all we know."

She shook her head. "Michael, I just woke up. Tell me again."

His voice calm, he repeated it.

"Say it all again—what happened?"

He spoke slowly, spacing the words in his sentences until her head began to clear and she had registered it.

"We were at the club and there was an explosion, a fire. We were all in different places, but we all got out, except Elinor. She was injured. I couldn't find her at first, but then the paramedics got to her." By the end, Michael's voice was shaking.

"And how bad is she hurt?" Saffron felt her own voice starting to shake. "I have to go!"

"Saffron, it's—not good."

"How bad? How did this happen?"

"As far as we know, no one was killed, but several have been seriously injured. Elinor was one."

"I have to see her!"

"Yes! I'm coming to take you to the hospital."

"Where's Tonio?"

"He rode with her in the ambulance. He's fine."

"Are you okay?" She suddenly realized he was in the blast too.

"I'm fine, and what you need to do now is wake up and get dressed. I'll be there soon."

"Is Ellie conscious?" Gripping her phone hard, she got up out of bed and started looking for her clothes in the dark.

"No. But she's stable. Hurry up. I'll be there in ten."

She was about to hang up when she thought to say, "Thanks."

Michael said, "Pack a small bag, whatever you'll need in case we're there all night and day."

After she hung up, she stared into the darkness and then turned on the light. She reached for her clothes from yesterday. No time to make choices.

Elinor, explosion, emergency, hospital, stable. These weren't words she could put together, but like pieces in a difficult puzzle they slowly cohered, until at last they were forming actual sentences. Elinor was badly hurt—very badly, because they had used the word stable. As in, she might at any time become unstable. And what did unstable mean—that she could die?

She put on tennis shoes. Weren't people on their feet a lot in these situations? Making herself a coffee, and one for Michael, Saffron realized how desperately sleepy she was. Even the shock hadn't awakened her completely. How could it have happened?

Saffron wanted a better word than "stable." She wanted them to use words like, "injured but fine", or "seriously injured but going to be fine." Stable was not a good word. It sounded like a warning.

She drank leaning on the counter, and then remembered she hadn't packed her backpack. She ran upstairs. What if Ellie died before she got there?

She realized her turquoise top was on inside out. She pulled it off and threw it on the floor, swearing at it. Then she put it on right. She needed a sweater. What would she tell Betsy? She'd have to call.

Ellie was usually the one to handle these crises.

Life without an Ellie to handle them. That wasn't possible.

Why wasn't Michael here? She packed up and looked around to see what else she might need. Scooping up her bulky sweater, she found one sock under the bed to match the other on the chair. She grabbed them and went downstairs. Still groggy, she remembered something and went back upstairs for her laptop, stuffing it into the pack.

She might scream all the way to La Spezia.

To calm down, she stepped onto the patio to listen to the ocean. It was still dark. The hum of crashing waves and the whisper of leaves soothed her until caffeine flushed through her. She located several stars in the west above the branches, and tried to be grateful that Ellie was alive.

She'd keep her alive with the force of love, keep her "stable." *Please, please, keep her alive!*

A rustle that was more than leaves. A voice that was hardly louder than a thought.

I watch over you both. Elinor will be all right. But the danger isn't over.

The doorbell made her heft her backpack and step inside to open the door to Michael. She hurried out, locking the front door behind her.

He gave her a quick hug and grabbed her hand to lead her up to his car.

On the way, Michael told her more about what had happened. There had been an explosion in the nightclub's boiler room. It caught Tonio in the men's room, where he was protected from the blast. Michael was on his way there, and he was protected in the hallway. But Elinor had been on the floor, in the path of a flying beam. She had been unconscious when they found her in the debris. They didn't yet know the cause of the explosion.

"I don't know how to deal with this!" she said, and turned onto his shoulder, sobbing.

He patted her hair. "I know."

"I should be the one injured. Ellie doesn't deserve this."

Michael stared at the road, driving as fast as safely possible.

Saffron stared out the window and tried to imagine a world without Ellie. She remembered saying that awful thing as her sister left last night. "I hate you."

The car came to a light and stopped.

"There it is," he said, pointing at the ruins.

The black-painted storefront with a neon sign shaped like an electric guitar was a bloom of black shards, jagged and ruptured beams at odd angles, bricks scattered like pebbles. Somewhere inside Ellie could have died.

A fierce will blossomed within Saffron. She wasn't going to let this explosion have Ellie.

Mingled with determination was the strong sense that if she had been there, she could have lifted the beam off Ellie herself. If only she hadn't been such an impossible brat she would have forgiven Ellie and never let her sister go off on New Year's Eve without an apology. She should have been the one to catch the flying rubble.

The car started again and turned a corner. They sped away, onto the wider road toward La Spezia.

In the dim light, every building was crystalline-edged, every harsh light pole a statue of the world with her sister in it. It must stay exactly this way, a world with Ellie alive. In these last three months, she had made so many mistakes. Shelley had been right. She'd behaved badly. She had been awful to Ellie on absolutely the worst night. She had thrown roadblocks in Ellie's way while her sister dealt with lawyers, realtors, and contractors. Ellie had tried to take care of them both, while she had made secret plots. Saffron had always known herself to be a terrible person. But she had never seen the consequences so clearly. If only time allowed, she'd make it up. If only Ellie would live.

They parked at the hospital. Leaping out, they ran into the emergency entrance, Michael holding her hand, to find chaos inside. Many people had been injured at the club. Gurneys bearing patients stood at odd angles along the hallways as green-clad doctors and nurses dashed around. A cacophony of beeps, bells, chimes, buzzers, and electronic noises made it hard to think.

No one paid any attention to them, except to push around them. What were they all saying in rapid Italian?

With her minimal grasp of Italian, Saffron would have a hard time understanding anyone here. But she had Michael, and he spoke some Italian.

He held her arm and led her to the reception desk. "*Dové la Americana*, Elinor Greene?"

Busy at her computer, the green-suited nurse didn't look up. He repeated the question. She continued to type and at last rattled off a sentence that made Michael nod and pull Saffron away.

"She told us to ask at another desk."

Navigating them past obstacles in the hall, Michael steered her to a desk where a small, dark-haired woman in a silky gray blouse looked up immediately. She gave Michael a quick, formal smile.

Michael said something. Saffron heard Elinor's name.

The woman then answered in English, directing them to wait in a row of chairs. The chairs were empty, except for a man who appeared very drunk. But it was quiet down here, and Saffron was relieved to be waiting in this area.

Saffron looked up at the wall clock. It was exactly 1:12 in the morning.

She had only been in an emergency room once, when Betsy had lacerated her knee, falling on rocks at the park. That Berkeley hospital ER, with its gray-white walls, rude nurses and doctors, had been scary for the young sisters. The staff made the girls and their mother sit in a row of chairs like this one while they took care of more urgent needs. After an hour, they stitched Betsy's knee, but not before she had been in pain a while, clutching the girls' hands. The medicinal smells had frightened Saffron.

Sitting here, Saffron wished the tedium could overcome her fear. Italian strangers controlled her sister's wellbeing while she knew nothing. Maybe they'd come out and announce that Elinor had died. If only the last thing she had said hadn't been so mean.

"Break a leg while you're dancing!" she had said. "Oh, wait, that's for performing, isn't it? Well, break a something."

Break something. Just because she was mad at Ellie. To say such a horrible thing to her own sister. If Ellie survived, she'd always remember Saffron's words. What if—but she stopped herself. She couldn't go there, sitting in this hard-plastic chair.

As Saffron was about to jump up out of fear and guilt, Tonio came out and came over to them. He picked up Saffron's hand.

Terrified, Saffron said, "Is she—?"

"They believe she's going to be okay. But she's not awake. They need more time."

"Why are they allowing you in? She's my sister! I want to see her."

Tonio's deep voice was gentle. "They allow me because I know many people. I used to work here. I explained that I'm a family friend. This is a very good hospital. Let the doctors and nurses do their best, and you'll see her soon."

He sat next to Saffron and nodded to Michael. Time clicked by with the sound of a wall clock's meaningless tick.

"I'm going to go back and check on her," Tonio finally said. "I will let you know."

Sitting there, unable to do anything for her sister, she alternated between falling asleep and waking. The pale green walls began to feel prison-like, and that merciless clock's noise ground into her.

She felt as much in alien territory as she had that first year on the school playground. Kids loved teasing the new

Greene girl. She had arrived in Berkeley speaking a smattering of French from her mother, and they began to call her the Weird Girl, then the Weird Greene Girl.

One day on the playground, George had pushed her down in a game of pitch and held her head down so her cheek ground on the gravel. He knew it hurt; she had squealed. He held her down anyway until Elinor rushed up and bounced the ball on his back so hard he yelled and jumped up off Saffron. For a moment, Saffron watched, afraid Elinor might punch George. But he shook his head in disgust and backed away from her, then ran toward his friends.

"Coward! Bully!" Ellie had shouted.

The boys raced away. They had never again tormented Saffron to that extent, and it was because of her sister. Had she ever thanked Ellie for that—had she?

Saffron came to herself in the plastic chair. "Check with Tonio," Saffron demanded of Michael. "He's been gone so long!"

She looked up at the clock. It was 2:00 exactly. Too long.

Michael went over to the reception desk and inquired. She could see his head bending to hear the woman reply. He nodded, and came back shaking his head.

"No news."

Saffron thought she might cry. Michael said, "Remember, Tonio said she's going to be okay. He was told that. The nurse said it would be probably another half hour before we can see her."

Saffron stood up because he was still standing.

"Could we find something to eat?"

He liked that idea. "Yes, surely there's a cafeteria around here."

He was such a gentle, considerate man, charming, with his nasal English accent, and she had been an idiot to dislike him. Would she have liked Michael better if he were aggressive, intimidating her and handling every situation with arrogance, the way Justin did? "Yes, I want to eat, and I don't want to spend another minute in this chair. Will they know where we are?"

"The nurse said she'll text me when we're needed. Let's go."

Michael asked the receptionist where to find a cafeteria. She pointed down the hallway.

"Hospitals are the same everywhere in the world," he said as they walked. "But she said this one has espresso!"

"Good. I need about four."

Thirty minutes later, nourished on sandwiches, they went back to the reception area. Now there was a different receptionist. Michael asked if they could see Elinor yet, and she said they could go to the recovery area.

An emergency doctor met them before they found Ellie's bed. A thin, short, dark-haired man in his thirties, he introduced himself and said Elinor wasn't yet awake, but she was stable. That word again. Meaningless, threatening.

He led them to an area filled with beds presided over by machinery. In her tilted-up bed the sleeping Ellie looked tiny and yellow. Her skin was the color of a paper towel that had soaked up oil, her cheeks sunken, and her lips compressed. Her forehead was heavily bandaged. Plastic tubes ran from hanging bags to her arms, under the covers. One port below her shoulder was visible.

For a moment, Saffron felt queasy. It was as if Ellie had died after all, she looked almost corpse-like. But then her eyelids fluttered. They didn't open, but it was enough.

Saffron rushed forward and bent over her sister, grabbing her hand.

"Ellie, we're here. Don't leave me!"

Elinor opened her eyes and gave the smallest nod. She closed them again and was still as a doll. Her shallow breathing gave Saffron comfort. She couldn't let go of Ellie's hand.

Saffron was bent forward in an awkward half-crouch, watching. Michael pulled a chair over and she sat, without releasing Ellie's hand.

Tonio came in and joined them. "She's going to pull through," he said. "They say she's stable. And from stable, you improve. That's what stable means."

His deep voice washed over her, calming the electric nerves that frayed all over her body. Saffron let herself believe him. A rush of gratitude made the tears well up and slide down her cheek.

"I will go and check on her nursing schedule. You should go home and get some rest."

After Tonio left, Michael put his hand on her shoulder. At last she let go of Ellie's hand. Her sister was deeply asleep.

A different doctor came in and adjusted one of the many plastic bags hanging from the metal rack.

After he had briefly examined Ellie, he repeated what Tonio had told her. "*Signorina*, your sister remains stable, which is good. Her kidney has been damaged. It cannot be repaired. We will need a donor."

Saffron nodded as if she understood, though nothing he said made sense.

Michael asked, "Her *one* kidney? But don't people usually have two?"

"Of course, people generally have two, but it occurs

that some are born with one. This patient was born with one, according to the records that were sent from the U.S."

Saffron was incredulous. "How can that be? Why wouldn't I have known?"

In good English he said, "The doctors delivering her wouldn't have found it important for all family members to know. It's not usually a great danger. A person can survive quite well with only one."

"So she'll need someone to give her a kidney?" Saffron asked.

"Exactly," he said. "She has acute kidney failure. She must be on dialysis until the transplant."

A sudden burst of realization told her what she needed to do. She could give her sister something that would make up for her rottenness.

She grabbed the doctor's arm, surprising him. "Give her mine. I have two—I think. Even if I don't, she can have it."

The doctor patted her hand and gently pushed it away. "We wouldn't take your only kidney. You will need to be tested to see if you are a match. Not every kidney can be donated."

"Then test me. How long does it take? Can we do it now?"

She wanted more than anything for Ellie to live, and she wanted to give Ellie the most precious thing she could. Her kidney. Of course!

"Test me now," she said again.

"Yes, *signora*. Because of the urgency, we can begin testing you right away, but it can't be completed in one day. Let me contact the department. Please wait."

Michael put his arm around her shoulders and steered her back into the hallway where they sat down to wait.

She held onto Michael's arm and couldn't stop holding on. She felt the love she had rejected flowing in and keeping her upright.

Grayish-green wisps of fear seemed to cloud the air as people rushed past. It was terrifying to feel these clouds from patients, family members, and medical staff. Saffron wished for the millionth time that she wasn't so sensitive to emotions.

She remembered Shelley's visit last night, followed by her father's. She suddenly felt dizzy, as if she were falling backward.

Michael took off his jacket, folded it up and put it behind her as a cushion. Saffron looked at him with surprise. He was sensitive too. How had she not known?

"I didn't know Ellie had only one kidney," Saffron said. "Why didn't Betsy ever tell me? Did Ellie even know?"

Saffron put her face in her hands, her long hair around her like a shawl. He leaned over, pulled aside her hair, and whispered, "You're full of love. That's your problem."

He reached his arm around and held her. Saffron let herself be hugged hard and then reached around him and hugged back. She could feel his ribs beneath her hand.

He breathed into her ear, "She's going to be fine. One step at a time. First see if you're a match. If not, they'll find someone."

"What if he doesn't? Maybe they just say that!"

She didn't want to let go, but after a few minutes, the pain of reaching around and next to the chair zinged a nerve in her arm and she pulled it back. He let go and smiled his wide, irresistible smile. Where before its eagerness annoyed her, now his kindness warmed her. He cared about Ellie almost as much as he cared about her. She was such an idiot. As usual, she had ruined everything.

Life was always on the edge of disappearing. First her mother, then Dad. Now maybe . . . She felt the weight of an accident that could suddenly change your life.

As if he could hear her thinking, Michael said, "Just take the test and see. You've got me. You'll be okay."

She let Michael's strength seep into her. "I can do that. One step at a time."

"We'll find out today. And then we can move forward, however it's going to go. We'll face it and she'll be fine. I feel it."

He had said 'we'. He said he 'felt it'. She wasn't alone. He was making that clear. When Nathan died, his death was distant. He had been distant to her for so long—really for most of her life. Crossing the geographical distance to come to Italy, she had pushed Nathan even further away, but the finality of never seeing him again rushed into her in a way she couldn't have predicted. Now the thought of never seeing Ellie again was as sharp as a blade.

"What would I do without you here?"

He inclined his head and she saw tears at the corner of his eyes. He said nothing.

She was ashamed of her meanness to him. "Don't leave me, Michael! Even if she does."

His eyes opened wide. He reached over and took her face in both his hands. She thought he might kiss her, but instead he simply said, "Never."

Slumping, cushioned by his jacket and the certainty of his presence, she leaned her head on his shoulder and closed her eyes. He let her rest.

She awoke to the sound of the doctor's voice. "Please come with me."

The clock read 4:35 a.m.

They rose and followed him down a different hallway to the laboratory. He gestured for Saffron to come inside.

"Can I come too?" Michael asked.

"No need. The first test is simple. Wait here," the doctor said, pointing to yet another row of chairs. "It won't take long."

He informed Saffron that the tests consisted of a blood test and an ultrasound, and that they would analyze it quickly. If she tested positively for blood type and antigens, they could proceed to the next step. She would know within the week whether or not she was a match.

"Go in there and check in at the reception desk," he told her. "They'll have my order for your tests."

"Doctor, I need another test. I need to see if my sister and I are really half-siblings."

The doctor stared at her as if he thought his English had failed him.

"Can you perform that test as well?"

"That isn't a test we can do here. Why don't you wait until you're finished with the series of tests to be her donor?"

Saffron thought about it. "Maybe I don't need that one." She thanked him and he left.

Michael turned to her. "What makes you think you're not half-sisters?"

"Something Shelley—oh, I don't know. If I'm a match, it doesn't matter anyway." She didn't add that if Ellie wasn't her real sister, donating a piece of her body would make them blood sisters.

She was summoned into the laboratory and came out an hour later. Michael was asleep. She touched his shoulder to wake him.

He sat up. "Well?"

"I'm on my way to being a match! We can go home. The doctor will call me tomorrow about scheduling the rest of the testing and surgery."

As they rode back to Lerici, he said, "Tell me why you asked for the sibling test."

"I'm not ready to talk about it."

"Who suggested to you that you might not be sisters?"

"Someone." She reconsidered. She needed to trust someone. "Okay, it was Shelley. Shelley suggested I find out."

He didn't reply. What could he say? He had never disparaged her Invisibles. Did he think this was just too weird? And there was the discovery, sinking into her, that the list of her biological siblings totaled zero. As far as she knew.

Saffron stared out at the dawn light coming over the hills to illuminate the sea. It had taken on a greenish-blue tint and shimmered as if translucent.

She shivered. What exactly had she agreed to, and where along the line had she said she was fine with giving her sister a piece of her body? And where had she signed up to possibly die from doing it?

The doctor had told her the DNA test couldn't be run now. Why pursue it? What mattered was whether she could save her sister's life. Whatever happened now, she was going to give Ellie her best.

Chapter 32

Drifting—Elinor

The drip and click of the machinery kept lulling her to sleep, but then a nurse would come in and wake her up. Elinor couldn't give in to sleep yet. She had to figure out how to persuade her stubborn sister to back out of this idea of giving her a kidney.

Elinor was sorry she'd gone that night—how long ago was it? Last night? Last week? She was sorry she'd planned to leave Saffron, upsetting her so much. Saffron wasn't strong the way she was. She shouldn't have to go through all this.

While she was having these thoughts, Tonio appeared at her side. She hadn't seen him come in. She smiled, sinking back into warm fuzziness.

Someone—a doctor?—had said she had to have a transplant. Her sister had volunteered to test as a match. Elinor couldn't let Saffron put herself at risk! But she needed to sleep again.

Waking up with a jolt, she knew something. She had to stop Saffron from giving her a kidney. It could kill her little sister. The doctors said the risk was low, but it was there.

Warm darkness. So good. Vague pain, letting it go.

Elinor never wanted anything from Saffron—and certainly not an organ.

When she had taken Saffron's poetry book and hidden it, she did it to protect her new sister from an obsession with their father. Elinor wanted her new sister to let go of the Shelley book given to her as a parting gift. She wanted to spare Saffron from the suffering of Nathan's abandonment. Of course, it hadn't worked. She could never manage to protect her sister well enough, and Saffron's feelings grew and overflowed.

Elinor couldn't accept this sacrifice from her sister. There had to be another organ donor out there. But if not, Saffron would be fine after Elinor died. Her energy and survival instincts were powerful. In Elinor's will, she'd left everything to her mother and Saffron. That would now include her share of the house. It would fix everything. Saffron could stay in their house, and maybe she'd get together with Michael.

Before she could reach the button to summon a nurse, sleep again pulled her under.

Chapter 33

Matched and Ready—Saffron

Three days later, Michael was making sandwiches for them at Casa Magni after another day spent at the hospital keeping vigil over Elinor.

Saffron sat cross-legged on the sofa, peering into her laptop while she was reading the scary but necessary article, "Preparing to donate a kidney."

Tonio had taken them to a transplant center in Genoa for the rest of the testing. It was kind of him, sparing a half day away from Elinor, to help them navigate the Italian healthcare system.

Yesterday they got the word—Saffron was not just a match, but a good match. Elinor was still hardly in any condition to be transported to Genoa, but when the time came, that's where the transplant had to be done.

Michael came out with two plates. His strength was as dependable as ever. Though he had been up for too many hours and had little sleep, he showed not a sign of fatigue. She knew she had bags under her eyes after four days of waiting to see Elinor during the brief minutes her sister was conscious.

She decided not to look in a mirror. She felt ten years older. She couldn't imagine how bad she looked, especially without a shampoo since last week.

"Wouldn't you rather have a nap instead of food?" Michael said.

She shook her head and he set the plates on the coffee table. He sat next to her and leaned his head back against the sofa back.

He was devoted, she had never realized just how much. Staying with her through all this was something she'd never imagined from anyone. Someone caring enough to stick with her through the bad times. Only Mom-Betsy and Ellie had ever done that, and now she was the only one who could take care of Ellie.

"Let me read this to you," she said. "This is a website explaining kidney transplants."

Michael was clearly exhausted, head leaning on the back cushion as he stared up at the ceiling, but he said, "Read to me," without a trace of annoyance.

He probably hadn't slept for over a day. Saffron put a hand out, finding his fingers and stroking them. He turned his head to look at her, smiling.

"I'm going to read," she said, "but feel free to fall asleep. This is maximum boring, but I have to learn about it."

She read to him as softly as she could about transplants and the center in Genoa, the number and type of transplants they performed each year, about transplant survival rates, recovery processes and timing, and then just as his eyes fluttered, she stopped.

"Michael, am I crazy to do this?"

"Of course you're not crazy. You want to," he said without opening his eyes.

"The doctor said there could be other donors."

"But you want to be the one." He was smiling.

"They're going to take good care of us." She hoped she sounded convincing.

He opened his eyes and looked at her. "You're really worried."

She realized how much she had come to rely on him. That meant she could confess her fear. "I've never had surgery."

He lifted his head. "Don't worry. I had a torn ligament once. You spend all the time beforehand being nervous. Then they put you out and you wake up. And it's all done. All the worry for nothing. Some pain, but they give you drugs. You're loopy-happy and then you go home."

"Really?"

"The worst part is imagining what you'll never even experience. I was out cold before they finished wheeling me into the surgical suite."

"Is there a lot of pain?"

"Depends," he said.

She appreciated his honesty. She could rely on that too. He said, "I doubt there will be much pain. They're good with medications. You will probably wake up singing a silly song at the top of your lungs."

She laughed. He put his head back down and closed his eyes. "Nothing to worry about," he mumbled.

He stretched his arm over the back of the sofa and she put her hand on his.

"Michael," she said, the words not yet coming.

His fingers caressed hers. "It's okay," he said, and fell asleep, his sandwich untouched. She bent to her computer, eating hers as she read through the hospital's website, and more sites devoted to kidney transplant surgery. Facts soothed her anxiety until she could close the lid, set the computer on the table, and put her feet up. Resting against the sofa back, she stared, doing something she could only call praying, and then she drifted off herself.

When she woke up, she took up the laptop again. The surgery she would undergo was called a nephrectomy and was listed as major surgery. Major. There was no long-term risk for the kidney donor, provided she was healthy. Was she? Saffron had never thought much about whether or not she was. She rarely went to a doctor, except for routine gynecological checkups. She had tested as healthy, and that was good. Elinor should have the healthiest kidney, to become her only functioning kidney. That meant she too would now live with only one. That was irreversible. You couldn't grow another.

The article she had been reading said your remaining kidney would enlarge after one was removed.

Michael was snoring. She would have liked to give him a bed upstairs so he could stretch out, but she hated to wake him. But then he stirred, made a noise somewhere between a hiccup and a gulp, and his eyes flew open.

"Are you okay?" he asked.

She smiled. "Yes. I slept. Why don't you go upstairs? You need real sleep."

"What time is it?"

"Two-thirty. Go upstairs and sleep more."

He nodded, lurched into a standing position, and staggered away. The man was beyond exhausted. He was doing all this for her.

Her own fatigue was at the stage that made her body

feel fizzy. Saffron lay on the couch, stretched out her legs, rolled on her side, and was gone.

Michael woke her. The sun was low over the ocean, apricot and gold clouds gathering. She looked at her phone. Six-fifteen.

She swung herself up and yawned. Michael still looked groggy, his clothes beyond wrinkled, but he was lively.

"I'll make some coffee." She got up.

"I'd kill for coffee." He winced. "Sorry, that wasn't the right way to put it."

She said, "I'd kill for some, too."

He followed her into the kitchen, saying, "We should get back soon." He got out the milk and steamed it.

"Yes. I hate that hospital. I hate that she works in them. It must be like working in hell."

Michael foamed the milk. "Here, let me do this. You're still groggy. Go back to the couch. I'll bring it."

She was inordinately grateful for this simple gesture. All his gestures were declarations of love. Why had she resisted him so long? She remembered being in bed with him all those weeks ago. He was tender and exciting, and she had been an idiot to him afterward.

"I hate hospitals too," he said gently from the kitchen, "but we have to be glad for them because this one pulled Ellie through. God, I feel like the cat's spit-up. Probably look it too." He checked his reflection in the chrome on the machine, noticing his sticking-up hair and the confusion of his eyebrows. "Yup."

Working the espresso machine expertly on two cups, he poured out the foamed milk and brought two mugs to the table.

"I did some research after you went to sleep," she said as he sat down. "After they take my kidney out and put it into Ellie, it will take us both sometime in the hospital and at home to recover."

Michael put his hand on her knee. "I'll take care of you both."

"But don't you have to go home at some point? To England, I mean."

"I can tell my parents I need to stay for two extraordinary women who need my help."

"You mean you'll tell them about Ellie and me?"

"You especially."

The glow in his eyes told her things, and the message found its way inside her heart, wide open and wrecked as it was. Michael was a life raft in this raging ocean. She wanted to grab him and hold on, but she held back. She felt the urge to express the love burning in her and she reached out and put her hand on his cheek, but didn't say it.

He put his hand over hers. "How long will it take you to recover?" he asked.

She was sorry he had changed the subject. "I don't know exactly, but on these websites it says it can take up to a few months. But I'm ridiculously healthy. It's another matter for Ellie. Of course, we had different mothers. Different genes."

She hadn't ever talked about Samantha to Michael. "She was wonderful, my mother. She must have been so unhappy with Nathan to do something like that. She was sweet, and he was so hard to be with. For everyone."

"It's good to know more about your background. It matters to me, you know."

"Yes. That's why I told you."

She drained her cup, looked at her phone, and said,

"I got a text. We have to go. A new doctor needs to meet with me. He's the transplant specialist."

The doctor met them in an office near the waiting area on the floor of Ellie's room. He was a large, slim man who seemed to be from Africa but educated in England, judging by his lilting accent and the lack of contractions in his British-sounding speech. His coat was white against his beautiful dark skin. His color calmed Saffron, reminding her of the Bay Area where people came in many different colors. Here in Italy people were almost all white.

Dr. Ikande told them about the "nephrectomy," the procedure to take Saffron's kidney out and place it in her sister's body. He phrased it like that, "place it in your sister's body."

His musical voice made up for his serious, expressionless doctor face. Because of a lilt in his accent, everything sounded simple. "There is slight long-term risk for you. You will finish a more complete medical examination to confirm that you are healthy, with no health problems that have arisen since your first exam."

Despite his lovely voice, Saffron listened, paralyzed as the surgeon detailed the risks.

"Kidney donation involves major surgery, and the risks include uncontrolled bleeding and infection. The risk is small, but it is there."

"Uncontrolled bleeding? Is it likely or unlikely?" Saffron asked, confused.

"Yes. It is unlikely that you would suffer death by internal bleeding."

Like a fanged cobra, a new fear rose up in Saffron. Suffer actual death. She just couldn't.

After your kidney is removed, you will spend about eight to twelve weeks recovering, but only a few days in the hospital, and then you may recuperate at home. Do you have a home here?'

"Yes, we do. In Lerici."

The doctor didn't exactly smile, but he looked pleasant. "Do you have any questions?"

Her kidney—removed!

"Why will my recovery be so long?"

"It takes time for your remaining kidney to enlarge as it takes on additional blood flow and filtration of wastes."

"Oh. And how long does the surgery itself take?"

"I will perform the operation through a series of small incisions in your abdomen. It will take four or five hours, longer because it's laparoscopic, but that shortens your recovery time."

She felt nauseated. Michael took her hand and squeezed it. It didn't help much.

"Your long-term survival rate, quality of life, general health and risk of kidney failure are about the same as for people who aren't kidney donors. You'll need regular checkups and monitoring of your kidney function and blood pressure."

They left and Michael asked if she wanted to see Elinor, but she shook her head.

"Home. Sleep."

As they drove back, Saffron was half-asleep, her head leaning on the open window. The dream, unspooling from her hair as it riffled in the breeze, was of the poet, his sad eyes and curly hair also moving in the air.

"Does Shelley go on telling strange Stories of the Death of Kings?" Keats had written. "Tell him there are strange stories of the death of poets."

How absurd! Keats' death was so mundane, whereas mine had the distinction of being frightful.

Shelley said it with contempt, as he hovered outside the moving car.

Saffron's hair fluttered her reply. *I don't want to think about death. It's negative thinking and won't help Ellie. I reject your death. Besides, here you are.*

We always give our best, he murmured. She opened her eyes and saw only the Italian landscape streaming by.

Chapter 34

Waiting for Surgery—Elinor

Stuck in this hospital bed. Immobile with fatigue that weighed down every limb, down to her toes. Elinor didn't know what to do. She wanted to prevent Saffron from taking a big risk, but she was helpless. She squirmed, reaching for the call button, but she couldn't remember what she wanted to say. Something about her will?

An instinct to care for Saffron pounded in every pulse beat as she lay there. The doctor had said the donor's risks were low. He had said she urgently needed a transplant. He said she couldn't wait too long. And Saffron wouldn't listen to her about the risk. Her little sister seemed to have developed her own sense of protectiveness and was now determined to take care of her.

But there had to be another way. She should ask the doctor.

As she was again reaching for the button, Saffron and Michael came in. They looked like they had slept at the bottom of a laundry hamper.

Elinor stretched out a hand and Saffron rushed over

to take it. Michael got a chair and pushed it under her. Elinor squeezed her sister's hand as hard as she could, which wasn't very hard.

"Don't talk, dearest," Saffron said. "You need to keep your energy and get well." Saffron grinned. "It's miraculous. I'm going to give you a piece of me! It's way better than being blood sisters." She reached to gently hug Elinor.

"You're miraculous," Elinor said.

"We're the miraculous Greene sisters." Saffron's tears spilled.

Michael put a hand on Elinor's shoulder and she smiled up at him. "Take care of her after."

"You have my word," he said.

Saffron turned to Michael and said, "Would you give us a few minutes?"

"Sure," he said and left.

Elinor managed a smile. "Okay, so why did you get rid of him?"

"I have to confess something. But I know you worry."

"I'll always worry about you."

Elinor licked her dry lips. Saffron reached for the water glass, handed it to Ellie, and guided the straw into her mouth. She sucked down a few sips.

Saffron said, "I don't want you worrying. So I have to tell you."

Elinor rolled her eyes. "Are you looking for a drumroll? Because I left my drum in Berkeley."

"Cute. Okay, you know my Shelley visits? I know you worry about my mental balance."

"Yes, sometimes."

"I figured out who Shelley is. He's a—what? An animated symbol of something for me."

"He's dead. But he's real for you. Go on."

"He's—he compared himself to a guardian angel. Does your subconscious give you those? And before you say I'm too old for a guardian angel, think about how often I've needed one."

"Yes. I know."

"Well, sometimes Shelley is also . . . the last time I saw him, he told me a lot of the things you'd tell me."

Elinor watched her sister carefully. "Such as?"

"The whole long list of how I've been an awful sister."

"Long list?"

"I'm sorry, Ellie. I'm so, so sorry." Saffron bent her head to their clasped hands and began to cry.

Elinor shook her hand and said, "No, you're a great sister. Let's get back to Shelley. What else?"

She was running out of energy, but she had to say it. "We'll find him. Our brother."

Saffron bent her head again and sobbed.

Elinor knew her sister's heart was helpless to resist the idea of a new sibling joining their family. She wanted to say more, but she was so tired. She faded out and then came back as Michael appeared at the door.

Elinor squeezed her sister's hand. Saffron looked so vulnerable, just as she had when she was eleven or twelve, a bright, sensitive girl who cried quickly and smiled even quicker.

"I just want to help you get well," Saffron said.

Elinor felt her strength going. "Have to sleep now."

Chapter 35

Mom-Betsy Arrives—Saffron

Two days later, Betsy Greene arrived at the Pisa International Airport. Saffron and Michael met her at the baggage claim area. Saffron was happy to see her mother emerge, and at the sight of Mom-Betsy's smile, Saffron waved energetically. Mom-Betsy rushed to them in a fluster of tapestry bags, mismatched suitcases, with a hat and sweater-coat over her arm.

"Darling!" she cried as she tried to run.

Her long gray hair was braided into a thick tail, and as always fastened with a colorful variety of hair clips and bands, no colors of which matched her dangling silver and turquoise earrings.

Michael shook her hand, which surprised Betsy, Saffron could tell. He then went over to the luggage carousel and soon swung her last suitcase off and onto a cart. Saffron took her stepmother's coat and hat. Unencumbered, Betsy hugged Saffron so hard Saffron couldn't get a breath. She pulled back, laughing.

"Mom, I'm so happy you're here. Elinor's friend Tonio

is with her in the hospital. We can go straight there, or stop at the cottage, whichever you'd like."

She had seen Mom-Betsy only a few months ago, but her mother looked older, with more curly gray hairs popping forward around her face like wiry renegades.

"Straight to the hospital, please."

"But you've had a long flight."

"You're fussing, dear. Like Elinor. Have you switched places?" Betsy was smiling.

"Mom, this is Michael Shelley. He's my . . . good friend who's helping with everything."

"Pleased to meet you, Mrs. Greene," Michael said, offering his hand.

Betsy took him into a hug. "Don't stand on ceremony, dear. Call me Betsy. I'm grateful you've been helping my girls. Especially this one."

Saffron warmed under a cozy blanket of motherly care. Where Elinor sparred with their mother, Betsy and Saffron always melted together.

Michael wheeled the bags out to the sidewalk and asked them to wait while he brought the car around to the curb.

After he left, her mother said, "You picked a handsome one to get rescued by!"

"Yes."

"What's the problem?"

"He's too good for me."

"That always did ruin it for you." Taking Saffron's hands, she held her away, scrutinizing the way she used to while getting the girls ready for school. Betsy would take off an ornament Saffron had added, not knowing that Saffron was trying out jewelry paired with new names.

Betsy now studied Saffron's black pants, off-white sweatshirt, and simple silver hoop earrings. She nodded.

"You've finally learned to dress yourself without going over the top!" she exclaimed.

"The struggle is real," Saffron said, noticing there wasn't a limb of Betsy's that hadn't received a whimsical accessory—an African recycled electronics bracelet, dangling silver and turquoise earrings, a lavender crocheted scarf, and a macramé belt tied around her hips.

"We must get to your sister," Betsy said, dropping Saffron's hands and turning toward the curb just as Michael pulled up. He got out, shoveled the bags in the back seat with Saffron and opened the front passenger door for Betsy.

"You'll do fine," she said, smiling flirtatiously.

Michael laughed. "I'm glad to know that!"

At the hospital, Michael took Betsy's arm and steered her to Elinor's room.

He stopped outside, at the hand sanitizer dispensers. "Take a big breath and let it out," he advised Betsy.

Saffron was so grateful that in this short time he had become good at reading Betsy. She could see that her mother was terrified and not letting on. She never let on about her feelings, until they came pouring out in a deluge.

Betsy walked in, immediately rushing to her thin, yellow, and only half-awake daughter.

"Oh, my darling girl!" Betsy rushed to grab Elinor's hand with both of hers.

Saffron could tell that Betsy's alarm bells were ringing, even though she had them on mute.

"Mom," Elinor said.

Betsy knelt on the floor, pressing her forehead to their hands. She gave a quick, dry sob. Michael brought over the one chair in the room and gently lifted Betsy into it.

"Sweetie, I'm so glad I got here before—" Betsy checked herself.

"I'm fine, Mom," Elinor said, sounding so weak no one would have bought it.

"Tell me the truth!" she said to Elinor. "Never mind, don't talk. Saffron and Michael told me everything."

"Did you have a good flight?" Ellie was making an effort.

"Sure, okay, yes I did. I'll talk, you rest." Betsy patted Elinor's hand and kept patting gently as she continued. "It was a long flight in economy. I'm going to upgrade to business when I go home. But I'm not going back anytime soon." She looked up at Saffron meaningfully. "I'm going to see you girls through all this. I know there are surgeries. I came to help, and to be sure you're getting the best care."

Michael had quietly found another chair and brought it in. He offered it to her, and Saffron sat in the opposite corner. Betsy was in a state of fatigue and distress. She looked at Mom-Betsy, and their gazes held. She felt her mother wanting to take over, and that made her feel judged as incapable of handling Elinor's care. No matter what she did, she would always seem to her family to be the flighty, unstable daughter. But what Betsy didn't know was the strength Michael brought to the situation, and the experience and contacts Tonio had.

At that moment, Tonio came in. "Mrs. Greene?" he said, offering his hand. "Don't get up. I'm pleased you have come."

Betsy did rise, though, and took Tonio's hand. "I understand you've been helping my girls. I'm so grateful!"

She was glad Mom-Betsy had met Tonio and Michael. They all needed to be together now.

"I've spoken to her doctors," he said softly. "They

want to do the surgery in a week, if possible. Sooner is better, to give Elinor the best chance of full recovery."

He took a long look at Betsy. "How was your travel from California?"

Betsy shrugged, "I'm not a fan of planes, but I have to be here." She looked more closely at him, and from her smile, Saffron could see she liked what she saw. "Do you live here?"

"Yes, and I've worked in hospitals here. So I can help, if you'd like."

Saffron intervened. "Tonio knows we'd like his help."

Betsy turned to her daughter. "Why is she sleeping?"

"She sleeps most of the time," Saffron said. The doctor said pain medication can do that."

"She's so pale." Betsy leaned over for a closer look. She stroked Elinor's cheek and let her hand linger on it.

The doctor came in and Saffron introduced her mother.

Betsy rose again, reaching out for the doctor's hand. He didn't shake. In one hand he was holding a pen and the other one a clipboard.

When he shrugged, Betsy came right to the point, "I want you to give her mine."

Saffron, Michael, Elinor, and the doctor all looked startled.

"Your what, Mrs. Greene?" the doctor said.

"My kidneys. Both of them."

The doctor said, "You know, you can't . . ."

"I want my daughters to have the best chances, so take my kidneys. I'm consenting."

The doctor raised his eyebrows and silently appealed to Saffron with a shocked gaze.

"Mom, you can't do that," Saffron said. "It would kill

you and that's against medical ethics. Besides, she only needs one, and I'm a match."

Betsy was irritated. "She's my daughter. I'll be the best one to give her a kidney."

Elinor, weak as she was, opened her eyes and said, "Mom, listen to the doctor." She closed her eyes and took another nap.

The doctor filled in. "Mrs. Greene, I understand your desire to protect your daughters, and you can be tested, of course, but you may not be a match..."

"Nonsense! I'm her mother."

"Not all relatives will match," the doctor said patiently, now scribbling on his clipboard.

"You have to match me. I'm not letting either of my daughters be in danger."

The doctor looked confused. He began backing out. "We'll test you. I'll be back later."

"Fine. Go and save other patients," Betsy said.

"Mom," Saffron said, "I'm going to be her donor. It's done. Accept it." She relished the surprised smile on her mother's face.

Saffron looked up at Michael, who shook his head and smiled.

At that moment, Elinor woke up. "Mom, why don't you go to Lerici and rest and eat? Saffron and Michael can take you."

Saffron smiled. It was a good sign that her sister was again trying to take care of everyone.

* * *

Michael dropped them off and went home to change clothes. Saffron was learning that he could be sensitive to people's feelings. How had she missed that before? Maybe her own feelings had blinded her.

Betsy dropped her purse and shoulder bag, shrugging off her coat, and went straight through to the living room. She pushed open the patio door and stepped outside.

Saffron went outside with her.

Her mother said, "That view! I can see why you want to keep it."

Saffron hugged her. "Isn't it wonderful? But Ellie says we can't afford to keep it."

Betsy shook her head. "Let me talk to her."

Just like the old days.

They went back inside and sat side by side on the couch. Saffron made them cappuccinos.

They drank in silence until Mom-Betsy turned to look at her. "You don't look good, sweetie. But I can see that Italy agrees with you."

Saffron smiled. Mom-Betsy could always tell what was going on with her.

"I'm scared, Mom." She hadn't realized how much she had missed her mother's intuitive way, a quality of sensing people's feelings that they shared.

Mom-Betsy said, "Someone here agrees with you too. Is it Michael? He's great. Too eager, but I like that in men. It makes them behave."

Saffron laughed. Her mother always cheered her up. She thought of the impossible challenge her father must have been as a husband.

Though she and Mom-Betsy weren't biological mother and daughter, they looked so similar, even to their curly brown hair and green eyes. People always had commented on how much Saffron looked like Betsy.

Comforted by her mother's presence, Saffron said, "Why didn't you ever tell me how much you hated Dad?"

"Hate Nathan? I'd never say that to you! You're his daughter. Besides, how can you hate a hurricane or a geyser? He was a force of nature."

"Dad must have hated me, to leave me that way."

"You should never think that. He loved you. He knew he was no good as a single parent. He wasn't much good when we were raising Elinor. We agreed it was a good choice."

"What kind of person gives up their daughter?"

Her mother's smile lit up. "You inherited a lot of his spirit, darling. He just couldn't be tamed, and neither should you be. You need to be with someone who understands that."

Saffron started to say she couldn't find anyone like that, but then she thought of Michael.

"When you first arrived at our house," Betsy said. "Nathan said you were still in shock. He told me you were handling it, but I didn't know what he meant until you told me about your Invisibles. I understand why you can't talk to your sister about this.

"Mom, she's so literal. It's hard to talk to her about anything except money."

Betsy shook her head, heavy turquoise and silver earrings making a tiny music. "I know. We have to do something to help her. But most of all, honey, I want you to know I'm so proud of you."

"Proud?"

"Offering her your kidney. But I won't let you. It's too much of a risk!"

"Mom, don't start," Saffron said, but a quiver of fear ran up her spine. "Why didn't you tell me Ellie only had one kidney?"

Her mother became defensive. "Why would I tell you such a thing? It's medical. Medical things are meant to be private."

"Dad left it in his will that we were to find out his secrets. There's a manuscript, and there's ..." Saffron stopped, looking at her mother. Baby Boy. What would it do to Mom to tell her?

"Are you sure this is the best time to go treasure hunting?"

Saffron was sarcastic. "What time is ever the best in our family?"

"Oh, Saffron."

"You don't know how hard it's been, being here with Ellie. She's always controlling everything. Like always. And the worst is, she won't let herself enjoy life, even in this beautiful place. All she does is work."

"Elinor is who she is. You two have never understood each other. Oil and water, I guess. You must make peace."

"How exactly?"

Betsy shook her head, lips compressed at Saffron's sarcasm.

Saffron was immediately sorry. Her mom had come all this way. She smiled.

Betsy held out her arms, and Saffron fell into them. She again confessed, "I'm so scared! What if she—what if I..."

"I won't let either of you die," Betsy said firmly, stroking Saffron's hair.

"Mom, I've never done anything ..." Saffron trailed off, thinking she couldn't say "life-threatening" because her mother had to be brave, too. She had to accept that Saffron was the one to donate the kidney.

"I'm here, honey. You both need me."

Saffron stood up and held out her hand. "Come on. We need to get you settled."

While her mother complained of creaking joints and long flights, Saffron led her to the chaos room.

Betsy put down her bags and looked around. "Feels homey. What an elegant clock! Not like your father's taste, though."

"And keeps losing time."

"I think you have to wind it every week," her mother said, going back to the living room and returning with her sweaters. "Is there anywhere I can hang things?"

"You'll have to . . ."

Saffron realized Elinor wouldn't be in her room again for a long time. She grabbed her mother's bags and threw one of her sweaters over her shoulder. "Come upstairs. You can have Ellie's room."

Betsy followed her into the room, carrying her large purse and dropping it on the chair. Saffron put everything else on the bed.

Betsy went to the dresser, where Elinor had arranged small ceramic Christmas figurines Tonio had bought for them on Christmas Eve. "You girls always did love Christmas," she said.

"Tonio bought them. Elinor's special friend. He came to Thanksgiving dinner, and Christmas Eve. He and Michael took Ellie out dancing on New Year's . . ." Saffron stopped and swallowed a sob.

Tears rolled out of the corners of her mother's eyes. "I'm glad you girls had holidays together."

"Let's unpack you, Mom. Do you want to lie down?"

More of Elinor was seeping into Saffron. Someone had to be practical, and it clearly wasn't going to be her mother. It felt strangely good to be taking control.

"No, I napped on the plane. Now tell me more about Tonio," Betsy said, sitting on the bed. "Does Elinor like him?"

While she unpacked and put away her mother's things, she said, "Yes. Ellie met Tonio in our grocery store. He took us on a day trip to Portofino, and then he showed us a Ligurian Christmas festival. He's a friend. I don't know if Ellie thinks of him as more than a friend, but I think she will."

Betsy smiled and patted her hand.

"Mom, you should have a rest."

Saffron left her mother lying down. She called Michael, asking him to take them back to the hospital in an hour.

They came into Elinor's room. She was still asleep, with Tonio sitting beside her. He stood and greeted Betsy in his courteous English, with a gallantly European nod of the head. Betsy smiled and put both her hands around his. Then she hugged him.

Tonio offered her the chair and she sat.

He said, "Even though she's asleep, I've stayed nearby, to be sure her care is consistent. And to give you time to rest."

Betsy smiled and thanked him. Saffron could see she was offering her best smile. She liked him.

"I don't know if I can bear having two daughters undergoing surgery," Betsy said. She hugged Saffron. "You are a good sister, sweetie."

The word rang in her mind. Saffron knew that she wasn't. She never had been *good*. But apparently, they both thought she was.

Tonio said, "Let me be of help. I know everyone in the transplant center. I can ensure that communications go well."

Saffron reached around Tonio's tall frame for a hug.

He was startled but pleased. "I cherish your sister."

Saffron saw the truth that Elinor couldn't. It was courtly, friendly manners that seemed at a slight distance, but Tonio was in love.

He volunteered to stay with Elinor, and Betsy wanted to stay too.

"Go home and rest, honey," her mother said.

Michael drove her back. As soon as they went inside, she plopped onto the couch and he sat next to her. Saffron slipped off her shoes to lean her feet on the table's edge and recline into the soft pillows. Her head was swimming with fatigue and shock.

As if he knew what she was thinking, he took her hand. "You know, it's a routine surgery, donating a kidney. Entirely routine. Done all the time, everywhere. You'll be fine."

She didn't want to talk about the transplant. "All my life, everywhere I turned, I'd see things I'm afraid of. But I've never been more afraid than now."

The squeeze of his hand was nice.

"Afraid your sister won't make it?"

"And afraid I won't. I've never had surgery. Do you think I'm awful?"

He wasn't shocked. "Of course not. You have more courage than you realize."

"I don't. I'm afraid."

Michael sat up and looked at her. "What do you usually do when you're afraid?"

She was honest. "Usually I go away. I escape. I don't look back."

Michael sat back, absorbing this. It obviously wasn't what he wanted to hear. "Even if you aren't her donor, you have to stay. You have to see Elinor through this."

"Of course I do." But as she said it, Saffron wondered what would happen if she died. What would it be in *The Room Over There*? To be an Invisible like Shelley, who didn't seem able to go forward, who had been stuck for more than a century. Why would you get so stuck? And did dying hurt? She ought to ask him.

Michael took her hand again. She smiled as he squeezed it and then gave her arm a light caress, but one that flared her senses into heat. Or was it the warmth in the house? It seemed unusually warm. She had a fleeting memory of their afternoon in bed, but she let it dissolve into anxiety.

"You don't know what a screw-up my family thinks I am," she said, her voice dropping into a monotone.

"Mine thinks the same of me. Adult children in their twenties are always considered by their parents to be demented."

He was being funny, and she laughed. They lay back on the couch side by side, not talking, for a few more minutes.

"You don't know what it's like to be this afraid," she whispered.

He turned his head without raising it and watched her for a moment before answering. "Don't let your fear scare you."

She wheezed in exasperation. "That proves you really don't."

"No, I mean it. Don't let it shake you. You can go right past it. I know you can."

All at once, Saffron needed to sleep. "I have to go to bed. Now."

He was comforting. "You need to rest. I'll come and get you in the afternoon to go back to the hospital."

He was so good, always being there for her. After he left, she climbed the stairs wondering why being good had made him less attractive. She didn't feel that way anymore. She couldn't even remember it.

As she got on her bed a whisper of memory echoed, *One of you won't be here in the new year.*

Chapter 36

A Festival in Viareggio—Saffron

Saffron startled awake. Had she slept too long?

Early morning light slanted across her bedroom wall. She stretched and sat up. Taking off her tee shirt and jeans, she went downstairs, wondering if Mom-Betsy had already gone back to the hospital. When she reached the foot of the stairs, she saw that the tapestry handbag wasn't next to the door. She was alone for the first time in three days.

She stretched her arms over her head, and then she went to the front door and opened it. A freakishly warm January breeze blew in. It was going to be beautiful. Checking the weather on her phone, she saw that the northern Italian coast was having a heatwave. As unpredictable as the Bay Area's climate.

Suddenly it all came back to her, the upcoming surgeries—the possibility she'd die while donating her kidney. Dread came over her like ice in the hot air. She faced what now seemed a certainty that she would die. One of them might, Shelley had said. It was going to be the cost of sisterhood, and she was expected to pay it.

Lying on the chaise, she looked up as if the sky had answers, or at least consolation. So pretty a sky, a light breeze cooling the warm sunlight. She was getting tired of being here or in the hospital, day after day. Especially the hospital. She was so ready for something different, for a break. What could she do this morning? She was due back at the hospital this afternoon.

It was adventure weather. If she had more time, she could have gone to the train station, hopped on a train, and ridden until she felt like getting off. She could see something new in Italy. She'd never get enough of this beautiful, happy place. But surgery in two days didn't allow for spontaneity. She had to avoid being exposed to germs. No crowds, no travel. Rest.

But the light was beaming on her face, relaxing her will to do the things she was supposed to do. Soon she'd be cooped up in the hospital, hopefully getting over surgery. Or else she'd be dead, in *The Room Over There*, having not survived. Was there a next life to look forward to, or would she be endlessly waiting, the way she'd waited in the hospital waiting rooms, anxious, uncertain, out of control of her own life?

They didn't need her today. Mom was there with Ellie. Maybe she could skip one day. Before she went to sleep last night, Michael had said he'd come back and take her to the hospital. But he could go, or he could take a day off too. He must be tired.

She sat up. The sea now seemed bleached, its sparkling aqua paler than ever, like a fantastic world beyond this one. She realized she could go anywhere she wanted today. No one would know. The sense of adventure ruffled up her spine and widened her eyes.

Everything looked so beautiful. A rare day. A single

cloud hovered in the pale blue, a thin streak of white. A lust for adventure zinged through her. Just one more exploration. It couldn't hurt to walk down to Lerici for a lingering hour in the café. Especially if there weren't many people. Few germs.

But no, she'd be good. She'd get up and wash and dress. She'd call Michael to come and take her to the hospital, where she'd meet with the surgeon and hear more about her preparations. As soon as she finished another cup of coffee, she'd do it. One more cup. Saffron made more coffee and extra foamy milk. It felt amazing, being the good one in the family.

With a quick shiver, Saffron knew she needed to be excused from being good, if only for this one day.

Two birds called back and forth across the hillside. They swooped across the ocean view like flying ribbons. The landscape was untying tiny bows of leaves from branches. A perfect day.

Always try to give your best.

Saffron remembered her last summer, spent mostly at Point Reyes Station, with dazzling afternoons on Limantour Beach, walking along the cliffs and watching the seabirds swoop down from their high nests, giving her a feeling of being one of them, a creature of nature living in nature, perfectly independent.

She grabbed her backpack and ran upstairs with it. Stuffing in a pair of slacks, a blouse, a light sweater, and underwear, she told herself it was just for a day and maybe a night. Wherever she went. Two days—was that day after tomorrow, or the day after that? She should call and find out. She grabbed the tee shirt—didn't smell too bad—skipped the shower—hot today anyway—and put on a fresh pair of jeans.

At the railway station, she got out of the taxi and soon found herself on a train. The conductor announced they were going south. Small stucco buildings flipped past like postcards from Arizona, stark white or beige against a beige landscape dotted with Mediterranean shrubbery and a cypress here and there.

Saffron relaxed into the plush seat. Feeling its deep, faded rose-colored pile between her fingers, she rubbed back and forth to raise a soothing softness on her skin. *Going somewhere, something happening.* This would change everything, but it wasn't her fault, and it was all her fault. The wheels hummed with a rhythm like a galloping pony under her. *Keep moving, keep speeding away.* Where? *Figure it out later.*

She had stared out the window for a half hour, she realized. The train turned inland and then headed south again through rolling fields. The sky was white. The strange January heat that had come over Lerici was following her inland. Boringly similar white or tan buildings streamed by, as if poured out of a single vat of concrete. She thought of writing her apology letter to Ellie, but she couldn't find words to begin. Her phone rang many times, calls from Michael and Betsy. She turned off the ringer.

There must be food on this strain. She stopped a porter and asked. He shook his head. She said, *Dove?* and made the gesture of eating. He nodded and pointed, saying "Dining car."

She made her way down the shimmying train until she found vending machines. Good enough, she thought, for someone like me. I don't deserve to eat. She bought herself a tuna fish sandwich, a Danish roll-looking thing, and a Coke, then sat at one of the tables and made her way through a soggy sandwich and limp sweet roll. Feeling sorry for herself, she sipped the soda.

"Do you mind if I join you?"

The voice made her jump. A dark-haired man who must be a little older than she was slid into the seat across from her. He wasn't Italian, judging from his accent. Danish?

"Are you going to Viareggio?" he asked, unwrapping his own sandwich.

"What's in Viareggio?"

He smiled, friendly without leering. "The famous *Carnevale* of course! Most famous in Europe."

"Today?"

"Beginning today. You mustn't miss it. It's worth a stop."

Though he had a pronounced accent, his English was fluid. His open face and smile made her feel she could trust him. He wasn't offering to take her, simply recommending a stop.

"Why?" she asked. "Are you going?"

"No, sadly. I have a business appointment in Rome tomorrow. But this train goes right by Viareggio. You must see the spectacle, at least for a few hours."

Perfect. She could see it for just a few hours and then go back. If she could manage to return. After the Christmas events, she knew Italy had great pageants.

"Each year the Viareggio *Carnevale* attracts more than half a million people over the month. They have masked parades, huge papier-mâché floats that make political statements. It's like nothing you've ever seen."

"Wow. I'll do it. I'll go."

"I've been many times," he said, offering his hand across the table. "My name is Finn. I work for a Danish travel agency's Rome office."

"I'm Saffron," she said, taking his hand.

"When you go, don't get swallowed up in the crowd. Be careful. So many people!"

His kindness reminded her of Michael, but that wasn't a good association. "Thanks, Finn. I would have liked your showing me the parade."

He looked at his phone and said, "You know what? I'm going to get off with you! I can spare one hour, and there's another train for Rome later. I'm going to make sure you at least get to where the parade is."

She thought of Elinor lying in her hospital bed, but it was just one day. Saffron said, "Great!"

They sat together until the conductor announced Viareggio.

As she gathered her bag, she looked quickly at her phone's missed calls and a few frantic texts from Michael. She chose not to read or listen.

They walked into town from the station.

Finn said, "We will take the *Passagiata*."

Saffron saw a wide promenade that hugged the curving, sandy beach. The coast stretched all the way up until it shimmered into the distance, overlooked by cliffs. It was filled with crowds. The swarm slowly passed them by, with fantastical floats and enormous balloons riding along. A float passed by, a leering, clown cartoon image of the U.S. president. The Italian sense of humor combined with outrage. The loud music and boisterous chatter were deafening.

"Today, you're very lucky!" he shouted. "It's the grand parade."

A mob of costumed people followed the float, families, actors, and spectators dancing along to the slowly progressing float.

Finn looked pleased. "This is the soul of Tuscany."

After it passed, Finn said, "I have to catch the next train." And he dashed away into the crowd.

Suddenly she was surrounded by people running fast, jostling her. Alone and excited, she felt a delicious sensation of danger, a feeling that always oddly soothed her. Another rock band started up, raucous and harsh. It was getting closer. The crowd thickened and then parted to the sides of the street as a giant float came toward her, an Italian clown with a gaping mouth. Dancing on its tongue were two more clowns, male and female.

Above, on the clown's hat, another clown waved the Italian flag. A stream of shiny metallic stars bobbed above the flags. She was in the middle of a parade of enormous, leering balloon clowns floating overhead. People in masks and costumes streamed past her like bad dreams, cheering as they danced forward.

This is true Italian spirit. Who whispered in her ear?

Her hand was brushed, as if by another hand. But no one was near.

"Are you Shelley?" she asked the air.

The crowd was dancing wildly, merging into the parade, becoming part of the theater of allegory. A man thrust a paper cup of wine into her hand. Surprised, she looked up at him. He wore a half-white, half-black mask. What she had thought was Shelley's touch on her hand was this man, who had grabbed her hand from behind to give her the cup.

He swirled away into the throng.

She took a sip and then finished it, and she felt the wine's effect almost immediately. Her head felt light and the atmosphere grew bright, almost effervescent, as if its molecules had enlarged. Panicking, Saffron stepped away into the standing crowds alongside the parade.

Her phone rang. It was the hospital. Cupping a hand over her other ear, she could barely hear as a male nurse came on the line.

He said he was extremely sorry to have to tell her, but Elinor had just died. She hadn't been strong enough for the transplant, and her heart had stopped. His voice was neutral, heavily accented but fluent in English.

Saffron asked him to repeat what he had said.

"I am very sorry, but *Signorina* Greene has passed away. Your relatives are here waiting for you."

Saffron's heart gave a knife clutch and her knees gave way. She sank onto the pavement, but quickly pulled herself up. It was dangerous to fall under a moving crowd. She had to get back.

How had it happened so fast? And she wasn't there. They were all right about her. She was a waste of space, always the ruin of her family.

Saffron had lost her chance to have a sister again. Instead, she had done what she always did—run away from the fear of surgery. She was going to be haunted for the rest of her life by this stupid choice. And not by an Invisible. She doubted Ellie would come to her now. She'd never give Saffron a chance to say, "I'm sorry. I love you."

Standing under the eaves of a shop, she watched as hordes of costumed revelers streamed by, making her feel even more faint and miserable. What was worse, as they passed, they twisted and warped, not quite solid, like Invisibles going crazy. The suspended floats swelled and rose higher in the air. It came to her. She was hallucinating.

There was no phone in her hand now. Had she taken a call? What was in that wine?

Saffron felt in her pocket and couldn't find the phone. Frantic, she zipped open the bag, found the phone at the bottom, and remembered she had zipped it into an internal compartment for safekeeping. All that stuff on top of it meant that she hadn't taken it out. There had been no phone call.

Slowly she came to feel her feet on the ground and the tingle as she pinched her fingers together.

Walking away, she dodged through the crowd, hoping to get somewhere quiet so she could call Michael. The call from the hospital might have been a hallucination, but what if it were a premonition? What if Ellie really was dying and she'd never see her sister again?

This had been just a mistake, the idea of spending the day away. It wasn't just a day, it was the entire risk of not being able to be there for Ellie, who had always cared for her. This was her chance to be a real sister when she was needed.

She had to get out of here.

The moment she had that clear thought, Shelley was in front of her, dressed in his nineteenth century clothes. Or was this another hallucination, just one of the costumed revelers? She shook her head but still she saw him, his pale face slightly transparent.

"I haven't seen you for weeks!" she shouted. "Where were you?"

And where were you? Where should you be?

Shelley was accusing her, as she stood there, hair wild and thoughts fuzzy. She was a maker of huge mistakes. Shelley's gaze swept her up and down. But instead of judgmental, he looked sympathetic. He knew she loved Elinor more than anything.

"You said one of us must die. It's me, isn't it?"

Shelley continued to look at her silently and sadly, with that sympathy that now chilled her.

"I knew it," she said. "But can't you tell me where I'm going when I die? After all, you're my guardian ghost. You're not like the others. You're supposed to help me."

How can I know the place I haven't yet seen?

She was relieved he was finally talking, but his image thinned and wavered. He was leaving. Why just now? Why wouldn't anyone ever tell her where they were going—where she was going?

Saffron suddenly thought of that first night in Ellie's home, in her bedroom. How she had sobbed, more alone than she thought anyone could ever be, until a touch on her shoulder roused her and the offer of a doll to cradle changed her. The loss of her mother, the gain of a sister. How quick life was to rearrange you. How quick was death.

Her head cleared. The din of the crowd became a hum rather than a cacophony. She was ready. She'd make this change of life that was coming to her, if only she could save her sister's life by doing it.

Shelley was holding something out to her.

We always give our best. Even if it's a kidney.

There had been no phone call from the hospital. There was still time to go back, to change, to be a different person.

She turned around, trying to figure out which way to go. Music and shouting voices poured over her in rhythmic waves. The papier-mâché floats receded.

What had she been thinking, being in a sea of people, exposed to all their microbes? If she caught something, she couldn't go through with the transplant. What had she touched, and what had she drunk? Her tongue was furry. Was that a symptom?

She stopped a man and asked for directions to the railway station, but she couldn't think of a word of Italian. He didn't understand, so he shrugged and rushed away. Maybe she could find a map of Viareggio on her phone, but she couldn't get network. So she turned and ran in what might be the right direction. She had to do something.

Revelers streamed around her in both directions, pinning her into the crowd. Knowing what she had to do with a burning clarity, she was trapped and helpless. Saffron tried to gain momentum, dodging and pushing people, sweat flying from her face. Tears too.

Saffron ran along the beach promenade, every breath burning until she was gasping. Where was it? She was sure she had come from this direction. She tried to remember getting off the train and heading to the festival, coming to the promenade and seeing the majestic floats and being danced into a crowd of masked revelers. She remembered having walked for at least ten minutes from the station.

The intense smell of chocolate nearly stopped her as she passed the artisan chocolate festival shop, with its exhibition of handmade chocolates. The temptation assaulted her nose and her stomach grumbled in sympathy, but she made a quick left turn and found her way out of the parade and spectators to a side street that paralleled the beach promenade.

As she got away from the hubbub, she found her way through the streets to the station. She went inside and asked about schedules. A train was leaving for Lerici in twenty minutes. It would take two and half hours to get there. Then she'd have to get to the hospital.

The moment her foot hit the first step of the train, a bolt of shame sent tears running down her face. She found a seat where she could avoid being seen, turned to the window, and pressed her hot, wet cheek against the glass. She had come so close to blowing—blowing everything. Her life. Her sister's. But it was okay, she'd soon be back.

As soon as the train neared the station in Lerici, she called Michael.

"Saffron?" he said. "Where are you?"

"I'm in Lerici at the train station. Is Ellie—the same?" She couldn't bring herself to ask if her sister was alive.

"Of course she is. Where the hell have you been?"

It was the first time she'd heard anger in his voice, but she couldn't care about that now. Ellie was alive. And after all the things she'd done that should have made Michael furious, this was the absolute worst. He had every right to be salty.

"I went just for a day trip. To Viareggio. There was a carnival." She could hear how unbelievably lame it sounded.

"What the bloody hell! I'm coming to get you. You're needed, remember. A little date with surgery? Stay there."

"At the train station? But I need to change."

"Stay at the station. We have to get back to Genoa and make sure you're still viable as the donor." His voice was hard, monotone, different than ever before. She deserved it. And more.

He hung up without waiting for an answer. As she waited, Saffron was finally satisfied, thinking of the inevitable and somehow perfect conclusion to all this. She'd be the sister that died. After all, what did she have to offer anyone? Nothing but flaws and mistakes, and hopefully one good kidney. She was the mistake in her family, and undergoing the operation might happily erase that mistake.

She had the presence of mind to grab a coffee and try to clear her head before Michael arrived.

Once she was in the car, she endured twenty minutes of Michael's furious silence. He wanted to stop for a sandwich on the way, saying he hadn't eaten since breakfast, but he rushed through, insisting they take sandwiches back to the car and eat while driving.

He drove in a way that normally would have unnerved her. She could feel judgment pouring from his silence, seasoned with a whiff of disgust.

"I'm so sorry, Michael. I'm sorry you got tangled up with me."

He didn't look at her. His voice was still harsh, his grip tight on the wheel. "Someone else might say they've had enough and can't keep rescuing you, but the truth is I can keep doing it. If that's what it takes."

She reached for his hand and caressed it. Although he flinched, she said, "Sometimes I could rescue you."

He understood, but his frown remained deep. She was on thin ice. Her breath was short as she said, "I hope you'll forgive me sometime."

Ever since she could remember, Saffron had only ever tried to survive the disasters in her life, but what was the point of merely surviving and going on, like a leaf drifting on a storm? What was the point, if she didn't have a sister? But she had a sister who was alive, and now she had Michael, too. Angry as he might be.

But after another hour, it seemed that Michael might not ever speak to her again.

"Michael, I know you despise me now."

"No." Face averted, and again he sped up. He wanted to frighten her. She was.

She waited. "I don't know why I ran away. It just happened."

It had been a silly, selfish whim, to get away for the day right before their scheduled surgeries. Saffron thought back on the morning and the urge to run away. She hadn't thought about being exposed to germs in crowds, or that it might delay the surgeries. But how could she know she'd be drugged? But things tend to go wrong. That was why Ellie was such an organizer. It wasn't her fault. But it was. She had to learn to think ahead for the people she loved, as Ellie did.

Michael slowed the car down, his anger subsiding, though he was still silent.

What had happened to 'I will always rescue you'? Maybe he meant he'd always rescue her and then punish her for it.

A flush spread through her chest. She didn't deserve this anger, yet she realized it was more complicated than simple judgment and indignation. He must have been worried about her.

"I panicked," she said, "but I only meant to take a day away. I just got on a train and then I heard about the festival."

He gave her a brief, cold stare. He changed again to the fast lane. She gripped the door as the car swerved.

"It's all about you, isn't it?" Michael's voice was harsh and rough. "Were you even thinking of Elinor?"

She wanted to protest, but she knew he meant to ask if she was even thinking of him.

* * *

The day before the surgery, Michael drove her to Genoa, still talking to her as little as possible.

Saffron leaned against the window. "Why are you punishing me?"

"I can't bring myself . . ." He stopped.

"Because now you know what a jerk I am? Had I failed to convince you before?"

"Yes. No." He stared at her with a disapproval that made her shrink. "How could you do that? Are you going to run again?" Once started, it all came out. "You scared us all to death. Did you think of Elinor? Of me? I thought you were gone for good. How could you make me feel like that?"

She couldn't look him in the eyes. "I'm sorry. I should have told you where I was going, but I was afraid you'd stop me." The truth felt surprisingly easy to say, and now she could look at him. "What did Ellie and Mom say when they found out I was gone?"

He relented, looking at her with some sympathy for the first time since she'd been back.

"Elinor slept through it," he said. "We never told her you were gone. Betsy was beside herself, but I told her the Saffron I knew wouldn't just disappear. I lied to keep her calm."

She was losing Michael. He thought she was a terrible person.

Tests at the hospital determined she was still able to be Ellie's donor. Saffron came out to find Michael in the waiting area. She sat with him. The place was deserted, except for the interminably coming-and-going medical people who passed by.

"Should we go up to see her?" Saffron asked.

"You're an unbelievable idiot!" Michael shouted. "A fucking jerk!"

She had a strange sense of calm, feeling his tirade was necessary and might change things. She nodded.

"Don't agree with me, and don't ever fucking do that again!" he shouted.

Nurses turned their heads as they rushed past. Michael stood up, facing her.

For some strange reason, Saffron wanted to giggle. It was better to have him furious than icy. "What, don't ever again run out on my sister before donating my body part?"

"Don't run out on me!" he said. He grabbed her hand and pulled her into a fierce kiss. She was almost shocked enough to resist, but of course she didn't. She had forgotten how much she liked the feeling of his lips smashing hers with passion and now fury. She had wanted his anger. She deserved it. Perhaps it would change her back to being good.

"I won't ever do it again," she whispered. She had an odd sensation of being brave, to face surgery, possible death, Michael's fury, and yet feel calm.

"Don't leave," he whispered into her hair. "Don't die on me."

He was taking a cruel pleasure, reminding her of the risk. She decided that if she didn't make it and became an Invisible, she'd haunt both Ellie and Michael. She wouldn't ever leave them.

"I won't," she said, pulling back to look into his eyes. All she saw there was love. She melted into it, feeling his strong body pressed to hers, as if to ensure that she stayed alive.

It was all up to her. Her turn to make things right. Shelley had said she could do it. And Dad had always known she had to take care of her sister, as much as Ellie thought she was taking care of Saffron. He'd said so in his last letter.

She was going to try her best not to die, but if she did, she hoped she'd run into someone who could see her and help her on her way. To wherever they went, with their smiles and waves.

SPRING

Chapter 37

Healing in the Spring—Elinor

When Elinor woke up, the most immediate sensation she had was that everything had changed. She knew she had had the surgery, but she had the weird sensation that her body was strange, not really her own.

Groggily she asked the nurse, "Where's my sister?"

But the nurse didn't seem to understand her. Had Elinor spoken in English or Italian?

The nurse left. Tonio came in, wearing scrubs and a mask. Had he been part of the surgery? She had never fully appreciated his kindness. She felt it now. A surge of warmth in her throat told her she was erupting in tears. Dizzy stars spangled her vision. She felt so weak and so grateful. And so woozy.

Miraculously, Tonio had gone from being a neighbor to someone very important to her. But Elinor wasn't in a mood to question miracles.

"How did they let you in to see me?" she mumbled.

"I once worked in this hospital. I still have good

connections." He smiled, more handsome than she remembered. "I'm coordinating your care."

"Mom needs someone like you."

"And Michael is making sure Saffron gets the best care. He's ferocious with the nurses."

"Saffron? Where is she?" Elinor tried to sit up, but Tonio gently pushed her shoulder and she lay back.

"Your sister is fine. She's recovering and not well enough to get up. But she will be, soon. Her doctor is pleased with her—and your—outcome."

Elinor smiled as she fell asleep.

The next time she woke up, Saffron was beside her, wearing a hospital gown. Her sister reached down and kissed her cheek.

Saffron held up a brochure. "Listen, I'll read to you about our recovery!"

Elinor pulled her sister's arm until Saffron collapsed over onto her for an awkward hug.

"You're such an oddball," Elinor said, weeping. She looked up at her sister and with a gentle thumb, wiped tears off Saffron's cheeks.

Her sister whispered, "I'll be less of an oddball if you'll get well."

"No, don't ever stop being yourself. I promise to be more like you. And get well. How's that?"

Saffron laughed. She began to read aloud from the brochure. "You should eat a diet low in salt and fat to prevent high blood pressure. However, you can now eat more fruits and vegetables and drink more fluids than you could when you were on dialysis. You will be assigned a dietitian to make an eating plan that works for you and your new kidney."

Saffron stopped. She looked into Elinor's eyes. "I love you."

"I love you, Saffron. I'm sorry . . ."

"Don't. We're sisters. Go back to sleep."

"Yes. Happy," was all Elinor could manage.

The next day, when Saffron came in, she said, "Ellie, I've forgiven Michael."

"What did he do?"

"He chewed me out for . . . oh, never mind. It's all good now."

Elinor managed to sit up. She saw that Saffron was thinner. "Did you lose weight?"

"I don't think so. Why?"

"What does your doctor say?"

Saffron smiled. "He says I'm absolutely fine. I haven't lost anything except the weight of one kidney."

Elinor laughed.

"And one other small ounce."

"An ounce of what?"

"Of anger. I'm not angry at Dad anymore. If he hadn't brought me to live with you, I wouldn't have you and Mom."

"He was being a good father."

"Yes." Saffron reached over for a careful hug. Elinor lay her head on Saffron's arm, trying to stay awake and savor this bloom of happiness in her heart.

* * *

For days, Elinor could barely wake up to eat and talk. They made her get out of bed and walk a little every day, and that exhausted her.

The doctor talked to her about her fragile condition. She expected that from the preparation for the transplant, but she hadn't imagined how precarious she'd feel, how on the edge of going to sleep for good.

The doctor again emphasized that her long-term survival wasn't guaranteed. Many recipients survived less than two decades after a transplant. "Your chances of living longer are good," he said, as if this were a consolation. And he added, "You may not travel any long distances for at least six months."

That meant going home to recover in Berkeley was impossible. And why would she want to endure the trip just to live there alone? Here she had Saffron and Tonio. And Mom was here, however long she'd stay.

Uncertainty about living put a different color on every single moment in Elinor's day. She treasured the silliest things—an extra fresh glass of orange juice, first thing, brought by Tonio. It made her weep. Saffron's christening her new kidney *Saffrellie* also made her tear up, but through her laughter. *Saffrellie*, the tests confirmed, continued to do well.

Rest was right now Elinor's full-time job. Whenever she awoke, Saffron, Betsy, Michael, or Tonio was beside her. She especially liked when it was Tonio. His smile as she opened her eyes made her heart burst into bloom.

One day, she told him what the doctor had said.

Tonio took both her hands. "I know," was all he said, but he kissed the back of each hand gently, and then put one down. He stared at her and their gazes held. He leaned over and kissed her lips.

She wanted the kiss to linger, but she felt herself fading back into sleep.

Three weeks after surgery, Saffron and Michael came in holding hands.

Saffron came over and bent to kiss Elinor's cheek without letting go of Michael. "How's the patient?"

"Happy to see you both," Elinor said as she sat up.

She had given up on Saffron appreciating Michael, but now they were holding hands.

"We're going back to Lerici," her sister said. "Can we bring you anything?"

Elinor thought they must be sleeping together again, the way they held onto each other.

She said, "I'd like to borrow your book on Shelley. Would you bring it?"

Saffron was surprised. "Sure! Anything else?"

Elinor had a thought. "Bring me my Christmas notebook and pen."

They brought the notebook, pen, and the Shelley book, as well as Michael's silver bracelet of seashells and beads that said *Lerici*. He put it on Elinor's wrist, on the arm that didn't have tubes, and he tightened the string.

"I hope your doctors will let you keep it on," Saffron said. "They're so careful about germs."

Elinor said, "I'll tell them I've been tagged for Lerici."

Saffron grinned.

Elinor kept losing track of dates. After working in a hospital, being marooned in a patient bed was a new experience. The doctors assured her she'd get better soon, but soon never seemed to arrive. But one day, it did.

Saffron and Michael came in while Elinor was sitting up, eating.

Saffron took Elinor's hand, glancing back to Michael. "We're engaged."

Elinor sat up straighter. "About time!"

Energy shot through her. Something to get well for—her sister's wedding!

"We're not getting married until you're strong," Michael said.

"Strong enough to be my maid of honor." Saffron held Elinor's hands. "Though of course, we don't want anything formal."

Of course.

After this news, Elinor healed as fast as an opening bud in spring. A week later, she walked outside in time to see spring blossom in Liguria. She was so weak she had to push against the wind, but with her physical therapist on one side and her mother on the other, she made it around the hospital campus. That was the signal to her doctors to send her home.

Betsy had stayed to help care for her girls. She had called a neighbor, who agreed to take care of her cats, which spent half their time at the neighbor's house anyway.

Michael took charge of Betsy, driving her back and forth from Genoa to Lerici as needed. Betsy was living in the cottage helping Saffron recover.

Betsy's help to Elinor consisted mostly of entertaining Michael. He found in Saffron's mother many of the qualities that made Saffron unusual and charming.

"You always gave Saffron freedom to be herself, didn't you?" he asked one day as they sat in the room with Elinor, who was slowly eating her lunch.

"I didn't give it to her. I simply never took it away from her," Betsy said with a smile. Elinor could see she was pleased to take what he said as a compliment. "Children are natural geniuses at being themselves, until adults squash it out of them. I didn't squash her."

"You did a great job of not squashing."

"Does that mean you squashed me, Mom?" Elinor laughed.

"You wanted a little squashing. You took to it so fast I couldn't help supporting that."

On discharge day, in early March, Elinor awoke with a clear head and more energy. Out her window was clear blue sky, the rooflines of Genoa clear and sharp. She got out of bed and dressed, shedding the hospital gown on her sheets like a crumpled tissue. She sat in the side chair like a visitor. Before everyone came to take her home, she had one last thing to do. She called Cosma and told the realtor to take the house off the market. They weren't going to sell. For now, Elinor was going to stay in Lerici.

The decision was made simple by her condition. Now her job and money worries seemed absurd. Working would have been impossible .

Betsy, Saffron, and Michael came in just as she hung up with Cosma. "You ready to go?"

Elinor sat up. "I'm going home. To Lerici. When I feel better in the fall, I'll come home to Berkeley. But I've got savings, and for now I'm staying."

Betsy's smile preceded her warm hug as she bent over her daughter. "Now you're talking! And I can stay to help you get better."

"So much for planning ahead, Mom."

Betsy picked up Elinor's bag. "I've always thought planning was overrated, dear."

"I'm going home!" Elinor said, rising. She turned and kissed her fingers, then planted them on the sheet. "*Ciao*, bed with rails and tubes! Bye-bye, hospital food!" She stood up straight and strong.

"Mom's going to stay for another couple months," Saffron said.

"Mom, what about your cats and club?" Elinor asked.

Betsy said, "My neighbor's taking care of the cats already. My club will gossip about me while I'm gone, so they'll be happy. I need to be with my girl. Both my girls!"

Saffron handed Ellie a handmade card. On the outside was a photo of their cottage. Inside the card Saffron had lettered in italics, *Make a thing of feathers and let it fly with hope.* "The Romantics. Your favorite card."

Saffron took Elinor's elbow. "The one you made me. I'm taking care of you now. You don't have to plan or do anything."

Elinor shook her head. "Who are you, and what have you done with my sister?"

"Tonio is renting a hospital bed for you at home. The doctor says I'm well enough to help you."

"Let's take a lap around the hospital while I wait to be discharged."

Betsy said she'd wait, so Saffron and Michael helped Elinor walk out of the room, down the hall, and outside the hospital. They held her hands as she took not one, but two slow and careful walks around this building. It was a brisk, beautiful day and the hospital grounds were spring like.

When they returned to the room, Saffron said, "You never understood how much I wanted to be your full sister, not your step-sister."

"We're not stepsisters. We're half-sisters. Be precise, Saffron."

"What's the difference, a step or half, we're sisters." Saffron shrugged.

"That's settled then."

They both broke up.

In the late afternoon, they got Elinor home to Lerici, where Tonio was waiting.

"I will run your errands and buy your groceries," he said. "I know how to shop for you."

Saffron turned to her sister and gave her a look that said, *He's in love*. Elinor shook her head, but she was smiling.

Chapter 38
A Wedding—Elinor

March in Lerici turned quickly into the delicate, trembling edge of spring. Saffron and Elinor settled into their healing routines at the cottage. Betsy with cheerful creativity made meals and cleaned. Michael and Tonio ran errands and Tonio showed off his culinary skills by making some spectacular dinners. Elinor enjoyed how impressed her mother was by his talent.

Elinor rested every morning on the chaise, watching their garden unfold in a tapestry of brimming buds and pale green leaves. Even on her hikes in the mountain trails at home, she had never felt the earth so close and tender.

Healing in springtime took her as away from her compulsive nature. She couldn't move quickly. She couldn't think for long. The doctor had said it would take a year to get well, and that she'd be at high risk of getting a life-threatening infection, due to the anti-rejection drugs. The job was far away now, and her friends in Berkeley had agreed to sublet the condo for her.

There was little to do but sit on the patio, enjoy the

greenery and flowers, and read until Tonio's next visit. She had just finished reading Saffron's book about Shelley when she heard the sound of hammering. It must be afternoon, as Cosma had agreed to keep Matteo from working on the house until later in the day. But Elinor enjoyed the sounds of repair. She enjoyed Matteo's dark face with his soft eyes peering around the corner of the house, his deferential tilt of head and nod, silently saying hello. In silence, he was a gentle presence. She had no idea what he was working on, and didn't care. Matteo had become part of the house, like Saffron's Shelley spirit. Part of their lives. Surely the house needed whatever he was doing. Oddly, she trusted Matteo, without ever having communicated with him in words, except to learn his name and say *Ciao* a few times.

Elinor had slowed down to the pace of a silent plant growing new shoots. She existed in a lovely, drifting state she hadn't known since that first day in Rome, when she and Saffron sat in a trattoria watching the afternoon grow golden. She wound the wall clock every Friday, when she could remember it was Friday. *Venerdì*, in Italian, Tonio had taught her. She was picking up bits of the language from him, nothing like lessons, just random words and phrases that slowly knit into Elinor's sense of belonging here.

The weather warmed, day after day. Elinor sat on the patio soaking up the light and the scents of lavender and damp soil wafting to her on the salt breeze. She couldn't fix anything or anyone now, not even herself. She could barely get up to make a sandwich. Mostly she had to lie still, yielding to healing processes that were like spring unfolding its tentative new green leaves. She was encouraged to see buds on the camellia, but would she ever bloom again?

This afternoon, she had indulged in a long nap when a slight sound roused her. She raised her head and turned to see a man in a long black jacket just inside the patio door. He wore a flowing white cravat. His dark, curly hair was long.

Startled, she raised her voice, realizing she was alone, with a stranger in the house.

"May I help you?"

He could be a salesman who had found the front door unlocked.

I've come to help you, she seemed to hear. Had he spoken?

Your father sent me.

Elinor knew she was half-awake, and yet she had no doubt of what Shelley was saying, and that Dad had sent him. This was what Saffron's rambling reports had been about: Shelley was part of the family. He always had been, and now he was going to help her recover.

As she gazed back at his pale face, silently thanking him, the door opened.

Tonio walked into the place Shelley had occupied.

"I thought I saw someone come in before you," she said.

"I saw no one," he said.

"Oh. Doesn't matter."

Tonio handed her the heirloom tomatoes she loved, mozzarella, and fresh-picked basil. He showed them off and went into the kitchen to make a salad.

They had lunch on the patio, as they often did, now that the weather was warmer.

After he left she blissfully stretched out again on the chaise. No sooner had she drifted toward sleep than her phone rang. *Signor* Capelli, sounding agitated, told her that he had consulted with an American colleague and discovered information about inheritance taxes that might affect them.

"New information?" Elinor said, jolted by the phrase. "What taxes?"

"If you sell your house," *Signor* Capelli said, "You would be subject to both Italian and American inheritance taxes, and Italian real estate sales taxes as well. It could be quite costly."

In her weakened state, Elinor's mind flew in two directions, instead of the ten it might have. She let the two directions battle it out before answering.

"But that makes it almost impossible for us to afford to sell, ever!" she exclaimed. "We can't afford the taxes. What's the point of inheriting property if we can't sell it?"

Signor Capelli's voice became mellifluous. "*Signorina*, you should consider carefully that it might be more advantageous to retain the house. You might lease it, since it is in a vacation area, to gain income. You could eventually earn enough to pay the double taxes and then you can sell it, if you wish. But no matter how long you wait, you will have to pay taxes to both countries."

She marveled at how quickly Saffron had devised the idea of leasing the cottage in the summer. Her intuition was rarely bolstered by logic, but it had a way of leaping over reason to arrive at the right answer.

The next day, Tonio found her sitting at the table. He pulled out a chair and sat close beside her. "I let myself in. The door was open," he said.

Elinor rubbed her eyes. "Of course."

Tonio had become someone she expected to walk right in, without knocking.

He had brought a tangerine, which he began peeling. His long, well-manicured fingers delicately tore off the rind in one single circular strip. He had perfected this small art, and he smiled at her briefly as she watched. She could see from the way he looked up that he was proud of this feat. He split the tangerine and offered her half.

"Thank you." She took her half and the napkin he offered with it, and bit into the exquisitely juicy fruit.

"This is fabulous," she said, licking a drop of juice off the corner of her mouth and then dabbing at it.

He watched her and smiled that unexpectedly brilliant smile of his. What mirth lurked inside him that she hadn't yet discovered?

Suddenly, Tonio leaned over and kissed her. She remembered his kiss in the hospital, which she'd forgotten until this moment. His lips lingered on her mouth, and she didn't pull away until he did.

"I've wanted to do that ever since the day I met you in the market," he said, holding her.

"And I've wanted you to, but I thought I was leaving. Going home forever, leaving Italy behind."

"I'm so glad you didn't! Though I wish you didn't have to stay because of what happened."

She laughed. "The universe had to hit me over the head to get me to do what I needed to."

He released her and asked, with some anxiety, "How are you feeling today?"

"Well enough. Saffron's kidney is trying to change me. I'm becoming happier and more whimsical."

She loved making him laugh. It was an ability she decided to practice. Along with kissing him.

"So it feels good to have a part of your sister within?"

"It's like having my guardian angel implanted in me. Keeps me ticking."

"You are each other's guardians. If I had a brother, I do not know if he would have done as much for me."

Elinor hesitated, and then let the secret out into the warm air, trusting Tonio. "Funny you should say that, because Saffron and I learned that we have a half-brother, but we don't know where he is. We found adoption papers here in the house."

Tonio was shocked, she could see. But his response also shocked her.

"I know," he said softly, looking down to avoid her gaze.

"What? How can you have known?"

Tonio got up and walked a few steps away, looking out toward the ocean. He came back. "This was something I was sworn not to say. And then I met you. I was going to tell you about this at Christmas, but then I hesitated, and then . . ."

"What? Tell me!"

Tonio had been keeping big things from her. She looked at him as if he were a stranger, and possibly a dangerous one. How could he know such a thing and keep it to himself? And why?

He stood above her, somber as that first day they'd met. His large eyes were sad. But she was sadder, losing this lovely cocoon of trust in him.

"I knew your father, of course. Residents of Lerici aren't strangers. When he moved here, Nathan came often to the hospital because of his wife's cancer. We met in the cafeteria and discovered we were neighbors."

Elinor tried to imagine a good reason why Tonio

345

wouldn't have told her this as soon as he learned who she was. She failed to find one.

He went on. "Gradually, we became friends, and when Alessandra died, I visited him often. During that time, he confessed to me that he had a lost son. He felt extremely bad about it. He didn't know if anything could be done now, but he wanted to do something for him."

Elinor jumped up and walked away from him, wanting distance, wanting him to stop talking, but not wanting him to. She turned to face him and shook her head, glaring. "And then what?"

Tonio's head tilted as he tried to understand her expression. "*Cara* Elinor, you must not think I would ever have kept this secret from you if your father hadn't insisted on absolute secrecy. And then when I met you, I didn't want to admit I knew him, because it would be so hard to hide this from you. You would have asked me a lot about him, and I was afraid I'd tell you."

Elinor wanted to hit him, but she wanted to kiss him more. She didn't move. "And I suppose you know about the hidden manuscript Dad told us to find here at his house?"

When Tonio looked her in the eyes and shook his head, she had no choice but to believe him. This man couldn't be a liar. He could keep things to himself, but he couldn't outright lie. Her anger crumbled.

Saffron and Michael rushed out onto the patio, hand in hand, and beaming.

"We've decided to set the wedding date for next month!" Saffron proclaimed.

Michael held up their clasped hands and kissed hers. "This beautiful woman makes me exquisitely happy!"

Pivoting emotionally, Elinor managed to say, "Next month—April—how wonderful!"

She held out her hands. They each took one, while Tonio clapped Michael on the back.

"What exactly are your plans?" Elinor asked.

"Ellie, you should know me by now well enough to know the plan isn't exact. We only just decided."

"You must get married here." It came to Elinor easily. Of course they had to. Right here on the patio.

After that wonderful news, they left.

Tonio said, "I'm sorry I had to withhold things from you. Knowing you as I do now, I wouldn't have done it."

Elinor wanted to forgive him, and so she did, holding out her hand to invite him into an embrace.

"I'm going to rest now," she said after he embraced her. He kissed her and left.

After all these revelations, Elinor lay down on the soft chaise, forgiving Tonio with all her heart. His trouble was that he was too sensitive, like her sister. Too easily opened up and touched. And full of respect for others. He had respected her father. He respected her. She loved that about him.

She intended to ask Tonio everything she could think of about Nathan's time in Lerici. How well they must have known each other, if her father had confessed his biggest secret—well, she hoped it was the biggest—to this neighbor.

When she saw Tonio next time, he assured her that he and Nathan hadn't been very close. They had met often in town at restaurants and cafes, as residents all went to the same places, not the tourists ones. Tonio thought perhaps Elinor's father had been lonely after his wife died. He seemed to wish for a close friend and confidante. Nathan's confession had surprised Tonio.

Elinor recognized in the story Nathan's clumsiness with relationships. She let go of the hope that she'd know her father much better through Tonio's memories. He didn't have that many.

A week passed, with Elinor more energized every day. Maybe it was the healing atmosphere, maybe it was the new friend. The new kidney. The sister she'd always wanted to have. On her chaise, she had time to think about her life and to make notes in her journal. She perused every new shoot and blossom that emerged, purple pansies with puppy-like faces and violets starring the ground underneath the rosemary's green spikes. Her Thanksgiving camellia was covered in buds, and she was sure something should be done for it. Feeding it, possibly. How often did you water camellias? How often did you water *everything* here? She could buy more plants and learn about gardening.

She could use this energy to give Saffron and Michael a wonderful wedding. But even the simplest wedding involved planning. Details and planning weren't Saffron's skills, but they were as natural to Elinor as breathing.

There was only one problem. The doctors had said to avoid crowds for a full year. She was to be careful when going out, avoiding anyone who might be ill because the immune system suppressant she took could leave her vulnerable to infection. She wasn't to become overtired, either. She should carefully regulate her fluid intake and take her medications religiously, never missing a single one. It was a lot to think about, even at home.

But to put on a wedding, she'd have to go out. She could pace herself. She could be careful, maybe wear a surgical mask. She could send Betsy on small local errands, but to shop for the rest, she'd need Tonio's help, with only a few weeks to put it all together.

She could keep it simple. Saffron would want an informal ceremony. But simple and informal or not, Saffron's nuptials had to be gorgeous and full of flowers—cascades of them. Saffron herself was a flower, a wide-open white rose whose golden stamens blazed back at the sun. Flowers would be the theme. And Saffron had to have a special dress. If Elinor had to, she'd go all the way to Genoa to get a dress in which her lovely sister would shine.

Nothing elaborate, of course, but the dress had to be simple and exquisite, and Saffron had to hold a spectacular bouquet. Even if Saffron wanted to get married barefoot, she should have the most romantic dress. After all, they were The Romantics.

Elinor did a search on weddings in Lerici. She found out about weddings in the famous fishermen village and others with the colorful setting of a palazzo. Words like *enchanting* and *picturesque* dominated the website, which promised the history of the medieval town as a memorable backdrop. But these were tourists' weddings. She and Saffron were residents now, and besides, there was the issue of her going into crowds.

Elinor would have to hold the wedding here, on their lovely patio. She'd ask Tonio about the legalities. It would have to be a civil wedding, surely, as they weren't Catholic. A ceremony here in the garden, with a canopy over the patio, to protect against the sun and in case it might rain. That meant figuring out how to get a big enough canopy and how to put it up. Again, Tonio could help. And Betsy.

The food. She would have loved to spend days preparing a wedding feast for them, but she knew she didn't have the energy. After the Thanksgiving meal, she was humbled by the finesse of seemingly simple Italian recipes. She'd order a catered meal. Lerici or San Terenzo would surely have a wonderful restaurant that could cater a small event. She would ask Tonio.

Tonio. She kept thinking of him. It would be impossible without his help. It was an interesting feeling to depend on someone. Even if he'd kept an enormous piece of information from her, she trusted him. Maybe she could persuade him to give the bride away. It was a family thing, but he was feeling more and more like family. But she thought of Tonio's reserve, and she wondered if it was acceptable in Italy to ask such a thing. Would he be flattered? Or feel imposed on? Saffron wouldn't need such a formal gesture as being given away, but her romantic side would love it.

Elinor got up and walked to the edge of the patio, looking out to the endless silver-blue scalloped waves of the sea. To have such a backdrop for the ceremony would give it a symbol of permanence, framed by flowering plants. She'd add more, so that by that magical day, the garden would be bursting with beauty.

Elinor knew now that she belonged here. Saffron had been right, this was a perfect home. She might even persuade her mother to live here in Lerici. She inhaled the sea air and the garden's green and earthy notes. Saffron should wear a crown of flowers. They'd have prosecco and seafood for the reception.

On an impulse, she called Tonio.

"*Ciao*, Elinor!" he exclaimed.

She could feel herself blushing.

She told him what she wanted. "I want to arrange their wedding, and I need your help. Lots of it."

He agreed so readily that she went on to say, "I picture

a ceremony right on our patio. Simple, but lovely, in the afternoon."

"You'll need someone to officiate," he offered.

"Yes. I guess I have to talk to the American consulate." Complications reeled through her mind.

Tonio agreed. "Yes, there are formalities to look into. You have no idea about Italian bureaucracy. It can be tricky."

"Can you help me find out?"

"*Certo*. It will be my pleasure to help you in any way. In every way, dear Elinor."

That 'dear,' spoken in his deep voice, not only calmed her fears but warmed her.

"There are legalities, I know. Especially for a wedding between two people who aren't Italian," he continued. "I will make some calls for you."

She was so grateful. She thought of all the romantic pictures she had seen of weddings on the Ligurian coast, weddings between Americans. Surely it would be possible, even if it was short notice. If Italy wasn't selling its atmosphere to formalize romantic bonds, then what were all those photos about?

"The most important requirement I know of," Tonio said, "is that they must make a public declaration. It's a document called a *Nulla Osta*, or Affidavit, and it's required by Italian law for all weddings."

"Sounds simple enough. Is it made at city hall?"

"Yes. A *Nulla Osta* literally states that there are no impediments, and that they are free to marry."

"Thank you, Tonio. I appreciate your helping me with this."

Later, he called back, sounding less confident. "The

Nulla Osta must take into account the laws of the American state where the citizen resides."

"So, Saffron has to prove that she can legally marry under Italian and U.S. law."

"Yes. To obtain a *Nulla Osta* she and Michael must have their birth certificates."

"Birth certificates! But we didn't bring them, and Betsy is here. The birth certificate is in Berkeley. Surely they can't expect her to fly all the way back to the U.S. to get it!"

"I'm afraid that it's a requirement to have it, and not a copy."

Elinor was afraid to ask him to refer her to a lawyer. Her dreamy, simple ceremony was going up in smoke. But she persevered. "I think I need to consult a lawyer."

"Yes, and to visit the Consular Section nearest Lerici. The *Nulla Osta* will be valid for six months. It costs approximately fifty euros per person."

"Well, if we can get past the birth certificate requirement, it sounds not too bad."

"That isn't the end. Then, you must present these documents to the Wedding Hall in Lerici, if this is where the marriage will be performed," Tonio said. Elinor was quiet, so he continued, "It's usually required to make a *Declaration of Intention to Marry* before an *Ufficiale di Stato Civile*. That's in your language, I believe, a registrar."

Her silence must have told him that he had surpassed her ability to absorb details. He asked, "Is this not what you were anticipating?"

She wasn't anticipating any of it. "But Saffron didn't bring her birth certificate. Just her passport. Isn't there a way around all this?"

Elinor waited as Tonio thought. Finally, he said, "I will talk to a lawyer friend and see."

She was about to despair, when he offered an idea. "What about having an informal wedding here, and then they can finalize it when they go back to the U.S.?"

"They're going to live in London, but maybe they can finalize it there more easily."

That was the first moment it had sunk in with Elinor that Saffron wasn't going to live here at home afterward. After these months in this cottage with her sister, Elinor wasn't sure it would feel so much like home with Saffron gone.

Saffron refused to shop for a special wedding dress. "That's an antiquated ritual," she protested when Elinor proposed helping her find something.

"It's an age-old tradition. There's a difference."

"I'm not an age-old kind of woman."

"But you're going to be a bride!" Elinor couldn't prevent her tears from welling up. Ever since the surgery, she'd been ready to cry at the drop of a hat. Very unlike her old self. It must be *Saffrelli*, Saffron's kidney.

She wouldn't have pushed the issue, but her big worry was that Saffron might wear that lavender thing, the dress she'd worn at Dad's funeral.

"Let me handle it," she said, taking her sister's hand.

Saffron melted, on one condition. "Nothing fancy, and I'll kill you if it's frilly."

She told Tonio she needed help to shop somewhere nice, probably somewhere not in Lerici.

Tonio took her to Genoa to see a high-fashion dressmaker. He had made an appointment, and he said she should wear a mask when walking through the streets.

"A woman is most radiant when she's pleased with her

appearance," he said, as he drove. "But she is most beautiful when made to look more spectacular than she ever has in her life. The best dressmaker in Italy is, of course, in Liguria."

Signora Ferroni's small shop had curtained windows with no fancy displays.

She met them at the door. "*Veni*," she said curtly, leading them inside. "You are welcome," she added over her shoulder.

The shop had shelves all the way to the ceiling, bearing bolts of fabrics in every color Elinor could imagine. A few small cards in easels on the counter showed simple, basic designs with draping, one gown with a train, and others short. All looked understated, but in one of these luxurious fabrics, any design would be gorgeous.

"*Signora*, thank you for making the time to see us," Elinor said, wondering how to explain her request. While she had stood alone on the patio envisioning the marvelous dress for Saffron, it had seemed so clear. Now she couldn't think of how to describe what she wanted.

She was surprised when Tonio stepped into the void. "Luisa, *Signorina* Greene would like to treat her sister to the most lavish wedding gown possible, but for a small, informal, and yet imaginative ceremony. It will be on a hillside overlooking the port of Lerici."

Elinor couldn't imagine a more perfect description of the setting, what she wanted, and the tone of the event. She looked admiringly at him.

"Yes," she said. "That's exactly what we want."

"Color?" *Signora* Ferroni asked.

Elinor was quick on that one. "Pale peach would suit her. She has pale skin, with a blush in her cheek."

Elinor took out her phone, scrolled through her photos, and showed *Signora* Ferroni pictures of Saffron.

"Ah!" said the dressmaker, who clearly hoarded her English vocabulary. "I have the perfect fabric for this gown."

She walked to the end of the shelves and pulled a ladder along to the right shelf. Anchoring the ladder with a brake, she climbed up. Abruptly, she threw down a bolt of peach crepe de chine with raised floral patterns in the same color. It landed squarely on the counter, as if it dared not fall anywhere sloppily.

Elinor reached out to touch it, but Tonio put his hand on her arm. He shook his head. *Signora* Ferroni pushed herself sideways while still on the ladder, and threw down another bolt, this one of dark teal Thai silk. Then she stepped carefully down the ladder, her spike heels missing the rungs, and turned to face them.

"You may touch now," she said to Elinor.

Elinor smoothed her hand carefully over each bolt. "The peach is lovely. What's the blue for?"

"The tiny edging, so that we may feel how warm is the peach, as if the ripe fruit itself hung against a panorama of the twilight sea."

Elinor smiled and nodded. "Marvelous."

"Style?" asked the woman of monosyllables.

"I was thinking something loose and lavish, as she likes her clothing to swirl around her. And she likes loose clothes."

The dressmaker groaned a little. She pulled out a pattern book from below the counter and began flipping through, past the traditional gowns, past the slim-line gowns that swirled out around the feet, and into the section on short dresses. She kept flipping, despite Elinor's occasional comment of "That's lovely" or "Oh, that one is great!" She flipped on, until she found what she wanted. She turned the book around to show Elinor and Tonio the tightest, most high-fashion silk suit with a skirt that had a back slit so high Elinor wanted to gasp.

"This is your sister's wedding attire," said *Signora* Ferroni, using the most syllables she had uttered since they walked into her shop.

"But it's a long gown! It's much more the choice I'd—" Elinor stopped herself as Tonio tugged on her sleeve and she looked at him. He gave the slightest nod.

"Your sister becomes a wife on this day," the dressmaker said. "She will put aside her comfortable clothing at this time and take on the sophistication of a grown woman, perhaps soon to be a mother."

Elinor persisted. This was a mistake. "I'd love her to be elegant, *Signora*, but this isn't her style at all."

"She will grow into it."

"In one day?"

"At the moment she takes her vow. She is a beautiful young woman. She will become in full possession of her beauty in this dress."

And that, Elinor could see, was that. If she wanted *Signora* Ferroni, the best dressmaker in all of Italy, to create Saffron's spectacular wedding outfit, she would say yes and pay for the suit it would be hard to persuade Saffron to wear.

"You may email me her measurements and return to pick up the suit next week," was all the signora said.

Elinor looked at Tonio. He nodded.

"Yes," Elinor said, and got out her credit card.

Elinor spent the ride back to Lerici wondering how Saffron would like the dress. All she had to show her was a small card with two tiny swatches of fabric stapled to a drawing of the design.

"Have I made a mistake?" she asked Tonio as they drove home. "It looks so formal. What if Saffron looks at this and doesn't want it?"

"You can't return it now," he said.

"I'm not going to show this to Saffron. It's going to be a surprise."

* * *

It was barely a week before the wedding, all the plans in place, and the dress wasn't finished. Elinor took her coffee out onto the patio early on a breezy morning, wrapping herself in Betsy's warm shawl. While she was looking out anxiously toward a few wispy clouds on the horizon, there was a knock on the door.

It was the dress. Elinor was delighted to watch a stunned Saffron open the large bag and take out the handmade gown. As Saffron held up the peach-colored, pearl-ornamented dress with its long skirt, her eyes filled with tears. "Oh, Ellie," was all she could say before gently laying it on a chair and hugging Elinor.

All of Elinor's fears about Saffron's reaction melted into their hug. Feeling her sister's pleasure gave her a rush of warmth. She hugged Saffron harder.

"Make a thing of feathers and let it fly away with hope," Saffron whispered.

"You're my brightest hope," Elinor whispered back.

Elinor couldn't wait to see Saffron walk toward Michael in this confection, her little sister looking all grown up and blushing like the peach she was.

Summer

Chapter 39

Until Now—Saffron

April in Liguria was magical. No wonder Elizabeth von Arnim's book was titled *The Enchanted April*. Their patio was enchanted this morning, overflowing with flowers, and Saffron could sense the sprites dancing underneath nodding hydrangea and between the daisies.

She wasn't supposed to see any of the decorations yet. Ellie had forbidden her to even glance out the window, so naturally Saffron had tiptoed downstairs early to have a look. Standing on the flagstones in her bare feet, she sighed. Her sister's love sprouted from each stem and garden bed. It looped overhead, where Tonio's helpers had entwined the pillars with ropes of roses and jasmine and made a flowery arch under which they would stand to give their vows. Pitchers of roses and jasmine stood on the tables, their scents wafting out.

Saffron stood on tiptoe, her face turned up to the perfect sky, she reveled in the sunlight and sweetness. The trees seemed to be whispering about her day, and she knew they would give them the right amount of shade at the hour the wedding and reception. Saffron knew trees communicated with each other, and this morning she felt their happy conspiracy for their joy.

In late April, Lerici had just enough warmth, but the light sea breeze would keep it from getting hot. Even at this early hour, Saffron could tell what magic the weather gods had created for her and Michael.

The round table was moved to one side, and the caterer had set up a rectangular table to serve cake and refreshments, with more jasmine strands twining around on the white tablecloth. A single row of chairs was set facing the ocean, which would be the backdrop for the ceremony.

Saffron held her breath as she walked up to the flower-draped arch where they would take their vows and be sealed together. It was hard to believe only eight months had brought her to this day. And to Michael. How could she have been so completely unaware that he was perfect for her, when he walked into the café that day, and she tried to brush him off. How could she not have felt it when he saved her life? But then, she never had been good at boyfriends. She picked all the wrong ones and shooed away the good guys. Until now.

Vivian and Harold, Michael's mother and father, had arrived two days ago, in order to meet their new daughter-in-law. Saffron and Michael had taken them around Lerici and even up to Portofino to enjoy the area. They were frequent travelers to Italy, and Vivian even spoke some Italian. She had been the one who suggested to Michael that his year away be spent here.

Saffron sat in the single row of chairs arranged in a semi-circle, and for a moment envisioned the ceremony to come. She'd stand under the rose-twined arch with Michael, facing the sea and the minister, as they said vows they'd written together. Included in them was a poem she'd asked Elinor to write.

Since they weren't Catholic, the local priest couldn't officiate, but Tonio had again saved the day. He had quite a knack for helping the Greene family. Tonio knew a local Methodist minister, an elderly English ex-pat who agreed to perform the ceremony. It wasn't to be their legal wedding because Italian law prohibited people getting legally married in Italy if they weren't Italian, except with a long and tedious number of bureaucratic hoops to jump through. So this was to be their "true" wedding, with a legal one to come later, in London.

It would be a real wedding day, her feelings already beginning to spill over like the profuse blossoms. Could be that's why people always wanted flowers for their nuptials, and why the bride traditionally held a bouquet.

They had started their time in Italy with a funeral, also full of feelings, but such different ones. Saffron remembered the autumn colored roses they had bought to strew petals on Dad's grave. They'd been scentless and nearly wilting when purchased, the best they could do in the short time between landing in Rome and the burial. Today the garden was full of scents and fresh flowers. As a wedding should be, for feelings that rose into the air like bubbles, buoyant and bright.

When they had come to Rome to bury their father, she and Ellie had been virtual strangers, and their father a stranger who lived in a distant country. Now she felt she knew Dad for the first time.

Betsy and Elinor would be coming downstairs soon, so she had to get back upstairs before they caught her having a look at the patio. Maybe they were up there sharing first thoughts of this special morning. Saffron hoped so.

She was grateful to have had her first thoughts of the day alone and serene in the Italian home she'd be leaving.

After this, the rush began. She went up to get dressed. While dressing, she heard Michael and his parents arrive. Then the minister came, along with the few guests, including Cosma, Ellie's doctor in Lerici, a few neighbors. Michael and his parents came in and were waiting downstairs when she and her mother and sister descended, and everyone clapped.

The ceremony was as charming as she'd hoped. Saffron stood holding Michael's hand with a bouquet of jasmine, roses, daisies, and narcissus. Afterward, she turned and tossed it straight to her sister, but Tonio caught it. He turned around holding the spray of flowers and everyone laughed.

Vivian and Harold, laughed the loudest, which Saffron found charming. They didn't of course know the nuances of why it was funny the bouquet landed in Tonio's hands, as they had met everyone only a few days before the wedding. But unlike the stuffy, upper-class people she had expected, Vivian and Harold turned out to be affable, open, friendly, and casual in their dress, like their son. They created the impression of being the last people in the world who would judge their son's choice of a wife. Which was amazing, since he had only told them about her a couple of months ago, when he called them about the transplant surgery.

Having done one shining thing in her life, Saffron decided she had earned the right to be given the benefit of the doubt. As Michael had explained, his parents were people who had "good hearts as Americans would say," as shown by the fact that they supported many causes not only with donations, but also with their time. She volunteered as a tutor to disadvantaged children, and he was a trustee of an environmental organization.

Saffron hadn't expected them to be so warm and so... American in their way of joining the party. It was promising for her adventure moving to London. If Londoners could be like Harold and Vivian, she might well feel at home there. And if she didn't, she could always get Michael to move back here. He would do anything to make her happy, and knowing that made her supremely happy, and made her wish to reciprocate and do things that pleased him.

The light grew golden as the sun lowered. Saffron went upstairs to change out of her lovely dress and into her traveling dress. They were going to Rome tonight, for their honeymoon. Saffron wanted to stay close to Ellie for a while, so they planned to come back to Lerici and stay until July, when they'd go to London.

She watched Tonio and Elinor talking, as they sat together in a corner, with beveled flutes of sparkling water in their hands. Ellie wasn't yet allowed to drink, so Tonio was not drinking with her. Her sister looked beautiful and not at all frail now, her color warm and a little flushed. He leaned over and kissed her quickly, as if to do it before anyone saw. But Saffron saw.

Saffron understood that Elinor was going to stay in Lerici permanently. She saw the healing force of the land working now on her sister's tissues, lightening them and making them pulse a brighter pink. And most of all, Tonio was healing her.

When they turned to look at Saffron, she held up her own glass in a salute to them.

Elinor got up and came to her, as Michael drifted over to talk to his parents.

"I loved it!" Saffron said. "This was the perfect wedding for us. And perfect because it came from you. My sister. The sister I almost didn't have."

"Dear little sis, I was never going to die. They would have found another donor. But you being my donor, saving my life—it makes my life precious."

Saffron let her sister sweep her into a hug. She said, "A piece of me is inside you. Now I'm really your sister."

Ellie pulled back and was a little surprised. "This trip made us real sisters again."

"When I thought I might lose you, I realized I needed to give you everything. You always took my stuff, but now I've given it to you."

Elinor smiled. "Like I gave you my best doll that first night."

"I gave you my best kidney."

"We always give our best."

Laughter shook them so hard they had to lean on each other to stay upright.

At that moment, an Invisible arrived between them. The small boy with a shimmering transparency reminded Saffron of illustrations in her favorite fairytale books. A child soul—perhaps it was to be hers and Michael's. Did the Invisibles ever come back?

But then the boy's form faded.

Saffron looked over at Ellie, who said, "Perhaps he'll be yours."

Saffron's heart thumped. Her sister's heart was open again. Tears welled up in the corners of Saffron's eyes as she watched Ellie go back to Tonio.

She dabbed at her eyes and returned to her charming, quirky in-laws.

She had a family. Her dad might not have been the

perfect dad, but that didn't matter anymore. The things people called real were the things that were merely tangible. Her Invisibles had taught her that wasn't the whole story.

She was ready for a new country. Italy had changed her, but now she needed a change. Any doubts about living with her new family had been erased when Vivian said to her, "You'll like the old homestead. It's roomy enough for four and more. And you and Michael will have your own floor."

And Harold added, "It's a place with history. You'll hardly notice that it's haunted. Really, our spooks are quite friendly."

The Shelleys were her kind of people, and London would be her perfect new place. Come to think of it, the whole of England was filled with Invisibles, if their traditions and literature were anything to go by. As Michael squeezed her arm and they continued chatting with his parents, Saffron was sure that the swirling pale lavender clouds above their heads were friendly.

Then Dad flickered in and quickly out, saying a swirly goodbye, and she thought to him, *See you always.*

As she and Michael left, she caught Elinor's hand. "I'll be back to see you soon. For now, I'm leaving you Shelley."

Elinor kissed her cheek and then her forehead. "I know."

Chapter 40
Olio d'Oliva Redux—Elinor

In July, Lerici's charm ripened. The onshore breezes sometimes reversed to flood the pastel town on the Gulf of Poets with scents of lemon, orange, and rosemary. An excess of delicate pink, blue, and orange wildflowers bloomed down the hillsides. Lerici was at her finest in the seaside and countryside that drew the tourists. But they hadn't yet arrived in large numbers, and it was the precious moment between spring and early summer that was for residents to savor their magical piece of coastline.

Saffron's wedding had been so beautiful that Elinor had spent the entire week after crying off and on, amazing Betsy, who wasn't used to seeing her older daughter so emotional.

Everything had changed since the transplant. Saffron had become surprisingly mature. She was even dignified during the wedding. Afterward, when she and Michael had hugged everyone, and then gone to Rome, Saffron had been—simply all the things Elinor had always wished her to be. Poised, calm, beautiful, generous, and happy. Most especially, the thing Elinor had always wished Saffron to be—happy.

Two weeks later, Betsy went home. With everyone gone, and Elinor's health almost back to normal, she relaxed into the beauty of her Italian house and new life. Her boss had been kind, giving her a four months' severance. And that cushioned her recovery, which the doctor said would occupy six more months.

Michael and Saffron had gone to live in London. It wasn't far from Lerici, only a train to Genoa and then a short plane ride. On a particularly fine morning, Elinor decided that despite the financial risk, she was going to use her retirement fund to live here and keep the house. It was home, now that she had grown well inside it.

Saffron had generously told her not to worry about her half-share, because Michael's family home enabled them to live and work in London. Saffron told Elinor if she decided to buy out Saffron's half, it could be in widely spaced installments, so long as she and Michael had family visiting privileges whenever the weather was fine. She said they wanted her to stay in Italy.

Her phone rang. It was Tonio, suggesting a walk to town. The day's early warmth promised a beautiful afternoon, and Elinor was growing so strong that vigorous walking was a help to her recovery.

She had a deep sense of this rightness. After nearly dying she'd begun living, and begun it here in Lerici. Poetry had come back into her life. The silence of healing days and the joy of solitude were new discoveries. Elinor had never realized you could savor emptiness and just being alone. Each morning brought a fresh page along with deep breaths.

Starting to write again was natural, and keeping a

journal too, because everything that had happened was extraordinary. She could still die, the doctors had been clear to warn her. She didn't want to forget anything.

Italian air was more healing than any she could remember. The water and food were full of taste and seemed to promote a new kind of happiness. It also promoted creativity. The minute she set pen to page, she began to hear rhythms in her sentences, and poems emerged from her journaling like shy deer at the edge of a forest. She tried not to startle them. She let the words take the lead, without judging them. And they led into mysterious pathways inside her.

Tonio arrived and came out onto the patio. "What have you been doing to heal today?" he asked, as he always did.

She showed him the couple of poems she had played with today. Tonio said they reminded him of an Italian poet named Sevrino, and he was a fan of her writing.

They went out for their walk. At the promenade, they turned north and walked up to the door of *Olio d'Oliva Superbo*. "I have something to show you," he said.

By now Elinor was prepared to always be pleasantly surprised by Tonio, but she held back on this one. He didn't know about her earlier encounter with the proprietor.

"*Ciao*, Giorgio!" Tonio called out.

Elinor was glad the surly owner seemed to be absent. She had avoided the shop ever since their exchange months ago.

But he emerged from the back, through a small curtained doorway. Amazingly, he was smiling. He hadn't smiled at her once when she and Saffron had visited the shop. He probably hated women, as well as visitors.

She was embarrassed to see him, and worried that he

would again insult her, but soon she realized he didn't even notice her. He shook hands with Tonio and came out from behind the counter.

"Old friend!" the proprietor exclaimed as they shook. Real residents of Lerici. It must be a club.

"Giorgio, I'd like to introduce—"

"We've met. Several months ago, I believe, eh *signorina*?"

"At least several." Elinor couldn't help looking over at the little bottle that was still on the counter exactly where it had been. "And your bottle is still here."

This time instead of being belligerent, the proprietor laughed. He seemed a different man.

Tonio said, "The *signorina*'s name is Elinor Greene. And she's become a resident of Lerici."

Giorgio was surprised. "Congratulations, *Signorina* Greene!"

He held out his hand. Elinor took it and he shook hers vigorously.

"You're welcome, *Signorina* Greene, any time."

"Please call me Elinor, *Signor*."

"Giorgio. You may call me Giorgio, and you're welcome to purchase my olive oil. Any of it."

Tonio walked over to the small bottle that Giorgio had forbidden Elinor to buy in November. He picked it up, looked at it with the light behind it, and brought it over to them.

"Is this the bottle she wanted?" he asked Giorgio.

Giorgio nodded.

"Did you explain to her the rules?"

"*Non, certo*. She was an outsider. It's no business for outsiders to understand," Giorgio said, smiling. He turned to her. "The rules, *Signora*—Elinor—are that only permanent residents are allowed to buy certain of my stock. It's been this way for generations. It's part of our pride in Lerici."

"Giorgio means generations going back to medieval times."

"Yes. So you see why I was determined that you could not buy this bottle. But now . . . *Signorina* Elinor! You are one of us."

Giorgio held his arms wide, smiling.

She smiled and then frowned. "Why isn't there a price on the bottle? What if some resident wants to buy it?"

Giorgio smiled. "It's not a price, Elinor. It's a subscription. You join the *commune* and you help with the harvest. Then you are allowed to subscribe. We use so much olive oil every month. No point to buy one bottle at a time."

"You get your own bottle, for refilling," Tonio added.

Elinor was astonished. "So what's this?"

"That's merely for display. You would not want to cook with the contents of that! It's colored water."

Elinor began to laugh and found she couldn't stop. Tonio joined her. Giorgio did too, and they were all laughing hard.

Giorgio brought out a bottle of wine from under his counter. He followed that with three glasses. He uncorked the bottle and poured each of them a drink. "Salut!"

They raised their glasses and drank, three fellow residents of Lerici, Italy.

Chapter 41
The Manuscript

Matteo came around the corner of the house holding a metal box. He held it out to Elinor, silent as usual, and when she took it he disappeared again.

She took it, brushing off dirt encrusted around its hinges. It was unlocked. She opened it to find another box inside, a wooden box wrapped in plastic. Inside that box was a manuscript. This must be what Dad had left for them to find, on the treasure hunt he'd planned for them. It had to be a new murder mystery by her father!

But the moment she unwrapped the silk fabric around the manuscript it was obvious this wasn't his book. She couldn't believe the script she was seeing on the yellowed vellum pages.

Poems for a New Dawn. Percy Bysshe Shelley.

It couldn't be. But who would write an entire poetry manuscript by hand in this florid script, on antique paper? Could it be a forgery of an imagined manuscript, something someone—perhaps Nathan—was planning to sell as if authentic?

It was improbable that it was a lost Shelley book, but if it were, this one page she was holding would be worth more than the house itself. It could be sold at auction for—who knew, but possibly more than Elinor had ever dreamed of having in her retirement account.

The note Dad had written to Saffron came back to her. *I want my girls to come back together as sisters. A treasure hunt will help.*

Their father had been willing to hide a priceless literary treasure, one he must have prized not just for its value but for what it meant to him as a Shelley scholar, and to hide it at risk of its being destroyed by the soil, if not found in time. Dad had been willing to erase part of history in order to bring "his girls" together. Ironically, when *he* had never come back together with them.

Her sob was sudden, and then the tears streamed. Their father had always loved them, however miserable he'd been as a parent. There was his love like a backbone of their history, and it was more important to him than the other things in his life, things Elinor had always thought he valued above his family. Things like his literary reputation and his precious Shelley.

Matteo's hammer tapped steadily. He was nearby. Elinor put away her emotions, in case he came back onto the patio.

She'd have to let Dad's literary agent know right away. He could advise her and possibly arrange for an authentication, and if it proved genuine, an auction. Carefully inserting the page back onto the top of the manuscript, Elinor carried the crumbly box into the house. She laid it gently on the dining table and then went to find a towel and a plastic bag to wrap the whole thing in. The box itself was perhaps an antique, though she couldn't be sure.

It might be something Dad had found in a local shop and used to bury the manuscript.

The more she thought about it, the more amazing this treasure was, and the hunt he'd arranged for them. But they hadn't found it together! Did that invalidate the stipulation in his will?

She called Saffron. Her sister said she'd book a flight and get there as fast as she could. Two days later, she arrived. Elinor unwrapped it. As she opened the box and took out the front pages, Saffron's eyes glistened.

"Oh, Ellie! This is the treasure Dad gave us. It really is a treasure!"

They agreed that they had found it together, judging by the months and ordeals they'd gone through here, all their searching, and the way they'd finally repaired their sisterhood.

"After all, if you hadn't insisted we stay longer, I'd never have hired Matteo, and we'd never have found this."

Saffron nodded and hugged her sister. "Michael and I talked it over. We don't want the money. We just want an original Shelley to be discovered in the right way."

"You mean, even though we found it, we donate it to the university?"

"Don't you think that's best?"

Elinor studied her sister for a moment, seeing this newly logical Saffron. She hugged her again. "I think Shelley would want us to do the best for his manuscript."

"Yes, Michael thinks so too."

"He'd be glad his descendant feels that way."

Since Elinor couldn't travel, they arranged a video call to *Signor* Capelli. Holding up pages of the manuscript to show him, together, Elinor and Saffron announced their decision to donate it.

"Very good. I will inform the university. And *Signor* Greene has left another provision, a reward for your finding the manuscript together. His unpublished manuscript, *The Death of Shelley*, is awarded jointly to Saffron and Elinor Greene."

Two weeks after they called the lawyer, Elinor contacted their father's literary agent, who talked to his publisher. They offered a seven-figure advance for the manuscript.

Elinor hung up, stunned. Now that they were going to be very well off, she found she didn't care as much as she used to. With her fragile health, who knew how long she'd need the money. Elinor was happy at last with taking things one day at a time. For the first time, she understood why Saffron thought it was the only way to live.

Of course, being spontaneous was a nice philosophy, and she enjoyed long hours of it. But there was a lot to do, and that required making plans. Lists. Getting married was full of complications, as well as sheer happiness. You couldn't rest on your laurels too long, or things wouldn't come together perfectly. And though Saffron was hosting their wedding, she'd need a little help organizing.

Elinor smiled to herself as she went to the desk to get a pad of paper and a pen. She'd jot down a few thoughts and later turn it into a spreadsheet.

Chapter 42

Two Journals—Elinor and Saffron

Elinor. August. Lerici.

Saffron always brought us trouble, so why did it hurt so much when she said she hated me that night? Right before we went to the club and then the explosion. It was typically dramatic of her to say it, and I knew she was exaggerating. But it hurt. Maybe I felt I deserved it.

Now I see the differences between me and my sister, and how we've learned from each other. Thanks to Dad, for bringing us here, trying to make sure we stayed together until we figured out how much we need each other. Our connection is solid now, it's steel. It carried us through sharing a body part, and it can carry us through anything. We're sisters because she showed how much she loves me. Not half-sisters. There's nothing half about us.

Mom asked me to watch over her, and I did my best. Dad asked her to watch over me! Now she has Michael and his family. So why can't I quit feeling protective of her?

Here's the thing. She and Mom are all the family I have left. I'm on the edge of early retirement, with no kids. My mother is now someone to take care of, not someone to take care of me—not that she ever was. Having a sister is not just one thing in my life, it's everything. For those years when we barely talked, I missed her crazy, romantic heart. Her genuine sweetness. And now I have her for always.

I finally learned that love never goes away, no matter what happens. No matter who dies, who gets angry, or who nearly dies. It's deeper than death. Italy brought me my family and a life I couldn't have imagined. I got so much more than I ever was smart enough to want. Part of me is in London now, but it feels like London and Lerici are next-door neighbors. Sister cities.

And then, as Saffron says, there's Baby Boy. When I'm better, we've agreed, we have to find him.

But first, our wedding.

* * *

Saffron. October. London.

London is cold a lot of the time, but I have Michael, and I know my sister's a short plane ride away. I love our London flat. It's full of overstuffed furniture, replicas of classical statues, Victorian prints, and plants that don't get quite enough light to become that yellow-gold-green color of a new leaf.

Michael and I were planning to set up a small animal shelter, until we hit a bump in the road. A baby bump. The project may have to wait, even after all our planning—at least until after our child is born. We're going to call him Nathan Percy. I have to send Ellie a copy of the ultrasound. And the name. She'll want to rush right over.

But first, I've proposed hosting her wedding to Tonio.

And I have to tell my sister that Michael may have found a way for us to find our brother. Baby Boy may finally gain a name and a face! But will he want to see us? I'd think so. We're a pretty great family now. Maybe he needs one as much as we do.

A Word from Rachel

I hope you enjoyed *The Invisibles*. If you did, please consider posting a review on the book's Amazon page. Reader reviews help others discover my books. Thank you! For my author news, sign up on my website to be part of Rachel's Readers & Writers: https://racheldacus.net. Find my other books on Amazon: https://www.amazon.com/Rachel-Dacus/e/B001K7SZ2C/ref=dp_byline_cont_ebooks_1

Acknowledgments

This novel wouldn't exist without the support and editorial gifts of my husband David Dacus. Few writers are blessed with a spouse who's a talented editor. I call him the Plot Whisperer.

My great thanks to early readers for invaluable feedback and encouragement: Donna Stadtler, Elaine Gallant, Elizabeth Penney, Elizabeth Sumner Wafler, Jodi Lew-Smith, Kathy Dodson, Suanne Schafer. Especial thanks to my mother-in-law Dottie Dacus, an enthusiastic early reader.

Huge thanks to Robin Facer Taylor for her astute comments, ideas, and generous encouragement. All helped sustain my belief in this book and energy to complete it.

ABOUT THE AUTHOR

Rachel Dacus's first novel, *The Renaissance Club*, was praised as "enchanting, rich, and romantic . . . a poetic journey through the folds of time." A touch of the supernatural also runs through *The Invisibles*. She writes about women, relationships, history, and love.

Find Rachel on Twitter: @Rachel_Dacus and Facebook.

Also by Rachel Dacus

The Renaissance Club (2018)

Timegathered, a prequel to *The Renaissance Club* (forthcoming 2020)

Time's Wily Thief, a sequel to *The Renaissance Club* (forthcoming 2021)

Arabesque (poems)

Gods of Water and Air (poems, essays, and a short play)

Femme au Chapeau (poems)

Earth Lessons (poems)

For Book Clubs

Reading discussion questions on Rachel's website: rachel-dacus.net/for-book-clubs. Please email Rachel if you're interested in her joining you for a meeting. She can also attend by Skype.

Don't miss

The Renaissance Club
Book 1 in the Timegathering Series

on Amazon

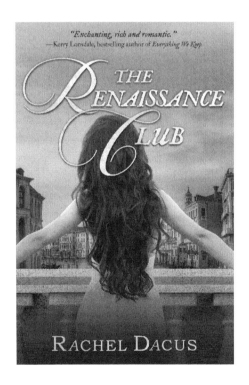

Made in the USA
Coppell, TX
21 July 2021